In a
Heartbeat

Books by Rosalind Noonan

ONE SEPTEMBER MORNING

IN A HEARTBEAT

IN A
HEARTBEAT

ROSALIND NOONAN

KENSINGTON BOOKS

KENSINGTON BOOKS are published by

Kensington Publishing Corp.
119 West 40th Street
New York, NY 10018

ISBN-13: 978-1-61664-782-7

Printed in the United States of America

IN A
HEARTBEAT

PART I
July 2010

Chapter 1

Kate McGann
Woodstock, New York

That night Kate McGann slid between the cool sheets of her bed, thinking of ways to escape her life. Her job, her daily routines, her ragtag marriage . . . the whole package cried out for an overhaul, a radical makeover, Pygmalia to Princess. She turned on her side, her body aching from planting the small pine trees in the yard that day. Heavy work, desperate work designed to exhaust her physically and keep the hillside around the house from eroding. Now, as she lay awake despite her exhaustion, she worried that her plan would fail on both counts.

She thought of those houses on television that were gutted, a new design rising on the same lot. If only you could employ architect, designer, and carpenter to remake a life. Her dark hair, now streaked with white, seemed mousey, the A-line cut far too cute for a woman of undetermined age. She wasn't fat, not really, but the flesh on her petite frame had shifted and pooled in ways she didn't want to face in the mirror. And her wardrobe, faded denim or khaki shorts with washed-out T-shirts, would qualify her for that other show, the one where the fashionistas wrest your favorite pair of jeans from your hands and toss them into a trash bin. Apparently, she'd spent too much of her free time this summer watching television, but movies, books, and even her survival gardening helped her avoid the task at hand, the challenge that probably faced every woman on the threshold of fifty.

Finding Kate.

It seemed to her that she was in need of one of those lyrical twists of fate, the proverbial lightning strike that blocks the familiar road with a felled tree and lights up a street you've never considered traveling. Her thoughts flowed to various pockets of possibility: a move to Baltimore to live with her sister, a tour with the Peace Corps that would take her to a small village in Africa or South America, a fellowship at some university that would allow her to do, well, something creative. Resident artist-gardener.

She tried to concoct the perfect fantasy, but each scenario had its thorns of trouble, tight vines that would inevitably choke off all possibility.

And why was that? she wondered as the full moon bled bold color through the stained-glass windows in her room. *Her room* now; her own personal space. It had been that way for almost a year, ever since she had dropped Ben off at college in Boston and returned to find Eli's drawers emptied, his jeans and sweaters and T-shirts piled into boxes in the guest room. It had happened so quickly, or at least it seemed that way at the time. Strange how Eli, a passive-aggressive person, had stepped up and taken action on the one thing she'd hoped was negotiable.

The vacuous disintegration of their relationship was unlike her parents' divorce, which had been a hot, passionate drama. Funny, but she still remembered that terrible scene some forty years ago. Although at the time she was just a kid in second grade, she remembered the loud argument of that momentous night. Voices quivered in rage, and profanity was flying, lots of "bad words," some of which she'd never heard before. Her father turned up "Moon River" on the hi-fi so that no one could hear the arguments, but Kate moved to the top of the stairs where, peering through the balusters, she caught the words, flying like shards of glass.

"That woman," her mother kept saying. "Moon River" was punctuated by smashing glass and sobs before the needle ripped across the record. That ended the song.

"Now you've done it." Her father's growl was low and deadly. Kate shrank behind the balustrade at the sight of his face, beet red with fury. A railing monster in her seven-year-old world.

Even now, nearly a decade after his death, that image of her father was branded in Kate's memory. It seemed shameful, unfair to define a man by one bad moment, maybe one of the worst moments of his life, but Kate didn't have a vast collection of memories to draw from, as he had packed a suitcase the next day and withdrawn from Kate's life. Although she'd seen him many times after that night, his visits with Kate and her sister Erin well staged and sweetened with little gifts, their relationship was always distant, two people reaching across a fence, their arms straining, the connection only halfhearted.

Yes, her parents' divorce had been explosive and quick, so different from the slow, torturous fizzle she'd been going through with Eli, who said there was no reason for divorce. He liked things the way they were, status quo.

Methodical, infuriating Eli.

Kate punched her pillow and flopped over in bed.

When she finally found sleep it was the restless variety; the purgatory of sleep where fitful dreams have you kick or cry out for the turmoil to end.

Night was still wrapped in itself when the bleating phone sliced into Kate's subconscious.

The noise split the night, a clear division between life as she has known it and uncertain jeopardy on thin ice.

Instinctively she turned toward the digital clock on the nightstand, her eyes straining to focus in the dark. Just after four a.m. Who would be calling in the middle of the night?

Maybe a wrong number . . . or something important. Eli calling from the sheriff's office, or Ben out of gas.

Pushing up from the mattress, she stretched to reach the

phone, snatched it from the charger. It took her a few seconds to find the right button, her mind racing even as her body lagged.

"Hello?" A jagged vein of sleep ran through her voice.

"I'm calling from Cross College in Syracuse, trying to reach the parents of Benjamin McGann."

No one called her son Benjamin. Only strangers. She threw off the sheets and slid out of bed.

"Who is this?" Kate raked back her hair and paced to the wall of windows as the man gave his name, said he worked security at the school, and that he needed to speak to one of Ben's parents.

Moonlight fired the colored glass, slanting colored patterns on the fabric of the chaise. Blue and green diamonds. Eerie light. The stained glass seemed inordinately bright, but then she remembered there was a full moon tonight.

"I'm Kate McGann . . . his mother." Her rapid heartbeat punctuated the momentary pause.

"Mrs. McGann, your son was injured in the dormitory. He just left here by ambulance, and I suggest you meet him in the Emergency Room at Good Samaritan Hospital."

"Yes, yes. Of course." The wood floor felt cold and grainy under her bare feet as she opened her bedroom door and headed down the hall, past Ben's old room, which had remained intact since he left for college. Her heart pinged in her chest as she raced through the open living area. It wasn't until she flew into the guest room and approached the couch that she realized where she had been running: to Eli, her husband.

Thank God he was there. A blanket sloped over his back, his face pressed into the pillow, he was lost in sleep.

"Eli, wake up." Her voice quavered as she held the phone to her chest. "Something happened to Ben. He's in the hospital."

She felt him come awake even before his arm swept the blanket away and he sat up. "What happened?"

"I . . . I don't know." She asked the man on the phone, "What happened to him?"

"I'm sorry, Mrs. McGann, but I don't have the details."

"But he's okay? I mean . . ." She closed her eyes, searching for the reassurance that would allow her to shake loose from this thorny panic. "He's going to be okay, right?"

The silence on the line was like a weight dropped on her spirit.

Panicked, Kate scurried back across the house, back to her room to get dressed and go—fly!—to her son's side.

"You'll want to talk to the doctors at Good Samaritan," the voice on the phone said.

"Good Samaritan," she repeated, finding it difficult to hear him over the roar of her heartbeat. "Yes, yes, we're on our way."

As she crossed the dining room her gaze fixed on the circular stained-glass window in the living room, Eli's masterpiece. It was a mandala, Sanskrit for "essence," and the intricately designed circle was said to contain a primal pattern, this one colored to reflect Eli's past, present, and future. Moonlight fired its panels of pearlized and colored glass, brilliant triangles of orange, inlaid amber, and brown surrounding crescents of ruby-red glass. Although she had passed that window a thousand times, never before had she seen moonlight strike the glass so that it resembled a crimson heart, engulfed in flames, aglow with anguish.

An illumination of the terror swelling in Kate's chest as she darted down to the hallway to dress and go after her son.

Chapter 2

Dr. Theodora ("Teddy") Zanth
Good Samaritan Hospital

So much blood . . .
When the doors flew open to reveal paramedics wheeling in a man strapped to a backboard, the blood was all Teddy could see. Red and clotted, it covered the man's entire head, which looked sticky and slick.

Teddy let her eyes shift back to the entrance to keep from gaping at the patient. She wished she could escape to the cool night beyond those doors, but she was held in place by subtle reminders: the button-down smock hanging loosely around her, the stethoscope around her neck, and the ID card that read, as of yesterday, "Dr. Theodora Zanth, Good Samaritan." She was a resident now, a doctor. Before someone on the trauma team at Good Sammy smelled her fear, she had better step up and take charge.

Especially with interns like Max Sanchez around. Teddy had been here little more than a week, but she already had a solid handle on the players in Good Sammy's ER. What she lacked in medical savvy she more than made up for in observation skills, and her powers of observation indicated that Max Sanchez was a risk taker, a self-promoter, and a bully. Not very endearing qualities in Teddy's book. If Max didn't have those dark, exotic good looks going for him, he surely would have been bumped off by the nursing staff in his first year.

"Bay three is open," Goldy shouted as she pointed behind

her, grabbed the gurney, and tugged it her way. Goldy had probably prepared bay three when they got the call that the male trauma patient was in transit from a dorm at the college. Nurse Tonya Goldman was almost psychic in her anticipation of the next step of trauma medicine. Teddy suspected that Goldy could run this place single-handedly if the doctors would let her.

"What do we have?" Teddy asked.

"Head trauma. GCS is two-two-five." The petite female paramedic had to shout to be heard over a beeping monitor and an argument in the waiting room between two intoxicated men. "The guy who found him said that he was talking, but we haven't gotten a verbal response. Sounds like someone came at him with a baseball bat."

Teddy processed the information as she hurried alongside the gurney. "GCS" stood for the patient's Glasgow Coma Scale, a standard assessment of how the trauma had affected his consciousness. The GCS measured response to stimuli, such as whether the patient could close or open his eyes on command or respond to questions. Two-two-five meant nine out of fifteen; not so good. This guy had suffered a major injury. His verbal responses were poor, though he was still responding to physical stimuli.

"What's his name?" Teddy asked.

"Ben. Benjamin McGann. Nineteen years old," the female paramedic answered. "He's at Cross College for the summer. Plays for the Lakers."

"Ben, can you hear me? Do you know where you are?" He was unresponsive as the trauma team hustled him down the hall. His left eye was swollen, the skin bruised blue. "Let's get a CT scan," Teddy said, wanting pictures of his neck before she took him off the backboard and removed the collar.

Glancing up, she saw Dr. Chong, the ER attending physician, catch up with the moving gurney. Cold and reserved, Dr. Chong had a schoolmarmish approach to overseeing her staff that rattled Teddy's nerves. "Go ahead," Chong said with a quick nod, indicating that Teddy was to run the procedures.

Teddy's heartbeat quickened as they pulled the gurney into the bay and one of the paramedics locked the wheels. For the first time in her career since she'd walked across the stage and been given the name of "Doctor" at med school graduation, she was the lead doctor calling the shots. It was scary.

"Cross match! Let's get two units O negative in here," Teddy called. Although his blood pressure was in the normal range, they would replace some of the blood he'd lost, just to be on the safe side. While they worked, the lab would match his blood type; in the meantime, he would receive two units of O negative, the blood type that was compatible with all blood.

"Any other tests, Dr. Zanth?" Chong prodded.

"Get me a CBC, coag panel, Chem seven, and a tox screen," Teddy ordered. She interpreted Dr. Chong's silence to mean that these were the right tests. The CBC would measure the red and white blood cells and the platelets in the blood. The coag panel would test his blood's ability to clot, the Chem 7 would record seven aspects of the blood chemistry, and the tox screen would test for alcohol and drugs in his blood.

Teddy helped Goldy and the paramedics lift the patient and backboard onto the bed, then the organized chaos began. First the portable CT scan. Then Goldy took vital signs while another nurse, a guy they called Welch, started cutting off his clothes. Goldy inserted an intravenous line in his right arm. Welch started a Foley catheter. The paramedic was still pumping oxygen from a bag mask.

Members of the trauma team were well versed in their duties.

Teddy was the rookie here.

What's next, what's next? Each second was loaded with decisions, jam-packed with activity. Panic teased the edge of her confidence, but she tamped it down and gloved up.

Primary survey. She needed to stabilize any immediately life-threatening injuries. First things first: ABC. Airway, Breathing, Circulation. "How's his breathing?"

The paramedic squeezing the bellows of the bag mask shook his head. "He's struggling."

"You'll have to do an emergency trache," Max offered. "With his facial injuries, his airways will be compromised. We need a trache kit," he ordered, stepping on Teddy's toes.

Max was going to drive her crazy. "I've got it," Teddy told the intern, looking over to the computer monitor behind her. "Results of the CT scan?"

"He's clear," said the radiologist, a young, bearded man Teddy had never met.

"Okay, then." Teddy removed the c-collar and examined the patient's neck for soft tissue or ligament injury that wouldn't show up in a picture. So far so good. She leaned over to assess the patient, his face tinged red from dried blood. Not a man, but a boy. A kid. A laceration near the patient's left eye oozed fresh blood into a coagulating black scab. His breaths were shallow and rapid.

"Let's move him off the backboard," she ordered. "In three, two, one." Together the staff lifted and shifted the patient onto a gurney.

Airways, airways! a voice in her head prodded Teddy. A sensor clipped onto his finger measured his oxygen level at 88 percent. Normally a person's 0_2 stat measures 95 percent or better. "Oxygenation is not good," Teddy said.

"And it's falling. Don't waste your time and his," Max advised. "Order a trache kit and tube him. Do it now."

"I'll be calling the shots, Max." Teddy tried to sound authoritative but knew her agitation was slipping through. She didn't want to look to Dr. Chong for advice, felt sure the attending would cut in if Teddy chose the wrong thing, but she sure as hell didn't need a med student like Max shouting orders.

Besides, right now a trache was the last thing she wanted to do. Panic sizzled under her skin at the thought of performing a tracheotomy, an incision into the neck to insert a breathing tube into the trachea. It was surgery, damn it, and she'd learned from her surgical rotation that she had not been gifted with the "beautiful hands" her mother possessed.

"Let me take a look," Teddy said.

"Dr. Chong, you're needed at curtain two," someone called, but Teddy didn't acknowledge the interruption. She needed to focus on the patient, filter out the unnecessary.

The paramedic pumping the ambu-bag removed the breathing device, and Teddy opened the patient's mouth, her purple-gloved hands floundering on his chin for a moment before she reached into his mouth. "No foreign object blocking his airway." The bag mask went back on his mouth as she placed her stethoscope on his chest, checking both sides. "Good breath sounds. No sign of lung collapse," she reported.

Could she intubate? It would be difficult if there was blood or swelling in the throat. She looked for Dr. Chong, then remembered that the supervisor had been called away. Damn.

"I don't think the airways are compromised." Teddy held out one hand for the laryngoscope, announcing, "We'll intubate."

Although she felt Max's disapproval, he kept quiet as she positioned herself behind the patient and gripped the cold metal tool with her left hand. Trying not to think, she took a deep breath and inserted the curved hook of the laryngoscope into the mouth, past the larynx. Forty-five degrees and lift. She looked for the vocal cords, but she couldn't see a thing.

"We'll need to suction him," she said.

Welch handed her the tube, and she extracted maybe a half pint of blood.

"Blood oxygen is dropping," Max warned. "He's down to seventy-five percent."

Dangerously low.

Teddy wasn't sure if she should remove the scope and bag him for a bit, or proceed. He needed oxygen soon, but if she removed and reinserted the laryngoscope, all the poking and probing could cause swelling, making it impossible to establish an airway.

"You're out of time," Max said.

He was right. Well, maybe exaggerating a bit. What to do? She peered in the patient's throat, and this time the tiny light on the laryngoscope revealed the vocal cords, situated like two fleshy flaps at the trachea entrance.

"I'm in." She reached for the plastic tubing and quickly fed it through the device, just enough tubing so that the cuffing tube would seal off securely at the larynx. She removed the laryngoscope.

There. "Inflate the cuff," she ordered.

All this in seconds, her heart thumping in her ears.

Goldy responded as Teddy listened for breathing sounds in the lungs and stomach.

"Breathe," Goldy said sternly.

With a smile worthy of a toothpaste ad, Max folded his arms. "You don't have to worry about that; he's intubated."

After hearing strong breath sounds in both lungs, Teddy lifted her chin and met Goldy's stern gaze as the woman repeated, "Breathe."

Teddy took in a welcome breath, realizing that Goldy had been talking to her. She had been holding her breath, but she had made it through the procedure, her first successful intubation. For most interns it wouldn't have been such a big deal, but for Teddy, it felt hopeful.

Baby steps.

Chapter 3

Greg Cody
Cross College

As he stopped for a red light at the edge of campus, Greg Cody had to wonder what the hell he was doing. There were no other cars in sight. Why not blow the light to get to his crime scene, or at least ease through it?

He rolled down the window, hitched his hand on the car roof, and reconsidered. Nah. It was the stolen hour, that time after the drunks have gone to bed and before the joggers are out, and he didn't mind soaking it all in for just a moment.

The smell of grass and cool night reminded him of how far he'd come in the last year—264 miles, to be exact—from the only home he'd ever known. New York City to the smaller city of Syracuse.

Big difference.

Different culture, different weather. Different smell on a summer night, he thought wryly as he recalled the choking odor of the well-baked subway platform at Times Square in July. Now *that* was something you definitely did not want to soak up at two in the morning.

Not to put the Big Apple down. Some nights he longed for the crazy pace and the noise. He missed taking his daughter to dinner, missed late nights hanging out with friends from the job at Donovan's or First Edition. Right now he'd kill for real bagels and pizza. He missed sitting in cheap seats at a Mets game—never gonna happen again, now that they had the new stadium. He missed taking mass transit to work when it snowed, which it did a lot here in Syracuse. A lot. One of the cops who grew up here talked about sewing Halloween costumes that would fit over her kids' snowsuits. Snow in October, and they said New Yorkers were crazy.

From what he'd seen in the last year, Syracuse was a different kind of crazy, but his brother Joe had warned him about that. Joey was a cop, too, NYPD, though he was younger than Greg and still a ways from retirement. Always the Yoda of the family, Joe had warned Greg not to think that law enforcement would be any sweeter in Syracuse. "People are people everywhere," Joey had said. "You got good ones and bad ones. Just not so many of them in Syracuse, I guess." In the year that he'd been here, he'd learned that Joe was right. Syracuse's culture was different from New York City's, but the public, the perps, the jobs . . . they were about the same.

He'd left NYPD on a dare of sorts. Got sick and tired of hearing that he would never summon the nerve to leave the job. "You old-timers are all alike," a young buck named Filch had razzed him one night in the precinct locker room. "You just can't let go. Give it up, Gramps. You got gray hair."

Cody had raked back his short-cropped silver hair, thick hair that still grew like a weed. "Better to have snow on the roof than a hole in the roof."

"D'oh!" One of the other cops laughed, pointing at Filch, whose shiny pate gleamed in the fluorescent light. "You've been served!"

Filch's jaw hardened. "Yeah, well, I can handle myself out there."

Greg Cody sucked in a breath through his teeth. "I may be pushing fifty, but I can still do the job."

"Yeah, yeah. You'll be fat and bald and still tracking down perps when you're ninety," Filch warned. "They'll have to carry you out of here in a pine box."

Even after the kid had slammed his locker and left, Greg

had been unable to shake the feeling that the kid was right. He was a hamster on a wheel, same old, same old. Nothing new, nothing to learn, nothing to look forward to.

The next day Greg had put in his retirement papers and started filling out online applications to other police departments, figuring that a change of venue would do him good. He'd been smarting from the divorce, still feeling like so much of New York was defined by the man he'd been with Carol as a wife. Their first apartment, their first house. The buildings she'd worked in at Rockefeller Center and down on Water Street. The Police Academy down on East 29th. The hospital where their daughter had been born. And the precincts—each place Greg had been assigned, Manhattan, Queens, and the Bronx—each had its own tilt, a distinct character. He'd loved that city—still did—but everywhere he looked he saw reminders of how his life had gone sour.

Enough already. He had to get out.

A month or so later Syracuse called, he answered, and long story short, here he was a year later, detective on the rotating shifts.

Greg Cody liked Syracuse because it was a smaller department. *Smaller,* not small, with nearly five hundred uniformed cops. He'd come here hoping to make a difference, to *feel* the difference he was making, though the jury was still out on that verdict.

Hawthorne Hall was easy to find; it was lit up like a Christmas tree. The four-story building had been constructed in that unfortunate era when brick and glass cubes were thought to be the design of the future. The poplar-lined circular drive in front was now blocked by a fire truck and a handful of police cars, their flashing lights mesmerizing in the cool night. Cody pulled his unmarked unit into a parking space, wondering at the way law enforcement types loved to pull up at skewed angles on curbs and sidewalks. Aside from the first vehicles on the scene, there was no need for it.

He passed a few students, one of them barefoot and curled into a jacket, who had engaged the firefighters in conversation.

Good thing it's summer session, he thought as he passed into the lobby of the dormitory. When he'd been on campus in April to investigate a date rape the place had been swarming with students.

The two square seating areas at the front of the lobby were overcome with sleepy students in pajamas and hoodies and fluffy slippers. Here and there some of the students gave statements or spoke with officers; others huddled in groups, talking quietly. Someone let out a laugh, and he scowled. This was not a sleepover.

Toward the rear of the lobby was a security desk and two turnstiles, the modern ones with retractable arms that whooshed open when you scanned your ID card. Impressive. Cody approached the desk and recognized Mal Rosenberg, another NYPD exile. "Sarge. Looks like you caught a crime scene. What you got?"

"Baseball player, summer league, one of our very own Syracuse Lakers. Injured in an assault. Kid goes to bed, next thing you know another player finds him bleeding on the bed, bloody baseball bat beside him. Looks like someone whacked him good."

Greg took out his notebook. "Who found the victim?"

"Kid named Gibbs. Isaiah Gibbs. Said McGann was moaning, even talking to him. He's really spooked." Mal nodded toward the staircase. "He's talking with one of the uniforms upstairs."

Greg scanned the room, glared at two girls giggling in the corner. "Sounds like one of my daughter's sleepover parties."

"Yeah, once the residents saw the flashing lights they scrambled down to get a peek. Can't blame them for being curious." Mal scratched at the graying hair behind his ears. He was losing it on top, but the fringe of curls around the side, coupled with his reading glasses, gave him a professorial aura, which fit well here on campus.

"You put the campus in lockdown?" Greg asked.

"Nah. This is the first incident of its kind, appears to be someone the kid knew. Devin Mains, director of campus secu-

rity, is on his way here. I'll take care of coordinating the incident impact with him."

"Who's living in this building right now?" Cody asked.

"Summer school students and all of the guys on the team.
It's mandatory if they want to play. Supposed to be a bonding
experience."

"Did you ID the victim?"

Mal unclipped a BlackBerry from his belt and tapped his
fingers on the screen. "Benjamin McGann, nineteen. Student
at Boston College. Parents are on their way from Woodstock,
New York."

Cody took out his notebook and jotted down the name. He
was a paper and pen man, trained by the NYPD with carbon
copy reports and too old to change now. "No kidding? Like
the rock concert?"

"Unless there's another Woodstock."

"Next of kin notified?"

"Security guard here at the college made the call, 3:22
a.m.," Mal read aloud from the screen of his device. "Victim's
parents, Kate and Eli McGann. They're on their way to meet
him at Good Sam."

"Are your technicians here yet?"

"They're upstairs, sweeping the scene as we speak. There
was a lot of blood, but then head wounds tend to bleed a lot.
No obvious fingerprints or shoe prints." Mal poked at the
screen of his BlackBerry again and turned it toward Greg.
"Photos of the scene."

Greg took a look, nodding as Mal narrated and switched to
the next picture. "Most of the blood was on the bed. Looks
like the victim was either sitting or fell back onto the bed when
he was attacked. Which could be lucky for him, seeing as the
dorm has a linoleum floor."

"You take those photos yourself?" Greg asked.

Mal nodded. "Sure. This thing is like a portable office. I'd
be lost without it."

"Not me." Greg extracted his cell phone from his pocket
and grimaced. "Personally, I'd like to toss it into the Hudson."

"The Hudson? Now that'd be quite a toss from here. You're one of Syracuse's Finest now, Cody. Try tossing it in the lake."

"Either way, it's one more way for the department to reel you in. One more way for the ex to nag."

"One way for your kids to reach out when they need you."

"Yeah, maybe," Cody admitted, thinking that Jessica had texted him twice since they'd returned from Florida last week, and yes, it had actually been sort of cool to read messages from his daughter on the phone. All those years of school, at least she'd learned to write. Come September she'd be a high school senior, but it had to be hard for her when he and Carol had split up when she was just starting high school. He scowled at his phone. "I don't even know if this thing has a camera."

Mal flipped open Greg's phone and laughed. "You kidding me, Cody? How long you had this dinosaur?"

"It works."

He handed it back. "Do yourself a favor. Step into your Verizon store and step into the twenty-first century."

Tucking his phone away, Greg waved his small notebook. "Everything I need, I got right here, and I can still read it when the battery dies."

Mal grinned, his dark eyes twinkling behind his reading glasses. "Yeah, well, you'll be wanting to haul that dinosaur upstairs to the fourth floor. Only one elevator in this building, need the staff key to use it. When I wanted to go up, the paramedics had it tied up. Pain in the balls on a summer night."

Greg glanced toward the open staircase at the back of the lobby. "Had a feeling about that. Looks like I'll be getting my aerobic workout early today. Hey, have you seen a floor plan of the building?"

"Talk to Marcus, there," Rosenberg said, pointing to the uniformed campus security guard. "He's got some behind the desk."

"And where will I find this Isaiah Gibbs, the kid who found the victim?" Cody wanted to talk to the guy while the details were still crisp in his memory.

"Fourth-floor lounge. Every floor has a sitting area, just across from the stairwell."

Cody nodded, headed toward the stairs. "You say Gibbs is on the team? What position does he play?"

"Hell if I know. I gave up baseball when the Dodgers left Brooklyn."

Greg Cody shook his head. "You're too young to remember that."

Rosenberg was already sliding a finger over his BlackBerry screen. "Don't flatter me."

"Catch you later, Mal."

Mal Rosenberg nodded. "Later."

Chapter 4

Kate
New York State Thruway

It took three calls to Good Samaritan Hospital to extract the sparse news.

"I'm sorry, but we don't release patient information over the phone," was the first response. Kate had argued, cajoled, and redialed twice to negotiate a release of precious information.

The voice on the phone seemed harried and reluctant. "I'm not supposed to say anything over the phone. Liability and everything," said the woman from Good Samaritan's ER unit, "but seeing that this is the third time you called and you're down in the paperwork as next of kin, I'm thinking I might just tell you how it's listed on the board?"

"Yes, please," Kate said, desperate for a nugget of information.

"Head trauma."

The words stole the air from her lungs. Kate hunched forward, grateful for the distance of the phone, the anonymity of darkness in Eli's car.

This was serious. Ben was hurt.

Head injury.

Kate mulled over the possibilities. Now that they'd ruled out a car crash, she could fantasize that it was just a minor injury. Some minor bump or bruise, as Eli kept purporting.

"Head trauma," Kate relayed to Eli, unable to look up at

him as she sought to process the information and get more. She wanted some reassurance, some casual comment that would help her believe everything would be fine in the end. Unfortunately, the young woman told her she would have to talk to one of the doctors to get more information. "And they're all busy right now."

She could not imagine it, did not want to picture it. Being a fifth-grade teacher, Kate was not well versed in advanced anatomy, and she didn't want to go there.

Eli moved his right hand from the stick to the stubby growth on his chin. "How does a nineteen-year-old guy hit his head in a college dorm room?"

Kate shook her head. "He's always been so healthy. Never a broken bone. No surgeries." While other moms sweated through ear tubes and tonsillectomies, Kate had counted herself lucky that Ben always got the thumbs-up from Dr. Palmer, his pediatrician.

She pushed panic away, forced herself to stay positive. Ben was physically strong, in perfect shape. Wouldn't that help him heal quickly?

Kate knew the obvious scenario would involve drugs or alcohol, but she didn't think that was likely with her son. Ben had always been appalled by professional baseball players who tested positive for drug use, disappointed when the big stars like A-Rod and Barry Bonds were connected to steroids. When Ben emerged as a strong, skilled athlete in high school, he took the initiative to develop healthy habits, eating the right foods, exercising, and training. When other parents worried about their kids experimenting with drugs and alcohol, Kate had confidence in Ben, who was determined not to let anything get in the way of his success in baseball. "I've been at parties where there's beer," he had admitted to her once when he was a junior in high school. "It's not my thing and people are okay with that. Everyone knows that Dylan and I are just baseball nerds."

Dylan and Ben . . . they'd been inseparable as kids. People had joked that Dylan was her second son. At times, Kate sensed him veering off track and she'd pulled him back in line, as a mother would. There was that time Dylan had too much to drink, and Ben brought him to their house to sleep it off in the guest room. Having known Dylan since he was a gap-toothed second grader, Kate let him crash there, but greeted him the next morning with tea and toast and a firm parental lecture.

"Thanks, Mommyson Two," Dylan always told her with a big bear hug.

Having just his grandmother at home, Dylan often joked about being adopted into the McGann clan, and there was truth in comedy. In many ways, he was Kate's second son, and Ben was the older brother, modeling good behavior for Dyl.

"Hey, man, your body is your temple," Ben had told Dylan one day. Kate overheard them talking about trying a caffeinated energy drink to give them a boost before the game. "You're going to pour in that garbage?"

Dylan . . . he would know what was going on.

She slipped her cell phone out of her purse and went to the phone directory.

"Calling the hospital again?" Eli asked.

"Dylan. I'm sure he's on top of things. Maybe he's with Ben right now. He can give us a better picture of what's happening."

But the line kept ringing. When his voice mail clicked on, Kate ended the call.

"No answer," she said.

Eli tugged on his beard.

"Maybe he fell in the shower," Kate said absently, desperate to fill in the blanks. "Or tripped on the stairs."

"Kate, he's nineteen, not ninety."

"Maybe he got into a fight."

"Our Ben?" Eli was skeptical. "Mr. Diplomacy?"

"I know, he's not an instigator, but things happen. Sometimes guys just get dragged in." Kate had seen it happen at school.

"You know, we're probably overreacting." Eli drove with

one hand on the wheel, the other on the stick shift that he'd covered with black duct tape when the original knob broke off. "We'll get there and he'll con us into taking him to lunch. We'll have to buy half a dozen burgers for Ben and Dylan."

"That would be great." *But I doubt it.* The leaden feeling in Kate's stomach would not allow her to indulge in that fantasy. Somehow her body knew the seriousness of the situation. A mother knew these things. She just knew.

Their car sped along the interstate moving in sync with two other vehicles far ahead, seen only by the red disks of their taillights. "Red candy lights," Ben used to call them when he was seven or eight. Once, while their car floated through the night in a traffic jam, he'd talked about reaching out the window to snatch up the red candy lights and eat them. Cherry lights, he'd said. Sometimes strawberry or raspberry. Never mint or cinnamon, which he hated.

Kate pressed a fist to her mouth to staunch the tears that threatened. Although it seemed that they'd been on the road for an eternity, they'd barely made a dent in the three-hour drive to Syracuse.

Three hours. An eternity to wait and worry.

And to think that she'd been thrilled when Ben had landed in Syracuse for the summer. "So close!" she'd told him. "Dad and I will be able to drive up and catch some games."

Eli's ancient BMW smelled of oil and leaf mold. Needing some fresh air, Kate pressed the button to open the window. The glass did not move. She pressed it again.

"That one's broken," he explained. "I have to take a look at it."

She marveled that the engine purred smoothly at seventy-five miles per hour on the interstate, but then Eli had always told her the engine was perfect. "It's the rest of the car that's falling apart," he used to joke. Not such a funny joke to Kate, given that it was true.

A few years ago when they got a good-size tax return she had campaigned for Eli to buy a new car, but he had refused, horrified at the prospect of change. Eli did not cope well with change. And so, sixteen years after they had moved Upstate, he was still driving the same route to teach at the Woodlands Academy four days a week, still making the same patterns of stained glass in his studio each weekend. His short, dark beard was trimmed to the same length, and he probably would have kept the same hairstyle if hair were still growing on the top of his head. He found security in the routine of it, wrapped himself in the sameness of each day as if it were a blanket worn soft with familiarity.

There was a time when Kate felt that she was right beside him wrapped in the same blanket . . . but not anymore. Now, at a time when she needed some source of security, she was outside, looking in.

Suddenly she felt cold. She huddled into the gray hoodie she'd thrown on before they left the house.

Eli shot her a look. "I can turn the heat on."

"That's okay." God knew what would fly out of the vents if he cranked the air on.

"You know, I question whether we did the right thing, letting him play summer league. He's only nineteen, and it's a lot to be on your own for the summer."

Kate hugged herself. "He's learned a lot this year, living on his own in Boston."

"College is different." He stroked the hairs on his chin, a sign that he was waxing philosophical. "There's a modicum of security in collegiate life. You've got that safety net of professors and student life. Ben's good at learning the limits and staying with the pack. But this summer ball . . . it's such an odd program."

"He's playing with other college kids. He's got Dylan on the same team. For God's sake, he's living on a college campus. It's not like he's juggling an apartment and a job somewhere."

Eli shrugged. "Maybe it's me. I guess I just don't understand the politics and competitiveness of college athletics. I've always told you straight out that I don't get baseball."

You can say that again, Kate thought, though she restrained herself. This little lecture was Eli's passive-aggressive way of pointing the blame at her. Now it would be her fault Ben got hurt, because Eli didn't *understand* competitive sports.

Why did he always do this?

Here they were driving into God only knew what kind of a nightmare, and already he was shuffling away from culpability, distancing himself from the situation.

"Yes, Eli." She tried to temper the agitation in her voice to resignation. "We all know you don't care for baseball. Big of you to go along with it this far."

"I'm not trying to make this about me; this is about Ben."

"That's right. It's about Ben, and he loves baseball. It's his passion." In her mind Kate could see the way her son moved on the field, like a dancer surpassing his choreography. She recalled the hours of practice, fielding grounders and shagging fly balls, batting till his arms ached and the palms of his hands blistered, slipping through the cold mud time and again so that he could perfect the ultimate standing slide. Ben loved the game, and Kate had always been determined that no one, not even Eli, would stand between Ben and his passion.

"He's worked so hard to be the best . . ." When her voice cracked she paused and took a calming breath. She did not want to break down and cry in front of Eli. He would try to be consoling and compassionate—not his gift—and she would want to smack him away all the more. Besides, giving in to grief right now would be admitting that Ben was in trouble, and she wanted to hold on to the illusion of safety as long as she possibly could. "I just want him to have the chance to realize his dreams," she said finally.

"And he's had every opportunity," Eli said.

"Yes, he has. He's had every opportunity, despite you." Her cutting remark wasn't entirely fair, given the situation, but it did put an end to the conversation for the time being.

She turned away, turned to the black landscape inked against the night. The empty highway stretched on forever.

How many miles left? She checked the dashboard clock and sank down into the seat.

Miles to go. Miles to go before I sleep.

Chapter 5

Teddy
Good Samaritan ER

For head trauma victims, the first hour after the injury occurred is often called the Golden Hour. That brief hour is a window of sorts, a time when proper medical intervention might prevent a medical catastrophe like permanent brain injury.

Knowing that, Teddy did not leave Ben McGann's side after he was brought in. As soon as she established a clear airway she ordered a head CT, then continued examining him, looking for other problems that might pose a difficulty if he needed surgery. She'd been assigned an elderly patient who needed his leg sutured and a teen with a persistent nosebleed, but she knew those two patients could wait until Ben's X-rays were complete. She had already paged Dr. Pruett, the neurosurgeon on call, who was on his way.

Although Teddy had been doing procedures in hospitals during her last two years of medical school, this was only her first week as a doctor—even if she was a resident. Last week was "transition week," as they called it in the medical community; the time when the house staff got replaced with totally inexperienced residents, fresh out of med school.

Teddy was a brand-new doctor, along with thousands of others who had endured four years of med school. Unfortunately, the word "new" placed before "doctor" did not have the same cachet as "new car" or "new condo."

Some people joked that the first week in July was the absolute worst time of year to be in the ER, but Teddy liked to think differently. If she screwed up as an intern, it wouldn't be for lack of trying. Didn't determination and earnestness account for anything?

Apparently not when you couldn't establish a clear airway in a trauma patient.

She went to the computer monitor on wheels and brought up the patient's lab work. The results of the CBC looked good, with normal counts for red and white blood cells and platelets. His tox screen showed no alcohol, but a prescription drug was detected in the blood. Valium.

Teddy's gaze moved from the monitor to the patient, who breathed in and out with the machine, his vital signs displayed as electronic peaks and valleys on the monitor behind him.

"Oh, Ben, say it ain't so."

In truth, she knew so little about him. Why had she been disappointed to learn about the drugs? She checked the clip on his fingertip for the oximeter, checked his breathing, though none of this was necessary at this point.

She was hovering, trying to get a sense of him that superseded Western medicine with its analysis of the anatomical, of blood chemistry and systemic functions.

The Eastern approach was less complicated, though equally complex. Teddy knew about chakras and elements. Although she had never studied Eastern ways, her Balinese grandmother had always told Teddy she had a gift for it.

The vision.

Teddy took a deep breath. Sometimes insights and a sixth sense got in the way. They tripped you in the Western world. People here wanted answers; they wanted a diagnosis and a cure, not a recommendation on how to restore balance in their lives.

No one wanted to hear that this young man had too much fire in his composition, too much frenetic, electric energy. Americans would not understand that he needed to find the earth in himself, that he needed to get in touch with his water and air.

She checked his pupils for dilation, hearing Nyoman's voice in her head.

"Ooh, look at him! He's all fire, yes?" Teddy's grandmother would have said of Ben McGann. She would have passed her splayed hands over his head and lifted her brows in that expression of surprise that always seemed genuine. "He's a fireball, this one. He needs some water to calm the fires, bring him balance."

Nyoman had been in her thirties when she left Bali for the States, and although her daughter, Teddy's mother, had decided to pursue the study and practice of Western medicine, Nyoman remained embedded in Balinese culture. Ether, air, water, fire, and earth . . . to Nyoman's way of thinking, those elements held the keys to good health, to happiness, to life.

"Dr. Zanth?" Teddy was interrupted by Rashid, the tall, olive-skinned technician who had taken the head CT. He brought something up on the computer and motioned her over. "This is your guy. Do you see the right side?"

Teddy leaned over the counter beside him, her eyes greedily taking in the image of her patient's brain. In a healthy person, the brain is usually symmetrical, filling the skull cavity. But here, the right wall of the brain buckled away from the skull. The dark spot that seemed to be swelling between the skull and the dura mater was a collection of blood from the injury. "An epidural hematoma."

"Yes, on the right side."

"We've got to get him up to surgery." Teddy straightened and called to Goldy, "Would you please page Dr. Pruett in neuro again? This patient needs surgery to relieve the intracranial pressure on the right side."

Dr. Chong poked her head out from the curtain of bay two. "Ordering brain surgery, are we?"

Teddy opened her mouth and closed it, wishing she could still her racing pulse. Of course, only attending physicians could order a surgical procedure, and that with a consult from the neurosurgeon. "I'm sorry, but I don't want to waste any time with this patient."

Chong stripped off her gloves, tossed them aside, and stepped out of the bay. "All right, Dr. Zanth. Show me what you think you have."

Talking fast, Teddy went over the head CT results and the course of treatment with Dr. Chong. "If they drill a hole in the skull to alleviate pressure and allow the brain to swell without being blocked, underlying injury to the brain may not be severe. He has a chance at recovery *if* we get him to surgery stat."

"That part seems accurate. Have you gone over his labs?" Dr. Chong stood straight, her hands resting in her deep pockets as Teddy went over her labs. As they were talking the air shifted, and she sensed someone joining them.

Pruett, the neurosurgeon.

"Is this the head trauma?" Carl Pruett pursed his lips as he studied the image of Ben McGann's brain on the monitor.

"Dr. Zanth has diagnosed an epidural hematoma on the right side, but of course, we need your opinion," Chong offered. "Are you taking this boy upstairs with you, Carl? Have you time to fit in a surgery before breakfast?" The whimsical tone of Dr. Chong's voice, the cavalier way that she mentioned surgery as if it were nine holes of golf, reminded Teddy that she still had much to learn about the many levels of the medical culture.

"Absolutely. Let's get this patient prepped for surgery." Pruett clasped his hands together as he studied the images a moment longer. "I'll leave it to you to notify next of kin, Dr. Zanth." He headed off . . .

And that was that.

No pat on the back, no accolades. In fact, Chong and Pruett were so matter-of-fact about it, Teddy had to replay the whole scenario in her head and remind herself that she had, in fact, made a correct diagnosis.

A successful intubation and an accurate diagnosis, all in one day. Maybe she was on the right track.

As if on cue, Goldy materialized and started hooking the patient up to portable machines and monitors so that he could be transported up to surgery.

With one last look, Teddy backed away. She felt oddly reluctant to let him go, wished she could follow him through surgery and monitor his progress, but she didn't dare say that to Dr. Chong.

"Did you take care of those sutures in five?" Chong asked.

"It's next on my list," Teddy said as they both moved toward the open office, command center of the ER.

"And the family? Did you talk with the head trauma patient's family?"

"As I understand it, they're on their way from out of town."

"See if you can call them on a cell. I don't like to send anyone into surgery without next of kin being informed first. Especially not a kid this age." Dr. Chong crossed to the board to update a case.

Teddy was heading toward her patient in bay five when Paulina waved her over. Fortyish, blond, and obese, Paulina Krakowski moved with great difficulty, and Teddy suspected that was one reason she had been assigned a stationary spot manning the phones and the main reception area. Reason two: Paulina was the ultimate mother hen. Paula Deen, Mrs. Claus, and Mother Goose all rolled into one.

"Teddy, dear, I have a bunch of phone messages for you!" No one but Paulina could get away with calling doctors by their first names. "The family of that young man, Ben McGann? They're still on their way and very worried."

"I need to speak with them," Teddy said, accepting the pink slips. Could she keep the elderly suture patient waiting that much longer and take care of this first?

She leafed through the pink slips, all three from Kate McGann, the patient's mother. Hmm. These people needed information. She snagged Max and assigned him to do the sutures. After so many years of being assigned the scut work, she felt guilty at passing it on, but warned him, "I'll stop in to make sure you've done beautiful stitches."

On her way back to the main desk, she ran into Dr. Pruett, consulting on another case. He advised Dr. Stafford to start the patient on an antiseizure medication called Keppra, then turned pointedly to Teddy.

"You know," Pruett said, "I was in my surgical residency with a Dr. Angela Zanth. Any relation?"

A deer in the headlights, Teddy felt her eyes grow wide at the mention of her mother. She thought of the obvious comparisons, the complaints of nepotism she had heard in the past. "No," she said. "No relation."

"Too bad. She was a crack surgeon. Beautiful hands, as they say."

As Dr. Pruett strode off at a brisk pace, Teddy smiled.

She would be her own Dr. Zanth, and damn it, she had made a correct diagnosis her second night as a resident in the ER. She had acted expeditiously and competently. That had to account for something.

If she were sick, she would almost want to be treated by a doctor like her in the ER . . . almost. Just not during the first week of July.

Chapter 6

Greg Cody
Cross College

If you could categorize a detective by a distinct crime-solving creed, Detective Greg Cody would have said that he came from the "Everyone's a Suspect" school of law enforcement. Granted, the culprits of most violent crimes were patently obvious. The husband or wife. Son or lover.

Sometimes the evidence took you off on a tangent, and you got a chance to dig a little deeper to build a case against a swindled partner, a disgruntled employee, a creepy neighbor. That was when things got interesting for Cody.

The way he saw it, if a person had the opportunity to commit a crime, they had to be considered a suspect. You could argue that it's ludicrous to look at someone just because they happened to be the janitor assigned to that building that night, or because they happened to be walking down a certain street at the time of the crime. You might even say that it's a waste to take time out of the investigation to interview such "witnesses." Even Cody's supervisors had their doubts over his methodology from time to time. But when all was said and done, Cody almost always extracted valuable information from witnesses, and a handful of times, he had snagged the perpetrator of the crime just because the perp was hanging out at the crime scene.

That saying about how a thief never returns to the scene of the crime?

A load of crap.

As a detective in NYPD Cody had seen some perps actually stick at the crime scene like groupies at a stage door. His favorite story was the guy they'd found hosing off the crime scene in Brooklyn. When the uniforms responded to the 911 call, they found a man on the street in front of a row house. He was unconscious, but there was no blood, no obvious injuries. The paramedics packed him up and sent him to the hospital, and the sergeant decided not to set up a crime scene, thinking that there'd been no crime committed.

Twenty minutes later, a cop at the hospital phoned the detectives, asking that they get a crime scene set up right away because the docs x-rayed this guy and there's a bullet in his brain. From the angle of the bullet, the docs figured someone put the barrel of a gun right up to his nose and squeezed one off. When Cody returned to the scene with two nervous uniformed cops, they found one of the neighbors hosing down the area. He was pretty resistant when the cops told him to shut off the hose. The hoser gave the cops a statement, and wouldn't you know, a week or so later they took him into custody for sending a bullet up a man's nose. Supposedly a drug deal gone bad.

You'd think the hoser would have known not to carry on a dirty business right in his own front yard. But that was the misconception about criminals; people assumed they were clever. Not true. Criminals were people, some smart, others not the sharpest pencils in the box.

But, long story short, you had to look at every single individual as a suspect when a crime went down. Otherwise, guys like the hoser might get away with murder, literally.

Downstairs, Cody had gotten a floor plan from the security guard and figured out that there were twelve rooms on each floor, all of them single occupancy for the summer. Now as he climbed the stairs Cody did the math, figuring if they canvassed all four floors at twelve rooms a floor, that'd be forty-eight rooms—a nightmare by anyone's standards. He hoped he could get another detective and some of the uniforms to help with the canvass, as well as with the other tasks like checking the college's security tapes, inspecting records from the dorm's ID scanner and security system, and combing through the community garbage heap—whether a Dumpster or incinerator—for bloody items.

On the fourth floor of the dorm, the crime scene was apparent. One door in the north corner was open, the doorway tied off with yellow crime scene tape, and Cody could see a tech from CSI squatting down to remove something from the floor with tape. As he headed that way, he soaked up the basics. The center of the floor was a community bathroom. The rooms appeared to face the outside, their doors clustered in threes in each corner. Tile floors, painted concrete walls. Smells of floor wax, urine, shaving cream, and ramen noodles. Ah, college life.

Inside what must have been McGann's room, Samira Goldwyn could have been a college student in her burgundy capri pants and white knit shirt, working the scene with intelligence and energy despite the god-awful hour. Cody was relieved to see that Goldwyn and Shaggy had pulled the duty tonight. Samira Goldwyn was one of the best, an efficient worker who obsessed over every detail. Although only in her twenties, she possessed a degree in forensics and the wisdom of an ancient yogi. Her partner, Len Conklin, whom everyone called Shaggy after the Scooby-Doo character, was equally on task, despite the slacker appearance with his soul patch, oversized Quicksilver T-shirts, and perennial earbuds clamped in place. Wearing gloves and paper booties over their shoes, the technicians worked in tandem collecting evidence. Tuned into his iPod, Shaggy lifted blood spatter from the tile floor with tape, while Samira, on the other side of the single bed, sketched on a clipboard.

"How's the art class going?" Cody asked.

Shaggy looked up and grinned, but Samira's dark eyes did not flinch. "I am making you beautiful sketches, Cody. The DA will love you for this."

"Photos, too?"

"Of course. Sketches. Digital photos. Some video. We have

it all. Do you want to trail the scene before we start bagging?"
She gestured toward the bed quilt, a lightweight cotton printed
with green, blue, and brown circles, now stained with a thick
pool of brown, as well as spatters.

"Nah, I won't get in your way. It looks like a fairly straight-
forward scene."

She paused behind the bed. "You never know, Detective."

"You're right, Samira. That's why I'm happy to have you
doing the digging. Any idea what the perp used?"

"We've got three baseball bats, one with blood and hair on
it. Probably the weapon."

"Brand?"

"A Louisville Slugger."

"Any nice fingerprints?"

"From the bloody smears on the bat, I'd say the attacker
wore gloves." Samira tucked the clipboard under one arm.
"Points to premeditation."

"Did the attacker leave any blood?"

"Can't say yet. However, there is a lot of blood here. Most
of it on the bed." She lifted the corner of the quilt to show him
the sheets. "Soaked through the quilt. The victim must have
ended up here. Did he survive?"

"Still alive. Head trauma."

She nodded, dismissing him. "We'll keep you posted."

"Thanks." Cody noticed a uniform cop halfway down the
hall, leaning in the doorway, talking to someone. Mal had said
that the uniforms had stayed on the scene. The cop stepped
back to include Cody.

"Good morning, Detective."

"Officer Alvarez." Greg nodded. He'd never worked a case
with Alvarez, a full-faced man with a flabby neck that sat on
his collar. At least Alvarez's collar was starched, his uniform
pressed smooth. Cody wished he'd had a clean shirt to wear
when he'd been yanked out of bed thirty minutes ago by the
cell phone summons. "So what's happening?"

"We're just talking to people, seeing if anyone saw or heard
anything unusual."

Good. "Making my job easier. Thanks for that." Cody glanced down to catch the name on his pad. "Right now I'm looking for Isaiah Gibbs, the student who found the victim?"

"That brother is freaking out." The voice came from inside the room. "Every which way but weird. He acts like he's never seen blood before."

Cody stepped up to the doorway and came face-to-face with a broad-shouldered African-American youth wearing boxers and a tight tank top that revealed the sculpted curves of his upper body. The guy had six-pack abs, all right, and it wasn't from downing six-packs of beer.

Alvarez consulted his clipboard. "This is Kevin Webber, plays on the Lakers."

"I'm Detective Cody."

Kevin Webber cocked his head to the side, his bleary-eyed look making it clear that he really didn't care.

"How're the Lakers looking this year? I haven't made it to a game yet."

"We're twelve and four," the player said, almost begrudgingly.

"That's pretty good. So you saw Isaiah Gibbs freaking out."

"Crying and shit. It's embarrassing."

"Violent crimes can be a tough thing to see," Cody began. "It can really rock your—"

"Yeah, well, you can save your speech for the Boy Scout over there in the lounge." Webber paced over to the single bed built into the cove by the window and sat down on the edge. "Can I go back to bed now? We finished with the questions? 'Cuz we got a game today and I'm gonna be dragging my ass if I don't get some sleep."

"Go on and get your beauty rest." Cody backed away and made a notation for Kevin Webber: brawny, strong, will not suffer a fool wisely.

Alvarez pointed Greg to the lounge. "I got a statement from Gibbs already, but we figured someone from the squad would want to talk to him."

"Thanks," Cody said, approaching the lounge, a small

room with a wall of windows that looked out over the dark campus. Even before he laid eyes on the kid, he could smell the fear. Yeah, this kid was rattled.

Isaiah Gibbs sat hunkered down in his hoodie. The fluorescent lights cast a pearly sheen on his chocolate-brown skin, and he wore his pain in his red, owlish eyes. His legs stretched off the sofa and covered most of a solid pine coffee table; legs so long they didn't seem to fit the upper half of Isaiah's body, spare beneath the voluminous sweatshirt. A flat-screen TV was mounted on the wall by the archway, the volume muted, though Gibbs didn't seem to be watching.

"Isaiah Gibbs? I'm Greg Cody, a detective with the Syracuse PD."

Gibbs nodded. "How's Ben doing? Is he okay?"

"Last I heard he was at Good Sam, but I don't have any other details." Cody took a seat across from the student. "I know you spoke to the police about what happened, but I'd like you to go over it one more time."

Gibbs pursed his lips and turned his gaze down to the floor. "I'd go over it a million times if it could get these images out of my head. Man, he was in bad shape. His head, it was all wet with blood."

"Yeah, that's hard to see. Let me ask you, how'd you run across him in the middle of the night?"

"I got up to hit the can. I was on my way when I heard this noise, like a sick cat or something. It was Ben, moaning. The door to his room was open a crack, and when I pushed it, I saw him there, all messed up on the bed."

"He was on the bed? Like, was he in bed, under the covers?" Cody asked.

"Nah. It wasn't like he'd gotten into bed. He was sort of situated at the bottom of the bed, on top of the comforter. Like he was sitting there when he got whacked, and he fell back onto the bed."

Which would have been better than falling on the unforgiving floor tiles. "Right." Cody nodded. "What exactly did you see when you opened the door?"

Gibbs shook his head, as if he could shake off the memory. "It was a nightmare. The skin by his eye looked like . . . like raw meat. He was moaning. Real creepy. You ever see *Zombieland*?" Gibbs wrapped a large hand over his jaw and mouth, as if to contain the horror, then let his fingers slip down to his chin. "At first I couldn't believe it. I mean, I thought it was some kind of joke. Like he was wearing a mask or something. Then I flicked on the light."

"And you saw it was the real deal." When the kid nodded, Cody went on. "You said he was moaning. Did he say anything to you?"

Gibbs nodded, squeezing his eyes shut a second. "He asked me to help him get up, that he was going to miss the game." His voice cracked, as if Ben's words were the saddest thing he'd ever heard. "He was worried about missing the game. That just killed me. I mean, his head is covered in blood, his face all screwed up, and he thinks he's going to get out to play ball."

Cody glanced down at his notebook, waiting a moment while Gibbs cried. He felt bad for the kid, whose wounds were real. In his wayward career Cody had seen some sociopaths put on good shows of remorse, but this was not one of them. Gibbs's shock was the real deal.

He also sensed that this young man felt out of place here on the Cross Campus. Gibbs didn't possess the smug sense of entitlement that glazed the eyes of most students.

"Listen, I know this is hard for you, but there are a few more questions I have to ask."

Gibbs nodded and swiped at his tears as Cody went on. "Did you see anyone else in the room or in the hallway?"

"No. It was quiet. Middle of the night."

"Was the room trashed?"

"The dresser—where Ben keeps his bats—it was all messed up."

"Messed up how?"

"Ben likes to keep his favorite bats in his room. He props them on the dresser on top of towels, nice and neat. Guys are always making cracks that it's a baseball shrine and that Ben probably takes his sticks to bed at night, but Ben didn't care. He wasn't about impressing people."

"Do you have any idea who might have done this to Ben McGann?"

Gibbs shook his head.

"Did Ben ever cross any of the other players? Ever argue with anyone?"

Isaiah Gibbs seemed to curl farther inside his baggy hooded sweatshirt. "Yeah, they had some words. The Lakers aren't really a team, except on the playing field. Summer ball isn't anything like what I expected."

"Is Ben unpopular?"

"Nah, most people like Ben. But some of the senior guys, Turtle and Rico, they have issues with McGann. Mostly they're jealous. Ben's better than them, and he's only going into his sophomore year."

Cody suspected that Rico and Turtle were nicknames for two of the players, but he would extract that information from someone else. "So Ben has had some friction with these two guys. . . . Turtle and Rico?"

"Yeah. Last night Ben and Turtle went at each other."

Cody wrote the names in his notebook. "Where was this?" he asked, trying not to sound too interested.

"At the Regan Hotel. Ben's girlfriend threw a big party and invited the team."

"What was the party like?"

"Pretty fancy. Had these appetizers, bacon wrapped around scallops. Really good. I never had those before."

"Any booze there?"

Gibbs's eyelids closed slightly, suspiciously. "Some, but I wasn't drinking. Emma was dishing out these tropical drinks with coconut milk, but she ran out of rum fast."

"Did you see Ben drinking?"

"Yeah, but only after the booze ran out. Then he let Emma make him one of those froufrou drinks."

"You said Ben and Turtle got into a fight . . . at the hotel?"

"Yeah, they were tumbling. I didn't hear what they said. I try to step away from things like that. I wasn't raised that way, jumping people and taking a shot at them. They seemed to settle things after a bit. But as soon as that died down, in comes Rico, yelling at Ben because some scout is supposed to be at the game tomorrow." He rubbed his eyes. "Actually, that game's today. It all runs together when you get no sleep. Anyway, Rico was yelling, saying that as long as Ben is around, Rico won't be playing first base."

"Really." Cody stopped writing, knowing that he would remember these details. He was on to something . . . definitely getting warmer. "Tell me, was there bad blood among these guys before tonight?"

"They had issues," Gibbs said.

"Did you ever see them or anyone gang up on Ben?"

"Nah. And I don't think guys like Turtle and Rico would pull something like this. Just because you want a guy's place in the roster doesn't mean you beat him up. Not like what happened to Ben."

"You know, Isaiah, not everyone sees it that way. I suspect that someone around here doesn't share your moral code. Certainly, the person who attacked McGann is of questionable integrity."

"I didn't mean to rat anyone out." Isaiah shook his head warily. "I told you I don't know anyone who would hurt Ben."

"We're just having a conversation here," he said, circling the lounge area with a pointed finger. "A routine part of my investigation, okay? Nobody else gets my notes."

Gibbs pressed a hand over his mouth, closed his eyes. "Okay," he said, though he didn't sound okay. "Can I go now?"

Drawing in a breath, Cody noticed a tinge of pink in the landscape outside. Dawn? It wasn't even five in the morning yet, but the days were long this time of year. "You can go, Isaiah. You going to try and get some sleep?"

Gibbs shook his head. "No, sir. I need to check the train schedule and get packing if I'm going to get home. Back to North Carolina."

"Don't you have a game today?"

"I got no game left in me, sir. Maybe, once I'm back home . . . I don't know, maybe I'll play again when I feel safe. I'm scared. Whoever did that to Ben is out there. There's a psycho dude out there, and I don't want to be anywhere near here. I'm going home, back where people are decent Christians and all."

Cody didn't have the heart to tell the kid that "psycho dudes" could turn up anywhere, even in decent Christian communities.

In the window beyond Gibbs's head, the sun emerged behind a stand of leafy trees. A bright orange ball.

Another day, and it was going to be a hot one.

Chapter 7

Kate
New York State Thruway

Although he was annoying the hell out of her, Kate reminded herself to be grateful for Eli's presence as the white lines at the edge of the highway became a blur and her head bobbed toward her right. Falling into a drowsy sleep, she tried to recharge as her mind combed through images of Ben and Eli. Like the jittery projections of her father's Super 8 movies, the early days of the McGann family trudged through her dreams.

There was Ben falling back on his diapered bottom in front of a kneeling Eli.

Eli carrying him on his shoulder, Ben drooling down into his father's hair.

The two of them dozing on the couch while an old Beatles album played on the stereo.

Those early days, a magical time that had surprised both Kate and Eli after the bumpy years of battle over the baby question.

First, there had been Kate's campaign to have a baby when Eli was convinced that he would not make a good father. He had argued that he was too passive-aggressive, too aloof, that he did not feel any stirrings of paternity, that he was well aware of his family's dysfunctions and had no intention of reenacting that madness with a child of his own.

Kate had danced around Eli's reservations, to no avail.

When it became clear that he would not commit, she forced his hand with an ultimatum: *I will not be happy without a child in my life.*

Eli had rolled his eyes at what he perceived as Kate's weakness, then agreed to give it a try. "If that's the only thing that will make you happy," he kept saying.

So began the years of trying, those short weekend getaways to country bed-and-breakfast inns or candlelit dinners in their SoHo loft. The tedium of determining ovulation with a basal thermometer and marked-up calendar.

After three years of trying, Kate grew discouraged. It wasn't going to happen for them. She was convinced that she was not going to get pregnant, and Eli appeared to be not just content, but smug about it.

How she came to revile him in those days! For a time she worried she would never move past that hatred and then . . .

It washed away the day she learned that she was pregnant. She was able to forgive him his snide comments about not "feeling" paternal. She changed the subject when he worried that their relationship would be ruined by a shrill, needy intruder. For every negative projection Eli made about how they would be as parents, Kate was able to create a more cohesive scenario, a portrait of a family woven together by communication, openness, and love.

Nine months later when Ben was born, a true miracle transpired. Eli learned that he was not only a receptive father, he actually enjoyed taking care of an infant who needed him. Although Kate had worried about staying sane with a baby in their loft apartment, Eli was happy to have Ben's bassinette close by. "It actually makes the apartment feel like a home, having him here," Eli had said. "It's our family nest in the city."

Eli had been a capable father. He had been able to differentiate cries of hunger from cranky moans. Each milestone in infant development had inspired awe, as Eli cried: "He's learning to use his hands now!" or "Did you see him roll over?"

Ben was a cheerful baby, a predictable napper, rarely fussy, and easy to soothe when he was teething. When he was just a week old Eli brought him to the gallery where he worked, and Ben seemed to find the airy, open space comforting. When the baby's presence warmed up a wealthy buyer to the tune of fifty thousand dollars, even the gallery owner agreed that Ben gave them an edge on the competition.

When Ben began to crawl and explore, Eli was the one to initiate a move from Manhattan. "The city is full of hazards for him," Eli had observed, as if seeing the world with new eyes. The noise of street construction could hurt Ben's ears. Trucks belched exhaust fumes just inches from their baby's stroller. Cars jumped the curb, old buildings were lined with lead and asbestos, and the bathroom at their favorite brunch place in NoHo was too disgusting to take Ben into for a diaper change.

When a news account appeared in the *Times* about an indigent, deluded man who leaned into a stroller to put his cigarette out on a baby's forehead, Eli cracked open the real estate section and took action. He drew a wobbly circle around the island of Manhattan, thirty miles in all directions. "There's a lot within a stone's throw of the city," he told Kate.

Some of this worried Kate, who wondered what sort of house she and Eli could afford on the salaries of a schoolteacher and an assistant manager at an art gallery. Occasionally Eli made substantial money when he sold a stained-glass piece, but much of those profits had to go back into the business to pay for the studio space he rented with another artist, the kiln, the lead mill, supplies, and tools. Kate worried not only that they might fall into debt, but that they would land somewhere they did not want to be, on a suburban cul-de-sac, a slave to fast foods and satellite TV.

In the New York area, house hunting on a budget was depressing. They looked at many stodgy row houses in Queens and the Bronx. On Long Island they saw boxy Capes on treeless lots. In New Jersey there were houses that backed up to railroad tracks, houses that bordered highways or choked in the smoke from the factories along the river. Cancer Alley, they called that area. The outlook was bleak.

Two years passed, and during that time Kate began to accept her lot as the parent of a toddler in the city. Sometimes things were difficult. The horror of watching Ben reach for broken glass in the park. The shrill stares of restaurant diners when Ben got cranky. The indignation when someone absentmindedly flicked cigarette ash in his direction while waiting to cross the street. But they were surviving, and Ben was certainly a happy kid.

Then, one afternoon, Eli came home from the studio in a swirl of joy. Julie, the gallery owner, had some architect friends who were desperate to unload their house in Woodstock because they had already relocated to the West Coast. Julie said the house was fabulous—a glass and wood design built by the architects themselves. "And Woodstock is loaded with galleries and craft shops. Julie's looking into buying a gallery there."

For Eli, this was unbridled enthusiasm, definitely worth exploring. They strapped Ben into a rental car that weekend and drove out to Woodstock, to the glass house on the hill.

"It's more than thirty miles from Manhattan," Kate pointed out as she folded the map in her lap on the way there. "A lot more. A hundred miles from civilization, Eli."

"But it's Woodstock, Kate. Woodstock has its own civilization. Do you know that this place has been a hub for American artists and craftsmen since the nineteenth century? The Byrdcliffe Colony was established here back in 1902. Woodstock's had an international art reputation since long before the music festival."

"I didn't know that," Kate admitted. "I just think of that big rock concert in the sixties."

"The concert was actually held at some farm, miles away, but it really put Woodstock on the map. After that, many artists and musicians and revolutionaries ended up settling in the Woodstock area."

She laughed. "Does that inspire you? God, Eli, that was some years ago. I was seven, and I didn't have a clue about any revolution beyond 1776. You were only ten or eleven."

"Eleven, and much more socially conscious than you, apparently. I wore a bracelet with the name of a POW on it. I wrote to soldiers in Vietnam."

"I was saving my allowance for a Malibu Barbie," she countered. Though that probably wasn't true, sometimes she liked to play devil's advocate with Eli, who could become myopic when on a campaign.

The center of the little town was quaint and artsy, with galleries, candle shops, and bookstores. A banner hanging from a lamppost boasted: WOODSTOCK, COLONY OF THE ARTS.

Eli was hooked.

The house itself, a modest, rectangular prism of glass and wood, was perfect. Set back from the road, the house was built at the base of a hill on three acres of property—plenty of space. There was an old tractor garage by the road that Eli could set up as a stained-glass studio. An acre of the hillside had been cleared to build the structure, but three large pine trees on the property had been milled on-site and used to construct part of the house.

It felt right.

Before they closed on the house, Kate found a teaching job at a nearby grammar school, and Eli, surprisingly, was offered a contract to teach art at the prestigious Woodlands Academy.

They moved in the summer of 1993. For Kate, the first few years in the Woodstock house were bliss. Here was a place for Eli to create his art, a yard for Kate to plant bulbs and daisies, a hillside for Ben to toddle in grass free of cigarette butts and broken glass.

Each morning on her way to work she dropped Ben off at a Montessori school. They hiked as a family and had breakfast in the sunlight of the little windowed nook. Eli turned more attention to his stained-glass art and started creating custom pieces for their little house on the hill. Some nights he worked late in his studio, and though Kate missed his company, she was always reassured by the lights of the studio at the bottom of the hill.

Gradually, as Ben began to assert more and more independence, Eli withdrew. As new milestones were reached, when Ben could read aloud or write a sentence, Eli grew surly. It was as if he'd been terminated from fatherhood, been relieved of all duties when Ben learned to feed and clothe himself.

Once Ben started grade school, Eli took the estrangement one step further by criticizing Ben's teachers and coaches. Miss Riddle certainly didn't know how to teach math, or Coach Shawn was hopeless at multitasking. At the time, Kate had dismissed his comments, thinking that he was just being protective of Ben and overly critical. She didn't realize Eli's derision took root in those years and later blossomed into estrangement from his son.

By the time Ben turned ten or eleven, Kate had found her own way with her son, figured out her own patterns and parenting skills, and learned to keep Ben away from the man who considered kids a buzzkill and a nuisance. Eli was always lost in his work at the studio, running behind deadline on a stained-glass window commissioned by a church or engrossed in a new design that required intricate cuts of glass. On weekends when Ben had games or picnics, Eli contended that he needed to mind the shop—referring to the junk pile in an old garage that Eli liked to think of as antiques and collectables.

And now . . . this was what they'd become: two strangers traveling to rescue their son. Although Kate wasn't sure precisely how Ben would need rescuing, she would do everything she could for him.

And what about Eli? Could he find it in his heart to reach out to his son and reconnect? Was he capable of giving Ben what he needed in this crisis?

Kate's cell rang, and her breath caught in her throat. She snatched it from her bag and flipped it open. "Hello?"

"This is Dr. Zanth from Good Samaritan Hospital. I'm trying to reach Kate McGann."

"Yes, yes, this is Kate." Kate's pulse accelerated, blood thrumming in her ears. "I'm Ben's mother. How is he doing?"

"They've just taken him up to the OR for surgery."

"Surgery?" This was not what Kate was expecting to hear. She had not consulted with the surgeon or signed any papers. Not even a consent form. "This is all going so fast."

"Yes, I know, but the emergency surgery is necessary. We had to move quickly in an attempt to maintain full brain function. With injury, the brain swells and pushes against the skull. The swelling and constriction can actually cut off circulation and damage parts of the brain."

"Brain damage?" Kate's voice was just a whisper, but she could feel Eli tensing in the driver's seat. Was his heart breaking, too? Was a frisson of dread creeping down his spine, squeezing his stomach, piercing his core? "Is he . . . brain damaged?"

"That's what we're trying to prevent," the doctor said. "Dr. Pruett, the neurosurgeon, is doing a craniotomy. He will drill holes in the skull, or remove a small part of the skull, to relieve intracranial pressure. Mrs. McGann, I'm sorry to have to give you this information over the phone. Are you okay to drive? I can explain this all to you later."

"My husband is driving," Kate said absently, her thoughts focused on Ben, in surgery already. Did they shave his head? Was he frightened? "Doctor . . . I'm sorry, I've already lost your name . . ."

"Zanth. Teddy Zanth."

"Dr. Zanth, was Ben conscious when you saw him?" The thought of her son being told he needed brain surgery cut Kate to the bone. To think of him navigating the strange faces of hospital workers alone, being wheeled down those strange halls without any family by his side . . .

"He was unconscious," Dr. Zanth answered.

Thank God . . . that was some relief. "It's so frustrating not to be there. We should be arriving within the hour."

"He might be coming out of the OR soon after you arrive. The procedure usually takes two to three hours. You'll want to come straight to the surgical waiting room, ninth floor in the Grace Pavilion. Have the receptionist page me and I'll do my best to answer your questions."

"Yes, I will. Thank you, Dr. Zanth." Feeling like she now had more questions than answers, Kate cut the connection and turned to Eli. "You need some wings on this car," she said.

"I can make it fly," he said, stepping on the accelerator. "I was just waiting for you to say the word."

As Kate sat back and stared through the window at the pink sky of dawn, she breathed in relief. It was good that Eli was coming with her. Whatever the crisis ahead, Eli belonged in this scenario, a father to his son.

Chapter 8

Joe "Turtle" Turturro
Cross College

In the campus dining hall, Turtle straddled a chair at the team table, leaned forward, and plucked a sausage link from Trevor Dozneski's plate. "Thanks. I need a wiener."

"Hey!" Dozo growled, cradling an arm around his plate. "Get your own."

Ignoring him, Turtle devoured it in two bites, his gaze combing the half-empty table for more. He hadn't paid for the meal plan yet. He'd figured out a way to divert the fifty-dollar-a-week meal allowance to his checking account, and so far he'd been getting enough just by finishing off the food items the other guys left behind. They wasted so much food, probably because half of them didn't have to pay.

On the one end you had those rich guys like Ben McGann who were bankrolled by Mommy and Daddy. At the other end of the spectrum were guys like Rico Valpariso, kids who came from nothing and went through programs like this on full-ride scholarships. If you came from poverty, everything was paid for.

It was the in-between guys like Turtle who got stuck. His old man was into the wind and his mother made sixty grand a year as a nurse. Not enough to finance her son's summer ball but too much for Turtle to qualify for financial aid during the school year. Stuck in the middle, that's what he was. No one was allowed to get paid for playing summer ball, and that hurt guys like Turtle.

Eyeing the piece of fruit on Kenta Suzuki's plate, he snapped his fingers in the air. "Hey, Turning Japanese! Toss that peach this way."

Kenta gently took the fruit in one hand, squinting at Turtle in confusion. The Japanese kid was an okay guy, though nobody knew what he was thinking. Maybe he was just shy. Maybe he hated them all. Turtle assumed it was the language barrier and not some weird psycho factor.

"Yeah, yeah, underhand it," Turtle coached him. The ripe peach flew and Turtle caught it with a soft splat on his palm. He licked it, swiped Dozo's knife to slice the peach.

"You know," Turtle said, feeling philosophical, "it's too bad McGann won't be in the dining hall for a while. McGann is a great food provider, good for a sandwich or salad." He slid a sliver of peach in, turned it in his mouth. "Yeah, too bad."

Across the table, Rico Valpariso coughed over his oatmeal. "What do you mean? Is McGandolf sick today?"

Turtle grinned. "Well, you should be the first to know. Better get your glove ready, my man. First base is yours tonight."

Valpariso rubbed the stubble on his jaw, his eyes red rimmed and haunted. "What are you talking about?"

"Hello?" Turtle snapped his fingers. "Like you don't know?"

"Don't tell me you missed the whole show last night," Dozo said. When Rico shook his head, Dozneski added, "The ambulance. Fire truck. Flashing lights and cop cars? Didn't you answer the door when those friggin' storm troopers banged on it?"

"I talked to the cops, but I didn't let anyone in my room," Austin Harold said.

"Nice thinking. When they filled out their little form, did they keep asking you what your last name was? 'Is it Harold? Or is it Austin? Austin or Harold?'" Turtle liked to tweak Harold, calling him Double First, on account of the guy had two first names. It drove Double First crazy, but Turtle didn't really care. Double First was a benchwarmer. "So, Rico, how'd you miss the whole show?"

Rico poked at his oatmeal with a spoon. "I don't live on the team floor."

"Well, neither do I, but I caught the action." Turtle hated it when Rico got evasive like this. "So you didn't notice anything weird this morning?"

"I thought that was a cop car parked outside the dorm, but whatever. So what happened?"

"Somebody snuck up on McGandolf and cracked him over the head with a bat," Dozo explained smugly. Like the story wasn't all over campus. "The paramedics took him away, and he ain't coming back anytime soon."

"Yeah?" Rico's tired eyelids lifted a little. "Wow. Bad break for him."

Turtle and Dozo exchanged a look of disbelief.

"Yeah," Turtle grunted. "His misfortune, your lucky break."

"You got first base now, Rico." Dozo grinned his feckless smile. Jesus, he could be a stand-in for Alfred E. Neuman on the cover of *MAD* magazine. "Everybody's going to be watching you."

"Yeah, yeah, great. I got what I wanted." Rico threw down the spoon, which clattered against the bowl. "Can you shut up about it now, Dozo?"

"What'd I say?" Dozneski's freckled face scrunched defensively.

"Just stop. I'm done talking about it, okay?" There was an edge to Rico's voice.

An edge that halted all conversation at the team table.

Ooh, conflict.

Turtle curled his lips into a sick smile as he turned his attention to Rico, whose dark eyes glittered dangerously. "You're a little sensitive about this, Rico. If I didn't know any better, I'd think you and McGandolf were best of friends."

"I said, let it go." Rico glared at Turtle, then looked away to break the deadlock.

But Turtle fed on confrontation. He tapped a fork against the table, aware that he held everyone's attention. "But wait . . . you and McGann both play first base. That's right!" He touched his forehead. "You two are rivals. How could I forget? You're rivals and, in fact, you threatened him last night, didn't you? In front of God and the world."

"Are you accusing me of something?" Rico's gaze snapped at Turtle. "You trying to say I'm the one who attacked McGann?"

"If the shoe fits . . ." Turtle shrugged. "Or, maybe I should say, if the bat fits." He was only half joking. The police were going to be sniffing around players on the Lakers, looking for the guy who attacked McGann, and if the trail led to Rico Valpariso, well, it would make things easier for Turtle, who had a few issues of his own.

"McGann and I exchanged words last night," Rico said, talking fast. "*Words,* not punches. You were the one who fought him, Turturro. Rolling on the floor like animals. Did you go after him a second time last night? Sounds like you fucked him up real good."

"We had a misunderstanding, but we cleared it up before the end of the party. However, you and McGann ended on a sour note. What was it you said? Something about taking him out of the lineup? Or did you just threaten to knock him out?"

The air was thick with tension as all eyes went from Turtle to Rico. Everyone at the team table was waiting for an answer, Dozo, Suzuki, Double First, Sager, Webber, and Steiner.

"Wow." Rico sucked on a front tooth, then smiled, revealing one flash of gold in his dental work. "I guess I did threaten him. My bad."

Turtle let out the breath he'd been holding and laughed at Rico's comeback. He had to laugh. Rico was a better strategist than he'd realized.

Laughter scattered around the table, and Dozo said, "And the plot thickens."

"Shut up, Dozo," Turtle and Rico said, almost at the same time.

Like minds, Turtle thought. But he and Rico had been allies before.

"You know, it's really not a joke," Zach Steiner said. His face was pale against the black stubble on his scalp. "Sounds like Ben got messed up bad."

"It wouldn't be so funny if it happened to you," Kenta added.

Turtle was about to say that he never enjoyed a pity party when he noticed Coach Ramsey coming down the stairs, his pale blue Lakers cap in his hands. "What's that about?" Ramsey did not show his face in the dining hall. Made all his players eat here, but Turtle figured him for a Denny's man. Or maybe the wife's homemade biscuits.

"I'll bet it's about Ben," someone said. "Looks serious."

Otis Ramsey paused at the head of the table, his hat over his heart. Was that deliberate? Turtle wondered. "Good morning. I suppose you've all heard about what happened to Ben McGann." He waited as people nodded. "I just had a meeting with a detective from the Syracuse Police Department and the director of campus security. This campus almost went into lockdown, but since it seems to be an isolated incident, we are proceeding with business as usual, though I'm making the morning drills optional for those of you who want to hit the hospital."

"What about the game tonight?" Dozo asked. "Is it still on?"

"Honestly, I thought about canceling, but since the other team is already in town, it's a go. McGann will be on the injured list." Ramsey walked along the table, as if counting heads. "I have offered the police our full cooperation. There will be a detective or two attending today's practice to meet with some of you."

Rico flipped his napkin on the table in disgust.

"I don't like cops," Turtle grumbled under his breath. And he was liking the coach less and less. Already they had to live and eat together like freakin' soldiers. Now Ramsey was going to offer them up to the cops like weenies on an appetizer tray?

"Wait." Ramsey squinted. "We're missing two. Where are Kroger and Gibbs?"

"You can take Gibbs off the roster, Coach," said Kevin Webber. "He's the one who found McGann. He's all fucked up."

"Where is he?" Ramsey asked.

"Last I heard, he was packed and headed home."

"And Dylan Kroger?" the coach asked.

A few guys shrugged. No one had seen McGann's best friend.

"Probably running after the ambulance like the loyal dog that he is," Turtle muttered under his breath. And finally, guys laughed. Best laugh of the morning.

Chapter 9

Eli McGann
Good Samaritan Hospital

Eli McGann was adept at disengaging from reality, a skill he employed every day. Whether he was in front of a class of pimply adolescents who liked his 3-D art class because he didn't give homework, or in his studio cutting glass over the light table, Eli had taught himself how to withdraw from the here and now, to shrink back from this deflating body of his and pass into a cerebral world untainted by annoyance and tedium.

Music, paintings, a certain slant of light through colored glass—these were stored in his mind as sanctuaries, a place to go when life grew flat and sour. On a humid summer night, the bejeweled emerald glass that formed a cluster of trees in a window he was leading provided cool escape from the heat of the kiln. When pockets of conversation erupted in his classroom, he was the indigo shadow on horseback of Kandinsky's "Blue Rider," roaring across the painting's pastures beyond anyone's reach. How many times had he slid into the timbre of Van Morrison's "Moondance" or faded into the bittersweet landscape of the Beach Boys' "Caroline, No"?

Sometimes the escapes came to him unbidden. Like now, in this institutional hospital corridor. The Beatles' song "Martha My Dear" played in his head in sync with the clogged footsteps of a woman in front of them dressed in navy scrubs. He didn't know why that song had risen in his thoughts. Maybe because she slumped and plodded along and the song lyric advised: "Hold your head up, you silly girl."

Or maybe it was the woman's multicolored shaggy hair, a style that reminded him of an Old English sheepdog, the dog that was supposed to have inspired the song for McCartney.

Whatever the reason, the song provided escape from the rhythmic plodding of feet, his and Kate's, on the hospital linoleum as they navigated up to the waiting area outside the OR, trying to find Ben in the elusive Grace Pavilion.

Good Samaritan Hospital was a box of dread, and Eli knew he would not last long in this environment without suffocating.

He needed a distraction, anything to keep from lashing out at Kate, anything to stop himself from contemplating the worst-case scenario for their son, and if "Martha My Dear" kept him moving ahead, it would suffice. The sheepdog in the scrubs stayed with them till the elevator stopped on the second floor. She stepped off, but the song remained.

At the ninth-floor reception desk a young Asian woman sat leafing through paperwork like some visiting auditor. When she continued to avoid eye contact, Eli cut in.

"We're looking for Ben McGann. He's having brain surgery. Are we in the right place?"

She flipped a stack of papers over with a sigh. "I'll check for you."

"We're his parents," Kate said, pressing her lower body to the desk as if she would collapse without it. "Can you tell us his status?"

"One minute. This isn't my station, but I'll see what I can find."

Kate pushed her sunglasses up so that they sat atop her head like a sixties headband. Marlo Thomas in *That Girl.* "And would you please page Dr. Zanth? Teddy Zanth from the ER. She wanted to meet us here."

How did she remain so calm and civil, when he knew she was quavering inside?

And damn it, why did they hire girls with elephant tusks glued to their fingernails to type on computers?

At last, the chick nodded at the screen. "Your son is still in surgery. While you're waiting, I have some paperwork for you to fill out. Looks like he came in through the ER." She handed a clipboard of papers to Kate, who stared down at it hopelessly.

"I'll do it." Eli took the clipboard and sat on the edge of a mundane oatmeal tweed chair. At least this was something he could do instead of sitting around torturing himself and Kate. This business of hospitals, the call from doctors to rush here, then wait, was all so maddening.

Paperwork was no friend of Eli's, but he'd become inured to it; one of those inevitabilities in life, like death and taxes. He managed the basic information, but then was stumped. "Any allergies?" he asked Kate.

She hugged herself, shook her head.

No. He should know that. A father should know, but then he was no Ward Cleaver.

"What's his address in the dormitory here?"

"Just put down Hawthorne Hall."

He jotted it down, frowning. Why bother? If Ben was at this moment having brain surgery, what were the chances of him returning to his dorm room anytime this summer? What were the chances that he would walk out of this place and return home at all? Under address, he should write: currently residing in your operating room.

Fueled by sour fury for a system that hits you with paperwork when you're down, he flipped through the pages on the clipboard, blindly signing on the lines marked with a canary highlighter. Yes, they could release information to his insurance company. Yes, the information on the form was true. Yes, he understood the sheaf of release and confidentiality papers that he really hadn't begun to read.

He handed back the clipboard, felt like flinging his insurance card into the face of tusk-nails but restrained himself and handed it over.

This floor wasn't quite as crowded as others, though Eli observed the traffic, the attendants with carts, the staff in scrubs. He watched and waited for a man in surgical scrubs who would have information about Ben.

"He should be out of surgery by now." Kate checked the time on her cell phone. "Do you think something went wrong? Some kind of complication?"

"Of course there was," Eli snapped. "We couldn't be so lucky to have things go smoothly. The only luck I ever have is bad luck."

Just then there was a flurry of movement at the desk. A new arrival. The exotic-looking woman in a white lab coat seemed far too young to be the doctor they were looking for. You know you're getting old when the people on the hospital staff seem like kids to you. When the receptionist pointed to them, Kate and Eli stood immediately.

"Are you Ben's parents?"

"Yes, yes, I'm Ben's mother, Kate McGann." Kate extended her hand.

"I'm Dr. Zanth, Teddy Zanth. I treated your son in the ER."

Eli noticed how the dark-haired woman didn't so much shake hands as clasp his hand for a moment and fix her penetrating amber eyes on his. What, were they teaching compassion in med school these days? Mind reading?

Motioning for them to sit, Teddy Zanth perched on a chair beside Kate. Her golden skin and dark hair were a stark contrast to her crisp lab coat. Not a classic beauty, Eli decided, unless you were Paul Gauguin. Definitely some Asian ancestry, maybe South Pacific or Indonesia.

"I stopped by the operating room on my way here. I was hoping to get an update, but learned only that they are still in surgery."

Kate's face was flushed now, her eyes glassy with tears, and Eli felt torn between rubbing her back and snarling at her not to cry now, when they finally had a shot at getting some solid information. "We thought he'd be out by now," Kate said hoarsely. "Was there some complication?"

"I really can't say. The procedure usually takes two and a half hours, but it's not a big deal for an operation to take a little longer. Carl Pruett, the neurosurgeon, has an excellent reputation. Ben is in good hands."

Kate nodded, her face crumpling into a full-fledged crying jag.

Eli looked away impatiently. He felt like crying, too. It appealed to him in the way that any stormy release can ease the suffering. A sneeze, a yawn, an orgasm. But honestly he hadn't cried for years now. It was as if that emotional core inside him had dried to a hard, knotty kernel, a lifeless, withered pit.

"If you like, I'll go over what I observed when Ben was brought in," the doctor offered.

Kate gasped, as if catching a sob. She had lost the ability to speak.

"Go ahead," Eli said, his gaze homing in on the young doctor who seemed far too sympathetic to have been doing this job for long. Maybe she was just a med student. Was that possible? Were students allowed to treat patients? He thought of his students at Woodlands Academy. What a nightmare.

"I don't remember exactly what I told you on the phone, but Ben came into the ER with head trauma. As I said, by the time we saw him he was unconscious. His GCS was nine out of fifteen, which indicates serious trauma."

Eli held up a hand. "Speak English."

"The GCS? It stands for 'Glasgow Coma Scale.' It's an assessment of how major trauma has affected a patient's level of consciousness. A score of eight or lower indicates serious injuries. Ben was a nine, which is not great, but I've seen patients come back from that."

Eli nodded, signaling her to go on.

"The first hour after a TBI—that's what we call a traumatic brain injury—that initial time is often called the Golden Hour. If we move fast with diagnostics and treatment, we have a much better chance of preserving the patient's brain function."

She paused, watched as Kate dug into her purse and pulled out a pack of tissues, then continued. "From the X-rays we could see that Ben had a good amount of brain swelling on the right side, right frontal lobe. One of the greatest dangers of a closed head injury is the tendency of an injured brain to swell. The human skull is fairly well packed with brain in a normal head, so when the cranium swells, there is no room for the brain to expand. The cranium might push into the eye sockets or press into the skull and damage the brain." She looked from Kate to Eli. "There's the possibility of brain damage, as I mentioned."

"So the surgeon is going to drill a hole in his skull to relieve the pressure?" Eli asked. He had tracked what the doctor had said as Kate relayed it after their phone conversation.

"Right." The single word held a slight twang, a touch of a British accent. "Dr. Pruett's plan was to burr holes into the skull to relieve cranial pressure. But once in the OR, he may have found that more extreme measures were necessary. Sometimes, if the brain swelling is extensive, the surgeon can remove a good-size piece of skull, an escape hatch for the brain, if you will. The piece of skull they cut away is called a bone flap, and generally the doctors will save the bone flap and replace it in the patient's skull after the swelling has gone down. They can store the bone flap in a refrigerator or they might make a small incision in your son's abdomen and tuck it in there for safekeeping."

Following the details of the procedure, Eli was struck by how it sounded so normal, as if it were an everyday event to have a portion of your skull sawed off and tucked into a fridge, between the pickles and the eggs.

He folded his arms, his hands icy from the air-conditioning, or maybe just from dread. He didn't want this to be happening to his boy. He didn't want to see Ben broken, a bloody mess of a science experiment sewn together by some type-A-personality doctor who thought he could play God in the operating room. Eli did not want any of this.

"So what's his prognosis?" Kate asked, her dark brown eyes opening wide in hope.

"It's really too soon to tell. Dr. Pruett will be able to tell you more when Ben gets out of surgery, but in terms of healing, time will tell."

Eli clenched his jaw. Next she was going to hand them the old platitude that "time heals all wounds." What a load of shit.

He sucked in a deep breath, trying to find some escape—a glimmer of colored light, a song in his head, *something*—but there was only vacant space, the box of this room, airless and so fucking monochromatic you could go snow-blind.

"I still can't imagine how this happened," Kate said. "I mean, in the dorm? Did he fall?"

Dr. Zanth linked her fingers together and pressed her knuckles to her chin. "I was told it was an assault. That a baseball bat was the weapon."

Eli's chest felt tight, his pulse quickening at the notion that Ben was a victim of malice. A violent act in the middle of the night . . . He had to force himself to keep breathing.

"How could that be? Ben is a popular guy." Kate shook her head, a fresh tear streaming down her cheek. "Granted, he hasn't been with this team long, but wherever he goes, Ben has this gift. People just like him."

"Perhaps the details I was given were inaccurate," Zanth said. "You'll have to speak with the police about that. I understand that a detective from the Syracuse PD is on his way."

"The police?" Kate held a hand up.

"Oh, great." Eli disliked cops. Even before he'd been jailed overnight for his DWI, he had an aversion to the rank-and-file who posed as heroes and played enforcer. "So now they're going to bring on the cops."

He had to get out of here . . . withdraw to another place.

Back to his studio, working under the flame, bending and melting lead.

He tried to go there in his mind, ducking under the clamor of his heartbeat, sliding into an old familiar pocket. The glimmering gem at the center of a whimsical design. The shiny button of a roundel that punctuated the sidelight panels he was working on for a dowager in Westchester.

Unfortunately, he could not disengage enough to block out their conversation.

"I can't believe the police are involved." Kate sounded distant.

"Ben's injuries were not accidental, Mrs. McGann." Teddy Zanth's voice was barely more than a whisper, but each word scratched at Eli's resolve. "Your son was assaulted."

Chapter 10

Marnie Epstein
The Regan Hotel

Why did I come here?

W Marnie Epstein was awake and trying to figure out what had brought her to this place, in a figurative sense. She pressed her pinky finger to her lips, still swollen from his kiss, and she wondered if that was the answer. Maybe it explained everything. As if her coming to Syracuse was one of those divine moments in which all previous paths of her life were destined to intersect.

She flopped over in bed and let her body sink into pristine fluff: feather pillows and comforter and exquisite white sheets.

It was no surprise to be up so early. When you wake up at five a.m. every morning to open the coffee shop, well, you wake up at five every morning even when it's your day off. No, the big surprise here was that she had plenty of time to doze off again and sleep in, but she could not because the feeling held her rapt.

She had thought the feeling would fade with sleep, but it remained so raw, edgy, and crisp.

As brilliant as the orange glow from the wall of windows, as swollen as her lips.

The feeling . . . hadn't faded overnight.

If anything, it had doubled and tripled, increased in magnitude and intensity.

It was totally crazy because it defied any realistic framework, and yet, there it was, deep inside her, flowing through her, resonating around her like an aura.

Why was she here?

The idea of the trip came to her when she realized she had the same two days off from Beantown Grind and from her summer job at Storemart—what were the chances of that?—and she had never been to Syracuse before. Well, that sounded like a good enough reason.

In truth, she had come to have a conversation with Dylan, to discuss something that couldn't be said by phone or e-mail. Of course, Dylan didn't know that yet because she hadn't dropped the bomb. Ironically, when Dylan found out she was considering the trip, he was all over her about it. "You have to come!" he'd insisted. "God, it'll be great to have a fan in the crowd." At the time she wasn't sure if Dylan was trying to guilt her into coming or if he was really that lonely here in Syracuse. Either way, she knew he was not going to be happy to hear what she had to tell him.

Then her friend Ben, who was her first connection to this whole crowd through Beantown Grind, called and told her Emma could give her a ride so she wouldn't have to take the bus. And then Emma insisted that Marnie keep her company in the suite as if they were new best friends.

"I've got the extra room, anyway," Emma said casually. "You might as well use it."

It was generous of Emma, and Marnie was grateful that she wouldn't have to rent a cheesy room in the visitors' dorm. And really, Marnie had never stayed in a hotel quite so grand before. Really. It reminded her of that hotel the Julia Roberts character stayed in during *My Best Friend's Wedding*. Floating in feather down, she did manage some sleep last night.

The soft, perfumed dreams of a princess.

So not me.

Marnie was a girl who put the jet-black henna in her own hair, plucked her own eyebrows, and made her own mac and cheese for dinner.

At home it was just Marnie and her mother, Jade Epstein,

who couldn't afford to house Marnie in the Boston College dorms, let alone set her up in her own apartment off campus like Emma. No, Marnie would be staying in the tiny second bedroom in their Brookline apartment, sharing a closet with her mother, who couldn't lose the bitter disappointment at being deserted by her well-off husband fifteen years ago.

How many times had Marnie heard what a disappointment Leo Epstein was to her mother? "What kind of man leaves his wife and daughter without a word?" her mother would ask all the time when she was little. As if Marnie had the answers. Although Marnie never dared respond, she could think of a few good answers. Maybe Leo Epstein wasn't happy with his wife. Or maybe he'd fallen into a ravine somewhere and his body was frozen under some dead leaves.

Then, when Marnie was in junior high, the mystery of Leo Epstein's disappearance had been solved, much to her mother's delight. "He's right here in Boston," Jade had gloated. "And I have an address. Ooh, I'm going to hit him so hard, his bank account will quiver for years."

"You're going to attack him?" Marnie had asked, taking it literally.

"The government will attack him for me," her mother gloated. "I'm filing for child support. Does he think it's cheap raising a kid on your own?"

Marnie had no idea what Leo Epstein was thinking and she didn't care to know. She was in junior high, and her top priorities were figuring out how to shave without her mother finding out and letting Jake D'Angelo know she liked him without being weird about it. But Jade Epstein sunk her teeth in like a shark and refused to let go until Leo agreed, out of court, to a settlement of just under a thousand dollars a month. "Tax free," Jade crowed. "Thank God. He's lucky I don't sue him for back pay."

While Jade Epstein was thrilled with the settlement, Marnie was shocked by the terms, which allowed her estranged father visitation rights. "He's lived without me for all these years," she told her mother. "Why do I have to do this?"

"Because he's your father."

The visitations lasted only long enough for Marnie to feel like a commodity sold by her mother to the strange man with a black-and-gray mustache who smelled of lime aftershave. Creeper, Marnie called him in her mind, though he had never done anything inappropriate beyond forcing her to go on outings with his six-year-old daughter from the new wife. Movies and ice-cream sundaes. The Boston Pops and Barney. Freakin' Barney! Marnie wasn't sure who she despised more, her father or his little chubster.

With some doing, the visitations faded away, as did Creeper's contributions when Marnie turned eighteen, which soured her mother all over again. "Just when you need money for college, he pulls it all away," Jade seethed.

In fact, Marnie's mother, Jade, was not in favor of her attending Boston College, even with the full-ride academic scholarship. "A mere forty grand a year," Jade kept saying, as if Marnie had taken a suitcase of cash from the college and dumped it into the Charles River.

Marnie had tried to explain her financial status to Emma a few times, but either Emma didn't get it or else she figured she could buy Marnie for the weekend, because she kept saying, "It's on me," when Marnie didn't want Subway sandwiches during the drive, or when Marnie declined shrimp and piña coladas from room service, or shots from the liquor Emma had brought.

The awkward part? Marnie got the feeling that Emma wanted to be her friend, which wasn't what Marnie had intended. When she accepted the ride to Syracuse, she didn't realize she was signing up for the buddy program. She thought it would just be, well, a *ride*.

Not that Emma Lenson was a bad person. She came off as kind and generous. She was a beautiful girl, definitely had Marnie beat in that category. There weren't a lot of bad things you could say about Emma, except of course, that Emma was all about Emma.

When Marnie first heard Emma referring to the family

housekeeper, she thought it was an inside joke, some reference to reruns of *The Fresh Prince of Bel-Air*. Emma's conversation was peppered with references to therapists, restaurants, and spas Marnie had never heard of. Emma told stories of the famous people she'd danced with in various clubs around the world, about the celebrity guys who were so "into" her, and about tweets from Paris. The city or the Hilton? Marnie couldn't really tell, and she definitely wasn't going to ask.

Less than twenty-four hours with the girl and Marnie was beginning to see the real Emma Lenson: a caricature of the stereotype people assumed a crystal heiress should be. There were moments when Marnie felt sorry for her, but then Emma would blurt out how Chris Brown wanted her to sing on his next recording and all empathy faded.

Marnie stretched, then scraped her long, dark hair back and twisted it into a knot atop the pillow. New best friend aside, she had come here to watch baseball. She'd been friends with Ben since the fall, but didn't have time to attend a game during the school year. And she didn't mind supporting Dylan's efforts, even if things were changing between them.

Last night's game replayed in quick bursts. Ben on first base, scooping up poorly thrown balls and tagging the base in a quick step that made it all look easy. Marnie and Emma had sat on the first-base side because Emma was all about proximity to Ben, as if she could keep a better hold on him by staying close enough to attach a leash or throw a lasso.

"That's my boyfriend, Ben," Emma always said. So many times that even the players on the Lakers had begun to mimic her, and they'd only been a team for a few weeks. "My boyfriend, Ben!" they'd chirp, fluttering their eyelashes or squeezing their cheeks together with the palms of their hands. The team dynamic was further evidence to Marnie that when guys in their twenties got together, they regressed five years.

At one point, during one of the later innings, the center fielder fobbed the ball and Dylan was sent in to take his place. As he trotted out, Dylan turned to the bleachers, his eyes searching against the field lights until he homed in on her. He looked like he was going to wave, but instead grabbed the bill of his cap and gave it a twitch, like a secret gesture.

"Ooh, look! He's pointing to us!" Emma's hand fanned the air as if the stadium spotlight had turned to her.

Marnie suppressed a groan. She didn't wave. She hated public spectacles; didn't want Dylan to embarrass himself. And God, she wished he wasn't looking up at her that way. With such pure adoration. You'd think she was the Virgin Marnie.

Shifting so that she was leaning against the padded headboard, Marnie pressed her lips together and covered them with her fingers, as if she could hold it all there—the good feeling, the magic—and keep it safe from a world where real-life connections were tugged and scraped away.

She had to choose her words carefully with Dylan, think about the best place to break the news to him. There had to be a way to break it off with him and let him down gently.

Telling him when they were in swimsuits on the steps of the hot tub last night?

Bad idea.

He had totally misunderstood her desire to be with him in private, and before she could say a word, he had grabbed her and started mashing his body against hers.

Big mistake.

He had talked about making her coffee in the morning. The guy had plans. Fortunately, she'd dodged that bullet.

But it was time to tell him. Maybe they could find a coffee shop—quiet but public—and she could set things straight with him.

Just then her cell phone chimed and she stretched to grab it from the nightstand. Dylan.

Had he been picking up her psychic attention?

"Good morning, Beantown," she said. It was the greeting she used at Beantown Grind from a joke so old, she didn't even remember how it had started.

"Hey, babe."

Marnie gritted her teeth. She hated it when he called her that.

"I waited to call you. Didn't want to wake you up."

"I was awake. Actually, I was just thinking that we need to talk. Maybe we could meet for breakfast?"

"Not today. Ben is in the hospital. He got hurt last night."

"What? What happened?" Marnie bolted up in bed. "He was fine when he left the party."

"They're saying he was attacked in the dorm." The timbre of Dylan's voice changed. "It looks bad, Marnie. I saw them taking him to the ambulance. I wanted to go along with him to the hospital, but they wouldn't let me."

"Oh, my God." Something told Marnie this was serious; she could hear it in Dylan's tone, sense it in his hesitancy.

Before Dylan, before Emma, or any idea of coming to see the Lakers play in Syracuse, there was Ben, sitting at the counter in Beantown Grind with a textbook open under his notebook.

The first day he showed up there in his jock jacket with leather sleeves, Marnie noticed he was reading the same textbook her anthropology class used, but she didn't say anything. She had learned that people who wanted to talk just launched right into stories or questions or small talk about the weather. Aside from some exchange with the other barista when she served him, this boy didn't look up from his coffee and notes, so she left him alone. As he left that first day, she tossed a rag in the sink and admitted that something about his thick brown hair and open face kept catching her eye.

"Do you recognize him?" asked Fiona, one of the other baristas. "He said he thought you looked familiar."

"The guy with the jacket?" Marnie shook her head. "Don't know him, but he looks like he just got released from *Happy Days*."

"The jacket is retro." Fiona chucked damp grinds. "Anyway, he said you look familiar, like maybe you have a class together."

"I don't think so." Marnie had been insistent.

The next day, as if to spite her, she walked into her anthro lecture hall and found him sitting alone in an aisle seat.

As she came down the steps he looked up and caught her staring. "Good morning, Beantown," he said.

From anyone else, that might have been creepy, but when Ben said it with that crumpled half smile and one brow arched over his steely eyes, Marnie just had to smile.

She sat beside him in the lecture hall that day. The next day, he appeared at her side of the counter. She served him coffee and three examples of creatures with exoskeletons. He asked her to study with him when she got off. She did, all semester. When it came time to register for the spring, they decided to take biology class together. Somewhere between that first cup of coffee and the anthropology final they became friends. Good friends.

"You still there?" Dylan asked, pulling her back to the here and now.

"Yeah, just a little worried. Ben is okay, right?"

"I'm heading over to the hospital as soon as I check in with the coach."

His nonanswer filled her with dread, a cold, jagged stone in her throat. "Dylan, do you think it was the guys from the team? Those two jocks at the party . . . Turtle, the one who was rolling on the floor with him? Or the other guy? Emma said another guy was threatening him. Rico. Do you think they sneaked up and attacked him?"

"Marnie, I don't know." He sighed. "I haven't really thought past checking on Ben."

"Right." She swallowed past the thickness in her throat. Dylan was right; Ben was the only person who mattered right now. "So I'll meet you at the hospital?"

"Yeah, and you're there with Emma, right? Would you mind telling her?"

Emma . . . of course; Marnie hadn't even thought of her. With a stab of guilt she realized Ben's girlfriend should be the first person to know.

"Sorry to dump this on you," Dylan said. "I know she can be high maintenance."

"I'll tell her." Marnie threw back the plush comforter and slid out of bed. Dylan was right; this wasn't going to be fun. "I'll tell her right now."

Chapter 11

Emma Lenson
The Regan Hotel

The knocks on the door rattled with impatience. "Are you awake?"

Emma's eyes felt pasty as she forced them open to check the time. Oh, no! Not even eight o'clock. Not enough sleep to wipe the dark circles from under her eyes or to keep her hands from shaking.

How rude of Marnie when she knew Emma had sleep issues. The girl had the whole suite to hang around in, and she was banging on the door, disturbing Emma?

Another tattoo of knocks.

Emma groaned and rolled over in bed. The bed was cushy and comfortable, but that was the nature of her insomnia prison. Sometimes, the more tranquil and elegant the surroundings, the more infuriated Emma became for not being able to relax and find sleep. She'd been through it a million times with her therapist Lucy: how the insomnia was directly related to the anxiety attacks that had begun some nine years ago. Even now Emma felt her face grow warm at the memory of that first paralyzing incident that had prompted her nanny to rush her to the Emergency Room. The freakish way her body betrayed her still made her squirm.

Marnie didn't know about the attacks. Of course she didn't! Emma had only recently adopted the girl, but even so, this was not something Emma would share, even with a good friend. No one outside the Lenson family knew, and Emma was determined to keep it that way.

Another series of knocks. The girl was dense.

"Go away!" Emma shouted. She turned her face into the pillow, nuzzling back toward elusive sleep. It wouldn't be easy. The Ambien was wearing off, and if she took another one now, she would be tired all morning.

A second later the door clicked open—why, oh,why hadn't she locked it?—and Marnie called, "Emma? You need to get up."

Cracking one eyelid, she watched Marnie edge in cautiously, black hair falling over one eye. Sometimes Emma could see that Marnie was beautiful in one of those ugly duckling ways, the way that unrefined coal could be sultry black, faceted, and shiny. Most times, she saw what the rest of the world responded to: bad dye-job, neck too long, and the nose piercing? Don't even go there.

"Emma?" Marnie peered into the shaded darkness. "Are you awake?"

"What are you doing in here? Are you crazy? I'm trying to sleep." Emma raked blond strands out of her face so Marnie could clearly see that she was pissed.

"You need to get up." Marnie came right up to the bed in some ridiculous plaid boy's boxers and a gray Boston College T-shirt with holes at the shoulders. "Emma? I'm sorry, but you have to get up. Ben is in the hospital."

"What?" Emma squeaked, forcing herself to open both eyes. "Are you talking about *my* Ben?" Her gaze scrutinized Marnie, the Goth black hair and nose ring and shabby clothes, and she had to ask herself how well she knew this ragamuffin. Not well at all. So there was no telling what kind of prank Marnie might pull, just because she was weird or because she wanted to get back at the rich girl. It wouldn't be the first time Emma was targeted by one of the have-nots.

"Ben is hurt. They took him to the hospital by ambulance."

As she spoke, Marnie opened the outer drapes so that the morning light spilled into the white and gold room.

A finger of pain hooked into the tender area just behind Emma's eyes, a dull headache that she knew would magnify if she didn't take something quick. But she winced around the thorn of pain and pushed herself up. "Oh, my God. What happened to him?"

Marnie turned back to face Emma, her skin ghostly white against her dark hair. "I don't know. Dylan said he was attacked." She shrugged. "So you need to get dressed. I'm going to throw on some clothes and we'll head over to the hospital."

The details fell over her like raindrops as Emma sat up in bed. "I can't go." Emma did not do well with hospitals, but she could hardly tell that to Marnie. "I just can't go out without a shower, and I have to fix my hair. And by the time I do that, he'll probably be released with a big Band-Aid, right?"

Marnie put her hands on her hips, her eyes on the ground. "I don't know, Emma. Dylan sounded pretty upset about it."

Emma could feel the other girl's worry, a dark cloud looming over the room. She pulled her knees to her chest, curled inward. "What can I do? I can't go out with this hair."

"All I know is, I'm going over there. Now."

Hugging her knees, Emma stared into the white sheets and pictured how things might play out if Marnie went to the hospital alone. There would be Ben, sick in bed, with Marnie and Dylan sitting beside him, feeding him milk shakes or laughing over magazines.

The whole collegial scene pissed Emma off. It was her place to be at the hospital with her boyfriend. She needed to go. Just suck up the freak-out feeling and go.

"All right. I'm going." Emma ripped back the covers and pulled her nightgown over her legs. "But I'm taking a shower first, so if you want a ride you'll just have to chill awhile."

"That's fine," Marnie said as she headed back to her part of the suite.

Big sigh. Then Emma padded into the marble bathroom and

leaned toward the mirror. Oh, puffy eyes! She really needed her sleep! At least her skin was looking better; those nasty, tender bumps under the surface were completely gone now. The antibiotics were doing the job.

She grabbed her silver cosmetics bag and snagged the tetracycline. She was due for a dose this morning, but not on an empty stomach. Ugh! Room service would have to bring her something quick, with no dairy. Snatching up the phone from the wall, she dialed and ordered two poached eggs with a sugar-free soy chai latte and a basket of muffins for Marnie, who seemed to think that carbs were her friends.

As she talked to the amusing man downstairs she dug through the brown prescription bottles until she found the Valium. Only two left! She'd burned through her supply in the past twenty-four hours. Well, she definitely needed one to get her through the hospital visit. The doctor would have to phone in a refill here. Now!

Stupid doctors. They could make life so difficult.

Chapter 12

Kate
Good Samaritan Hospital

Kate was disappointed by Detective Greg Cody. One look at the man who was going to track down Ben's attacker and her small kernel of hope crackled into dust.

From the dark stubble on his face, the track shoes and washed-out Levi's, the dog-eared notebook sticking out of his back pocket, it was clear that this man didn't give a rip what anyone thought of his appearance. His rumpled shirt could use "a good ironing," as her mother used to say, and his untamed silver hair reminded her of that old Disney movie about a wacky professor.

More revealing than his appearance was his low-key swagger, the way he walked down the hospital corridor and took charge without saying a word. It all added up to attitude and a certain lack of convention, which was not what Kate needed right now. She needed reassurance. She needed a representative of the law enforcement community who would: a. figure out what had happened to her son and, b. track down and prosecute the person who did this to him.

Kate pursed her lips as Dr. Teddy introduced the detective.

"Mr. and Mrs. McGann, I'm sorry about your son." Greg Cody sounded sincere enough. "I take it he's still in surgery?"

"Yes," Dr. Zanth answered for them. "I'm going to go check on their progress in the OR while you talk."

"Good enough," Cody agreed, as if Dr. Teddy were his to

dismiss. Just then his cell phone went off and he excused himself and stepped back. Holding his cell with one shoulder, Detective Cody leaned against the wall beside a sign that read CELL PHONE USE PROHIBITED and jotted something down in his notebook.

What was it about this cop that got under her skin? Kate wondered as she looked up at him and tried to see beyond the beard growth and disheveled hair. Maybe it was because she didn't want to be here at all, answering the wake-up call she'd gotten early this morning. Or maybe she blamed him for letting it happen, for security too lax to prevent the attack on a nineteen-year-old boy on campus.

On the other side of the wide corridor used as a surgical waiting room, Eli stood facing the window. He had been quiet for the past few minutes, withdrawn. Classic Eli. Joining him at the window, she realized he was examining a panel of inlaid colored glass depicting a chalice in lines so jagged it seemed almost creepy.

"Harry Potter's goblet of fire?" she said, her joke falling flat for both of them.

"I suppose the hospital was founded by the Catholics," Eli said, his fingertips tracing the soldered lead.

"Good Samaritan Hospital?" She shrugged. "Makes sense."

With a strained sound in his throat he pushed away from the window and leaned into the wall. Kate's jaw dropped as she observed him repeatedly banging his forehead into the glossy cinder blocks.

"Eli . . . Eli, please. Don't. Not now. Ben needs you."

"That's a load of crap! Ben is unconscious in surgery. He's in there losing a piece of his fucking skull, Kate. I am the last person he needs right now."

"Eli . . ." Kate felt her shoulders drop in despair. She wanted to say that she needed him now, but she and Eli had been down this path before and she didn't want to revisit Eli's tract on "competent Kate," the woman who did it all, managed on her own, needed no one.

"I have to get out of here," he said.

She nodded. "Why don't you go downstairs? See if you can get us both some coffee? Or get yourself some breakfast."

"You don't get it!" Anger rippled through him, leaving his eyes wide, his shoulders hunched. "I'm getting out of here, going home."

Panic beat like a winged creature in her chest. "But Ben's in surgery. . . ."

"You'll call me when he gets out. Let me know when I can see him. There's no reason to stay when I'm so useless here." He snatched his brown jacket from the chair, the old Carhartt that had prompted her to call him a sandhog when he'd picked it up in some secondhand store years ago.

"Don't." She dug her fingernails into the jacket, as if that could hold him here. "You need to stay. *Please.*"

"I just can't do it, Kate."

She sucked air in through her gritted teeth. "Eli, if you walk out that door—"

"What? You're going to divorce me?"

"I will never forgive you," she said quietly.

He wrested the jacket away and stepped back, though she read resignation in his eyes. "Fine. I'll stick around, but not here. I can't breathe here."

Tears stung her eyes as she watched him walk down the hall, that distinctive gait that reminded her of a boy who wasn't quite accustomed to managing his own body.

Coming from behind her, the male voice startled Kate. "Crisis can bring out the worst in people."

She pressed her eyes to the cuff of her hoodie, wished that she could honestly say that behavior was Eli's worst, but it was the tip of the iceberg. "Sorry," she told the detective. When she looked up at him, her eyes stung, her neck heavy on her shoulders.

His wave dismissed any worry. "Mrs. McGann, I've seen it all." He nodded toward the chairs. "Do you want to sit?"

"I can't sit anymore. And call me Kate."

"Do you like walking, Kate, or should we pull up a section of wall and lean?"

"Let's walk," she said, anxious to get some answers about the incident that had injured Ben.

They headed down a corridor with windows on either side, a skyway connecting two buildings. The day was bright, though the breeze that teased through the windows kept the corridor from being stuffy. As Kate gazed down at the green lawns, fountains, boxwood hedges, and tall trees, she realized she was numb to the beauty of this campus.

"So tell me, Detective Cody, do you have a clear idea of what happened to our son last night?"

"Not yet. He was found in his dorm room by another player. Apparently Ben was conscious, moaning. There was a lot of blood."

Struck by the terrible image, Kate steeled herself. A cold hollowness filled her chest now, a ghastly sick feeling. It hung there like a cloud of mist.

Stick to the details, she told herself. There was distraction in the details. "Was Ben found by Dylan Kroger?" she asked, wondering again why she hadn't heard from Ben's best friend yet. She hoped Dylan was okay. "He's Ben's friend. I think their rooms are close."

"The kid's name was Isaiah Gibbs, tall, skin and bones, African American. Do you know him?"

She shook her head. "But that doesn't mean much. This is summer league. Most of these players just met a few weeks ago."

He nodded.

"You didn't answer my question," she prodded. "What happened to Ben?"

"He was assaulted. It looks like the perp used a baseball bat, but we're still checking Ben's room and the dorm."

Despite his steady voice, fear tightened her throat, and her shoulders went rigid as if to ward off that terrible realization of violence, pure and evil. "I keep wondering how campus se-curity could let this happen. I mean, we were under the impression that Cross College is a fairly safe place. The city of Syracuse doesn't have a high crime rate. And I thought the college would weed out random strangers, like the psychotic man who broke into my son's dorm room and attacked him."

The detective took a pen from the V of his shirt and started clicking it. "We're jumping ahead here. What makes you think this was someone Ben didn't know?"

"Well, someone who knew Ben, even a little, wouldn't have done this to him. People like Ben. I'm not taking any credit for it; it is what it is. He's always been popular, or at least a guy that people want to get to know better. And when people have issues with him, Ben works them out. He's a diplomat."

"But you know that most personal crimes are not random. In fact, the majority of assault victims are attacked by people they know well. Husband, wife, father, son, brother . . ."

"Just stop, okay?" She held up one hand. "You can spout statistics till you're blue in the face. I still won't believe Ben was attacked by someone he knew."

"You can believe anything you want, Mrs. McGann. That won't change the facts of the case or the fact that most victims are attacked by someone they know."

"Please . . ." She tamped down her annoyance; she would not let him get to her. "Call me Kate. And you're going to have a short road to pursue if you're going to be hard-nosed about it. Ben doesn't have any siblings, and my husband and I were a hundred miles away. So it wasn't family."

"I didn't mean it that way."

When she looked up, his gaze was direct, no nonsense. At least he seemed to be tracking well. Maybe she'd misjudged him.

"I'm sorry," he went on. "I know this must be difficult for you."

She nodded. "So if you rule out family," she said, "who's left?"

"We're looking at the other guys on the team, the Syracuse Lakers."

"The other players?" Kate shook her head, doubtful that

those boys could have done something like that to a teammate. Apparently Detective Cody didn't understand camaraderie among teammates. Apparently Detective Cody never played ball.

They had arrived in front of two elevator doors, and Greg Cody paused there. "The other players have access to Ben in the dorm, since they all have to live there. They've got ID cards to get them in the door, and we know they have access to a baseball bat."

"But still . . . his teammates? If you knew Ben, you'd see how unlikely that is."

Cody scratched the back of his neck. "I can see you're not buying anything I'm trying to sell today."

"Because your line of logic is flawed," she said.

"Even so, indulge me. You've watched kids flock around your son all these years. You must know that popularity has its price. And few crimes are truly random. There's a reason this person went after Ben with a baseball bat. It may be a warped reason, or it might be something as simple as jealousy or rage or revenge. Magnify any of those feelings with alcohol or weed, and you've got a typical assault case. Whatever the motivation, it's going to lead me to Ben's assailant if I play my hand properly."

Kate tucked dark hair behind one ear. "I thought cases were solved through evidence and witness statements."

Cody smiled. "You've been watching *Law & Order*."

She scowled and cocked one brow. "So you're going to send someone to jail because of their motivation? Hmm. That does not sound like the legal system our founding fathers had in mind." She realized she was beginning to sound like the schoolteacher that she was, but she was enjoying this banter with Detective Cody.

"I don't send them to jail; that's the law part of the program. But in answer to your question, yes, sometimes you can work a case backward, find your perp, and then fill in with the evidence, hope it all matches up. But I'm getting off track here." He opened his notebook to a new page. "Back to the Lakers. Do you know many of the players?"

Kate bit her lower lip. "I wish I knew the guys better." When Ben was in high school, she prided herself on knowing all his friends and most of their parents. Between the guys who'd played ball with Ben and the hours she had spent volunteering at the school, she recognized most of the names when they were called upon to walk across the stage on graduation day. "I came for a visit back in June, and I met a few of the players then. The catcher, they call him Rabbit or Turtle or something. Turtle, though I think his real name is Joe. And Kenta Suzuki. He plays shortstop. I've met his parents." She sighed. "I'm sorry, but aside from Ben's friend Dylan, I just don't know these guys well."

"No problem. I'll get a roster from the coach."

"Coach Ramsey. He comes off a little cold at first, but Ben seems to like him. I don't think Ramsey wanted to be here this summer, separated from his family, but you see a lot of that in baseball. Sacrifices for the love of the sport."

"So you've met the coach."

She nodded. "I know Otis Ramsey and Ben's friend Dylan. Best friend, really. Dylan Kroger is my second son. He and Ben grew up together. They planned things so that they could be on the same team for summer league."

Detective Cody opened his small notebook and started writing. "I'll be speaking with Dylan later today, I'm sure."

"I hope he's all right. I got a text from him that he was fine, but I'd feel a lot better if I could talk to him. He and Ben are usually inseparable. I'm surprised that they weren't together when it happened."

"It happened in the middle of the night."

"That's true." When her mind went to the attack, unbidden images of bloodstains and yellow tape rose in her mind. "Oh, God. Ben's room must be a nightmare. Is it taped off, like on television?"

"Yeah. It's still a crime scene until our squad is done with it. I'll head back over after we finish up here."

"But it's secure, so no one besides the police can mess things up, right?" Kate wanted to go through Ben's room, get a sense of what had happened there.

"First of all, the police don't mess things up. We collect evidence. But yes, it's secure." Greg Cody rubbed his nubby chin. "Why do you ask?"

"I want to look it over. Something tells me I should go there, look for clues. Maybe I can pick up on something that your squad wouldn't notice."

The detective scowled. "Easy, Nancy Drew. Why don't you leave the investigation to the professionals?"

Kate bristled in annoyance. Granted, she was vulnerable, her thought processes compromised, but she still had enough awareness to realize that he was acting condescending. Was he going to try and keep her away from her own son's room now?

The elevator door that had opened beside them revealed Dr. Teddy Zanth, one small brown hand clasping a folder against her crisp white coat. She stepped into the crackling space between Greg and Kate, seemingly oblivious of the tension. "Oh, hello. I was on my way to find you."

"Is Ben out of surgery?" Kate asked hopefully.

"Not just yet. There were a few other things I wanted to go over with you, some paperwork to do."

More forms . . . Kate's energy shrank away, leaving her weak, a sapling in the wind. She needed to see her son, hear his voice, squeeze his hand. She ached to look in his eyes and see the Ben she knew and loved. She desperately wanted to put an end to this torturous waiting.

"One thing that you should be apprised of, Detective," the young doctor went on. "When Ben came into the ER we did a routine tox screen to identify any drugs in his system. Ben tested positive for Valium, not a huge dose, but present nonetheless. I had them run the test again, but it came back positive both times."

"What?" Kate squinted at Dr. Zanth as she felt the bottom drop out from under her for the second time that morning. "That's impossible."

Chapter 13

Greg Cody
Good Samaritan Hospital

Deny, deny, deny.

Kate McGann was so full of denial she could have run a very tight defensive strategy on a basketball court.

Cody started getting wind of her defensive stance when she insisted that the attack on Ben had to be an exception to the rule, that it defied statistics, that it would prove to be a random incident, a student attacked by a total stranger.

Possible, but highly improbable.

Given her frame of mind, what she'd been through this morning, he decided not to argue the point. He could have told her that he'd taken complaints on a hundred assaults in which people couldn't believe the perpetrator was someone who knew the victim. He'd heard countless testimonials about the victim's benevolence and popularity.

"This guy is good people."

"Everybody loved him."

"Who would hurt a guy like that?"

Yeah, he'd seen it during his years as a street cop and then a detective in the NYPD, but he didn't think Kate McGann would appreciate his old war stories, and she definitely wasn't able to be objective about her son's case. Right now her thoughts were all about taking care of her boy, which was as it should be.

Kate McGann loved her son, so she couldn't believe he had drugs in his system. That was her prerogative.

"My son does not take drugs," Kate said in a stern voice that would squelch any argument.

Observing her, Cody wondered what Kate McGann did for a living. Lawyer? Possibly. Not a nurse, or else she would be talking in medical gobbledygook like the staff here. Maybe a teacher or somebody's boss. She was a woman accustomed to being the authority figure, except with her husband, but that was another story.

"Mrs. McGann, I ran the test twice, to be sure," Dr. Zanth said. "Do you know if Ben was being treated for anxiety? Perhaps he had a prescription for the medication."

"He wasn't seeing a therapist," Kate retorted, then softened. "Ben would have mentioned that, and we would have seen the billing go through the insurance company."

"Unless he used the counseling services on campus," Teddy said. "I know they have such services at Cross College. Perhaps he was being treated by someone at his school. Where does he attend college?"

"Boston College . . . but I'm telling you, Ben did not take drugs. He wouldn't even take Tylenol PM when he couldn't sleep. With the recent scandals over athletes and steroids, he's been on guard about putting anything in his body that might be a problem down the road."

Greg Cody was impressed by Kate's conviction. She was one indomitable mama bear rolled into a cute brunette package. This was a woman who really believed in her son. But when the son is still a teen and you can't accept that he might do some experimenting . . . come on, Mom. Denial ain't just a river in Africa.

"Perhaps someone slipped him the drug without him knowing it?" Dr. Zanth suggested.

Kate was shaking her head no when Cody chimed in. "That's a possibility, especially when you factor in that Ben was at a party last night. I heard there was alcohol available, and it wouldn't surprise me if some drugs were scurrying around, too."

Folding her arms across her chest, Kate receded inside a shell. "A party?"

Cody flipped back through his notes to find it. "At the Regan Hotel." He shot a glance at Kate McGann, gauging her reaction, waiting for more denials. "That's a pretty pricey hotel in town. Apparently the whole bash was thrown by Ben's girlfriend?"

"Emma." Kate nodded. "I'd forgotten. Ben told me she was coming for a visit, to see the Lakers play."

"Have you met this girl, Mom?" Cody asked, thinking of his own daughter, wondering when she was going to give him a chance to meet one of her boyfriends.

"I met Emma once, in Boston. She and Ben have been seeing each other a few months."

"Are they serious?"

Thoughtful, Kate looked off in the distance. "Ben likes her, but I'm not sure how serious it is. He's only nineteen."

"Though she seems to like him . . . a *lot*. The girl threw a party, not just for Ben but for the whole team."

"That sounds like Emma. Her family is fairly well-off. Emma Lenson, as in Lenson Crystal. When Emma does something, she throws pots of money into it. For Christmas she gave Ben a trip to Barbados."

"Well, then," Teddy Zanth cut in, "perhaps there were some drugs circulating at this Emma's party last night. However, we found no alcohol in Ben's system, so he was behaving himself in that area."

Cody scrawled "Valium" and "Lenson Crystal" in his notebook. While he was familiar with the former, the latter meant nothing to him, so he would ask about Lenson Crystal at the station house.

Dr. Zanth's gaze went from Kate to him. "Are you about finished with the McGanns, Detective? I'd like to go over a few things with them."

"I'm good for now. I'll leave you ladies. Got to get back to work, anyway," he said. Fitz was waiting for him back at

Hawthorne Hall. He'd left two uniformed cops there to protect the crime scene and start canvassing, but this was his investigation, his call.

Still, the hospital had been worth the trip. He'd gotten a lot of background info on Ben McGann without really asking about the kid.

"I'll call my husband," Kate told Teddy Zanth. "He went downstairs for coffee." Kate reached into the pocket of her dark green hoodie and flipped open her cell phone.

He waited as she pushed the CALL button and slid the phone under the bob of her hair. He handed her his card. "Call me if there's anything I can do for you."

She nodded, her lips pressed together solemnly.

Cody also gave Teddy Zanth a card, thanked her for her help, and jotted down her number in his notebook. He had a hunch he would see both women again, soon.

When the elevator reached the main floor he stepped off and wove through the hospital traffic consisting of medical personnel in navy or bottle-green scrubs, an elderly woman toting a slim oxygen tank, a woman smelling an unlit cigarette as if it were ambrosia, a father corralling his toddler away from the automatic doors.

Just off the lobby the silhouette of a man paused in a doorway hooked him. What was it about the guy? Hmm. His lanky frame, the awkward gait . . .

Was it Eli McGann? Hard to tell from the back, but he was carrying that brown Carhartt jacket, which stood out on a July day in Syracuse. Had to be him, walking into the hospital chapel.

You had to wonder what was going on in that guy's head. Although Cody would have liked to get some answers, he'd witnessed enough of Eli McGann's surly attitude upstairs to know that he wouldn't get far interviewing the man. While on the phone with Fitz, Cody had witnessed the strained exchange between Eli McGann and his wife.

Something was broken there.

Granted, they had woken up to bad news in the middle of the night. Scary stuff.

But there had been no touching between them, no embraces or hand-holding. She hadn't leaned against him and he did not slip an arm around her. In fact, when he was trying to leave, Kate had clawed at his brown coat, an odd tug-of-war.

These things were telling.

You didn't have to be a therapist to know that this couple's relationship had been on the skids long before this morning's crisis.

He left Eli McGann lingering in the chapel doorway. It would be wrong to get between a man and his god. Besides that, he had an investigation to run back at the dormitory.

White light assaulted him as he stepped out of the hospital. He dug in his jacket but realized his shades were still in the car. Great. His eyes were going to look like a pair of cocktail olives that sat in a martini too long.

As he wove through the parking lot to the department Ford, he started a mental checklist of things to do in the investigation. When he pictured the actual crime scene in Ben McGann's room, he recalled Kate's comment about wanting to search for her own evidence. Goddamned Nancy Drew. Cute, but she could be a problem. Amateurs like that could get in the way, break the chain of evidence.

These days everyone thought they could conduct an investigation based on what they'd seen on a few television crime shows. They didn't realize that the TV drama only showed the scenes that were interesting, only played out the interviews that revealed some evidence. People didn't realize that for every interview in which you extracted new information for your case, you probably talked with a dozen people who gave you jack shit. One in twelve, maybe one in twenty, panned out. You could probably find better odds in Atlantic City. Which would not be a bad place to be, in this heat.

Squinting against the sun, he thought of Kate McGann begging her husband not to leave. Awkward.

Greg Cody was good at keeping a professional distance between himself and his cases. When you shoveled this crap for twenty-some years, you had to stand clear of falling debris. But today, for the first time in a long time, he let himself feel a little sorry for Kate McGann. She'd woken up to devastating news about her kid, a parent's greatest fear, and she was relying on a man pushing fifty to help her cope.

A man pushing fifty was a complicated beast. God knew he'd been there himself, surly and distant, buried in work for so long that one day when he tried to go home he'd realized it wasn't really his home at all. He'd probably known that for a long while, though he hadn't expected Carol to cop to it. He had expected her to keep on keeping on with her wry humor. "Middle-aged men," she used to say, "can't live with them, can't shoot them."

His eminently sane wife didn't open fire, but she did move on. Got new carpeting and carted his favorite chair off to Goodwill. For years it had been happening right in front of him, the dissolution of a couple, yet he had not seen it until the day Carol stood ready to hand back her set of keys to his car and sign off her rights to his pension if he didn't make a stink about the divorce agreement.

How easy was that? Carol had always liked keeping things neat.

A labeled pantry, a shipshape linen closet, a tidy divorce.

At times Greg felt a twinge of nostalgia for bygone days—mornings waking up with her hands smoothing his back, nights pacing the apartment to lull his baby daughter back to sleep, dinners of red wine and conversation. Seventeen years of same old, same old, and then, when at last you get the change you crave, it slaps you awake like an astringent after a bad shave.

Funny how you work your whole life to keep people at bay, and yet, when you succeed, you're completely surprised to find yourself alone.

Chapter 14

Eli
Good Samaritan Hospital

The chapel was intriguing.

Steeped in shadow and colored light from two arched windows flanking the altar, the chapel was probably the only room in the hospital that wasn't awash in fluorescent light and antiseptic smells. Eli liked the filtered light and the vague trace of incense in the carpet. He especially liked that the chapel was empty.

Two rows of chairs faced the altar and stained-glass windows. Well, at least someone here appreciated glass art.

He stepped inside, lured by the stained glass, of course, but surprised that they were even allowed to operate a chapel in a hospital in the twenty-first century. What about the Christmas tree that had to be taken down at a major airport? Why was that a PC offense, and not this? At Woodlands Academy the December show always contained generic winter songs and readings, "Frosty the Snowman" and "Let It Snow!" Emily Dickinson and Robert Frost. Yes, it was surprising to come upon any whiff of religion in a public place.

He supposed that a chapel in a public building would have to minister to Christians and Jews, Catholics and Unitarians. Atheists and agnostics too. Although a cross was carved on the door and a table draped like a Catholic altar stood at the front of the room, Eli recognized a mezuzah and prayer books, a quote from Kahlil Gibran, and a small gold Buddha beside a bamboo plant.

Leaning close to the Buddha, Eli rubbed the belly for good luck, thought about Ben, then rubbed it again. "I want him well," he told the statue, "and then, I want revenge."

He felt a fierce desire to hunt down the psycho who did this to his son, hunt him down, make him plead for mercy, then wring his slimy neck. Violence . . . he detested it. Most days he barely possessed the malice to crush an insect, but that had changed. Now the red fire in his belly roiled and spat, a medieval smelter.

He was ready to lash out, set to strike, but at whom? Where? He was not a medieval warrior but a middle-aged man killing time in a hospital holy room looking for someone to blame.

Who was responsible for this mess?

In his pocket his cell phone buzzed. He extracted it, saw that it was his wife.

Kate. He ignored the call and tucked the phone away.

Fucking Kate.

The sacrilege of saying that in another man's place of reverence made him want to laugh, but part of it was the laughter of release, the feeling that if he could put it on her head his burden would become exponentially lighter.

So yes, here in the room of crosses and stained-glass lotuses, rosaries and mezuzahs, he would lay the burden on Kate's shoulders.

Fuck Kate for putting him in this position, pushing him to have a kid, pushing him to give a damn.

Kate was the mastermind of his destruction. Kate was the one who'd wooed him to let his guard down. She had convinced him that something good could come of creating this person, that good things would come to the world through their son.

Kate had convinced him to view his son's future with hope and optimism. "He's really good," she used to say. "Just wait.

Someday I think Ben is going to earn a comfortable living doing something he loves to do."

Ben had been their light, their crescent moon in the sky, and they'd hung their hats on him with all the foolish optimism of an American dream.

An old song his mother used to sing lolled around in his mind. "Would you like to swing on a star," she used to sing, "carry moonbeams home in a jar." As a kid he had pictured the celestial scene with awe, a jar aglow with shards of moon brighter than any jar of fireflies he'd ever collected.

Ben had brought that jar of moonbeams into their lives.

And now someone had come along and killed the glow.

Eli fell back on a chair and collapsed forward, head and arms on his knees. How had it all come to this? So many mistakes. He had let his guard down. He had let himself care. He had been lulled into high expectations for his son.

Irony was a bitter taste on his tongue as he recalled the way his old man had tortured him with sports. And now the son of a klutzy artist had become a skilled athlete only to have it snatched away in a dark dorm room.

When Eli was a kid, sports had caused him nothing but anxiety, and the feeling lingered. Every August as the sun burned a hole through the sky and grass dried to pale stubble Eli still felt that cloying sense of dread at the coming football season.

At the age of eight he had lined up with his older brothers to go through the gear draw, where he was handed a hulking plastic apparatus to go over his shoulders, pads, and pants, and was fitted for a helmet. "Snug, but not so it's squeezing your head," the man said.

Tight enough to rip your ears off, Eli had thought as he pulled one helmet on.

"How's that?" The man smacked it twice, causing two global explosions in Eli's head. "That feel okay for you?"

It feels like my head is stuck in an iron bell, Eli had wanted to say. But he just grunted that it was fine, the way he'd seen his older brothers go along with it.

"Okeydokey. That's all I can do for you here," the man

said, smacking his helmet again. "You'll need a jock strap and a cup, but I can't help you with that. Got to get your own. Regulation. No freeballing allowed."

Eight-year-old Eli didn't answer. He couldn't admit that the helmet was too tight or that he didn't actually want to play football at all. When your dad was Bud McGann, coach of the high school JV team and volunteer coach of *your* team, you played.

And play he did. Through rain and headaches, mud and tears. Practice times were the worst, especially those late summer evenings when the heat melted your skin into rivers of sweat, pelted your head with a firestone. He could still feel the hits, like crackling thunder. Still saw the purple bruises on his arms and legs. Twice he was carried off the field, diagnosed with a concussion. He hoped the injuries would persuade his father to let him quit the team, but Bud McGann was galvanized by the incidents, more determined than ever to keep his youngest son in the game, let him learn the beauty of football from the inside out.

"What are you, afraid of the ball?" his father would ask, half chiding, half ashamed.

That was when Coach Bud designated another player to come behind Eli and hold his arms back, disabling him so that he couldn't deflect the ball when his dad tossed it at him.

Over and over again, Coach Bud would snap the ball and send it thudding into Eli. Into his torso, his legs, his hips. It bounced off his face mask, pounded as it made impact on his helmet. It dug into his bones and knocked the air from his chest. He had to bite back a moan when the ball bit into a sensitive part of his belly.

"See that? It doesn't hurt, does it?" his father would say as he waited for one of the other players to retrieve the ball. "The ball is inflated and you're covered with more padding than a living room sofa, so don't tell me it hurts."

"Yeah, it hurt, Dad," he said aloud, his voice resounding in the empty chapel. Only about forty years too late.

His throat thickened with all the things he never told his

son. Stories that might have explained to Ben why his father attended so few games, why Eli so rarely found time to have a catch, why there was no discussion of football or baseball at the dinner table.

Twisted, clotted words.

What an ass he'd been.

And now it was another missed opportunity. One of those things that might have sparked a connection with his son or certainly something that would have eased Ben's mind, if only Eli'd had the balls to go there.

He stood up, checked his cell. Four new messages, probably all from Kate.

Once again, it was difficult to breathe. Not even the colored panels of glass could bring him calm now. The edges of the lotus petals were far too pointed, and the red glass that was now backlit by sunlight seemed to be oozing crimson blood. Not the imagery you'd be trying to achieve in a hospital.

It was all wrong.

He couldn't stay here another minute.

He lunged toward the door, into the anonymity and noise of the hospital corridor. Pushed his way to the main entrance, his coat dragging on the floor.

Outside, the world was almost recognizable, a summer scene in patches of color, Impressionist splotches of green and yellow, blue and orange. Some van Gogh painting of trees in rows reaching skyward. People, grass, buildings—they all stretched up to the sky, barely tethered to the earth. So much movement in the landscape, people and vehicles, leaves and limbs.

He needed to keep moving, too, back to a safe place. Damn, his chest was so tight! He had to get back.

Their house on the hill.

Kate wouldn't understand, but it was a matter of survival.

Must breathe.

Chapter 15

Rico Valpariso
Cross College

Still on freakin' hold, Rico Valpariso held the cell to his ear as he kicked off his sneakers and dropped his jeans and boxers. McGann's injury had bought him some personal time, time to wash off the stink, the odors of sweat and smoke and booze. What did it take to get an answer from this place? How hard could it be to find someone in the fucking hospital who knew Ben McGann's status?

"Hello?" he snapped impatiently, pacing across his dorm room. Normally he'd take the phone right into the bathroom with him, but he didn't want the others to know he was calling about Ben. That was the problem with this team, everyone into everyone else's business. They were all a big group of candy asses.

How did it happen? In all those fantasies about nabbing McGann's spot on first base, this was not the way it went.

Rico wanted McGann off the roster.

Off the team.

Off first base.

Yeah, Rico wanted Ben McGann out, but not dead. *Dios!* This was insanity.

The voice returned. "Are you still holding?"

"Yeah, I've been holding." He leaned against the dresser, scratched the cleft in his chest where his gold medal of the Virgin Mother stuck to damp skin. La Alta Gracia, Our Lady of the Highest Grace, patron of every good Dominican. "A patient there, his name is Ben McGann. I'm wondering if you can tell me how he's doing."

"Sir, you need to speak to his doctor about that."

"I don't want to talk to his doctor. I'm just calling to see how the guy is doing."

"Are you his next of kin?"

"Nah, just a friend."

"We can't release personal information about a patient, sir."

"Can't a guy call to check in on a friend? What, I don't have the right to call?"

"Sir, you can call, but I can't give out information on the phone."

He pivoted and slammed a fist into the dresser drawer. It banged and rattled, piece of crap dorm. "I try to be a Good Samaritan, you know what I'm talking about? You're Good Samaritan Hospital, right? So I'm trying to do the right thing and check on my friend and you won't tell me how he's doing because of what? Because it's a policy? Have some compassion there, sweetheart. Can't you see I'm all hurting over my friend?"

"I suggest you contact his family for more information. Good-bye."

The click insulted his ear.

He lifted his head, closed the cell phone, and punched the dresser again. Fucking hospital. And it sounded like he broke the drawer the second time.

No importa. No matter.

So he'd have to wait to find out about McGann, just like the rest of the guys on the team. He wrapped a towel around his waist, grabbed his shower bucket, and yanked the door open.

If those pea brains said one thing about the words he had with McGann last night, he was going to take them down, too.

One word, and he would snap.

Chapter 16

Teddy was glad that she'd been able to secure a conference room for her talk with the McGanns. They deserved to have some privacy, and there was a calm though sterile silence in the room with its fake-wood-grain table, worn leather chairs on rollers, and a whiteboard covering one wall.

They had been waiting a good ten minutes for Eli McGann. Teddy's thumb worried the edge of the folder on the table before her as she turned back to check the door.

"I don't know where he is," Kate McGann said in a voice laced with disappointment. "Maybe we should just start? I'm sure you have a million other places you need to be."

"Actually, I'm off shift now, but I stayed on to monitor Ben's case."

Kate tilted her head, as if seeing Teddy for the first time. "Thank you for that. You've been so helpful."

"It's all part of my job. I'm a new fifth year," Teddy confessed. "I'm a doctor, but I still have a lot to learn."

"Do they cover this sort of thing in med school? Do they tell you how to talk to the parents of the trauma victim?"

"Not really." Teddy thought of the order of studies in med school. Anatomy and biochemistry. Surgery, psych, pathology. Western medicine possessed an aggressive personality, always on the attack, searching for the disease to be surgically removed or treated. "When really, there is no demon to chase from the body," her grandmother would say. "The body simply needs to find its balance."

"Are the papers in that file for me?" Kate asked. "Because I've already got a thick stack I haven't even looked at. Eli signed off on everything." She reached into her tote bag and waved a wad of papers.

"These are different." Teddy felt a weight pressing her throat, trying to strip her words of integrity. She pushed her shoulders back, opened her chest, her heart chakra. There, that was better. "These are forms we give our patients before they are admitted. In Ben's case, he was unable to sign, but then you and your husband are his health care proxy, entitled to make decisions on his behalf."

She opened the file and Kate's gaze stabbed the papers. Teddy noticed the masthead stamped boldy across the top of the page: *State of New York, Department of Health.*

A cry emerged from Kate's throat, and she quickly covered her mouth with one hand. "It's a DNR?"

"I'm sorry," Teddy said. "I know it must be difficult."

"I can't sign that." Kate pointed toward the door. "I want those surgeons out there to bring my son back. I want them to resuscitate him. I want them to put him back together, make him whole and healthy again."

"Of course! And right now the surgeons are doing their best for Ben."

"It's so frustrating, not being able to see him, not knowing what happened to him or what's going to happen. . . ." Tears filled her eyes as Kate lashed out, then sobbed.

Teddy waited, giving Mrs. McGann a chance to cry. And where was Mr. McGann in all this, when his wife needed some support?

All the while Teddy wished she could tell Kate McGann her story. Maybe it would help . . . or maybe it would upset her more. "It's not all about you," her sister Lily would say. Lily was a surgeon like their mother, already chief resident in a Chicago hospital. "A machine in the OR," they called her. So far Teddy had yet to earn a nickname.

When Kate was breathing steadily once again, Teddy went on.

"There are a few different options. You can choose not to sign anything. There's the DNR, which is simply a written order that resuscitation should not be attempted if cardiac or respiratory arrest occurs. Fortunately, that doesn't apply to Ben right now. In New York state, a family member may consent to a DNR, and it would only be used if one of four things is true. One, the patient is terminally ill." She counted on her fingers. "Two, if the patient is permanently unconscious. Three, if resuscitation would impose an extraordinary burden for the patient, and four, if resuscitation would be medically futile.

"Then there's something in the middle; you could sign advance directives that outline your wishes concerning medical therapies like feeding tubes or ventilators. The objective is to be allowed to die with dignity if the patient's condition is not reversible, to avoid being kept alive by machines. Right now I would say the advance directives are more relevant, as we don't know that Ben is going to be incapacitated in any way."

Teddy stopped herself as tears filled Kate's eyes again. Was she saying the wrong thing? She was sticking to the truth, but it seemed so callous to discuss this woman's child in such a calculated way. She swallowed, her throat dry. How did other doctors handle this situation? It wasn't something they went over in med school.

She closed the folder and laced her hands on top. "I don't mean to sound unsympathetic," Teddy said. "I'm just trying to explain your options."

Kate nodded, wiping one eye with the back of a hand. "I won't give up. He's my baby. Nineteen years old, but he's still my boy."

"Of course he is." Teddy met her gaze, brown eyes shiny with wisdom and pain. Kate McGann possessed an old soul, Teddy decided. Ancient and aware. "And you will do what is right for Ben."

Kate's eyes filled with tears again. "I don't know . . ."

Nervously curling the edge of the folder between her fingers, Teddy felt that pressure in her throat again. She recognized the heavy weight of conventionality, telling her to stop speaking, maintain a professional distance. Keep back.

"Maybe I should take a look." Kate pressed a tissue to her eyes and cleared her throat, trying to pull herself together. "I should know what the documents entail."

"Of course." Teddy slid the folder over and watched as Kate skimmed the top page. The urge to tell her story was strong, but Teddy bit her lower lip. Doctors were not supposed to share personal things with patients and their families. Beyond the intimacy of seeing a person naked, there was no personal aspect to doctoring, at least none that Teddy could see.

But this case unnerved her, brought her back to her childhood, back to a vivid summer morning when white sunshine lit the blinds and birdsong popped like bubbles outside the girls' bedroom window.

Teddy was five, her sister nine, and they awakened before any of the adults in the house had stirred. The girls bounced down the stairs on bare feet, then scraped sugary cereal out of the box with one hand in the kitchen.

Out in the backyard they found their bikes sunken in the grass like bones at a dinosaur dig. Wanting to get a ride in before it got too hot, the girls wheeled their bicycles around to the driveway, where Teddy discovered that her front tire was flat as a pancake.

Teddy recalled the way disappointment drained her enthusiasm. "Aw. Now I can't go."

Lily looked away, probably weighing the possibility of peeling out of there and cruising alone. But a moment later, she turned back to her sister and nodded toward the back of her bike. "Go ahead. You can ride on the back . . . but don't tickle me."

"Okay!" Buckling her helmet, Teddy swung her leg over the rear wheel and wedged her sneakers atop the wheel guard. When she placed her hands on Lily's shoulder, she was extra careful not to tickle or dig her nails in. Lily rolled down the driveway and into the cul-de-sac. Inspired by freedom, Teddy gave a hoot and smiled at the breeze in her face.

After that, the story went black, blessedly blank.

When Teddy regained consciousness a week had passed and she was in a rehab center and she was six years old without even having a birthday. She didn't remember much from that time, except that she had to go to a tedious hospital for months. She missed the start of first grade that year when she desperately wanted to escape from the antiseptic white walls, boring stretches of time, and painful shots in her clinical prison.

Neurology had changed since then, and the training of emergency responders had improved in most parts of the country. Still, sometimes Teddy couldn't help but wonder, what if . . . ?

Kate closed the folder, snapping Teddy's attention back to the here and now. "May I keep these forms? I need to show them to my husband."

Teddy nodded, wondering what was keeping Eli McGann. Alone with Kate, she sensed a certain intimacy developing between them that was unusual in doctoring. The stillness of the room, the lack of frenetic activity invited her to speak. "This may be stepping over the line, but I think it might help you to know. When I was a kid I suffered a traumatic brain injury."

Kate McGann sat back in her chair. "Really?"

"My Glasgow Coma Scale was exactly the same as Ben's. A little uncanny, isn't it?"

Kate shook her head. "I can't believe it. And you're so normal. Actually, you're probably well above normal, being a doctor." She pressed a hand to her chest. "Such a relief, though I don't mean to sound callous. It's just that you seem to have overcome your injuries. How did it happen?"

"I was five, hit by a car while riding on the back of my sister's bike. My sister was fortunate—just some bad scrapes. But I was knocked unconscious, my leg broken. The doctors think the helmet saved my life, but just barely. I don't remember anything about the accident, but they tell me that the first responders couldn't find any vitals at the scene. They attended to my sister, got her loaded into an ambulance, then zipped me into a body bag. The paramedics from a second ambulance were transporting my body to the hospital morgue when someone heard something—gurgling sounds, I think—coming from inside the bag. They pulled over on the side of the road, unzipped the bag, and suddenly I had vital signs again."

"And you made a full recovery?" Kate said.

"So it seems. I was in the rehab facility for months, and had to work through physical therapy for longer. I had to start first grade a year later." Teddy still had trouble imagining the crash site, the crumpled bike and dented car. Or the spine-tingling horror of the paramedic who heard raspy breath sounds coming from the body bag behind him. As a kid she and Lily had asked for the story over and over again, pronouncing it "creepy."

"My parents love to tell the tale of how their youngest daughter came back from death's door." Her parents, two doctors, did not indulge their girls in storytelling very often, but Teddy's return to life was a novelty.

"They must have been scared out of their wits," Kate said.

"I suppose." Funny, but Teddy never thought of them that way. Cautious, yes. Concerned? Sure. But if they were in the throes of a panic, Teddy couldn't tell. Mum and Dad were rocks.

But they had indulged Teddy in the months after the accident, cajoling her with favorite foods and surprise toys. "I remember when I finally was allowed to come home from the hospital, my sister had hung glitter posters around the house welcoming me home and my parents agreed to let us get a dog."

Probably because they felt sorry for Teddy, who had a pin in her thigh and a few months of physical therapy in store for her.

"We adopted a mutt from a shelter," Teddy said. "A little red dog who had some retriever in him. We named him Lazarus."

Kate snorted, half a laugh, and for a moment the air around them lifted, shaking loose the pathos.

"You know, Dr. Teddy, your story could be construed as a very good reason not to sign a DNR. Clinically dead, and somehow you came back to life without brain damage."

"You might see it that way," Teddy said. "I like to think of it as a miracle, but that's probably just because it makes me feel special."

"A doctor who believes in miracles?" Kate tucked a strand of dark hair behind her ear. "I wish you were operating on my son."

Teddy's face grew warm as the burn of shame descended over her skin. "I'm not a surgeon."

"Still . . ." Kate reached across the table and touched her forearm. "I appreciate your honesty."

Teddy focused on an oblong patch of sunlight on the tile floor as the image of the family dog came to mind. Old Lazarus, who had slept at the foot of her bed until Teddy went off to college. Although Teddy had fought her mother on it, the dog had a long list of ailments, and he was put to sleep that November—Thanksgiving holiday—while Teddy and Lily were home from school. Despite Laz's horrible breath and white mask, Teddy still saw that flash of intelligence beyond his eyes, even in his last moments. The flame of life force.

Sometimes she caught that same flicker of wisdom in the eyes of a deer on television or a dog on the street. It was sort of a peaceful nod that said, *I recognize your presence; I acknowledge your life.* Lately she had come to see that light in the eyes of some patients. Some, not all.

As of yet, she had not seen Ben McGann's eyes, but she felt his life force, the shimmering aura of silver and blue. If she were to guess, Teddy would think that Ben had many journeys ahead of him, but who was she to say?

"No one can predict the future," Teddy said aloud.

With a tired nod, Kate gathered the forms. "Ain't that the truth."

Chapter 17

Kate
Good Samaritan Hospital

The wait was the worst part.

Kate had begun to hate this empty waiting room that seemed removed from the rest of the hospital, as if they'd sealed off the opening at this floor of the elevator. Occasionally someone would step off the elevator and walk off in the other direction. No one approached the room with the vinyl chairs, steel-and-plastic tables, and a flat-screen TV showing an endless loop of pastoral images of trees and flowers, mountains and streams. If it weren't for the receptionist leafing through files—and even she was removed, listening to music through earbuds—Kate would have worried that she had landed in purgatory.

And where was Eli?

He'd missed the entire conference with Dr. Zanth. Afterward, Kate wanted to go downstairs and search for him, but the hospital complex was a vast cluster of buildings and she didn't want to take the chance that Ben's surgery would conclude while she was off chasing her husband.

She stood up and paced behind the black vinyl sofa, walking off her anger. For years now she and Eli had lived parallel lives in the same house. She had asked him for little, and now, when she needed him, when his son needed him, where the hell was he?

Where the hell was the Eli she had fallen for all those years ago?

Once, she had loved the smell of his skin after he had shaved, the warmth of his feet under the covers, the way they moved in tandem in the tiny space of their apartment. His scientific approach to art had stoked many satisfying arguments, and his wicked sense of humor . . . what had happened to that?

When they were first living together Eli initiated a comedic ritual that they played out every morning. While he was shaving she reached into the medicine cabinet of their narrow bathroom and popped her birth control pill out of the blister pack. As she tossed back the pill, Eli paused with the razor in his hand and let out a little yelp that resembled a cartoon baby falling down a hole. They both grinned, though Kate made a show of rolling her eyes. Once, early on, she had asked him why he made that noise, and he told her it was the sound of the baby being thwarted, which he found humorous despite Kate's disapproval.

After they were married, when Eli told her that he wasn't really up for having kids, Kate began to realize that he hadn't been joking. Eli really didn't want kids. Even when she finally got pregnant with Ben, he still was conflicted about the prospect of being a father.

Ben . . .

Her throat constricted when she tried to picture him beyond the series of closed doors leading to the neurological OR suite. Dr. Teddy had told her that Syracuse was only the second city to build such a facility, side-by-side operating rooms with a state-of-the-art scanner and MRI equipment that helped physicians accurately locate tumors and navigate the brain during surgery. How bizarre was that? Her son had suffered a traumatic brain injury in one of two cities prepared to deal with it.

Cold comfort, she thought as she flipped open her phone and went to her directory. Unable to restrain herself, she went to Ben's name, and a photo of him filled the small screen. Dark hair that grew like a weed, steely gray eyes, and that crumpled half smile that he developed in an attempt to hide his braces in junior high. When he was a boy, freckles had been scattered across his nose, but they'd faded when she wasn't watching. Somehow, her boy with dimples and freckles and a chipmunk voice had morphed into this young man pictured on her cell phone.

You're going to be fine. She willed the strength to him. *Please, be okay.*

She went to E for Erin and composed a text to her sister, asking her to call ASAP. She would have called, but Erin was never an early riser and she didn't want to disturb her. Besides, she didn't even have detailed news, anyway.

Just then her cell phone jingled, the screen revealing Eli's cynical grin.

"Eli, where are you? You missed the conference with Dr. Zanth."

"I couldn't stay there. The walls were closing in on me and . . . I couldn't breathe. I had to get out."

"Right." Kate hated how he made everything about himself. "So . . . are you refreshed now? Come back up to the waiting room and I'll fill you in."

"I can't do it, Kate. Haven't you been listening? I can't handle that whole scene, the white walls and know-it-all doctors. I couldn't take it. And really, I wasn't being much help, was I? So I'm on the road now. I'm going home."

"What?"

"Back to Woodstock."

"Oh, God . . . Eli!" This was the lowest of lows. Despite all of her husband's self-indulgence and bad behavior in the past few years, she had not expected him to walk right out from the middle of a crisis with Ben. But instead of pointing to the big issue, she stated the obvious. "So you've stranded me here."

"I guess I just assumed you'd be staying."

The sick feeling in her stomach thickened; up until this moment, Kate had not thought about how today would end. Would she sleep in a chair at Ben's bedside? In a hotel here in Syracuse, or back in her own bed at home?

Suddenly, her own bed seemed distant and unobtainable. She would never be able to sleep there, miles from Ben.

Eli sighed. "I didn't think about the car thing. But you can use Ben's car, right?"

Eli was not getting the big picture. "And you're okay with leaving Ben behind? Aren't you worried?"

"Don't start, Kate."

"Don't try to fling this back at me. I'm not starting anything." She glanced up at the receptionist, but the girl didn't seem to have noticed Kate's gritty, irate tone. "Eli, we still don't know about Ben. God, what if he doesn't make it?"

"Spare me the melodrama. Of course he's going to make it."

"How could you possibly know when you're driving in the opposite direction?"

"I've got to get back. Someone needs to take care of the business."

Kate gritted her teeth. The whole lot of junk in Eli's "antique" shop was probably not even worth the money it would cost to have it all hauled away. "The antique shop is more important than Ben?"

"Don't put words in my mouth. Sorry if I'm not the perfect father. I never wanted to be Ward Cleaver. I can't be perfect like you, Kate."

"Oh, please. Let's not go there now." She closed her eyes and let it wash over her, having played out this argument with Eli a million times before. She didn't have time or energy to battle it out with him, not now when they needed to make life-and-death decisions for their son. "Eli, I have a folder here with papers." Kate didn't want to go into this over the phone, but Eli didn't leave her any alternatives. "They want us to think about a DNR, or something like that. If he doesn't make it, if he's brain dead, we need to sign these papers so that they don't keep him alive with machines." Amazing how she could speak those words without faltering.

She waited for a response. The phone was silent.

"Did you hear me?"

"Yeah, yeah."

"And what do you think?"

"That the doctors are covering their asses. I already signed a stack of forms."

"This is different. This one means something." Kate could barely breathe through the thickness in her throat. "Back on point . . . I don't think Ben would want to stick around if . . . if his body is failing. I saw it with my stepfather for too many years." William Schiavone had suffered four years of dementia, weaving in and out of clarity, before his body broke down. In the end, Kate saw his death as a blessing—especially to her mother, the primary caretaker.

"You can't compare your stepfather's Alzheimer's to Ben getting hit on the head," Eli said.

And there she caught a whiff of his evasion, his way of minimizing things until they disappeared. Given a few more minutes, Eli would be calling Ben's injury "a little bump on the head."

"You know what? I can't discuss this with you."

"Good, because I think it's all an overreaction," he said.

"Fine. Good-bye, then. Go home. Go on. I'll handle this all on my own."

"That's right, Kate. Take it on, just like you take over everything else. Bulldoze right over everyone and pretend you can fix things. Make believe you can right all the wrongs in the world, though you can't. I know you can't."

"You know what? I'm glad you're going." She gripped the phone, tempted to fling it against the wall. "Have a nice trip." She sweetened her voice. "Drive safely."

And then, she flipped the phone shut, cutting him off.

So it would be her decision to make alone.

Kate massaged the glow of pain in her neck and stared at the folder on the chrome-and-plastic end table of the waiting room. She didn't need to sign anything. Dr. Teddy had assured her of that.

However.

In the worst-case scenario, would Ben want to be kept alive

if he was trapped in a stone shell? The idea of Ben's body, suddenly spiritless and without Ben's light . . . that equaled death. Or perhaps a fate worse than death. Life imprisonment.

She opened the folder and picked up the first page, but her vision was clouded by tears. Dashing them away, she felt questions rising inside her. Was there life still flickering inside a body that was dying? She had been raised Catholic and still believed that every person possessed a soul or spirit. When did the soul flee? How badly would Ben have to be injured for him to want to opt out of this world?

Of course, there were standards. She could see the criteria for a DNR clearly itemized on the document, four things listed concisely, scientifically.

But what about those circumstances that defied science? The Teddy Zanths of the world? The cold body of a girl thrown from a bike who woke up gurgling in a body bag. The skydiver with the chute that didn't open who picked himself out of a bramble and walked away? And what about the man who had survived being struck by lightning three times?

No one could predict whether or not Ben could defy science in the same way. Maybe he'd make a full recovery, come back from brain surgery. Maybe it would be his amazing story to tell down the road.

Damn it! She had always tried to do right by her son, even when it wasn't the easy choice or the most pleasant thing to do. She couldn't let him down now. Kate flipped open the folder and fanned the papers out.

She could not bear to let her son go.

But then, that wasn't her choice.

She signed the advance directives, her signature smooth for a woman in crisis. There. Done.

Pressing her hands to her face, she faced the doors to the neurological operating suite and willed him good health.

Beyond those doors was the boy she had loved since before he was born. Her only child.

"I'll be waiting, Ben," she whispered. "I'm waiting for you."

PART II

March 2010

Chapter 18

Kate McGann
Maple Elementary School, Woodstock, New York

"Is there anyone at home who can help Mei with her math homework?" Kate asked, trying to move things along.

"I'm sorry." Amy D'Angelo held up a hand to pause conversation as red suffused the edges of her eyes and a sob pinched her face.

Tears? Kate bit back her surprise. She hadn't expected an emotional response from this young parent with a diamond stud in her nose and a fat, snakelike braid down her back that clearly said, *I don't care that it's not fashionable anymore.* But then, Kate had always been better at reading her fifth graders than their parents, a diverse group, many of whom often came into these conferences with a list of things Mrs. McGann was doing wrong.

Kate reached for a box of tissues and put it on the small desk in front of Amy D'Angelo. They had already run over the fifteen minutes allotted for each parent-teacher conference, but now Kate made the executive decision that the clock be damned, she was going to give Amy D'Angelo the time she needed.

"I am so sorry." Amy pressed balled-up tissues to her eyes.

"It happens. My son was once failing math, too. Seventh-grade pre-algebra. Would you believe he's taking Applied Calculus this year and loving it?"

Amy sniffed. "It's not just math. It's everything."

"Under a lot of stress?"

Amy nodded. "My husband just moved out. He says he's not coming back and . . ." A sob choked off the sentence.

"I'm sorry to hear that." Kate had met Mei's dad a handful of times at after school pick-up, only enough to remember pale blue eyes behind very hip eyeglasses and a red truck that was so shiny clean you could serve food on the hood. Now she turned away so that she was facing the illustrated graphic of Shakespeare on the bulletin board instead of a full-frontal collide with Amy D'Angelo. It was one of those body language tricks she'd learned early on in her career, that the head-on stare feels confrontational to most people. "Have you told Mei that you're separating?"

"She knows her dad moved out. What she doesn't know is that . . . that she's the reason he left." Again she pressed the wad of tissues to her face, as if to push her crumbling façade back in place. "You know that we adopted Mei, right? We went to China to pick her up. It was such a wonderful time for us, the trip there with high hopes, and then coming home with our baby. Our first night with her, I remember we huddled in bed together, all three of us. Dave loved her so much, I know he did, but something's happened to him. He says that he can't see himself as her father, that he wants things back the way they were, the two of us. He doesn't want to be raising someone else's kid in the boondocks."

Kate gripped her pen. "I really am sorry."

"I don't know what happened to him. What could have changed the way he feels toward her?"

"Sometimes parenting is really difficult for men," Kate said. She thought of Eli's reaction when she got pregnant, which was less than stellar. "Am I supposed to cry?" he'd asked her, admitting that the whole idea made him feel like his shoes were getting tight. For so many years he had insisted that they didn't need a kid, and he'd watched to be sure she was taking her daily birth control pill. The only way she'd gotten Eli to try for a child was by telling him her life would be unfulfilled without one and, yes, threatening to leave him if he couldn't do this one thing for her.

It was the one time in their relationship that Kate had really pushed Eli. But it was worth stepping out of her comfort zone because in the end, there was Ben.

Sitting across from this distraught woman, Kate wanted to share the story about Ben. She wanted to let Amy know she'd been there too, hang tough! But the truth about how Ben had finally been conceived was much too personal . . . a family skeleton.

Instead, she said: "Listen, Amy, my husband and I have been on the rocks a time or two, and I know it's rough."

Amy nodded, now silent.

"No one can predict how things will go, but I do know this: You will make it through this. Your job right now is to look out for Amy, and Mei, of course. And I'll work with her on the math. I could keep her in for recess once or twice a week. Or how about before school? I'm always here by seven-thirty."

"That would work. I could cancel the sitter on Tuesdays and Thursdays and drop her off on my way to work."

Kate slid her calendar from her desk and penciled it in. Eli would call her a sucker, but Kate liked to make a personal connection with her students. She liked to feel that she could make a difference, or at least that she tried.

What Eli didn't understand was that you had to keep trying.

Chapter 19

Ben McGann
Boston

He wondered if she was trying to make herself look ugly. The black stud in her nose, the oversized sweaters, the dark, drab colors . . . Marnie dressed like ugly. Today she wore a baggy grandma sweater over a full brown skirt and scarred boots. Annie Oakley? She didn't really fit the Goth or preppy or nerd stereotype.

Marnie Epstein had a look all her own.

Despite the clothes that looked like hand-me-downs from a convent, there was no denying that she had some great physical features. Shiny dark hair and skin so white you just wanted to run your fingers down her cheek. She probably had a pretty good body, too, underneath all that fabric. Hard to tell with the way that sweater swallowed her up.

Amid the whir of grinders and the coffee odor so rich you'd swear the beans must taste like chocolate, she moved behind the counter. She was laughing at something Chaz said, not even looking at the equipment as she steamed the milk. It was second nature to Marnie, who'd been working here at the Beantown Grind even before college.

Sometime around the beginning of the fall semester Ben had been in the area shopping for cleats when he'd wandered into the Grind, a neighborhood place a few blocks from the touristy Faneuil Hall, and decided it was good to get off campus, away from the brass desk lamps and wooden desks of the library and into the real world where people had mud on their boots . . . or no boots at all. He didn't notice Marnie until his second or third visit, and then he realized they were in the same anthropology class. When she came over to wipe down a nearby table, she called him Jock and asked him how he did on the last quiz. Just like that, out of nowhere. He told her he'd done okay, but the new material was more difficult. She leaned over his shoulder and went step by step through a Yanomamo Indian ritual. When her shift ended, she curled up in the chair next to him and started quizzing him on stuff.

From then on, it was locked in: Two days a week he studied with Marnie when her shift ended in the afternoon. Toward the end of term they worked it out so they could register for the same section of bio in the spring, and they kept studying together.

Right now her pale arms were matchsticks poking out of the sleeves, her slender hands gripping two cups of café au lait, cups so wide they could be dog bowls. She crossed to him, her boots clunking on the wood floor, and set the two coffees on a table.

"Chaz said to remind you that the Celtics won again last night," Marnie said. "You guys have some sort of bet going?"

"I just made the mistake of letting him know I'm a Knicks fan." He turned toward the counter to flip him off, but Chaz was engrossed in conversation. "Might as well have declared war."

She sat down in the chair, her skirt swirling around her ankles. "Jocks and their teams. I can't keep them all straight."

"The Knicks are New York. I'm from New York."

"Well, I knew that." She rolled her eyes, wresting the textbook away from him. "So, Jocko, how many hearts does an earthworm have?"

"Are you kidding me? Five." They had dissected earthworms in biology lab. His flattened out and shredded; Marney's sliced open neatly to reveal the circulatory system. She was good at that sort of thing, knowing instinctively when to apply the right amount of pressure and when to ease off. Even their professor had told her she had skilled hands.

"What does 'megadrile' mean?" she asked.

"Big worm."

"Let's see . . . for twenty years G. E. Gates studied—"

"Regeneration. When certain segments are cut off, the earthworm grows it back—though never the tail."

She looked up from the book. "You're scaring me, Jock. How about reproduction?"

"The best part. The earthworm is a hermaphrodite, possessing both male and female reproductive organs. It's got two pair of testes, as well as ovaries and ovipores that release eggs via female pores."

Marnie turned to look behind her. "Are you reading this from a cue card somewhere?"

Ben shook his head. "Memorized it all. I was that impressed with the earthworm, the megadrile that can actually fuck itself."

She slapped the book closed and doubled over laughing. "You are one pathetic creature."

The sound of her laugh made him smile. "I knew you'd like it."

"I'll never look at another worm in quite the same way, little pervs."

"But here's the thing. If it can do itself, why isn't the planet overrun with these little string things?"

She nodded. "And wait . . . it can also regenerate, right? So it can reproduce on its own *and* recover if someone whacks the end off." She held her hands up. "What's to stop this thing? It's like an invincible superhero worm!"

He loved the way Marnie jumped aboard. "Exactly. I'm telling you, forget the cockroach; one day earthworms are going to take over the earth."

She sipped her coffee, then added, "Fear the earthworm."

"Fear the worm." It was his turn to quiz her, and as usual she aced every question. Ben didn't know if she was just naturally intelligent or if her powers of retention were aided by living at home, being away from the distractions of dorm life. Whatever the reason, Marnie had it together when it came to school. Sometimes he had to kick himself in the ass to stay on top of the material, just to keep up with her.

So unlike his girlfriend, Emma, who, people said, was majoring in "American Express." People were quick to criticize Emma Lenson, mostly because they were jealous. The private jet, the drivers, and the endless line of credit—Emma had privileges most guys and girls couldn't even imagine, and it seemed like the people who weren't trying to get a piece of her just sat back in judgment.

"Okay, hand over the book, Jock." Marnie waggled her fingers to get his attention, and he passed over his textbook. "Should we go over the labs we did for this section?" She was flipping through the book when two folded papers slipped to the floor.

"I'll never forget the fruit fly lab," he said. "The notes they gave us were like insect porn." They'd been given illustrations of fruit fly mating behavior—flies licking and copulating—so that they could record observations while watching them mate. The guys in the class had gotten a large charge out of that.

"Yeah," she said as she leaned down to pick up the fallen papers, "you guys all got off on that. What are these?" She unfolded the correspondence that Ben had been using as bookmarks. "They look like letters of acceptance."

"They're for summer baseball. Two programs have offered me spots, one in Cape Cod and one in Syracuse."

"But that's separate from college. So you're training to play for BC this season, and then after that ends you're going to play for another team?"

"That's sort of how it works. There's a short playing season unless you live in Florida. You have to squeeze the summer for what it's worth."

She scanned one of the letters. "And did you decide where you're going?"

"Not yet. It's sort of complicated."

"Complicated how?" she asked.

How could he begin to explain it? He was tempted to divert the conversation, but realized Marnie would be a good touchstone. She was his first friend who happened to be a girl, she had a good head on her shoulders, and she had no vested interest in what he chose to do this summer. Yeah, Marnie was the person to talk to.

"First, there's Emma. She's got big plans for the summer, and they all include me being arm candy in, like, Paris and Martha's Vineyard and the Hamptons."

Marnie rubbed the corners of her mouth. "Jock, I have trouble imagining you glued to anyone's arm. You're way too much trouble to be a good boyfriend."

He smiled. "Emma hasn't figured that out yet, but she's going to be pissed when she finds out I have to play summer ball, and there's no buying me off. I need to be out there playing so scouts can see my stuff. But Emma doesn't get that."

"The princess will get over it, as long as you're still her prince."

"I guess. Anyway, I'm leaning toward Cape Cod because it's closer to Newport and Martha's Vineyard and all those places. It's also a less competitive team, so they say they'll give my friend Dylan a shot at a starting position, maybe even in the pitching rotation. We've been playing together since peewee league."

"Okay, so you're liking the Cape Cod thing. Simple solution." Marnie brushed her hands together. "Next!"

"The only thing is, Syracuse usually fields a better team."

She squinted at him. "And that matters because . . ."

"It's challenging. You get better when you play up. And it's elite, draws MLB scouts."

"So why don't you go and play with them?"

"Because it's Syracuse. Middle of New York state. Emma's not going to like that, and the team can't guarantee that they'll pick up Dylan."

Marnie sighed. "Jock, you're making this more complicated

than it needs to be. Make your choice and commit. Once you do, Emma and Dylan will fall into place."

"And if they don't?"

She shrugged, bony shoulders rising under that tent of a sweater. "Are they your friends, or what? They'll live without you till next fall back at BC, right?"

He pulled out the letter from the Syracuse coach, Otis Ramsey, and read it over one more time. Maybe he was overthinking the decision. Hell, he couldn't make important life choices like this based on how it was going to work for other people. "You're right."

"Please, don't underestimate me. I'm fucking brilliant."

He smiled. "Confident, too. Okay, Einstein, back to biology. What were the behaviors observed in fruit flies?"

"You don't want to skip ahead to the pillbug?"

"And miss the fruit flies? They were my favorite lab."

"Okay. I will describe the mating dance of *Drosophila melanogaster,* but I will describe it only once."

"That's okay, I have the movie at home."

She snorted. "Some boys will do anything to hear the word 'copulation.'"

"I'm just trying to study for a bio quiz here."

"Right."

As they continued reviewing, Ben felt good about deciding to play for Syracuse. He'd been stuck, and Marnie had brought the salient details to light and set things in motion. It was like a window had been opened; something that had been jammed tight had finally budged.

Yeah, Marnie was a good friend. And someday he'd get close enough to understand why she hid behind the ugly clothes.

Chapter 20

Dylan Kroger
Boston College

"**Y**ou got a bug up your ass?" Dylan swung at the last pitch from the machine, then marched over to glare at Ben through the netting that separated the two batting cages.

"Just chill, okay?" Ben kept staring ahead, kept swinging at each ball that hurtled toward him, kept icing Dylan out.

Dylan stood waiting at the nylon netting, waiting for Ben to come clean. His best friend had been putting him off for a while now, keeping something to himself, and Dylan was sick of giving Ben space and all that shit. They'd been friends since they were little kids, played Little League together, shared clothes, nearly lived at each other's houses, so Dylan knew Ben McGann, and he wasn't backing off.

"I don't know what's going on in your head," Dylan said, "but I'm not going to let you push me away, bro. We've been friends too long for petty shit to get in our way. So you might as well come clean now."

Ben connected with the last ball, a satisfying smack, then cocked the bat in ready stance as the pitching machine beeped and shut off.

"Time's up." Dylan rattled the netting. "Time to spill your guts to your best bud."

Ben lowered the bat, his lucky Rawlings Blue Thunder, and cocked his helmet back. "Just back off, okay?"

"Can't do that, man." Dylan hitched the knob of the bat through a loop of netting and let it hang there. "Look, would you just tell me already? Whatever it is, you're better off telling me now than pissing me off by keeping secrets."

"You think?" Ben pushed his way out of the batting cage and sat down on the fake turf, leaning against a padded wall. "Because you're pissing me off, too. All the needling. Like I don't get enough of that from Emma? You're not my wife, Dylan, and neither is she."

Sliding down beside his friend, Dylan got a sinking feeling in his gut as he stared out at the hollow tin building that housed the college batting cages. "You're not being fair. Emma's the prima donna. This is me you're talking to."

"I guess." Ben's lips sealed tight as he turned the Blue Thunder bat in his hands, examining the barrel. "Here's the thing. I'm not going to play summer ball for Cape Cod."

"What?" Dylan winced, unable to imagine Ben ditching summer ball.

"I know we were going to do it, but I've been thinking about it, and the offer from Syracuse is a lot better. It's a triple-A team, as close as you can get to the pros. I can't turn it down."

Struggling to process all the facts, Dylan was stuck on one detail. "But they didn't offer me a contract. I'd have to try out for them."

Ben nodded. "I know, man. I'm sorry. But even if we don't play together this summer, we'll both be back here for fall ball. The summer will be just a short blip."

"Duh, yeah." Dylan's fingers dug into the artificial turf. This was what Ben was all warped about? "Summer goes fast. It's no big deal."

"Exactly." Ben let out a breath, obviously relieved.

"But hold on a second. Who says I'm not going to make the Syracuse Lakers?" Dylan went on. "I mean, who knows? Maybe they need a backup pitcher? A southpaw? I can be their summer closer."

"Maybe you can, man." Ben propped the Blue Thunder against the turf and rested his chin on the knob. "I'm sorry to screw up the summer. I've been feeling really rotten about it."

"It's not screwed up." Dylan had to think positive. "We'll be playing for the Lakers together, I guarantee it."

"That'd be great, but . . ."

"Just shut up with the negativity, okay?" said Dylan. He stood up and stepped away from Ben to take a few practice swings. Maybe he should bat a little more tonight, focus on his swing. "We're going to have a great summer. Really."

"Okay. I'll go with that." Ben hitched himself up to a runner's stretch. "You wanna hit some more?"

"Definitely. Gotta be a home run hitter to play on the Lakers."

Ben grinned, that smirky half smile of his. "Yes, you do." He straightened. "Let's get some water first."

As they went out to the lobby, Dylan thought about the information Ben had been keeping to himself. It pissed him off that Ben was keeping a secret, but now that it was out, he hoped things would be square between them. Ben was like a brother, and he didn't want anything to screw that up. With Dylan's gran getting on and forgetting stuff all the time now, Ben was really the only family Dylan had. Sometimes Ben didn't get that.

Not that Ben was trying to shake him loose. Dylan knew that would never happen. After all, he had practically lived at the McGanns' house through high school, having dinner with them, going home with Ben after school, and spending the entire summer sleeping in the top bunk in Ben's room of their house on the hill. Kate, Mommyson Two, as Dylan called her, seemed to like having Dylan in the house, and Ben's father spent so much time in his workshop at the bottom of the hill, he wasn't around enough to register an opinion. Dylan had always felt accepted by the McGanns. Even when Ben was tired or sick, he had wanted Dylan around. There had never been any question that they would go to the same college, so it did throw him a little that Ben was considering splitting up for the summer. Sure, it was just for a few weeks, but it felt weird.

A lobby connected the batting facility with the indoor track, where students ran laps when the ground was covered with snow. Dylan was filling his water bottle when he heard someone call out to Ben. A girl, and it wasn't Emma, because this girl had a low, honeyed voice.

"Hey, Marnie," Ben said. "How's it going?"

She jogged over to them and swiped at her sweaty upper lip with the sleeve of her T-shirt. "God, I'm soaked. The gym is so hot today."

Dylan stepped away from the fountain, smiled at her. "Wanna drink?"

"Thanks." As she leaned over the fountain for a sip, he noticed her baggy shorts and bleach-stained T-shirt. This was a real girl, a real runner, unlike the weekend warriors who went out in matching sweats and designer shoes. Her hair was shiny black like Cleopatra's, woven into tiny braids on the sides, all of it pulled back.

She stood up and wiped her mouth with the back of one hand. "So . . . did you hit chapter twenty-three yet?" she asked Ben.

"I was saving that treat for after batting practice."

"Well, you've got a fun evening ahead." She skipped toward the gym door. "Back to the sauna. See you tomorrow." And she jogged off.

"Who's that?" Dylan asked as Ben filled his water bottle.

"She's in my biology class."

"And her name is . . ."

"Marnie Epstein."

"She seems nice."

"Yeah, she is."

Nice, but not a Pop-Tart. Dylan didn't like those girls who always had glossy smiles stuck on their faces. How were you supposed to know what they were thinking when they never took off the happy mask? But this one was serious. A real person.

Dylan liked that about her.

Marnie Epstein.

For the first time this year, he was going to use the campus directory.

Chapter 21

Eli McGann
Woodstock

His teeth were locked together as he pressed the cutter into the panel of royal blue glass. The blade against the glass had the same cool whisper as a skater's blade cutting ice. This blue crescent would be part of a man's tunic in the replacement window for a church just over the Connecticut border. The window had been destroyed in a burglary, and Eli was one of four stained-glass artists on the East Coast who could do the repair.

"You're saving us," the pastor of St. Stephen's had told Eli. "I'm so grateful. Our parish's seventy-fifth anniversary is the first week in May, and the celebration would be a bit strained if our church had this big black eye in the front." Ironic that an agnostic artist would be the man to save St. Stephen's Episcopal Church.

Eli moved the sheet of glass over the cartoon to gauge the next piece. The blue tunic he was cutting belonged to a bad guy, one of two men hoisting rocks, ready to stone St. Stephen. The martyrdom of St. Stephen was just one story in the meandering tradition of Christianity, and Eli understood how stories were the things that held people together.

Was the same true of him?

Maybe. His original art didn't come alive if it didn't include some kind of contrast, that edgy conflict of black against white, smooth swirls against jagged thorns. Teaching paid the bills, but the glasswork in this workshop was his personal salvation. When everything was falling down around him, at least he was able to cut glass and fit the pieces together like a jigsaw puzzle and escape into color and facets and light. Turmoil roiled around him and yet he blocked and hammered and soldered lead between pieces of glass. His hands were strong from the work but scarred from stupid mistakes, and he sometimes kicked himself for not choosing an art form that was easier on the body. But then, he'd learned you didn't choose your art; it more or less bit you in the ass.

Something pinged in his mind. He felt her first, a soft, languid presence at the open garage bay.

He didn't know how long she had been standing there, watching, reading his thoughts. Tamara was able to read him well. "What are you doing here?" he asked.

"I was watching you work." She stepped forward, fingers tucked into the front pockets of her jeans, which were worn soft to a pale blue. The shirt tucked into the waistband reminded him of the chamois cloths he used to buff his BMW. Through the loops of her jeans was a wide cloth belt. Soft and touchable, that was Tamara.

He shook his head and bent back over his work.

"I like to watch you work," she said. "It makes me feel like something's being accomplished, and God knows something needs to happen around here. Do you know, I had three days in a row last week when not one person stopped into the gallery?"

"It's not tourist season," he said.

"True, but even in July, they're not breaking my door down."

Tamara Peak, owner of an antique shop and gallery in Glasco, the next town over, occasionally stopped by to search for collectables and rare items in the junk heap he kept on the closed-in porch of his studio. "But you're in here working like a fiend on something stained glass," she said.

"Yeah, but it's only because a church window got broken.

Business is slow everywhere," he said, "especially this time of year."

"It's spring, if you haven't noticed. People are supposed to be coming out of hibernation."

"It's March, Tamara."

"Almost April." She scratched at her neck where a blond curl teased the skin.

"Wait till Memorial Day," he said. "Things will pick up." He made the last cut in the blue glass. "Look, I'm kind of busy right now."

"I can see that. Don't mind me."

He lifted his goggles, stuck them on top of his head. "I mind. Glass cutting requires intense concentration."

She shifted to the other foot, her hips swaying. "Well, I was just wondering how much you'd want for that console in there. The one with the rose painted on the door?"

He rubbed his bristled jaw. "I don't even remember it."

She went to the door. "Come here and I'll show you."

With a frustrated breath he put down his cutter and followed her.

Tamara stood at the console and flicked dust from her fingertips. "You ever clean this place?" she asked.

"Never."

Beyond the trees, orange light of sunset pinched the sky, and Eli couldn't believe the day was over already. How long had he been cutting glass? He rubbed the bridge of his nose. When he looked over at Tamara, something was different about her. She was not looking at the console or any of the junk; her gaze was intent on Eli, as if she were trying to see into his soul.

Kate had not looked at him that way in years.

"You said you saw something you liked?" he said.

"Yes, I did." When she smiled her cheeks flushed, the pink dots of a china doll. She reached out and grabbed him by the lower arm, pulled her toward him.

She's a toucher, Eli reminded himself. But this was more than that. This was Tamara soft against him, his hands lost in the bunched fabric of her shirt. She pushed him to the threshold and he was her passenger, along for the ride. He felt the breeze from the open window frame, and he realized that she was right.

Spring really had arrived.

Chapter 22

Kate
Woodstock

Kate had kicked off her boots and tucked her legs under her. It was the only way to get comfortable at her desk after a long day when she wasn't quite ready to head home to a dark, silent house. With a steaming cup of tea at her elbow, she was correcting the spelling mistakes that riddled Jesse Miller's paper when Connie Pederson appeared in the doorway.

"I thought you'd want to see this." Connie waved a slip of paper. "Amy D'Angelo withdrew her daughter. She requested that we send Mei's records to a school in the Bronx, and the forwarding address is care of Mrs. Edward Lavinski." Connie crossed the classroom in her signature stance, shoulders hunched and eyes round and sorrowful. The eye thing was a result of hyperthyroidism, but it worked for a guidance counselor whose job required her to dole out sympathy on a daily basis.

"That's why she was out all week. I'd heard something." Kate scanned the request, the textbook cursive of Jan Scully, their office secretary, offset by Amy D'Angelo's scrawled signature. "Mei was talking about going to see her grandmother, but I assumed it was just a visit."

"I know Mei was happy in your class. What prompted the move?"

"The parents are separating." Kate handed the paper back. "Amy D'Angelo told me they were going through a rough time, but I'm sorry to lose Mei. She's made significant progress since September, when she couldn't string together more than three sentences. And now, look at this." Leafing through her stack of papers, she found Mei's essay. "She wrote this about her mom."

Connie leaned over her shoulder and read: "'My mother is the greatest hero in my life. She flew over the ocean to China to adopt me when I was a baby. My parents had to pay a lot of money to go to China and pay for my doctors, but my mom says I am worth all the gold in the world.

"'Whenever I feel bad because I was adopted, my mom gives me a hug. She told me that some children come from the mother's belly and some come from the mother's heart. I am a child of the heart.

"'My mom works hard at her job and at night she takes care of our home. She cooks my favorite foods like mac and cheese and peanut butter sandwiches. She is always very busy, but she is full of joy. She is a great hero, don't you agree?'"

Connie straightened with a sigh. "Wow, that's sweet. Kudos to you for bringing her writing skills along."

"I can't take the credit. Mei was diligent. She was one of my hardest-working students." Kate separated Mei's paper from the rest of the stack, then handed it to Connie. "Why don't you send this on with her records? I'd love for it to find its way to her mom. Sounds like Amy could use a lift."

"Good idea." Connie took the essay and headed out. At the door she paused. "Hang in there, Kate. Everyone has those old blanket days occasionally."

"Old blanket days?"

Empathy flooded Connie's huge, round eyes. "When you feel so bad you just want to curl up under an old blanket."

Kate was definitely having an old blanket day, without the security of a blanket to hide under. "You're so perceptive. Connie, the kids here are lucky to have you."

Connie lifted a hand, either dismissing Kate's compliment or saying good-bye. "Take care."

For a moment Kate stared at the empty doorway, trying to freeze her thoughts right there, knowing that if she indulged in self-pity one more second she would go over the edge. Her gaze lit on the bulletin board that held photos of her students, twenty-eight faces, a collection of gap-toothed smiles and braces, freckles, dark skin, and light, black, gold, or red hair. Her kids.

The floor was cool under her bare feet as she crossed the room and stood in front of Mei's photo. As she worked the staples out with a fingernail she wondered if Tori and Sara knew that their friend had moved away. It was hard on a kid to move in fifth grade, but then most children dealt with change better than adults. Mei would be fine. She had her mother's support, her grandmother's love.

I'm the one struggling with this.

Tears stung her eyes as she pulled the photo from the wall. Mei had a support system, but what did Kate have? Who was there to listen to her sad story of losing a favorite student? Her only son was away at college and her husband spent more and more time away from home, obviously drinking too much and drifting further and further away from her, though he insisted that was not the case. "I need my space right now," he kept telling her. "Sometimes I work so late that it just makes sense to catch some sleep in the studio." The studio was an old building once used to house tractors and animals. It hurt to think that he preferred that old garage to their bed, but then most of her thoughts of Eli were now shadowed in pain.

He used to be her best friend. What had happened to them?

And just as Eli drifted away Kate also felt her house becoming less of a home. Perhaps it was because Eli had poured so much of himself into it, fashioning stained-glass pieces for the irregular windows. When they'd first moved in he had spent hours sitting in the sunlight, accessing each window's personality and potential for color.

That was the Eli she fell in love with, the patient artist, the listener.

She sat down at her desk and pulled her knees to her chin, wondering how she had stranded herself on this lonely mountaintop, wondering how to reach out to her husband and pull him close once again.

Chapter 23

Emma Lenson
Boston

"Go in the lane! Go around him. Put it up—yes!" Ben shot to his feet along with the rest of the crowd, and Emma rose, clapping.

Emma wasn't really following the game, but she did realize that the BC Eagles had just pulled ahead with this basket and the BC fans were going wild. Beside Ben, Dylan and Marnie were on their feet, too, and for a Goth girl Marnie seemed to know a lot about basketball, whistling with her fingers in her mouth when important things happened.

"That's what I'm talking about," Ben shouted.

Dylan high-fived him. "Okay, let's see some D! Thirty seconds to go!"

Emma blinked. That meant the game was almost over? That was a relief, as this jam-packed gym was getting stuffy, the air damp with mass perspiration.

"No, no! Don't foul him!" Marnie shouted, then doubled over in agony when, apparently, the foul was committed.

A low murmur of disapproval rumbled through the home-team crowd when the players lined up for the player in blue to take two shots. Blue was the bad team, Emma knew that much. Blue got both shots in, and the game was tied.

"Ah, man!" Dylan winced, like the whole thing was painful.

Emma was getting interested in the game, but both teams stopped again for a time-out—they seemed to take breaks like this a lot. Then the players spread out on the court again. The BC players had the ball, but they just kept passing it around.

"Why don't they make another basket?" she asked.

"They're running down the clock." Ben didn't look away from the court.

Emma was grateful for the explanation, though she didn't really get it and she really didn't care. She just wanted to win.

Finally one of the BC guys chucked it up and, arching like a rainbow, the ball flew through the air and dropped right in!

The arena erupted in a roar. The buzzer sounded, and suddenly athletes and cheerleaders seeped onto the court.

Ben and Dylan threw their arms around each other, jumping and hugging. When Ben finally turned to her, Emma was ready for the fire in his kiss, the excitement dancing in his eyes. This was the Ben who attracted her, the wild-eyed, arm-pumping athlete who lived for the game.

But then, she'd always thought that game was baseball.

"Do you know how many of our starters are juniors?" Ben was saying to Dylan and Marnie. "It's phenomenal. They are going to be one tight team next year."

"Great game," Marnie said.

As they started down the bleachers, Emma realized that she'd actually had a good time. She had taken Ben to a few Celtics games using her father's season tickets, but those games had seemed tame compared to tonight's. Who knew that a college sport could be so . . . explosive?

When they reached the promenade Ben took her hand and squeezed it.

"You know, I thought baseball was your sport," she said. "How do you know so much about basketball?"

"It's a guy thing. Guys shoot hoops. Guys check scores online. It's in the XY chromosome."

Emma loved the bits of the "guy world" that she could see through Ben, the shorthand he and Dylan talked in, the way Ben could roll out of bed and be ready to go, the way they would both let go and double over in laughter, not even caring what people thought. That was the thing that really attracted her to Ben; he made his own decisions without a worry about being popular or gaining approval. Ben was brave that way.

They piled into Ben's red Ford and drove over to Faneuil Hall, that touristy place in town, where they got hot pretzels and watched as vendors closed up their carts. When Dylan split off to walk Marnie to her bus, Emma asked Ben why Marnie didn't live closer to campus. They headed back to Ben's car, walking through pools of light from the lanterns that lined the cobblestone streets.

"She lives with her mother," Ben said, "and they can't afford campus housing."

"Poor Marnie. I wonder what it's like to know everyone else is having so much fun while you're stuck at home."

Ben sipped from the straw, then handed her the lemonade they were sharing. "You don't think Marnie's having fun? She seemed to be liking the game today."

"That's not what I meant. I just think it's got to be hard, not having the freedom to do what you want when you want to. Dylan says she works at a coffee shop near here. That's got to be the pits. She probably smells like sour coffee all day, and when does she find the time to study?"

"She seems to do okay." He ducked into the car, suddenly distant.

The way that Ben just went cold made Emma backtrack. She climbed into the passenger seat and turned toward him. "Nothing against her or anything. I feel sorry for her."

His eyes were on the road as he pulled into traffic. "Marnie's doing okay. You're the one I worry about. You didn't get to History at all last week. You feeling better?"

Emma's muscles turned hard as steel, as if she'd been caught in a lie, which she had. Last week she'd told Ben that she hadn't been feeling well, when the truth was she'd been dodging that class because the professor, Dr. Tennison, reminded her of all the things she hated about her father. Refusing to make eye contact, his owlish eyes resting on some distant spot as if he longed to be transported elsewhere. Absent and disinterested. In her father's case Emma later surmised that he had been deeply unhappy with their family life and had wanted to be off cavorting with someone younger, thinner, and blonder than her mother. As for Dr. Tennison, Emma had no idea what he might be fantasizing about, but the man was definitely creepy. Major ick factor. She planned to get through that class reading the textbook and studying Ben's notes.

"I don't like history," she said. "It's boring."

"No way. The Revolution? The way they constructed a nation out of nothing but land. U.S. History is amazing. Besides, it's the only class we have together."

"I know, but Dr. Tennison is so weird." She tilted her head and gave a shrug, wanting to change the subject. "And it's no big deal to have a class together. We have more fun together outside of school. Which reminds me, summer plans are in the works and I'm putting together some great stuff for us. There's the house on the Vineyard, a little stodgy but the beach is gorgeous, and my parents have an apartment in Paris, overlooking the Arc de Triomphe. Have you ever been to Paris?"

He shook his head. They were stopped, waiting for a light, but he kept his eyes on the road. "I've never been to Europe. I don't even have a passport."

"Well, you'd better get your application in, because we are going places this summer, Ben." Turning in the passenger seat, she touched his arm, rock solid under the sleeve of the baseball jacket he wore even on the coldest of days.

"Not really." He stared through the windshield, avoiding her. "You don't need a passport to go to Syracuse."

"What do you mean?" Anxiety stole over her, flipping her pulse into a crazy acceleration and tearing at her stomach. An attack was coming on, pulling her down into the seat—into hell—right in front of Ben. Oh, God. Not now, please.

It took all her strength to turn her face toward the window and force herself to breathe as he dropped the bomb.

"I can't go to Europe this summer, Emma."

Oh, God, that was it. He was breaking up with her, ending their relationship. He would leave her behind without a thought, just as her parents had done so many times. Left her in the care of nannies, good, bad, and indifferent. They had enrolled her at elite boarding schools and sent her to exclusive summer camps so that they wouldn't have to sacrifice one minute of their day to worry about Emma.

The pain in her chest blossomed with each beat of her heart.

Ben was ending it, dumping her. She was losing her boyfriend.

Although it was tempting to melt into the seat and give in to the attack, somewhere beneath the swelling tide of panic was an undercurrent of logic. *Don't give in to this, Emma. Use the tools that Lucy taught you. Use positive thinking. Don't overgeneralize. Listen to what he's saying before you give in to catastrophe.*

"The thing is, I don't have the money," he said, "and I'm going to be playing summer ball. I got an offer to play in Syracuse on a kick-ass team, a team with the talent to attract scouts, and I accepted."

"Wait a second." She forced the words past the pain in her chest. "So you're transferring to Syracuse?"

"What? No, no, I'm just going there for summer ball. They always field an awesome summer team at Cross College."

"Oh." She tried to sound encouraged, though she was really just holding on by her fingernails. So he wasn't breaking up with her? The pain in her chest eased, allowing her a tiny breath. Just because he was changing plans didn't mean it was over. "So, if it's about the money . . ." She hesitated, not wanting to insult him. "You know it costs nothing to stay at my parents' place on the Vineyard."

"It's not about money. This is all baseball. I need to be seen by some scouts, get exposure. I need to play."

"Right." She wanted to point out that he did something baseball related every day. He was always lifting in the weight room or doing speed and agility clinics, not to mention actual practices with the team in the middle of winter when no one was playing baseball north of the Carolinas. Emma didn't understand why they had to go so crazy in the off-season, but Ben had told her that was the way you trained for a sport.

"Are you mad?" he asked.

"How could I be mad at you? I mean, I'm just disappointed. I've got some cousins who were really looking forward to meeting you." Though mostly she wanted to watch their jaws drop when they met Ben. Yes, she had been looking forward to gloating over Tiffany and Michaela, scoring a few points with the girls who'd bullied her when she was little, pushing her in the horse poop at their Rancho Santa Fe estate and lacing her lemonade with vinegar. Although Tiff and Michaela were older now, they were as bratty as ever, and she had looked forward to the day when she could get in their faces with Ben at her side.

Yes, she was disappointed, but a change in plans was much better than losing her boyfriend. She took a deep breath now and stretched her legs slightly, letting them relax. How stupid of her to freak out over the smallest thing. Stupid, stupid, insecure.

Ooh, she hated herself sometimes. But then it didn't help to beat up on herself. *"You need to be aware of the negative self-talk,"* Lucy always told her. *"Self-talk is your thoughts, it's all the things you think and believe about yourself. When your self-talk is positive, constructive things can happen. When it's negative, you are going to feel anxiety."*

Lucy had wanted her to keep a journal, and for a while Emma had written down her negative and positive thoughts. But really, when you've got a life the last thing you have time to do is write little notes for your therapist.

"Maybe you can have your cousins come to Boston," Ben suggested, bringing her back to the present. "We could hang out here."

"Or I could make them come with me to some games in Syracuse. They would love that." The last part was a lie. They would hate coming to a game, but Emma relished the thought of bony Tiffany and big-mouthed Michaela wilting in the hot sun of a smelly baseball stadium. Now that would be a sweet sight.

"I'm glad you understand." Ben dropped his right hand on her thigh and squeezed.

But she barely noticed. The weight had lifted from her chest, her pulse had slowed, and she allowed her mind to venture into a daydream of her cousins, two very unhappy girls who were about to learn what a mistake it had been to take advantage of Emma Lenson.

PART III

June 2010

Chapter 24

Kate McGann
Woodstock, New York

Kate tamped dark soil around the heather, then straightened unsteadily. The twinges in her hips let her know she was pushing fifty, but she wasn't going to let a few creaky joints slow her progress in the yard. Gardening was her therapy, and she possessed solid instincts on how to chase beetles from the roses and when to transplant the rhododendrons. She enjoyed nurturing plants and bringing color to the landscape.

But, really, this hill was a losing battle.

Every year she lugged in tons of soil and mulch in twenty-pound sacks, which she released onto the earth and spread over exposed tree roots and crusted flower beds. She built small rock walls and tried to grade the slope. And every year, rain and snowmelt scored down the hill, sweeping the soil and mulch away in what might be considered a textbook case of erosion.

"I don't know why you bother," Eli often told her, but Kate knew. The joy was in the doing. She could not stop the rain or the erosion. In truth, they needed to build terraces along the slope, but that would require a bulldozer to grade the hillside in to levels and buttress each terrace with stone walls or railroad ties. Who could afford it? Without an expensive landscape contractor she could not build a garden that would last forever, but she did have the talent and mettle to create a verdant patch of the planet for the duration of summer.

Today was a good day in the world of Kate's garden. The pansies bobbed lightly, the tiger lilies had unfurled into fat orange bugles, and the ivy, which she worked so hard to keep at bay, was no longer in danger of choking her roses—at least, not this week.

With a sure satisfaction she ran a blade through the end of a twenty-pound bag of potting soil. She tipped one fat bag over and let the rich, dark soil pour out in a mound beside the heather plant. Tomorrow she would till it into the crusty dirt on the ground and add some other perennials to this flower bed. Situated off to the side of the yard, it wasn't visible from the road, but this corner of the yard was the first thing she saw when she looked out her bedroom window, and this morning she'd decided that she deserved a calming splash of lavender, purple, and yellow.

Just then her cell phone buzzed in her pocket, and she yanked off her rubber-tipped gloves and pulled it out. Ben.

"Hey, there! How's it going?" she said, rubbing an itchy spot on her chin with the back of her hand.

"Good. I was just checking my grades online and I must have aced the calculus final. Dr. Stillwagon gave me an A."

"Ben, that's fantastic! I always struggled with calculus. It's the one class I took a pass/fail option on in school."

"It wasn't so bad. I had a great professor, and Dylan and I studied together, so that helped."

"I'm so proud of you." She picked up the empty sack and headed up toward the house. It was pushing two and she wanted to hit the market before dinner. "So I'll bet you're ready to celebrate."

"Sort of. I've still got one more final this week, but it'll all be over soon. Emma and I are going out to dinner tonight, some place she knows in Cambridge."

"Well, your father and I will raise a glass and toast you from down here." She shook her gloves off, then thought of Dylan. "Hey, how are finals going for Dylan?"

Ben was slow to respond. "Honestly? He's driving me crazy. Keeps pulling all-nighters."

Kate smiled. "He's always been obsessive."

"I really need a break from him. A *long* break." His voice faded out.

"I'm hearing some tension in your voice."

"Sometimes I just wish he would do his own thing, you know? He only took calculus because I was taking it. It's like he's my shadow. He'll follow me to places he doesn't want to go instead of make his own decision to do what's best for him."

"I thought you were happy to have him at BC with you," she said.

"Sure, yeah. That part is great. But he didn't get a baseball scholarship from BC, and he just barely made it on the team. Sometimes it's just awkward. And for this summer? He'll be wasting his time in Syracuse. He was only recruited as an extra. He's going to be warming the bench all season, when he could be playing if he signed up for another team."

"I get what you're saying." Kate felt a pang of sympathy for Dylan, who hadn't really found himself yet. "Have you talked to him about it?"

"I've tried, but he doesn't get it. He just keeps coming back to me with the 'brothers forever' crap."

"Oh, Ben." She felt for him. "Tough situation." Because Dylan's parents had left him, she suspected he had abandonment issues gnawing at his sense of security. She and Ben had discussed these things more than once. She'd talked at length with Dylan, too, but she was never sure what he came away with after a conversation like that. "Do you want me to talk with him?"

"I don't think he's ready to hear any of this right now. Maybe down the road. He's got to figure it out eventually, right?"

"I'm sure he will, though it puts a lot of pressure on you."

"Whatever. It's what you do for a friend. So, have you planned your trip to Syracuse yet?"

She told him she planned to talk to his dad about that tonight. "And I have to get to the market now or we won't have a dinner to talk over. But I'm glad you called, honey. Thrilled about your news. Stay on track and you might play for the Red Sox one day. . . ."

"Mom, I don't think they care about my calculus grades."

"The college degree is your fallback. In the meantime, I've got my eye on the prize. Long-term goals are a good thing."

By six p.m., Kate had set a grand table with fresh tulips, the good Limoges china, and twinkling white candles in cut crystal dishes. Tonight she planned to talk to Eli about the changing tone of their relationship now that Ben was gone. Like it or not, the dynamics between them had changed, and Kate was determined to talk about how they could find each other again.

She had stopped into his studio on the way to the market, wanting to share Ben's news and remind him that she was cooking a special meal tonight.

Music was blasting from his prized Infinity speakers. Vanilla Fudge, she thought. Kate passed one tall, coffin-sized speaker on her way in. Eli had a set here in the studio and one in the house, so that he could always have music. Those giant speakers and crates of LP record albums were Eli's anchor; he prized his record collection and worried about the day when the irreplaceable disks would be too worn or warped to play. She turned down the volume to get his attention, then passed on Ben's news, adding, "And dinner at six. I'm cooking tonight."

He stood there, bent over his light table, barely lifting his head to acknowledge her. "Good on both counts," he said.

"Oh, come on, Eli. Why are you such a bear?"

"I'm working, Kate. I'll dance around the kitchen later."

"I'll believe that when I see it," she'd said, heading out the door.

Now it was almost six and still no Eli. She took a swig of wine and was moving toward her cell to call him when she heard the door.

"You're home!" She smiled, stepping out from behind the kitchen island to greet him.

Stooped over the stack of albums in his arms, he seemed, well . . . old.

"Yeah, long commute."

"Do you want some wine?"

"Maybe later." He put the records down on the counter beside the spinach-cranberry salad. "I'm going to take a shower."

"Dinner's almost ready," she called after him, hoping he wouldn't take too long. She moved the records to an end table in the living room, then realized the chicken was about ready to come off the grill. She brought her wine outside with her and sat facing the green of the trees along the hill that rose behind their house.

Eli was in a foul mood, and maybe it was contagious. She swatted at an insect and took a long drink of wine. What was she doing, pulling together the perfect dinner, a Martha Stewart production, and expecting her husband to pretend he was enjoying it? What did she expect? That he would suddenly warm to her?

She opened the grill, forked the bird onto a platter, turned off the burners. Years ago Eli had enjoyed elegant, languid meals. He had relished her cooking, from the simplest stir-fry to the smoothest Hollandaise. These days he missed meals and didn't seem to care.

She carried the platter inside and saw that Eli was leaning over the old stereo, his hair damp from the shower. The album began to spin, playing the Eagles' song "Hotel California" at high volume.

He stood there, perusing the album cover, singing along. "On a dark desert highway . . ."

"Oh, my God." In a fit she let the platter slam onto the counter, but he couldn't hear over the music. "Eli!" she shouted.

He turned, cast her a cool look.

"Turn it down," she mouthed, miming the gesture with one hand.

He lowered the volume. "Rock and roll is meant to be played loud."

"And you can do that down in your studio. I need to hear myself think," she said, realizing how she sounded like her father years ago. Did people always turn into their parents?

Kate began carving the chicken, plunging the knife in with a vengeance though it wasn't necessary on the tender bird. She plated up the food, poured him some wine, and called him to the table.

"It smells great, but you shouldn't have bothered. Right now I'm buried in the studio. I should have started while school was still in session. I've got to get together enough pieces to do a display at that gallery in Glasco, and I need to do it now before the summer season is in full swing. I figure I can do a few more hours after dinner."

The gallery in Glasco was really just a dusty antique store on Main Street, owned by a thirtyish woman who'd burned out on Wall Street. "Why don't you just relax and enjoy the meal? You need to eat," Kate said.

"Americans eat too much. I can survive on granola and yogurt."

God, did he always have to be so contradictory? Kate put her fork down as she tried to savor a mouthful of wild rice. Even with Eli across the table, she felt as if she were eating alone. "This wasn't the way I'd planned tonight."

"Really? The chicken turned out fine."

"Okay, I admit, I had this special dinner planned so I could ply you with wine and good food and trick you into talking about us, about how we can make our relationship work in a new way now that Ben is in college."

He rolled his eyes. "I appreciate your honesty, but you know I'm not into the soul-sucking, open-heart conversations anymore."

"Soul sucking is a little extreme. I would settle for some friendly conversation now and then. Eli, we're like two strangers living in the same house."

"Not really. We know each other well."

She looked down at her half-eaten meal, no longer hungry.

"I can't do this. We used to be friends. Do you remember a time when we enjoyed each other's company? When we looked forward to reconnecting at the end of the day?"

He bit a piece of flesh from the bone. "That was years ago, Kate. Things have changed. Everything changes. You know how Don Henley says it; in a New York minute, everything can change. That's universal. Things change in a heartbeat. Close your eyes and when you open them, you might not recognize where you are."

"Maybe when you're drunk!" She clapped her water glass on the table with a thud. "Would you stop coming back at me with platitudes and get honest with what's going on here? I feel so alone."

"I can't help you with that. Why can't you understand that, Kate? No matter how we try to mask things or trick ourselves, we're all alone on this planet. We're born alone; we die that way."

"That's not true. You saw it yourself; you held Ben in your arms moments after he was born. We were a family, the three of us together in the same bed." She pressed her palms to her heart. "That bond . . . don't you remember how it felt?"

He drew in a deep breath, then rubbed his forehead with one hand. "I can't go there, Kate. I wish I could help you, but the guy you married, he was another person, a different man. The world has changed, and so have I."

Her throat was thick, knotted with emotion and anger. "So tell me, how do I go about getting to understand the new person you've become? I need a user's manual, a clue, a key to let me in."

"Now look who's talking in platitudes." He tossed his napkin onto the plate and stood up. "I have to get back to work."

"Wait . . ." She pushed away from the table and crossed to the door, physically blocking his way. "You can't walk out in the middle of our discussion."

"Didn't you hear what I said?" He pointed toward the studio down the hill. "I'm working against the clock here. This is not a good time to talk."

"There is never a good time with you, and don't just grin and try to shrug me off. I'm serious. I can't live this way."

Staring down at the ground, he tried to move around her, but she stepped in his way. "Don't you dare go out that door." She grabbed his wrist, his skin surprisingly cool and damp.

He lifted his arm and stared at her fingers clasped tight, a human manacle. "I'm sorry," he said. And then, without another word, he pried her fingers loose and ducked out the door.

Chapter 25

Ben McGann
Syracuse

The young men stood in two lines in the grass doing warm-up drills. They wore Lakers practice uniforms, white pants and flimsy practice shirts in a blue so pale you could paper a baby boy's room with it.

"Ladies and gentlemen," Ben said as he tossed a ball lightly to Dylan, "I give you the 2010 Lakers."

Dylan snorted, but no one else laughed.

Grim team, Ben thought. And probably the biggest bunch of babies he'd ever played with.

"Save the chatter for the locker room, McGann." That from the chubster who would be copping a squat at home plate. He was a senior; Turturro, his uniform said, though everyone called him Turtle.

"You know my name?" Ben said. "I'm flattered."

"I know every name. Didn't you hear? I'm team captain." Turtle threw back to his partner, hard, the ball rocketing into the other guy's glove with a sickening slap.

"Solid," Ben said, though it was a stroke job. What kind of loser needed to show off at practice? "You played here with Coach Ramsey last year, right?"

"I believe my reputation precedes me." Turtle took two steps back and jumped to catch the ball.

Fairly graceful for a two-hundred-pound hippo. Ben pretended not to notice.

"You must have heard about the awesomely skilled left-handed catcher, the first one who will make it to the majors," Turtle said.

"Really." A left-handed catcher would face a lot of obstacles, but Ben wasn't about to be one of them. "Good for you."

"Yeah. Good for me. Now everyone move back," Turtle shouted, and the players stepped back. Now Dylan and the guys on his line would be too far away to overhear.

"So, McGann. McGandolf. Mind if I call you McGandolf? Because they say you're a wizard at first base, and I'm wondering, what's the secret to your magic?"

Ben tamped down a swell of pride; he had a feeling this guy was setting him up. "No secret. No magic. I just get the job done."

"Really? No drugs? Steroids? Uppers?"

Like I'd confide in you if I did, Ben thought. "Nah. I just play it straight."

"Normally, that wouldn't be a problem. I can appreciate a first baseman who takes care of things. But the thing is, the Lakers already have a first baseman. A senior and an awesome athlete." Turtle caught the ball and stepped back, pointing a thumb to the player on his right. "You met Rico yet? Rico Valpariso. He's the best. Like he's got glue in his glove."

Valpariso turned toward Ben, a hungry glint in his dark eyes. He had a dark soul patch on his chin and a slight, broad-shouldered build. "Welcome to Syracuse, man," Valpariso said. "I hope you got a tough ass, because you are going to be getting splinters from the bench."

Ben pointed to Dylan, wound up, and shot the ball in a low arc. "I just came here to play ball," he said.

Turtle's response was a grunt as he caught the next ball.

As the team finished warm-ups, insecurity flickered through Ben. Coach Ramsey had promised him a spot in the starting lineup, his spot at first base, and it didn't sit well that the team had another experienced first baseman on the roster. Ben didn't want trouble with Valpariso, but he didn't come out here to sit

on the bench or play a position he didn't know. He was counting on Ramsey to make good on his promise.

What would Ben do if he got pigeonholed here, stuck on the
bench, second-string?

He didn't even want to go there.

They ran the perimeter of the field, Ben keeping pace toward the front of the pack alongside Dylan.

"What was all that about?" Dylan asked. "What was Turtle
saying?"

"Senioritis."

"What?"

"Tell you later." Ben pushed off from his toes and sprinted
to the end of the field. It felt good to stretch out and let loose,
and Syracuse was as good a place as any—hot, green, with
blue skies and plenty of sunshine so far.

A few other players lunged ahead to keep pace with Ben,
and Turtle called from the back of the line: "Let's see you run
the bases that fast in a game."

"Is he always that cranky?" Ben huffed through his teeth.

"Nah," answered the scrawny guy, Harold. "Sometimes
he's worse."

The guys laughed when somebody let one loose, and from
the back of the group Turtle complained, "That's just nasty."
This was the kind of shit that pulled a team together. Ben knew
it would take some time, but this team could be a force if the
guys could keep their egos under control and work with each
other.

And from what he'd gathered in the locker room before
practice began, the Lakers had ego to spare. Four of the players were going into their senior year, which meant they had
been eligible for the major-league baseball draft last week.
Sounded like the shortstop Kenta Suzuki had done okay, getting picked in the eighth round, though Kenta attended Columbia and was determined to finish college. A red-haired,
freckled, Norman Rockwell–painting kid with the last name of
"Harold" on his uniform kept getting ribbed because he'd
been picked in the fifty-third round.

Someone said: "If a tree falls in the fifty-third round of draft picks, does anyone hear it?"

"Really, when your pick is that high, good luck getting to the big show," Turtle added. Turtle was part of the group ribbing Harold, though he never mentioned exactly what his own pick was. That couldn't be good. Ben smelled a vulnerability.

"I got two words for you guys," Harold said. "Mike Piazza."

"Exactly." Ben grinned, being a baseball history buff. "Piazza was a sixty-second round draft pick. Last round, and he went on to be a twelve-time All-Star with the second longest RBI streak in major-league baseball."

"Really." Turtle licked the corner of his lips. "Maybe you got a chance after all, Double First."

"Yeah." Rico Valpariso grinned, his teeth flashing white against his mocha skin, dark shades. "A snowball's chance in hell." Rico had been chosen by the Pirates in the fifth round. Fifth round was pretty impressive, and Rico was making sure everyone knew it. He said he was staying in college, wanted to be the first in his family to get a degree, but anyone could see he was dying to be a star.

As he lunged forward to stretch, Ben worried about Valpariso, the other first baseman.

It could be a problem for Ben if Coach Ramsey was influenced by the draft.

And Ben wasn't about to waste the summer. What were his options if he got shafted by Ramsey? Ben thought about the offer he'd turned down to play in the Cape Cod League. Would they still take him?

Across the field Coach Ramsey and the assistant coach, Ash, emerged from the dugout and Ramsey summoned the players with the wave of a hand.

"Over to the dugout," Turtle ordered. "Move it."

Ben cut over toward the coaches, glad to be done with warm-ups. He was getting a little sick of hearing Turtle bark orders like a marine sergeant, and really, they were all here to play. Right now these guys didn't need much motivation.

The team huddled around Ramsey, who got down and told them all to take a knee.

"Welcome to Syracuse. I'm Otis Ramsey, your coach for the next few weeks, and this is Brent Ash, who'll be assisting me." He removed his cornflower-blue Lakers cap and ran one hand over the close-shaved stubble on his head. Ramsey was forty-ish, African American, and not missing too many meals from the looks of the paunch over his belt. "Nine o'clock in the morning and already it's a scorcher. Be sure to drink plenty of water today."

He replaced his cap. "Gentlemen, summer ball is an odd animal, a strange beast. It brings together players from all over the country, guys who may oppose each other during the regular season, players who may never see each other after this seven-week season. You will play at least one game a day, with a doubleheader most weekends and a day off during the week. We don't have the luxury of tryouts or weeks of practice, so I'm counting on you to do what you were brought here for.

"Now let's get real for a minute. I know you're not here because you want to run your ass off in ninety-degree heat. Some of you are here because you love baseball. Some of you are here because you can't get to the prize." He held one hand up high. "You can't get way up here unless you work your way up to it, and I'm okay with that. Summer ball can be your stepping stone to the pros. I'm banking on that myself. Believe me, I don't want to be the baseball coach at a community college forever. I'm looking to move up, too, and if we all work together, we can all get where we want to be. Or, at least we get closer."

So far, so good. Ben liked Ramsey's direct approach, unlike some coaches who acted as if they had some secret formula for coaching that they couldn't divulge until later.

Ramsey went on to go over "the rules," emphasizing that they needed to stay away from drugs and booze. "And that goes for you guys who are drinking age," the coach said, squinting against the sun. "I've seen too many talented athletes ruin their careers in barroom brawls."

As the coach finished up his talk, Ben slid his shades on and studied the faces of the other players. Hard to tell who was on board, though he didn't see any obvious dissension. For Ben the real test of Otis Ramsey would be whether or not he kept his promises, which was not to be divulged just yet. Ramsey went off to work with the pitchers while Coach Ash kept the others to practice fielding.

Two hours later, Ben lifted his cap to wipe the sweat from his brow when Coach Ramsey called them in again. Ben's glove was melded to his hand from sweat and heat, though it was not an unpleasant feeling.

Ramsey looked crisp and cool, shoulders back and hands on his hips. "I've posted the starting lineup in the locker room," he said. "I'll sub in replacements for injured players or for any players who fall down on the job. Tomorrow at seven begins a three-game series against Geneva. Be at the field in uniform an hour before game time. Now go and make sure you drink plenty of water."

Although Ben wanted to bolt off the field and into the locker room to see the list, he walked with the others, not wanting to reveal the baseball geek within. He loved this game, and he wanted first base so bad he could taste it, but he wasn't going to race in there like a two-year-old.

Once they were inside the cool air of the locker room, the team's energy level resurged and their whoops and laughter echoed through the shower chamber. Over by the windowed coach's office, guys swarmed the bulletin board where the paper with the lineup fluttered under two pushpins. Half a dozen conversations were going on at once.

Ben overheard a big guy everyone called Dozo, who was ribbing Turtle about being the only catcher on the team. "Must be nice not to have any competition."

Dylan was at the front of the mass of arms and heads, and Ben hung back as he saw his friend check the list, then pump his fist in the air. He squeezed to the side of the mob and sidled over to Ben.

"I'm on the pitchers' roster! A pitcher. I guess they needed a left-hander. Can you believe it?"

"Whoa. This is going to be a big change for you." At Boston College Dylan was second-string, and usually played in the outfield. "You up for it?" Ben asked.

"You kidding me? It's awesome!"

Ben nodded toward the list. "You see my name on there?"

"First base, of course." Dylan slapped him on the shoulder. "What did you expect?"

"It's all good," Ben said. Later he would tell Dylan about his confrontation with Turtle and Rico. Much later.

Just then Rico emerged from the crowd looking at the list. "Fucking third base." He threw his glove toward the wall. It hit a locker and bounced onto the tile floor. Conversation died down as Rico pushed through the crowd and marched to the coach's office.

"What's that about?" Dylan asked.

But Ben ignored him and followed Rico, thinking he could say something to take the edge off. Yeah, he wanted first base, but he didn't want to be the enemy. He peered into the coach's office, where Rico stood, his cleats planted on the worn carpet, his hands on his hips. Ben paused in the doorway, not wanting to interrupt but unable to tear himself away.

"There's been a mistake. A huge mistake," Rico said. "Coach, I played first base for you last summer, and you were satisfied, right?"

Coach Ramsey leaned back in his chair, considering. "I was."

"And did you see the draft?" Rico pointed as if the list were right beside him. "Pittsburgh picked me to play first base in the fifth round. Fifth round, Coach." He shook his head. "You gotta put me on first base."

Ramsey paused, biting his lower lip. "Can't do it, Rico, but I got you on third."

"No disrespect intended, but that's crazy."

"You'll be more valuable as a player who's familiar with more than one position."

"But what about first base?"

"You're my backup. If for some reason McGann misses a game, you're on first, I guarantee it."

"Coach, I covered first base for you last year, right? One of your finest players. No errors all summer. I got the runner out, every time."

"You're good." Nodding, the coach unwrapped a stick of gum and shoved it in his mouth. "McGann's better."

Rico continued to argue, but Ben quickly moved away from the doorway, not wanting to be caught eavesdropping, not wanting Rico to think he was rubbing in the fact that he'd won. Sure, he was relieved. Yeah, he needed to be on first base.

But it stuck in his craw that someone on the team had been wronged, and yeah, that's how the situation felt with Rico. The guy was a fifth-round draft pick; he deserved to play.

Coach Ramsey's words echoed back at him . . . *"You're good. McGann is better."*

Topping his teammate, that made it a hollow victory.

It didn't sit well with Ben.

He had to fix it, had to find a way to make things right with Rico.

Chapter 26

Rico Valpariso
Syracuse

Practice was over, the sun slanting low in the sky, but Rico wasn't quite ready to leave the field yet. As the other players headed off to the showers he went over to the third-base side, scraped at the course track in front of the dugout, stared at the uneven dirt of the baseline.

This part of the field was foreign to him.

Alien.

Like a strange, unforgiving country.

And yet, Coach Ramsey wouldn't budge, no matter that it didn't make sense.

He dug the toes of one cleat into the ground, right foot, then left. Bent his knees, assumed the defensive stance. Nah. Nada. It didn't work. It just didn't feel right.

He kicked at the sand, then headed over to the large orange cooler of Gatorade. Tomorrow was their first game and he didn't feel ready. Not if he was playing third base. As he tossed back the cool liquid he heard a thud in the sand.

Turtle was outside the dugout, peeling off his catcher's gear—his chest protector fell to the dust beside his mask and helmet.

He was in no mood for the big man. Rico had played with Turtle last summer and wasn't a big fan. Not a bad catcher, but the guy was always in your face. "You want some?" Rico asked, nodding toward the cooler.

"Nah, I never drink from the community well." Turtle took out a small blue cooler, his personal stash. Rico remembered it from last year; guys used to joke that the little blue cooler was filled with iced vodka. He took a sip, another, sighed. "So how's third base working out?"

"Sucks." Rico felt it rising inside him, resentment. "Fuckin' McGann comes in and robs me."

Considering all this, Turtle took another drink, swiped his hand across his mouth. "You want to take him out?"

"No, I don't want to take him out." Frustration bubbled and rose in his chest, hot as the yellow sun. "*Dios,* do you hear yourself? Like, what are you talking about? You going to kill him?"

"Easy, Rico. I was talking about drinks, man, take him out and get him good and drunk. But now that you mention it, you could put something together to end his season. You wouldn't have to get your hands dirty, you know. You could hire someone to do it."

Rico glared at the big catcher. "I'm here to get away from people like that."

"Okay. Then what are you going to do about McGandolf?"

"I just want him to go away so I can get first base back."

"Well, this here isn't a wishing well, and I'm no Santa Claus." Turtle tipped his head back and chugged a mouthful from the blue cooler. "You want something done, you got to take action, man. Make it happen. I'm not saying what or where; I'm just saying that sitting around and complaining is a choice, too. You get what I'm saying?"

"I get it, okay, Big Man?" He cursed in Spanish. "I'm not stupid."

"I'm just saying . . ." Turtle took another drink, then capped off the small cooler. "Food for thought." He bent down to snag his helmet and chest protector. "I wonder what they're slinging in the dining hall. Afternoon practices always make me hungry."

As Turtle headed off, Rico got another cup of Gatorade and turned to stare across at first base. What would it take to get it back? In some ways Turtle was right. If he didn't make it happen, he was giving up.

These past days, watching McGann guard the base, he'd come to hate that smug smile, the long stretch off the bag. The guy had long legs but he didn't get tripped up on them. McGann was just born shitting money. He had a rich girlfriend and a cherry-red Ford. He hated the way McGann tried to act like his buddy, sharing his expensive bat, a fine piece of work that felt so slender and strong in your hands. Rico coveted that bat, a Rawlings Blue Thunder. *That bat should be mine . . .*

First base, too.

He wondered what it would take to get McGann out of the picture.

Not that he would do anything, but just wondering, what if . . .

He thought of that ice-skater girl. What was her name? She went to the Olympics and won a silver medal after one of the other girl skaters tried to take her out. Or hired some guys to take her out. Something like that. Yeah, she got these thugs to do it, but they got caught and went to jail. At least, that was how he remembered it.

Those guys were stupid. No, he would never do something that stupid and evil. Pure evil.

He crossed himself, kissed his medal of Mary. *You can get me there, La Alta Gracia. Get me where I need to be.*

When he closed his eyes, he could see the prize, the dream fulfilled—his name on the MLB draft list in the first round. He could see it, all glowing and golden, like it was surrounded by halos.

Eye on the prize. He was a fifth-round draft pick, right?

The Lakers were just a team for today. Summer ball.

In the end, this team—this summer—it meant nothing. No big deal.

Not worth sweating over.

Chapter 27

Kate
Syracuse

As Kate climbed the bleachers she felt a tinge of self-consciousness, which she knew was stupid. Really, would anyone in the sparsely populated stadium notice the middle-aged woman sitting alone? "We Will Rock You" played on the speakers as she climbed to the top row—where you could use the rear wall as a backrest—and examined the hat she'd purchased from a small concession stand. The baby-blue cap featured a black cursive L worthy of a penmanship award. Hats did not flatter Kate—she had a short forehead—but she wanted to show her support; it would keep the sun off her face and disguise the fact that she had been crying. She carefully tucked her short hair behind her ears and plunked it on. With the hat and her sunglasses, she was well covered.

With school winding down, this was her first chance to see Ben play with the Lakers. She had to return to school Monday for a week of closedown, but those would be low-key, easy days. Game time was still twenty minutes away, and she could see the baby-blue uniforms of the Lakers over on a nearby practice field while Rochester warmed up down below. She could pick out Ben by the way he moved, or at least she thought that was him.

When she learned Ben would be playing summer ball in Syracuse, she had imagined herself making the trip with Eli, spending the night together in a little bed-and-breakfast inn, patching their relationship together. She had assumed he would want to come to a few games and cheer his son on. But no, Eli was swamped, in a bad mood, under pressure to create a dozen stained-glass pieces for some art festival he'd committed to. At the end of the school year he was usually able to kick back and move at a slower pace, but this year Eli seemed more frenetic than ever. Grouchy and distant.

Because it had started in September, she had thought it was a reaction to Ben moving out—empty-nest syndrome. But as the year progressed Eli drifted further away, skipping dinner to work down in his studio, sometimes coming into the house and going to the guest room without a word.

The guest room . . . that irked Kate. She had never expected them to be one of those couples with separate rooms. When they had shared a bed, Eli had always seemed physically accessible and sincere. Granted, the frequency of their lovemaking had waned in the past few years, but this . . . total separation?

And the feeling that it was all beyond her control . . . that wasn't fair.

This morning, while she'd been driving and trying to formulate a plan to save their relationship, the stark reality had come to her like a dark spirit in possession of her body.

It was over.

Tears had blurred her vision and she had quickly pulled onto the shoulder to cry. She had loved him once. She had thought their relationship would last, that they would grow old together, laugh at each other's jokes, take care of each other always.

But no, none of the details were adding up in their favor, and Kate was a detail person. Eli didn't want to talk and he refused therapy. He didn't want to be with her, and he avoided her nearly every day. How could she read the signals any other way? It was definitely over.

In those twenty or so minutes she tried to accept that, though she couldn't help but mourn the loss of what they once shared. At one time Kate and Eli were a couple who worked, and not only did it hurt to lose that, but also she questioned what would be left of her without him. After all these years of having her identity interwoven in their family, who was Kate McGann? Soon to be a divorced person, apparently. She shuddered in the sunshine. She'd never thought of herself that way, but she would get used to it.

Down below, the Lakers jogged onto the field and filed into the home team dugout. Kate clapped and waved, fairly sure she'd caught Ben's attention, and eliciting a salute from Dylan at the back of the line. Ben's expression was all business, but Dylan seemed happy, a big smile on his face.

She didn't feel out of place anymore. She was Ben's mom sitting along the first baseline, where she'd been sitting since the days of T-ball.

"Please rise for the national anthem." The teams lined up outside their respective dugouts, their hats to their hearts as the crowd rose. As music churned over the field, Kate saw before her a facet of her life that Eli could not take away. The diamond. She loved the irony of that. Green grass, sharp competition, the crack of a ball off the bat, the smell of popcorn and roasted hot dogs. And in the midst of it all was her son, standing tall and ready to play the precision game he'd been practicing all his life.

It was not her identity, but it was a substantial piece of the puzzle.

The first pitch was thrown, and though she tried to focus on the action at the plate her eyes always flicked back to his stance at first base. The Rochester batter hit an infield grounder, and the shortstop scooped it up and shot it over to Ben. . . .

Who stepped off the bag to make the catch.

"Sweet," she said under her breath as Ben returned the ball to the pitcher.

As the game went on, a couple sitting a few rows in front of her noticed she was clapping at the same time. The woman turned and they began to chat. Tak and Hoshi Suzuki were the parents of Kenta, the Lakers' shortstop.

By the end of the first inning the Suzukis had joined Kate in the top row so they could talk quietly during the game. Kenta was a senior, who had been chosen in the MLB draft this year.

"He is very honored," his father said. "However, he will continue at Columbia and finish university. Then he would like to play in major-league baseball." As Kenta had played summer ball in Syracuse last year, the Suzukis possessed tidbits of information about some of the players and the coach.

"The catcher, they call him Turtle," Hoshi Suzuki said. "And he is very superstitious. He only drinks from his own water cooler, and last year there was a pair of socks he was rumored not to wash."

"Oh, dear," Kate said, and she and Hoshi shared a smile.

When Will Sager snagged a fly ball in the outfield, Hoshi commented that she was glad to see him back again. "He is a very good player, but he had to end his season early last year when he got in some trouble. Underage drinking," she explained. "Sometimes it's so hard to keep these boys in the game. They don't understand what they're risking when they break the rules."

When Ben came up to bat, Kate turned her attention to the field. As he flexed his knees in batting stance, she saw that he was holding the Blue Thunder bat. "He's had that bat for two years," she told the Suzukis. "It was a Christmas gift. Crazy expensive, but it was all he wanted."

The pitch came and Ben swung. There was the crack of contact and then the ball sailed out, cutting through the gap between Rochester's left and center fielders. It bounced behind them, hit the wall, then ricocheted off to the left. By the time the fielder had recovered the ball, Ben was safely at third base, having driven in two runs.

"Very nice!" Tak Suzuki said. "It looks like Blue Thunder was well worth the cost!"

Kate laughed. Was it just last year that Ben had asked for the bat for Christmas? It seemed that he was so much younger then, a senior in high school. Sometimes he had asked her to proofread his papers, and he had thrown himself at her mercy when it came time to find something to wear for prom. Kate had enjoyed helping with the prom preparations, though she'd had to bite her tongue to keep from calling him sweetie and telling him how utterly handsome he looked in the classic black tuxedo.

As she watched him slide into home, it occurred to Kate that her "baby" was well into adulthood now, nineteen already. In the next few years he would need her less and less. It was one of those good news/bad news revelations: If you did a good job parenting, your kid went off on his own.

One of the teachers at school was always harping on how parents couldn't let go. "The human species is the only group of animals that doesn't know when to kick its young out of the nest." Kate would have to be extra careful not to cling to Ben just because she was losing Eli.

When the time came, she would have to sit on her hands and just say good-bye.

After the game Kate waited with the Suzukis outside the locker room. There was a break before the second game of the doubleheader at seven, and they were hoping to take the guys out for a bite to eat this afternoon. She had sent Ben a text, asking if he needed to check with the coach.

"Mom! You came to my game!"

Kate glanced up from her conversation with the Suzukis to see Dylan approaching, arms wide. She laughed as he swept her off her feet. "Geez, Dylan, we have to have a talk about knowing your own strength. You just about knocked me over."

"That's because you're withering away to nothing, Mommyson. So you saw the game. Did you see my catch in the fifth inning?"

"Of course, and it was fabulous." She didn't mention that she was surprised to see him on the field; Ben had warned her that Dylan would be warming the bench on this team.

"I got to play part of the game because one of our outfielders is sick," he said.

She patted his shoulder and introduced him to the Suzukis as "Ben's good friend. Sort of my second son."

Dylan shook hands with the Suzukis. "Your son is an awesome player. A human vacuum."

"That's good, I hope," Hoshi said.

"Definitely. Our infield really needs him." He turned to Kate. "I look out in the bleachers and there you are! Why didn't you tell me you were coming?"

Kate drew in a breath, not sure how to answer. She had planned to spend some time with Ben . . . just Ben. She was saved the embarrassment when Ben and Kenta appeared at the locker room door, and suddenly everyone was talking at once as they tried to sort out who would be going where. Kate invited Dylan to eat with them, pretending that it had been her plan all along. The guys wanted to go light, so they settled on a sushi place just a few blocks off campus.

"How's Ginger doing?" Kate asked Dylan as they perused the offerings going around on a conveyor belt. Dylan's grandmother had been his legal custodian until he turned eighteen.

"Ginger is Ginger. She works, and hangs at the Old Boar." Ginger worked the breakfast shift at a small Woodstock eatery. The job had been convenient as it allowed her to be at home for Dylan after school and evenings. Years ago Ginger had made a point of escorting Dylan to scout meetings or school functions, but when Dylan reached high school Ginger started spending most nights at a local pub, a pattern that brought Dylan to the McGanns' house for sleepovers, even during the school week. "I wish she would come to a game," Dylan added, "but I can't get her to leave her zip code."

"Ben's dad is getting to be the same way. He uses the stained-glass studio as an excuse, but I think he's just stuck in his ways, becoming inflexible." She shot a sidelong glance at Ben, wondering if it bothered him that Eli wasn't here. But he seemed unfazed, engrossed in gripping a piece of raw tuna with chopsticks.

Kate grabbed a large prawn from the conveyor belt, wanting to change the subject. "So tell me what it's like playing for the Lakers."

"Ramsey is one of the best coaches I've ever worked with," Dylan said. He talked about the coach promising to try him as a pitcher, and was saying something about improving his batting when Kate noticed that Ben was tuned out. "Summer ball is really just a chance to improve," Dylan finished.

"That's a great attitude to have, Dyl." Kate readjusted her chopsticks. "How about you, Ben? Are you liking the team?"

Ben nodded as he chewed. "Sure."

"The one-word answer," she said. "Always a warning sign."

"It's summer ball." Ben shrugged. "A short season."

Kate pressed a napkin to her mouth, surprised. This was not her son.

"Don't let them get to you," Dylan said. "They're idiots."

"Who?" Kate asked.

Ben waved it off, but Dylan answered, "Some of the guys on the team. It's all because Rico Valpariso isn't playing first base. Rico and a few of the others seem to think that Ben came in and deliberately took his place."

Although Ben had mentioned that there was another first baseman on the team, Kate was a little surprised that the issue hadn't settled down. Over the years she'd seen Ben play on countless teams, and he had always managed to win the other players over, even the guys who were initially put off by Ben's passion for the game and his determination to win. "Was this guy Rico playing today?" she asked.

"He was on third base." Ben stared at his chopsticks. "He's still in the starting lineup, but he's pissed, and he's directing it all at me."

"That's ridiculous." She sensed his tension. "You know, you would think that by the time guys reach this level, they would realize that it's the coaches who control things, not other players."

"Yeah." Ben's fingers rubbed at the condensation on his water glass. "It's pretty lame, but I get it. In some ways I feel bad for Rico. I don't know what he was promised, but he's a tight athlete, and he's a senior. He feels like I'm stealing first base away from him, and in a way he's right. If I didn't join the Lakers, he'd be playing first."

"Bummer." Kate put her chopsticks down. "And I guess there's no way you guys could go to the coach and ask him to alternate who plays first base?"

Ben winced. "Ma . . ."

"Sorry, I take that back. Just the nerdy schoolteacher mom trying to think of a solution that makes everyone happy."

"Yeah." Ben stared at his sushi. "Don't do that, Mom. You can't fix things for me anymore."

She bit her lower lip. "I know. You can handle it. You have that knack, a way of making people feel good about themselves. I know you'll figure something out." And she cut herself off before she called him sweetie.

Chapter 28

Marnie Epstein
Boston

Marnie hated Sundays. Even when she didn't have the Monday-to-Friday grind of school, she suffered on Sundays. Her body knew that it was the end of the week, time to feel blue and suffer remorse for all the things she did or didn't do that week.

You would think that her summer schedule working mornings at Beantown Grind and most nights at Storemart would have tricked her body into thinking she was on vacation; or that each day was eternally Monday, time to wake up and go to work. But no, she still hit that wall each Sunday evening.

Tonight as she lined up shampoo bottles in the cosmetic section, which Pratt, the manager, had told her to clean up, the focus of her remorse was Dylan.

She had to break up with him; couldn't stand being his girlfriend anymore. She'd thought it would be better once he was in another town, but Dylan wasn't backing off. Every day he sent a bunch of texts: He was thinking about her, wondering about her day, wishing she could have seen something he'd done. Every text reminded her that she didn't share his enthusiasm. The girlfriend role was choking her.

A whole row of Suave bottles fell back, and she bit her lower lip as she reached into the narrow shelf to right them one at a time, lining them up like cheerful soldiers in the war on greasy hair. Although her job at Storemart was mind-numbing she was grateful for the break it gave her from Dylan's texts that seemed to pop up every ten minutes, because Storemart employees were absolutely forbidden to carry cell phones during their shift. The texts ranged from "wassup?" to "love you" to "wish you could have seen the game," and each message compounded the guilt Marnie felt for letting their relationship go on for so long.

But really, it wasn't her fault. She didn't actually realize there was a relationship until after the fact. Her first clue should have been that Dylan would make sure she got home after they were out with Ben. Marnie had thought the three of them were just friends hanging out together, but suddenly Emma was included like a couples date, and Dylan was calling Marnie his girlfriend. Then the text messages started coming. Lots of texts, to the point where she didn't want to turn her cell phone on in the morning and weed through them.

"It *is* your fault," Marnie said aloud, which was okay, because the aisle was empty. Why didn't she just stop hanging out with Dylan and Ben when she got a hint of what Dylan was thinking? If she had cut it off then, she wouldn't be suffocating from him now. He wanted validation all the time. Didn't he have other stuff to do? Take a shower, go to batting practice . . . do something that didn't involve texting her?

Two girls turned into the aisle and started picking at the eye makeup. Marnie angled her body so that she wouldn't have to look at them, though she couldn't miss their animated conversation about gunking mascara and black flakes.

Because Dylan was really getting into this, she worried that he'd be devastated when she broke it off. She didn't want to hurt him. He was a good guy . . . just not for her.

So she kept on wimping out when she should have been telling him the awkward truth. She kept sinking herself deeper and deeper into this hole. But now that Dylan was off in Syracuse, what could she do? It didn't seem right to break it off in a phone call. What, was she going to text him that it was over? Only a heartless coward would do that.

And yet, she could visualize it. How simple it would be, a text message that said: "I think we should see other people."

She picked someone's wadded gum wrapper from the back of the shelf and fantasized that she could be free with one short text message.

"Marnie?" It was one of the girls down the aisle. "Is that you?"

The girl down the aisle was a two-tone blonde—sort of honey and mustard—and her eyes were an electric shade of aquamarine Marnie had never seen. Emma. Emma Lenson had to be the only student Marnie knew who could afford those fake colored contact lenses.

The other girl was so thin, Marnie could have outlined her entire clavicle with a felt pen. She was also putting the store mascara on her lashes.

"Um, you can't do that," Marnie said, closing the space between them. "Those aren't samples. Once you break the seal, we can't sell it."

The girl, who had her long brown hair twisted up on her head and held together with chopsticks, replaced the wand in the bottle. "How am I supposed to know if it works unless I try it on?"

Marnie sank her hands into the deep pockets of her ugly orange Storemart apron. "I don't know. Maybe go to Bloomingdale's and have one of their makeup artists paint it on?"

"Don't worry. I'm buying this for her." Emma snatched the mascara out of the other chick's hand. "But I've been thinking about you, Marnie. Guess where I'm going next week."

Marnie couldn't imagine. "Paris? Palm Springs?"

"I'm spending the weekend in Syracuse. I want to go to some games, and, you know, party with the Lakers." Emma turned to chopsticks hair. "That's the team Ben plays for. Just for the summer."

"Yah-huh." The girl stared at the glittery plastic tube, more interested in the mascara.

"You should come," Emma told Marnie. "I'm driving down since my father doesn't trust those little prop planes. I could make room in the car for you, and then you can visit Dylan. Have you heard from him lately?"

Every other minute. "He's been in touch," Marnie said. "But I wasn't planning to see him this summer." She lifted the strap of her orange apron. "Gotta work, but thanks for the offer."

"Really. I didn't know you worked here. Last winter you worked in a coffee shop, right?"

"Beantown Grind. I'm still there mornings. This is my evening job."

The skinny girl turned back to the cosmetics rack, as if Marnie were just too boring to hold her interest.

"Oh. Okay." Emma tossed her hair over one shoulder, changing tact. "Anyway, I'll tell Dylan you said hello." She turned back to her friend. "Do you want to go to Bloomie's for makeovers?"

The other girl vacillated, said something about being tired.

Taking advantage of the moment, Marnie said good-bye and made a beeline to the stockroom. Maybe there was a new shipment of cookies or toothpaste to put out.

Leave it to Emma to plan a road trip to Syracuse. From watching spring ball at BC, Marnie could tell that girl didn't know a baseball from a beach ball. Well, spend enough time around Ben the baseball junkie and she would learn fast enough.

She wished she could send a message with Emma, an easy way to get her off the hook with Dylan. She could just imagine Emma passing the word along in her bubblehead cadence. "Dylan? Just to let you know? Marnie is so done with you. 'Kay? Buh-bye."

Sometimes she wondered why Ben hooked up with Emma. Aside from the fact that she was heir to the Lenson Crystal fortune, Emma didn't seem to have a lot going on. Why didn't Ben see through Emma?

Guys could be so stupid.

Chapter 29

Ben
Syracuse

Ben knew what he had to do.

He had thought of ways to appeal to Rico Valpariso, ways to suck up. Most of them were too obvious and disingenuous. This would snag him, though it pained Ben.

He waited near the entrance of the batting cage as the pitching mechanisms whirred and balls slammed against the tarp dividers. Rico and Turtle were using adjacent cages, talking over the noise of the machines. Occasionally they called comments to each other, but Ben didn't want to hear what they had to say. He knew Rico was in a batting slump. He knew that the coach had told both guys to schedule extra batting practice.

They had the disease; he had the cure. Or, at least, he could present it that way.

"Hey, Rico." Ben stood at the netting behind Valpariso's cage and presented his favorite bat, the Rawlings Blue Thunder. "Why don't you try this?" Ben extended the bat with both hands, as if it were some kind of diploma. So benevolent, he wanted to gag.

His face was taut with a sneer when Rico turned, but his expression softened when he saw the bat. All the guys on the team had admired the Blue Thunder when they'd seen Ben use it. Rico emerged from the cage to squint down at the bat.

It took all of Ben's grit to keep a bland expression on his face when Rico's white-gloved fingers closed over the smooth wood handle. White batting gloves, what was that about? But Ben bit back his disdain. He had to rein it in if he wanted a shot at smoothing things over with Valpariso.

Rico gripped the bat to get a feel for it. "Not bad," he said. When he stepped back and took a swing, Ben detected the hint of a smile. "Nice stick, McGandolf. You selling it on eBay?"

"I'll be using it when I'm up at bat," Ben said. "But if you want, you can give it a try."

Rico lifted the bat and took another swing. "I might." He was trying to sound like he didn't give a rip, but Ben could see right through it. "But if I had a bat like this, I wouldn't be letting anyone near it."

"Maybe. Or maybe you'd want to make sure your teammates have an edge out there." Ben took the Blue Thunder back, ran one hand along the shaft. "There's no bat in the world that can make a good batter out of an incompetent. But when you've got a batter with some skill, the right equipment can make a difference."

Turtle, who had stopped his pitching machine and joined them, now stared down at the bat in Ben's hands. "Can I try?"

Ben handed it over. "Just take care of it, okay? If it gets wrecked, it's ruined for all of us."

Turtle took a swing, then grinned. "It's a thing of beauty." He moved the bat to the crook of his left arm and extended his right to shake hands with Ben. "Thanks, McGann. We might keep striking out, but we'll sure feel good as we do it."

Ben gripped the catcher's hand, no doubt shaking hands with the enemy. "It's cool," he said, though he sensed that Turtle wasn't completely won over.

Whatever. He'd made an attempt, and Valpariso was warming to him.

"You want to use it for practice, go on. I'll hang out for a while." Ben couldn't just leave the bat with them, but he didn't want to go into his ritual, the way he laid out his bats in his room at night. Not that it was so weird to take care of your equipment, but some guys left their stuff in the locker room, vulnerable to moisture or damage, sometimes theft.

"I'd like to try it out in the cage," Rico said.

"Go on." Ben folded his arms, settling in for a while. He didn't like sharing the Blue Thunder, but already the gesture seemed to be chipping away at Rico's animosity. "Give it a try. I'll wait."

Chapter 30

Kate
Woodstock

As usual, Eli dodged Kate's attack with his passive-aggressiveness.

Sunday night when she drove up the muddy hillside with a sound resolve to end their relationship, Eli was not in the house or his studio, and he didn't answer his cell. However, there was evidence that he had been there. The tenor of the house felt different; or maybe that was the thick humidity, the smell of mud and wet mulch. Apparently they'd had a good amount of rain here.

When she went to get a glass of water before bed, she noticed two wineglasses in the kitchen sink. Somehow Eli's dirty dishes never made it to the dishwasher. While she was loading them she noticed a pale film of lipstick on the rim of one glass.

Kate hadn't worn lipstick in years.

Another woman. Probably Tamara Peak, the woman with the antique shop in Glasco. Kate had noticed her car down at the studio a few times, but Eli said it was business.

The sinking feeling in her chest wasn't completely logical. It hurt, and she had thought she was beyond that. On the other hand, maybe Eli could handle a divorce with the help of another woman to smooth over the details of his life. Someone to make his home comfortable, keep his bed warm, deal with installers and banks and cleaning people. Someone to load the damned dishwasher.

Wanting to lash out, Kate called his cell, which went right to voice mail. Damn him.

She had to wait, though sleep eluded her. She took a Motrin PM and passed the time making a list of Eli's things that she would gladly pack and help him remove from the house. Boxes of clothes. Crates of record albums and old 45s. Two old stereos with turntables, and the giant Infinity speakers that reminded Kate of coffins for very thin people. She drifted off to sleep thinking of how she would paint the house in cheerful hues—buttery yellows, mocha, and pumpkin—colors that would embrace and warm her in the cold months ahead.

When she woke up the next morning, the signs of a deluge scarred their yard. One look at the trench of muck cutting through her rose garden made Kate sit back on the bed. What a mess.

She traipsed over the damp earth in her boxers and garden clogs, edging around two ribbons of mud where the rainfall must have broken through, forming its own path of least resistance. Eli could have called and warned her about the mess. Still, there wasn't much she could do about it now if she was going to make it to school to close up her classroom.

She showered, grabbed a breakfast bar, and stopped at the coffee shop in town to grab a latte to go. The cleanup at school was a welcome diversion from her issues at home. That afternoon when she turned into the drive at the foot of the hill, she spotted Eli's car parked behind his studio.

"Aha. Gotcha." She pulled in behind his car and cut the engine. Van Morrison's voice singing "Blue Money" danced through the humid air as she picked her way through the muddy drive to his workshop. When Ben was a baby, they used to dance him to sleep with this album.

Regret sniped at her, but she barreled over it and walked in through the open garage bay.

Eli leaned over a mess on his workbench, fragments of midnight-blue sapphire glass everywhere. One gloved hand held an oval window while the other squeezed a pair of pliers, trying to free a fragment of shattered blue glass at the center of the oval. He wiggled the pliers back and forth, like a dentist working a loose tooth. His teeth were clenched in concentration, his jaw grizzled with gray, which she had always found sexy. Now, it just made him seem old.

"We need to talk."

Without looking up, he said, "I'm sort of busy right now. Supposed to fix this one piece in the panel." His voice strained with the effort of yanking. "Only the lady who asked for the repair doesn't understand that it's easier to just make the whole thing brand-new."

"So charge her double. I don't care as long as you hear me out now. And don't tell me this isn't a good time, that you're tired or worried about finishing some piece so that your girlfriend can hang it in that dump she calls an antique shop. There's never a good time for you."

The shard of blue glass finally came loose, and he dropped it out of the pliers and finally looked up. "Feeling a little cranky?"

"I'm way beyond cranky. You could have called and told me how our yard was ravaged while I was gone."

"And what? You would have stopped the rain?"

She stepped into his line of vision. "It's called communication, Eli, but we're way beyond that. We need to talk about a legal separation. I've done some research, and a separation is the best way to go in New York state."

"And did you research the expense of divorce in New York state?"

"It's cheaper to go with a licensed mediator, though right now I don't care how much it costs."

"But I do. I'm not throwing money to the state so that a politician can buy some call girl. You want out, you can go, but I'm staying right here."

"That's not fair." And she'd been planning to stay in the house for the time being; she had thought he would gladly go off to the other woman's place. "But I'm not here to argue. The truth is, neither of us can afford to keep this house."

"Sure we can, if we keep things as they are. You got the master bedroom, and I keep to myself."

"And we're supposed to live as if we're two church mice sharing the belfry? That's ludicrous."

"Actually, it's more realistic than your plan to sell everything off and get two places. What do you think you'll find out there, Kate? You think the grass is greener, that you'll find something better? Someone better? The reality is that you're going to wake up bitter and angry wherever you go. Might as well save yourself the trouble and just stay here."

"That's not going to happen." She wiped beads of sweat from her brow. How did he work in this heat?

"Oh, no? Where are you going to go, Kate?" With a perverse smile he turned on his soldering iron. "The Bear Trap Inn is usually booked this time of year, and it is a little pricey for someone on a schoolteacher's salary."

"Why don't you just go, Eli? I know you've got a girlfriend, and you've been living out of boxes in the guest room. It's not like you use the house."

With a sudden movement that frightened her, he wheeled and pointed the soldering iron, a wicked tool that resembled a dentist's drill, toward the house up the hill. "My studio is here and that house has become my home, Kate. I created every damned window that's hung up there, and I'm not going to leave it now."

"Eli . . ." She had never seen him this way, hostility roiling behind his eyes. "This is not you. You don't get attached to material things. You're not part of the mercenary establishment."

"Try again, Kate. You made me this way. You wanted the house in the country and the kid."

"You wanted it, too! You fell in love with Woodstock. Remember how you couldn't wait to get Ben out of the city, how you felt a bond with this place? You said we couldn't live anywhere else."

"And there you have it. I've settled in here, Kate. I'm comfortable with my work, the house, my car. This is what I am, and if you don't like it, you can go off somewhere and leave me alone. In fact, I would prefer it."

Her hands balled into fists and she had to restrain herself from taking his ball-peen hammer and smashing the finished pieces hung in the corner. "Actually, I think I'll stay. Yes, I relish the thought of staying here and making your life miserable."

Her face burned with fury as she strode out the door. She gunned the engine, and dirt flew behind her car as it zipped up the hill. Inside the house, her hands shook as she dialed her sister's number. Erin would understand. Erin would give her a place to stay, time to regroup. Just as soon as she finished off this week of school she would fly down to Baltimore and make a plan. Escape.

Chapter 31

Joe "Turtle" Turturro
Syracuse

Night games were the best, cooler after the sun went down, and sometimes there was a breeze. Sometimes at night he could imagine he was in the big show, all eyes on the day-bright field, the players focusing so as not to lose the ball in the glare of the lights. And tonight, with people coming out to get in the mood for the Fourth, the crowd was hawking and sputtering, really making some noise like it mattered. Top of the ninth with two out and the Lakers ahead by three . . . Turtle savored moments like this.

Except for this pitcher. Turtle squatted at the plate, signaling the relief pitcher, who didn't seem to know how to read the fucking signals.

Dickwad. Dylan Kroger had never pitched for the Lakers before and now Turtle could see why. They needed one more out to win this game, but Kroger just kept shaking off the signals. And tonight of all nights, when Turtle knew there was a scout out there watching him. Andrew Greentree, from the KC Royals organization. Turtle would be fine living in KC. Turtle would be fine with living anywhere if it meant getting a paycheck for playing ball.

Perfect timing, 'cause he'd hit two doubles tonight along with an RBI. That sweet bat McGann was letting them use was working for him. Blue Thunder was printed on the side of the bat, but Turtle called it the Magic Stick.

Turtle tried to signal for a changeup, but Dylan shook his head again. Fine. Turtle flipped him the bird, then opened his mitt for the pitch. Let him throw what he wanted; hopefully it wouldn't be a fatty that would give this batter a home run.

Kroger wound up and finally pitched the ball, high and outside. It was a suck-ass pitch, but due to some random quirk in the universe the batter took a swing and struck out.

The ball slammed into his mitt and Turtle shot up behind the plate. "Yes!" Amid a smattering of applause in the stands he dropped the ball on the field and lined up to smack hands with the losing team—part of Coach Ramsey's ritual.

Turtle grabbed his small cooler and sluiced back cool water as Ramsey left the dugout and joined the scout. Coach caught his eye and smiled, a good sign, Turtle figured. Hell, he knew that it was a long shot to get in as a left-handed catcher. A huge obstacle. But he'd come this far without getting shut down, right?

Inside the locker room guys were shedding their uniforms, toweling off. Turtle caught McGann sliding the Blue Thunder bat into his bag. McGann always lugged that thing back to his room. Turtle leaned forward. "Take care of that magic stick, man."

McGann nodded, zipped the bag.

Straightening, Turtle watched Greentree follow Ramsey into the coach's office. Valpariso stood just behind the doorway, in position to listen. He caught Turtle's eye, waved him over with a casual gesture. Rico had been reeling Turtle in lately, as if he wanted to be his friend.

Turtle made like he was walking by, picking at his nails, then turned beside Rico.

"What's the deal with the first baseman?" the scout asked.

"That would be Ben McGann, but he's not eligible. He'll be a sophomore at BC next year."

"I noticed he connected with the ball every time he got up. A consistent batter."

"He's good, but I have a couple of seniors with significant potential. My catcher is solid, like a bull. Joe Turturro, best left-handed catcher you'll ever see. He's a senior, and he's got a hot bat now."

Turtle grinned and struck a strongman pose.

"A left-handed catcher . . . nah. Got any outfielders who can hit?"

And just like that, it was over for him.

Fucking scouts. They didn't know what to look for.

He kicked a locker, but Rico held his hand up to quiet him, still trying to hear the conversation in the office.

Ramsey went over a few players, said something about Austin Harold but admitted he didn't see that the guy had pro potential.

"And did you notice the third baseman?" the coach added. "Rico Valpariso, great infielder. He just came out of a slump. Now there's a consistent player."

"Honestly, none of them come close to McGann. They couldn't shine his shoes."

"What the—" Turtle raised a fist toward the coach's office, but Rico shook his head, jerked a thumb toward the other side of the locker room.

"Did you hear that? Fucking McGann is stealing from us. Getting all the attention." Turtle swung around toward McGann's locker, but it looked like Benny boy was already gone.

What had Greentree said? *"They couldn't shine his shoes . . ."* Turtle was ready to rip his shoes apart. "Did you fucking hear what Greentree said?"

"I heard." Valpariso's face was tense, a muscle in his jaw working. "And you're right: McGann is a problem."

"The guy's a fucking sophomore; he can't even be drafted. But he's out there every day doing his best to make us look bad. Outshining us. Distracting the scouts from the real talent."

Rico cracked his knuckles, stretched his fingers. "My bad luck that he plays first base. This is a wasted season for me."

"What are we going to do about it?" Turtle's voice was

booming, spit flying, but he didn't care. He was ready to throw a few punches to the next guy who crossed him. "He's wrecking everything for us. You think that's the first time a scout came in to see us play but got waylaid by McGann? I've had enough of him showboating. We got to do something."

"We're going to stop him," Rico said, then held up one hand to stop Turtle. "I don't know how. I don't have details. But we will stop him. Just chill for now, okay. Chill."

Chapter 32

Dylan Kroger
Syracuse

He was worried about Marnie.

He took a break from working his triceps on the weight machine and pictured her glossy black hair and dark eyes.

He sent her text messages all the time and she never texted back. Well, almost never. When she did send a message, she sounded annoyed. Complaining about how she wasn't allowed to text at work. Complaining that she had to work in the coffee shop all morning, then at Storemart at night.

Actually, that would suck. Was she jealous? Maybe it bothered her because he was loving what he was doing this summer.

Ben had told him not to text so much. "It makes you look needy," Ben had said.

Dylan had countered, "Real men text their girlfriends." That had to hit Ben, who didn't spend a lot of time talking on the phone or texting. Ben was a more in-the-here-and-now guy. Totally on if you were with him. Dylan would know, since he and Ben practically grew up together.

Now Dylan leaned down and swiped his cell phone from the floor, set it to text Marnie: "Big news. I pitched tonight. We won!" He sent it off and dropped his cell phone back to the floor as the door to the weight room opened.

Turtle and Rico Valpariso came in. Rico ignored Dylan and went to work on his pecs, but Turtle came over and flopped onto the machine beside Dylan. Turtle's legs were hairy tree trunks in his silken shorts. Dylan did a few presses, a little self-conscious with Turtle watching.

"Kroger," Turtle said. "I was glad to see you pitched your way out of that mess tonight."

"Yeah. Sorry I choked on the signals."

"No problem." Turtle nodded. "But do it again and I'll kick your ass."

Dylan snorted. "Yeah, right."

But Turtle wasn't grinning. "God, I'm thirsty." He went to the water cooler and poured himself a cup. "Where's McGann? You two are always hand in hand."

"He went back to the dorm," Dylan said. Ben liked his sleep. Most nights after home games he headed back to the dorm to unwind.

Turtle downed the water, wiped his mouth with his arm. "Yeah? He split pretty fast after the game. In fact, the coach wants to see him. Said they have some business to discuss."

"Really?" It was the first Dylan had heard of this, but then Ben didn't always fill Dylan in on things.

Turtle took another drink, nodded. "Yeah, I'm surprised that McGann would bag out like that. He totally wigged out on the coach."

Dylan released the weights. "That's not like Ben."

"He's going to want to get his ass back to the locker room fast," Rico said, as if he'd just noticed Dylan in the weight room. "Coach was getting pissed when we left, couldn't reach McGandolf on his cell. He's staying late just to work with him."

And Ben had stood him up? Dylan winced as he pressed the weights. Ramsey was going to pop an artery if Ben didn't get there.

Dylan got off the machine and picked up his cell phone. "I'll call him." He walked toward the door. "Thanks for the heads-up."

He dialed Ben's number in the corridor outside the weight room. By the time he reached the door, he was jogging, thinking he might have to sprint back to the dorm and roust Ben. "Come on, pick up!" he said.

But there was no answer.

He would have to run across the campus.

By the time he reached the dorm his shirt was drenched with sweat, his breath a harsh rasp in his ears. The four flights up were like adding a few suicides to the drill.

He nearly fell into Ben's door, knocking with one fist. "Ben, wake up! Ben! It's me."

He paused to listen over his racing pulse. No answer.

"Ben?" He turned the knob—nobody locked their door inside the dorm—and pushed it open. The room was dark, but light spilled in from the hallway, falling across the front dresser where Ben's Blue Thunder bat and his extra ribbed first baseman's glove were set on a cloth, a folded BC blanket.

There was motion on the bed—Ben stirring. "Go away, Dylan."

"Ben, you've got to wake up." Dylan went to the foot of the bed. "The coach is waiting for you in his office."

"What?"

"Coach Ramsey is waiting, and he's getting pissed. You guys had some meeting set up for tonight?"

"No, we didn't." Ben turned over, then sat up. "Did Coach send you to get me?"

"Turtle and Rico did. They saw him waiting in his office. Sounds like he's going to be really pissed if you don't get there soon."

"Turtle and Rico." Ben raked back his hair with both hands, then reached over and turned on a bedside lamp. "Dylan, don't you get it? This is some kind of prank."

Dylan shook his head. "It sounded pretty real."

"Sure it did, but it's a bag of bullshit. You know I wouldn't forget a meeting with the coach, and there's no way Ramsey is going to schedule something after a game, not this late at night." He scratched the stubble on his chin, sleepy-eyed. "They're setting us up, Dyl. Setting me up, really, but they pulled you into it, figured I'd trust the news if it came from you."

"I don't believe it." Dylan thought back to the two guys coming into the weight room, the concern on Turtle's face. "Oh, man, I was such a sucker."

"No, you're not. Look, you didn't get me to go meet the coach, so they were unsuccessful, right? That's all they're going to see in the morning."

Dylan sat at the foot of the bed. "I can't believe they pranked me."

"Listen, man, those guys are good. I would have believed them if I didn't know that I definitely don't have a meeting with Ramsey. Don't beat yourself up. Just chill a little and get some sleep. We'll think of a way to get them back tomorrow."

Revenge . . . Dylan couldn't go there yet. He could barely process that he'd run all the way across the campus for nothing. "Those guys are skanks. Don't deserve to be here." He rose and plodded out the door.

"Can you close the door?" Ben called after him. "Yeah, thanks."

Anger steeled his spine as Dylan slammed into his room. He could hear Turtle's cackling laugh, see the curl of a smile on Rico's stern face. He threw a few jabs in the air, imagining that they were making contact with Turtle's puffy face, then Rico's hard jaw.

Yeah, he would enjoy getting back at them. He'd talk with Ben in the morning, make sure they came up with a prank that would make those losers look like the assholes they were.

He peeled off his damp clothes, brushed his teeth in the sink, and got into bed. Yeah, he could wait. Revenge was a dish best served cold.

Chapter 33

Ben
Syracuse

"Gentlemen, we have a problem." Coach Ramsey paused, a heated gap during which guys coughed and squirmed on the dugout bench. Disgust flickered in Ramsey's eyes; he was pissed.

Dylan nudged Ben. "What's the deal?"

"No idea."

It was unusual for the coach to assemble the team this way on a game day, and they were fairly baking in the dugout, which caught the early morning sun.

"Someone sabotaged our locker room last night. Now I have no idea who would have done such a thing; however, I am not happy about it." He folded his arms, trying to squeeze them with more silence. "I don't like being pranked."

Isaiah Gibbs's hand shot up. "What'd they do, Coach?"

"Apparently some idiot buttered the hallway outside our locker room."

That explained the rubber runner in the corridor, as well as the orange cones with a "Caution: Wet Floor" sign. Ben rubbed his chin as he pieced things together. That prank was targeted at him. If he'd believed Turtle and Rico, he would have rushed over late last night, slipped in the corridor, taken a fall. He'd be the guy in the hospital now.

The coach crossed his arms as a few guys snickered and tittered.

"Yeah, yeah, very funny. So funny our custodian, Seth, took a fall when he came in to unlock the facility early this morning. This was not a harmless prank, guys."

"Is Seth okay?" someone asked.

"As far as I know he's still getting checked out by a doctor. What I want to know is, who did it?" His dark eyes combed the line of players, searching.

"Coach?" Zach Steiner spoke up. "What makes you think we would know? We wouldn't mess with our own locker room. I'd be looking at the visiting team."

"Coach Belmont from the Ithaca team has been notified, though of course, he defended his players. To be honest, I have never known a visiting team in summer ball to take it upon themselves to prank the home team. And the visiting team does not have unlimited access to our facilities." Ramsey put his hands on his hips. "Which takes us back to the Lakers. Really, gentlemen. If the culprit comes forward of his own accord, I'll be a lot more lenient than if I have to track you down. Don't make me waste time tracking you down. You know I've got no patience for that juvenile crap."

Ben tipped his chin down and shot a subtle look over at Turtle and Rico, who were sitting with Kevin Webber sandwiched between them. Great poker faces. Turtle stroked his soul patch as if deep in thought, while Valpariso's mouth was a slash of righteous indignation, though his eyes were hidden by shades.

You'd never know to look at them. . . .

"No takers?" Ramsey shifted from foot to foot. "I'll give anyone with information one hour to come to me. If no one comes clean, there will be a punishment for the entire team. Come on, guys. I hate having to play the big bad daddy. Let's cut the frat-boy shit and grow a pair."

As the coach turned away, Ash, the assistant coach, stood up and clapped his hands for attention. "Let's go through the warm-up drills. Grab your gloves, guys, and get on the field."

Ben didn't even risk a glance at Turtle and Rico as the men moved slowly but efficiently out of the dugout. It was a game day, and no one wanted to chance blowing their energy before the game even started.

"Ben?" Dylan stuck close, walking alongside him. "Should we tell? We know who it was."

"Don't say anything," Ben said, staring straight ahead.

"But we know who it was. They hurt the janitor. They were trying to injure you."

"So what? You want to rat them out?"

"We can't let them get away," Dylan insisted.

"Listen to me." Ben grabbed a bucket of balls and motioned Dylan away from the others. "Knowledge is power. We are going to keep the power and twist the screw." Ben didn't know exactly how to get Rico and Turtle in line, but he knew that no good would come of giving them up to the coach. He snapped a ball, starting a warm-up drill.

Dylan grabbed a ball from the bucket. "So what are we going to do?"

"Enough questions." Sometimes Dylan's persistence was irritating. "Right now, we just do the drills, and calm down, okay? You didn't do anything wrong."

Dylan took a deep breath. "I'm supposed to be a starting pitcher in this series. I don't want to do anything to risk that."

"Then shut up," Ben said. "Just shut up and do the drills."

Chapter 34

Rico Valpariso
Syracuse

Rico couldn't believe they'd kept their mouths shut. He felt sure McGandolf and his weasel sidekick Kroger would run right to the coach and give them up.

But it didn't happen.

No information about the oiled corridor was given to Coach Ramsey, who assigned batting practice to every team member immediately following practice. That caused a major snag in the batting cages, which could only accommodate five players at a once. He and Turtle got stuck in the second group, and by then McGann had split with Blue Thunder, so they couldn't even practice their batting with the right bat. By the time the guys batting in the second group made it to the dining hall, the servers were starting to put away the trays of food.

Rico was pissed. An extra batting practice without the right bat, and now, if he missed this meal, it wasn't like he had the cash to make a run into town for pizza or a hero sandwich. And he sure as hell couldn't live on peanut butter on stale bread from the sandwich station. He rushed into the cafeteria and lined up right behind Turtle, whose shirt was stained with sweat.

"Sweetheart!" Turtle whistled at the woman heading off with a tray of chicken scallopine. "That's right, you. Bring that on back. These big boys are starving."

She pivoted and returned to the steam table. "I don't know

about you," she said as the metal tray dropped into its bed of hot water. "Where's your meal ticket? You never have a meal ticket."

"Forgot to bring it." Turtle motioned her to keep going as she dished meat onto his plate. "I'll bring it tomorrow."

Both guys loaded up on mashed potatoes and green beans, then headed toward the team table. Their bad luck, the empty seats put them near McGandolf. Well, fuck him. Rico had a few choice words for the pompous first baseman. Last night Rico had experienced some regrets about setting the trap, but after it failed he felt only malice for this peacock who strutted onto this team and remained the center of attention.

"You." Rico slapped his tray down. "McGandolf. Did you forget something today?" Heads turned, everybody watching the end of the table. Dozo and Sager, Harold and Steiner, they seemed to smell the storm brewing, and everybody loved a good brawl.

Turtle shoved in a mound of potatoes, nodding. "Yeah. You split from batting practice with our bat, the Blue Thunder. A little inconsiderate, don't you think?"

Ben McGann wiggled a fork between two fingers. "Actually, that was no accident. I took it with me because I changed my mind."

Dylan Kroger's jaw slowed its chewing as all faces turned toward McGann.

"Here's the thing." McGann lowered his voice. "I've noticed in the last twenty-four hours that there's some bad behavior going on among members of this team. Present company included."

Rico stopped cutting his meat. "What the hell are you talking about? Coach has got us living so clean, we could be choir boys. Living and eating together, like we're in some kind of summer camp."

McGann leaned forward, his palms flat on the table as if he had to keep it from levitating. "Look, I got your invitation last night. I declined, thanks anyway. It's unfortunate for Seth that you guys don't know how to clean up your messes."

Rico cut off a square of meat, chewed slowly. He wasn't going to admit anything.

"You know, you got some pair of balls, coming in here and accusing us of stuff," Turtle said. "I'm still scratching my head as to why Coach even asked you to this team when we already had a first baseman."

"It's because he's good," Dylan said. Loyal as a Boy Scout.

"Really?" Rico turned his penetrating glare toward Kroger. "I didn't notice."

"It's over." Ben slapped the table, leaned back in his chair. "I've officially withdrawn the Blue Thunder from the team batting rack. From now on I'll be the only one using it."

Rico felt his lunch harden in his gut.

"You can't do that," Turtle growled.

McGann grinned, his upper lip curling on one side. "Sure I can. I already did."

"Yeah, and how's the coach going to like you fouling up the team's batting?" Turtle said. "Did you think about that?"

"The coach isn't going to hear about Blue Thunder." McGann's eyes locked on Turtle, then Rico, as if they were two targets at a firing range. "Didn't you learn anything from today? The team is supposed to keep the coach out of the petty shit. We're supposed to handle ourselves."

Rico stared, letting his hatred burn into McGann. There'd been a time when he thought they could be friendly, but no. That was impossible; he could see clearly now.

"Why don't you stop busting our chops?" Turtle said.

"I tried." McGann's voice was level, his face so neutral they could have been discussing the chicken entrée. "Unfortunately, that didn't work for me. Someone tried to bust my ass."

Kroger snickered, as if it were all a joke. What an idiot!

"Hey! Ben!" called a female voice. No doubt some annoying campus groupie. Then two girls shouted: "Ben! Up here."

The guys glanced up to the balcony that rimmed the entrance to the dining hall. Two girls waved, one a frothy blond pastry, the other cool with hair like licorice, some exotic witch.

Dylan rose from the table. "Marnie . . ." He seemed pleased, but not McGann. McGandolf set his jaw and stared straight ahead, as if he needed to mentally prepare himself for an inquisition.

Good, Rico thought. *Let him squirm. Anything to unnerve him. Anything to rattle his nerves.*

Eventually, these things would add up. McGann would screw up, and he'd be taken off first base.

Eventually, Coach will see . . . and I'll get back to my place on the field.

Chapter 35

Emma Lenson
Syracuse

Why wasn't he happy to see her?

She had expected a big smile, that half-crooked grin that wiggled her toes. She had imagined a real light in his eyes to let her know he was happy to see her. She had hoped for a little drama. He could have swept her into his arms and kissed her long and hard. Or at least he could have jumped out of his chair and shouted her name, the way Dylan did for Marnie.

But no. She had run down the stairs to the dining hall and gracefully squeezed through the turnstile, and her boyfriend, the guy she just drove a million boring miles to see, just sat there staring at her as if she'd just walked out of *Cosmo*'s Fashion Don't spread.

What was his problem?

"Hey." At last he stood up, touched her arm as she rose on tiptoe to kiss him. "How was the ride?"

"Five hours of torture. It takes forever, and you don't even go through any interesting places." She flicked her hair back over one shoulder and noticed that the guys seated at the table were all watching her. They were players . . . his teammates. A solid guy with a soul patch to hide his double chin. An intense Hispanic boy. A few who looked a little nerdy, or maybe it was those geeky uniforms they wore.

"Hey." She cocked her head to one side as she let it be known that she was checking out the guys. "You guys are on the team, I take it? Ben . . . are you going to introduce me to your friends?"

Ben touched her shoulder. "This is Emma," he said, "and these are some of the guys on the Lakers. Turtle is our catcher; Rico Valpariso plays third base. Dozo is on second. You know, Dozo, I don't even know your real name. . . ."

"Dozneski." He rose from the table, a moose of a boy with curly red hair. He must have been proud of his muscles because his tight shirt showed off his sculpted arms and broad chest. Trevor Dozneski shook her hand, as did Kenta Suzuki, whom Ben introduced as the shortstop. Finally, some boys with manners.

"Ben, you don't have to tell me what they all play. I'm not keeping score," she told him. "I just want to get to know your friends."

"Yeah, Ben," said the chunky one. Froggy? "What's the matter with you? Get social, already." Froggy was wearing some of his dinner in his beard . . . mashed potatoes, maybe? It grossed Emma out, and she turned instead toward the handsome firecracker with the mocha tan, Rico.

"You know, if you want to get social, I have the perfect place." The words spilled out before she even knew what she was concocting, but as the idea took shape she realized its brilliance. "I'm at the Regan Hotel, and they have this great pool that we could use for a party after the game. You can all come if you want."

"You don't have to do that, Emma." Ben's dark brows were stern, but she waved him off. He was always trying to stop her from spending her father's money, like it mattered.

"Ben, really, I want to do it. Nothing fancy, but I'm sure the hotel caterer can throw something together."

"We would love that," Froggy said.

"Turtle . . ." Ben stopped him.

Oh, Turtle was his name; wrong amphibian. And he was so enthusiastic that Emma was beginning to like him.

"A little party would be just the thing to pull this team together," Turtle said. He tipped his head down to Emma, adding,

"We've had a little friction lately, but nothing that can't be solved over some appetizers and cool beverages. You aren't twenty-one, are you? Nah. You won't be able to serve some cold ones to the guys who are drinking age."

"No one's supposed to be drinking during the season, not even the guys who are drinking age," Dylan interrupted. "Coach's rules."

"Shut up, Kroger," Turtle said, adding in a falsetto voice, "Coach's rules."

"Let me work on it." Now it was a challenge, and Emma ate up a meaty challenge when it came along—especially when the dare could be addressed with money. She loved icing the cake with gold . . . fourteen karat, of course.

Chapter 36

Kate
Woodstock

The soil was dense and rocky—like digging into cement—but with each shovelful Kate assured herself that she was preserving the hill, saving the house, maintaining life as she knew it.

She wedged the shovel under a stone and stood on the edges, throwing her weight into it. Last week when Kate had returned home from Syracuse to find that the sudden downpours had caused two mud slicks, she knew she had to take action. She was fighting the crumbling hillside—her nemesis.

Behind her, three small pine trees stood in their pots, sentinels waiting to stand guard on the hillside and ward off erosion. She had read that vegetation was effective in fighting soil erosion, as the stems and roots helped to hold soil particles in place on the slope. So Kate was going through the bone-jarring, back-straining process of digging three holes large enough to contain fertilizer and the root balls of the little trees, though the digging was slow going with the clay and stone just below the soil line.

After last week's series of thunderstorms, she had expected the soil to be softer, but the moisture only made each shovelful heavier.

As she worked, fat bees bounced in the heather, their buzz mingling with the hum of distant machinery from the construction site at the top of the hill. The noise of cranes and earthmovers had been so steady this summer that Kate had learned to tune it out. As the access road was on the other side of the hill, Kate had not driven to the top to see exactly what was going on up there, but the local newspaper had run regular features on the development over the past year or so. Mary Toloff, an elderly widow who had lived in a pink ranch house amid acres of forested hilltop property, had sold her land to Bill Shannon, who was building a community of luxury homes offering scenic rural vistas.

Eli had been highly agitated by the news. "I can't believe Mary Toloff sold out," he'd said when the development was announced. "In a couple of years we'll be looking up at a Burger King drive-through." His typical overreaction.

"It's not zoned for commercial property," Kate had replied. "They're building homes."

"The deforestation of America," he'd grumbled, and Kate had let the subject drop, knowing it was one of those things beyond their control that Eli would embrace and pontificate upon for months.

With the first hole complete, Kate dragged the small pine to the spot, turned the bucket on its side, and tapped the bottom and sides. Gripping the base of the trunk, she pulled, but it didn't budge.

Sitting back on her haunches, she noticed a small white vehicle on the road below—one of those hybrid minicars. Instead of passing their driveway, it turned and motored up the hill. As it approached, she noticed the decal on the side for Ulster County.

Kate rose as a heavyset man emerged from the car. His skin was weathered, a case of sun exposure, and his belly strained against an orange vest.

"Can I help you?" she asked.

"I'm thinking you could use some help lifting that tree out." He closed the door and came around the car. "Jerry Pyle. I'm with the county."

"And the county is providing drive-by garden assistance?"

"No, that's just me." He smiled. "I'm what you might call a

tree hugger, though officially I work for the Department of Soil and Water Conservation."

"Really? I'm Kate McGann, and I'd appreciate the help. What brings you out this way, Jerry?"

He nodded toward the hilltop. "Just circling the hill. That construction project up there is creating a buzz, maybe an erosion problem, too."

"I'll say. Your timing is perfect." She leaned down to tap a spade against the bucket. "We can get these bad boys planted and talk erosion."

After Jerry helped her remove the bucket and position the tree in the hole, she told him about the decaying hillside. He photographed the two trenches cut into the yard by the rain runoff and made some notes in a marble notebook.

"You're doing the right thing, planting these trees," he told her. "Though you could use a lot more. And things that you plant on your acres can only address part of the issue." He nodded to the top of the hill. "You can't stop the runoff that begins up there."

"Sometimes I worry that one of these days the entire hillside will come sliding down."

He touched his chin, squinting up the slope. "I don't think that's going to happen. You've got solid bedrock under here. But right now, with the crown of the hill clear-cut, we're seeing a good amount of soil erosion. It's to be expected, but there are ways to control it. I'd like to see some ditches or runoff pipes installed to divert the water. That way you won't be watching your yard slip on down the hill. It should actually be a city or town project, but like anything it requires money, and that's in short supply these days."

"Well, we'd be thrilled if the county would install some pipes for runoff. Erosion has always been a problem for us." Kate picked up the shovel and thrust it into the ground to start the second hole.

He held out a hand and took the shovel. "Please. I hate to see you torture yourself."

As Jerry carved out the second hole in record time she

learned that he was a geologist and that he loved his job, despite the budget restrictions. "I spend a lot of time doing feasibility investigations for pond sites," he said. "Not a terrible thing, but sometimes it feels a tad insignificant."

Jerry helped her plant all three trees; he insisted. "I'll feel like I've accomplished something today," he said.

She waved good-bye as Jerry drove off, then turned back toward the hill, the beast that mirrored her life. Out of control. Beyond taming. A foundation that seemed to be slipping out from under her.

And yet, the beast had such potential. A breeze rustled the lilac trees to the left, bringing their sweet scent to the warm air. Shoots from the fat hosta plants had formed pale purple buds, and the pansies were beginning to spread, fanning out in the sun.

The damaged rose garden caught her eye, and she went to the shed for a bag of mulch. As she lumbered over to the roses with the fat sack in her arms she thought about Ben and the problems he'd been having with the seniors on the team. Had he worked things out? In many ways Ben seemed more socially adept than either of his parents. Right now Ben was her only light in the darkness.

Stepping into the mud slick, she leaned forward to drop the sack and her feet slipped out from under her, sending her down to the ground with a thud. Ugh.

She closed her eyes, leaned into the soft mulch that had cushioned her fall, and allowed herself a moment to wallow in self-pity. This hillside was heavy work, a bastard when your heart was breaking.

With a deep breath she pushed up, sat back on the damp ground and pulled off her gloves. In a moment, she would haul her aching body up to replace the mulch under the roses, then she'd be done for the day. Hugging her knees, she wondered at the futility of pushing all this dirt around.

Was she fighting the laws of gravity?

Raging against the storm?

Sometimes you just had to ask yourself if it was all worth it.

Chapter 37

Turtle
Syracuse

Fucking McGann.

Turtle hiked up the path to the dorm, cursing McGandolf all the way.

The game had been a nightmare with a walk in the second inning, a pop fly smack into the glove of the shortstop, and two strikeouts. Miserable batting. Pathetic!

Coach was pissed at him, but Turtle couldn't help it. He felt lost without his lucky stick. Without Blue Thunder, he could only stand at the plate and quiver like a namby-pamby asshole.

McGann had screwed his game, ruined his batting average.

And now McGann was going to pay.

Turtle stomped into the dorm, swiped through the turnstile, and went straight back to his room—a choice dorm assignment on the first floor. Yeah, he was supposed to be up on four with the team, but he'd gone to the resident director and asked for a lower floor, alluding to a medical condition. That usually got them. "But keep it on the down low," he'd told the RD, a short, round woman named Darlene who had a preference for tie-dyed shirts and worn jeans. "You know, that personal confidentiality stuff?" he'd said. He actually didn't know the law about stuff like that, but Darlene had seemed cool with it.

So far the only guy to step foot in here was Dozo, and that was probably a mistake. The guy had followed him one day after practice, wanting to see if the rooms were the same on this floor. Turtle had thought he just wanted a look, but before he knew it Dozo had his fat ass on the beds. He tried on his lucky hats, touched his stuff. That was the end of that. Fucking Dozo.

Inside his room he washed his hands in the sink and removed a small vial of clear liquid from the fridge. Filling the syringe, he decided he'd need a little extra tonight, a little cushion for partying. They'd warned him against it, but who knew his body better than him?

Holding it up to the light, he tapped the syringe, knocking any air bubbles out. Twenty-one taps. That was his ritual, and it had always worked for him.

He pressed the pedal of the trash can and tossed in the syringe and gloves. There.

Before he opened the door he checked his face in the mirror, smoothed down the trimmed hair on his upper lip, the cool line that ran down to the soul patch on his chin. A fucking great Vandyke, that's what they called it, after some painter. After he'd read about it in a magazine he'd paid for a barber to lay down the track in his thick beard. Since then he'd made the style his own. Sexy bastard.

Party time.

A couple of beers later and—WHAM!—he was rolling on the floor with McGann.

It had started with a few jabs at McGann for being such a dick in front of MLB scouts and yanking away Blue Thunder just when Turtle had perfected his swing with the bat. Yeah, it had started with some beefs. But McGann ignored him. Told Turtle to back off. Said he'd been drinking. Which was true, but Turtle wasn't going to be shrugged off.

He hurled himself at McGann, took him down in a second. He reached for McGann's neck, fingers cupping his square jaw. Christ, he wanted to snap his head off. "Motherfucker! You are going down," he vowed. Or some such comment. He'd been drunk at the time.

Then McGann flipped him, and after that they were like a cartoon cloud of arms and legs and dust on the floor. They rolled in a forest of legs, players, and chicks. The girlfriend Emma shrieked like a squeaky toy and some of the guys egged them on. Turtle was so wasted, he wasn't sure how it stopped. Except that the damned beer was kicking in and he had to pee. And that—peeing himself in a fight—that would ruin his rep for the rest of the summer.

He flipped Ben off his back. They ended up face-to-face, hands to shoulders, so close he could see the steely gray of McGann's eyes and the tiny half-moon scar on the edge of his jaw.

"I'm sick of this," McGann said. "It's over. Done. I want to be left alone. No more tricks. Do you hear me?"

"Yeah, and I want my batting average back. I need the bat."

"Fine." Ben released Turtle's shoulders. "Done."

Turtle rolled onto his knees as the crowd grew quiet.

McGann stood up. Looking down on Turtle, he extended a hand.

In the swirl of emotions, Turtle could still taste hatred for Ben McGann, but there was also something else. A craving.

He wanted that bat. And even if he hated the guy looking down on him right now, taking McGann out of the picture would only take Blue Thunder out of reach.

Turtle reached for McGann's hand and pulled himself up.

"So we're square?" McGann asked.

"Bosom buddies." Turtle cocked his head, lowered his voice so that people had to shut their traps if they really wanted to hear. "Best of friends."

Chapter 38

Marnie
The Regan Hotel

Feeling like the outsider that she was, Marnie watched the large party crowd through a scrim of potted eucalyptus trees. Leave it to Emma to rent the entire hotel garden, complete with patio and swimming pool and hot tubs. And these other girls—like Jade, with the lace-covered cleavage, and Tracy, with hair so blond it hurt Marnie's eyes—where did they come from? Townies? Baseball groupies?

"I love this song," Emma shouted, tugging on Ben's arm, pulling him onto the dance floor. She strutted onto the patio, fists in the air, hips swaying in time to the music. "Come on, people! We need to be dancing." Emma stepped close to Ben and planted herself against him, grinding against him suggestively.

A handful of girls got up to dance, as well as two of the players, but Marnie could tell Ben wasn't into it. He planted a safe kiss on Emma's forehead and sat down again. Although he indulged Emma regarding a lot of things, Ben was not a dancer.

Observing the scene as if she were watching television, Marnie sipped Pepsi from the bottle and swirled it around her teeth like mouthwash. If she could just wash the taste of him away, maybe she'd be able to think straight.

This was not Marnie's scene. Really, she would have felt more comfortable serving up the food or collecting dirty glasses left behind on tables. She was one of those people; the anti-Emma.

God, what was she doing here?

Oh, yeah, she had come to break up with Dylan. And how was that working out? Not at all. Her presence seemed to be encouraging him. The way he came after her in the hot tub and mauled her mouth. Yuck. She took another chug of soda, another cleansing sip.

Dylan was acting like he owned her, and he was not good at reading people. Granted, she hadn't found the right moment to come out and say that it was over, but couldn't he see the signs that she wasn't interested? She could barely look him in the eye, but he didn't notice. And the way he'd laughed after he'd pulled her into the hot tub and soaked her shorts . . . as if it were hysterically funny.

Ha, ha.

And the boy didn't notice that he was the only one laughing.

From there she'd retreated up to the room, where she planned to hole up for the rest of the night. Just her bad luck that Emma had popped in and insisted that Marnie change her clothes and come back down. Marnie tried to decline, but Emma insisted. "I'm not leaving without you," she'd said. "You came all this way, Marnie, and I'm not going to let you miss my party." And she'd folded her arms and plopped down on an upholstered chair, acting like everything depended on Marnie.

"I'll be quick." Marnie had closed the door to her bedroom, plotting her escape. She would change into dry stuff fast, go back to the party, then shoot back here when Emma wasn't looking.

While she stripped off her wet shorts and swimsuit, Emma started talking about Ben.

"He seems really stressed about something." Emma's voice came through the door. "Do you think he's mad at me?"

Marnie had noticed that Ben seemed a little stiff; he'd barely said two words to her. "No."

"I don't know what's wrong with him. He needs to relax. I

wish he'd take something. I wish he'd drink a beer or something."

"Ben doesn't drink," Marnie said as she wriggled into black bike shorts.

"I know that. I should spike his punch." Emma laughed.

"Bad idea."

"I know." Emma sighed. "Now hurry up! Everyone's waiting for me." When Marnie emerged in the bike shorts, a white tank, and a black print T-shirt dress with an empire waist, Emma did not comment about Marnie dressing Goth; she didn't even flinch as she led the way to the elevator, down to the garden level, and back to the party.

Where all hell had been breaking loose, two guys rolling on the floor.

Marnie sipped her Pepsi and smiled over the whole scene. . . .

The way Emma squealed, telling people to call security until one of the players pointed out that, if the cops came, Ben might be banned from the team. Marnie had planned to grab a soda and head back upstairs, but witnessing this wrestling match seemed more appealing than the game of dodging Dylan. The fight didn't seem too serious. And when she caught a flicker of amusement on Ben's face and a mocking laugh from Turtle, she realized it wasn't a big deal.

Of course, Emma kept shrieking like a principal in a cafeteria food fight, but the crowd dispersed when the guys called some kind of truce. People headed off to the hot tubs or the food tables or the patio to dance.

Dylan came running out of the hotel, which sent Marnie diving behind a tree on the patio. And that was how Marnie ended up sipping a Pepsi and watching the party through the fat leaves of these potted trees.

"What's going on? You okay?" Dylan patted Ben's chest, as if making sure he was still in one piece. "Christ, I take a piss for one minute and all hell breaks loose."

"Yeah, the action was lagging," Ben said. "I figured I'd better liven up the party."

Dylan asked if he'd seen Marnie, and she pressed into the leaves of the tree to find Ben staring right at her.

Oh, God! She ducked.

"I haven't talked to her for a while," Ben said.

Daring to peek at them, Marnie rose and met Ben's eyes. He grinned that half smile, and asked Dylan if he'd seen the new bats Emma just gave him. "Awesome bats. Remember that DeMarini we saw, with the new endcap that's designed to dampen the vibration?" They headed over to take a look, passing an ice sculpture of a baseball mitt.

Again Marnie considered escaping to the room. She would fill a napkin with those tiny sandwiches and sneak them upstairs, change into the fluffy hotel robe, eat on the bed, and watch a movie. Tipping her chair back, she took the last swig of soda. Time to go.

Suddenly the plant shuddered and Ben stepped through. "Is this a private party?" Something inside her tugged at the sight of his twisted smile, familiar and irreverent.

"I'm taking my party upstairs." She set the bottle on the table. "I've drunk my limit of Pepsi."

He sank into the chair beside her. "Don't go. We haven't had two minutes to talk since you got here. I didn't know you were coming. Why didn't you text me?"

"I didn't know until the last minute. And even then, I probably came for the wrong reasons. I came to talk to Dylan, but so far that hasn't worked out."

He leaned back and crossed one leg, ankle on knee. In the wrought-iron chair he seemed gangly and tall, all arms and legs. "But you got to see a game. That has to make it worth the trip."

"Narcissist. But you were great, Jock. You always are."

"You're just saying that."

"I don't flatter people. You're awesome on a ball field. It's just biology you suck at."

"Thanks." He leaned forward, shifted his chair to face her. "I miss our time together, hanging out at the coffee shop."

She felt a stab of something. Sorrow? She missed those times, too, but she wasn't sure they would ever happen again. "I'm still there, just about every day. Good morning, Beantown."

"It's a lot funnier when you say it first thing in the morning." He scooted her chair to face him, Marnie's body jiggling as it dragged over the pavement.

She shook her head. "It won't be the same. You're practically married to Emma, and I'm breaking up with Dylan. It'll be different, sort of strained."

"You're breaking up?" His eyes were wide pools of gray. "You didn't tell me that."

She winced. "Well, really, Dylan should be the first to know, and when have I had a chance to talk to you?"

"My point exactly. You should call me."

She shook her head. "That's not gonna happen." She stood up to leave and suddenly he was a wall in front of her, his hands warm on her shoulders.

"Don't go. I'm not trying to make you mad."

When she looked up, his face was inches from hers and it was clear that he was waiting to kiss her, waiting for some sign that it was okay, that she wanted it. Which was so unlike the way Dylan had taken possession of her.

She reached for his shoulders, aware of the warmth between them. This felt right—to be in Ben's arms. It felt right as she leaned into him and he dipped down to capture her mouth. Their lips brushed once, twice, and then she opened herself. A sigh escaped her throat as his tongue moved along the inside of her lips.

This felt right.

But it was wrong.

Too many people could get hurt.

She ended the kiss, stepped back from the electrifying connection.

"I have to go," she said, turning away before she lost all resolve.

Chapter 39

Dylan tried to ignore the other guys as he checked out Ben's new bats on the table—gifts from Emma. He ran his hand down the shiny copper barrel of the DeMarini CFX, then stepped back to take a swing. Sweet. It was supposed to be balanced for a faster, more powerful swing, all to the tune of four hundred bucks.

"How did Ben's girlfriend know to buy him bats like this?" Kenta asked.

Dylan put the DeMarini back onto the tablecloth. "She probably just went to a specialty shop and picked out the most expensive."

"Must be nice to have a rich girlfriend," Will Sager said. "Where I grew up, that wasn't an option. You could get yourself plenty of pregnant girlfriends, no rich ones."

"Get out!" Zach said. "You're from Westchester. People are loaded there."

"You don't know shit about Westchester," Will said.

Dylan checked the grip on the Rawlings. Nice. "The question is, will Ben give up Blue Thunder for these bad boys?"

"Tough call." Zach buffed the barrel of the DeMarini with the edge of the tablecloth. "It's sort of like a brand-new car; you want to break it in, but you don't want to lose that showroom smell."

Dozo slapped down his can of beer. "Where did these girls

come from? Anybody know? That one Jade has quite the body, but nobody home upstairs."

"Who wants to dance?" Tracy strutted up to the guys' table and pivoted like a model. "Come on, guys."

Dozo's head swiveled toward the other players. "Can you spell 'bimbo'?"

There were a few laughs, though Dylan didn't think it was funny. These guys were animals. He looked over their heads, searching for Marnie. He hadn't seen her since the hot tub.

Tracy squared off with Dozo, a sheen of perspiration beading the makeup on her upper lip. "Are you rude, or stupid, or both?"

"Guilty!" Dozo said.

Tracy rolled her eyes and turned to Kenta Suzuki. "Wanna dance?" she purred.

As Kenta passed Dozo on the way to the patio, he muttered, "See how it's done? Watch and learn."

Will Sager smacked Dozo on the shoulder. "Man, do you have to sit with us? Scaring all the hotties away with your big mouth."

"She's just pissed because I called her bluff," Dozo said. "Told her I wanted to verify her hair color. The pubic test."

"Shut up, Dozo." Dylan pushed away from the table in disgust. Once he was on his feet he spotted her; or at least a dark-haired, thin girl who looked like her was standing behind the screen of white-lit trees lined up to divide the patio. She stood there talking to some guy . . . to Ben, actually. Her dark hair swayed as she tilted her head, listening. Marnie was a good listener.

And now she was talking. He tried to tune out the conversation around him to hear what Marnie was saying, tried to read her lips because it seemed important—a heavy discussion. Intense. But there was too much noise to hear.

And then Marnie reached up and leaned forward and the two figures merged into one.

A sour grit rose in Dylan's throat.

They were kissing. Not a friendly hug, but a walloping, sexy movie kiss that made him feel like a perv just watching.

Shit. What was that about?

He shifted, hoping that the view through the trees had distorted things. It was a speckled picture, fractured by leaves and tiny lights. A puzzle with important pieces missing. But no, they were still holding on. Major suck-face.

Marnie shouldn't have let him.

And Ben . . . come on, buddy. Where was the guy he'd grown up with, the kid who got him up at first light on summer mornings to have a catch? The friend who carried him home in a blizzard when he lost his boot in a snowdrift. The kid who dealt cards under a flashlight in the tent, the boy who shared his lunch at school just about every day because Dylan's grandma forgot half the time . . .

Where was that Ben now?

Shee-it.

Chapter 40

Ben
Syracuse

Ben had to get out of here.

The thing with Marnie, the fight with Turtle, the expensive bats from Emma—everything weighed him down, and with his head feeling twisted and dizzy he wasn't processing clearly right now.

Although people had begun to split, he knew Emma would want him to stay, and he wasn't up for an argument. Tomorrow was another game day; he needed rest. He waited until she was engaged in the "Soldier Boy" dance, and then cut away toward the pool. He was circling one of the hot tubs when someone stepped in front of him, blocking his path.

"Going somewhere?" Rico Valpariso's dark eyes flashed in the moonlight. "Like, maybe, back to Boston?"

Ben stuck his hands in his back pockets and looked up at the sky, searching the stars for patience. He was in no mood for Rico's whining. He looked down, noticed Zach Steiner and some girl watching from a small café table. They probably figured there'd be another show, another senior player squeezing Ben McGann. "Look, Rico, I'd like to give you a tumble, but Turtle already sucked the fight out of me. Can't we kiss and make up?"

"Don't talk to me like I'm some faggot. Turtle might have let you slide, but me, I'm not so forgiving."

"Hold on. You're talking like I'm the only one in the wrong, and we know that's not true. I didn't set you up, did I? Did I set a trap for you, Rico? I'm still scratching my head, wondering what you guys were aiming for. Something like a sprained ankle? Or maybe a broken leg?"

"Me? I was wishing you would break your neck."

Ben shook his head. "That's just mean. Didn't your mother ever tell you not to wish for mean things?"

"Let me remind you I was the Lakers' first baseman until you came along. I was it. Numero uno. And I was fucking good at it. I *am* good. Better than you'll ever be."

"Good for you."

"I belong on first base. That's the position I played all season long, fall ball, spring season, and summer ball, until you came along and stole it from me."

Ben scratched his chin. "Really? Last time I checked, you couldn't steal first."

"Shut up." Rico closed the space between them and dug his fingers into the front of Ben's shirt. "Just shut up and grow a pair. Be a man, McGann, and back off. Take yourself out of the lineup tomorrow, and I'll show you. Let me show you how it's done."

Ben stared into Valpariso's glittering eyes. "I don't think so," he said in a quiet growl. "And get your fucking hands off me."

Rico's fist clenched tighter, his nostrils flaring as he sucked in a breath . . .

Then let go.

Ben's gaze remained locked with Valpariso's as he straightened his shirt. "You know, I'd like to see you play first base someday," Ben said. "Just not on my team. Look, Ramsey may be certifiably insane for picking the two of us for his team this summer, but that's his problem. I came here to play baseball, and until the coach tells me otherwise, you'll see me out there on first base."

"That's not going to work." Rico pointed a damning finger at Ben. "No sophomore is going to take my place. I'm getting back to first base, and you know what I can do. You're lucky to be walking. I heard that the janitor broke his hip."

"Seth is fine. Slipped and got a bruise on his ass. He'll be back at work next week." Enough drama! Ben likened Valpariso to one of his father's skipping records, same thing over and over and over until you wanted to kill yourself.

"What happened to Seth . . . that should have been you."

"Woulda coulda shoulda. You know what? I'm beat, Rico. Tired of you and just plain tired." He pushed past Rico, staggering to the right. What the hell was wrong with him? He hoped he wasn't coming down with something. "I'm done here. I'm getting myself back to the dorm for some sleep." He paused, turning back. "Unless you and Turtle buttered the bottom of my sneakers."

Rico folded his arms, not amused.

Ben bent his knees and shifted his feet, doing the twist to check the soles of his shoes. "No butter tonight." He was only half serious, though he could tell his joke was wasted on Valpariso. "But I'll be watching you *and* the butter supply in the dining hall. Keep that in mind. I'm watching you."

PART IV

July 2010

Chapter 41

Greg Cody
Cross College

The case was beginning to take shape. As Cody perched on the vinyl arm of a couch in the fourth floor lounge of Hawthorne Hall, he was getting a picture of the incident, a few brutal swings of a baseball bat.

"This is coming together," Cody said. "In fact, it's starting to get way too organized. Which always makes me nervous." The Syracuse PD guys working on the case since early morning had taken over the lounge of the dorm for a short break while the team was out at practice. Blueprints, resident lists, notes, and a roster of the Lakers were flung in various forms of disarray on the coffee table in the center. "We must be missing something big."

"Don't look a gift horse in the mouth." Fitz leaned back on the sofa and took a sip from the paper coffee cup, courtesy of a campus snack bar. Detective Tom Fitzgerald had risen through the ranks in Syracuse, and Cody valued his knowledge of the area. A father of four, Fitz's schedule was usually built around the team he was coaching or the school event that couldn't be missed. "This is the result of a good morning of work," Fitz said.

"And half the night," said Wilkins, a rookie cop who was partnering with Alvarez for the graveyard shift. Cody had learned that, while Alvarez preferred working midnight to eight a.m., Wilkins was stuck there until he gained some seniority. Wilkins's brown fingers worried the plastic edge of the coffee cup lid. "The shift goes fast when you're busy. This is the first shift I didn't want to pass out around four a.m."

"Your body is getting used to working midnights," Alvarez said. He perched on the edge of a chair, his trousers hiked up to maintain the press in the seam.

"Don't tell me that." Wilkins ran a hand over his close-cropped hair. "I don't want this shift. Friggin' vampire life."

"Guys, I appreciate your helping me scrape things together last night," Cody said. He'd worked too many cases with just one partner and knew that witnesses tended to disappear or forget important details when a crime scene went stale. But last night Alvarez and Wilkins had been knocking on doors and taking statements soon after they secured the crime scene. "So we got statements from every guy who lives on this floor," Cody said. "Real quick, before we push to the next level, anything unusual we should follow up on?"

"Honestly?" Fitz lifted his coffee cup. "These are some of the nastiest guys you'd ever want to play with."

"Fitz, we woke them up at three in the morning," Wilkins said. "Someone did that to you when you'd been out partying in college, you'd be nasty, too."

Fitz scratched his thinning hair. "I'm just saying, no love lost here. These pitchers, Tobey Santiago and who was the other one? Chad, Chad Gilmer. They pointed out to me that it's summer ball. Every man for himself. It's all about getting attention from scouts to get a high draft pick as soon as you're eligible. So I take it with a grain of salt when these guys call Ben McGann a show-off. Still, they talk like they're jealous of the rich girlfriend, and yet they went to her party last night, ate the food, took a dip. Probably had a few drinks on her tab, though they won't admit it."

"The party." Cody flipped through his notebook. "Thrown by Emma Lenson. That's a key event. Anyone mention the fight between McGann and the guy they call Turtle?"

The men nodded.

"The guys I interviewed said they went at it," Alvarez said.

"Wrestled for a while, but called some sort of truce in the end."

"And that was one of two fights Ben had at the party," Greg said. "Gibbs mentioned a later argument, not so physical but pretty ugly."

"Yeah, I got the word on that one from one of my guys." Wilkins flipped back through his notes. "Zach Steiner. Says he was sitting nearby when Valpariso came after McGann. Apparently this Rico Valpariso played first base for the Lakers all last summer, and he's good. Pissed him off this year when the coach brought Ben McGann in to take his place."

"And there's our setup," Cody said. "Two awesome first basemen. A huge rivalry set up by the coaching staff. If you're sending a message, what better way to do it than with one of McGann's own bats? So we'll check out the big catcher, Turtle, and the other first baseman, Rico Valpariso."

"I have to say, I love the sound of that boy's name," Alvarez said. "Rico Valpariso," he said in a slight Spanish accent. "*Muy Bueno.*"

"He's a talented athlete. Bronx kid with parents from the Dominican Republic," Fitz said. "Saw him play last year when I brought the kids to a Lakers game."

"You've got an edge, Fitz. You saw them play." Cody lifted his cup, preferring the smell to the bitter taste of black coffee.

"The rest of us just saw them in their underwear in the middle of the night," said Wilkins. His comment elicited a few wry grins.

"Okay, pulling it together." Cody reeled the conversation back to the case. "We interviewed every resident of the fourth floor, including McGann's best friend, with the room next to him. Who talked to him?"

"Dylan Kroger." Alvarez lifted two fingers. "He's a wreck, and rightly so. Saw him try to hop into the ambulance downstairs."

"Did he have any guesses who might have come after his friend?" Cody asked.

"We didn't get that far. The kid's in denial, kept saying

everything would be fine, that Ben would come back from this, like he's Superman."

"He's worth talking to again. Sounds like he knows Ben McGann better than anyone." Cody added his name to the list. "And then there's the girlfriend. Emma Lenson." An obvious suspect, Cody's first choice after mother, father, or brother. McGann's parents had been miles away and since he had no siblings . . .

"Who is this girl?" Alvarez asked.

"Daughter of some millionaire." Cody looked back at his notes. "Does Lenson Crystal ring a bell?"

"I'd be willing to wager we got some of that in the china cabinet at home," said Fitz. "I'll ask my wife."

"And I'll reach out to Emma Lenson. Over at the Regan Hotel." Cody added the item to his to-do list. "She was nice enough to throw a party for the team. I suppose she can spare me a few minutes."

"You don't think the girlfriend did it?" Wilkins shook his head. "With a baseball bat? That just doesn't feel right to me."

Alvarez tapped the side of his paper cup. "The question is, could she get into the dorm? We all saw the gate down there, requires you to have campus ID."

"Though there's a manual override if you sign in a visitor," Fitz pointed out.

"And there's the possibility of someone piggybacking through the gate." Cody had seen that a million times. "Maybe the girlfriend came in with him. That takes us to the dorm security system." Most of Cody's discussion with the director of campus security had been about damage control. There had not been a security incident on the campus for more than three months, and that had been a date-rape incident. The college prided itself on maintaining a safe environment. "In my brief meeting with Devin Mains this morning, he told me there are security cameras in the lobby. Right now he's got his guys going through the digital images, starting with eleven o'clock last night. They're also printing out a list of students whose card was scanned from eleven to, say, four a.m."

"Sounds like Cross College has a fairly secure system," said Fitz.

"Maybe, but there's always some way to beat the system." Cody flipped through the blueprint until he found the grid of the first floor. "We need to check the emergency exits. Make sure there's no way someone could have slipped in through a locked exit."

"I can do that," Fitz said, making a note.

"Another thing . . ." Cody stared at the blueprint of the fourth floor. As he'd thought, bathroom in the center, three bedrooms fanning out from each corner. "Each floor except the first floor is the same, right. So the fourth floor has twelve rooms. Twelve rooms, but there are fifteen guys on the team, right? So where do the other three guys live?"

Alvarez picked up the team roster. "They're all required to live here." He scanned the list. "Looks like Valpariso and Pettit live on three. And Turtle . . . Joseph Turturro is on the first floor."

"We didn't get down to the third floor yet." Cody stood up. "Let's check their rooms now, while they're at practice."

"Whoa, what?" Wilkins pressed fingertips to his brow. "You want to check their rooms without permission? Don't we need a warrant for that?"

Cody shot a glance at Fitz, who shrugged as if to say, *Fine by me*.

"Ooh." Alvarez dropped his coffee cup into the trash bin by the door. "Can of worms."

"Here's the thing, Wilkins." Cody didn't want to disillusion the young rookie. "The issue of search and seizure in a dormitory is open to debate. It's not a private home. The school owns the property, and you could argue that they need access to rooms to protect their residents."

"Right," Wilkins said as they headed down the corridor. "But still, there is some expectation of privacy."

"True," Cody agreed.

"I'm impressed, Wilkins." Fitz put a hand on the rookie's shoulder. "Did you go to law school or something?"

"Thought about it." Wilkins touched the shield clipped to his uniform. "But I'm glad I didn't. I would have been a desk jockey, pushing papers. Got to be an urban cowboy instead."

Someday Cody would write a profile of the phases of disillusionment cops went through from their rookie years to retirement.

"So what are we looking for, exactly?" Wilkins asked.

"Blood," Cody said. "Bloodstains on a shirt or shoes or gloves. If the attacker used something sharp like a knife, he might have cut himself, too. Also Samira thinks he wore gloves. With the amount of spatter from the kid's head wounds, the perp would have gotten some blood on his feet or shirt, at least."

"Batting gloves?" Alvarez suggested.

"That would work, though they probably have their batting gloves with them at practice right now."

"Unless they're stained with blood," said Fitz.

"Exactly."

"And what if the rooms are locked?" Wilkins asked.

Alvarez held one hand up. "All these guys we talked to today, every single one said they left their room unlocked. Didn't want to get locked out, because the ten dollar fee is too much."

"I wonder if they're going to start locking doors after this," Fitz said as he headed down the hall.

The four men split into teams of two to tackle the room searches. Cody and Wilkins started with Kroger's room, right next to Ben's. A plaid quilt and blue sheets hanging off the bed. A one-cup coffeemaker and a few boxes of cereal, though no refrigerator. A bucket of toiletries sat beside his sink, and his closet housed a mound of dirty shirts, towels, boxers, and socks.

"That stuff is ripe," Wilkins said. "I wonder how they do laundry."

"There's probably a washer and dryer off the first floor lobby. But here's the thing, Wilkins. You got to get in there and check." Cody took out a pen and probed through the tangle of clothes.

"Checking some guy's dirty drawers? No, thank you. I'll look under the mattress."

"You need to do both," Cody said, "if you want to be a true urban cowboy."

After the best friend's room checked out, they moved on to Isaiah Gibbs's room, which was locked. A knock produced a sleepy-eyed Gibbs, looking sullen in his hoodie. Stacks of clothes sat beside two duffel bags that lay open on the floor like collapsed bladders. The bed was a tangle of sheets, the comforter tossed back on haphazardly.

"More questions?" he asked Cody.

"We're just doing a room check," Cody said. "Routine."

Gibbs stepped back, arms folded. "You can check, but I'm in the middle of packing. I was going to go get boxes to ship back some of my stuff, but my ma says to leave it here. Give it to one of the guys."

Cody passed by the clock radio, toaster oven, and stash of food sitting on the built-in desk. "This is a lot of swag to give away," he said.

"Yeah, well, I'm not going to stick around and try to sell it on eBay. It's not worth it. Nothing's worth ending up like McGann."

"True." While Fitz checked the bed Cody looked through a canvas laundry sack. "When are you headed back home?" Cody asked.

"I probably can't get a bus until tomorrow. But I'll tell you this: Till then, I'm keeping my door locked. Definitely locked. You can't trust anyone here."

"It's a good idea to keep your door locked," Wilkins said. "Just take normal precautions. You'll be okay, man."

Cody didn't expect to find anything, and when they left, he was glad to hear the dead bolt click behind them.

In the search they found that the other three guys kept laptops in their unlocked rooms, which miffed Cody, and Trevor Dozneski's room won the prize, furnished with a rug, a sofa, posters, an iPod port, and a fridge stocked with half a case of beer. Most of the guys had microwaves or hot plates; some had fridges and a decent supply of groceries.

Cody was noting the contents of Dozneski's room when he ran into the other team in the hall. "Anything?"

"Nada," said Alvarez.

"Damn." Cody shook his head. "We get a free search and still come up empty."

Fitz and Alvarez went down to the first floor to check Turturro's room while Cody and Wilkins checked out the players' rooms on the third floor.

In Riley Pettit's room, books were stacked on the dresser and floor.

"Library books?" Wilkins squatted down to check them out. "What kind of athlete reads library books?"

"The smart athlete who realizes he's probably going to need a job in the real world when college is over." Leaning over the trash, Cody stabbed at a cardboard sleeve with his pen. "Check this out." He fished out the paper on the end of his pen and held it up. "It's a Nike label for batting gloves. Looks like Pettit just got new gloves." He slid the cardboard into an evidence bag and labeled it. "I wonder if the attacker used batting gloves to cover fingerprints."

"Brand-new batting gloves?" Wilkins was skeptical.

"You use the old ones for the crime, the new ones for the game."

"Doesn't mean he attacked McGann," Wilkins said. "Could be a coincidence."

"Could be." Cody had never worked with the rookie before, and he found he was getting a kick out of it. Despite his lack of experience, Wilkins tried to think things through, a technique that would get him far as an "urban cowboy."

On the way to the next room, Cody noticed an open cutout in the wall along one hall. Inside the recessed area were a washer and dryer, both operated by quarters. "Aha. The configuration is a little different on this floor." He flipped through the blueprints. "So they have a small laundry room on the second and third floor." He stepped inside, opened up the dryer door.

"Catching up on your laundry?" Wilkins said.

"Just looking." The dryer was empty. At the bottom of the washing machine was a ring of wet items.

"It's probably nothing," Cody said. Nonetheless, he pulled a latex glove onto his right hand and pinched the edge of cloth to lift it up. "Looks like a T-shirt."

"A Lakers baseball shirt." Wilkins gaped as the wet shirt unfurled in Cody's grip. "And it looks like there're some bloodstains that somebody tried to wash off."

"And what else?" With his gloved hand Cody pulled out two opaque white surgical gloves and a small white towel, also marked with diluted stains. "Bingo."

"Do you think those were the gloves the attacker used?" Wilkins asked. "Can the CSU get the perp's fingerprints from inside?"

"I doubt it. Besides, these look like they've gone through a rinse cycle. But this could be a good find."

As they bagged the T-shirt, towel, and gloves, Cody noted that the shirt was a large—probably the most common size worn by the players. He called down to update Fitz as they headed to the next room. Fitz reported some problems getting into Turturro's room. "Apparently the guy put his own locks on. Not even the resident assistant can get in, and he's got a master key."

"Guess we'll have to ask Turtle for a personal tour," Cody said, then signed off.

Rico Valpariso's room was neat and spare, bed made, a small runner lined up beside the bed. Various shaving creams and aftershaves lined the ledge of his sink, and his dresser held half a dozen shiny bottles of cologne.

"Fancies himself a ladies' man," Cody said.

"Hey, Cody, check this out." Wilkins had turned Valpariso's hamper on its side and was fishing through his laundry. He jabbed his pen in and came up with a white hand towel dotted in brownish red. "Bloodstains?"

"Looks that way." They bagged the towel and lifted the mattress of the bed to search underneath.

"Nothing," Cody said as something clicked behind him. He wheeled around to see a young Hispanic man standing in the doorway.

"What the hell are you doing in my room?" Although the kid didn't raise his voice, Cody sensed an undercurrent of violence, a certain promise of it.

"We're cops," Wilkins said, though that much was obvious from his uniform.

"Greg Cody, Syracuse PD." Cody held up the leather folder that held his shield and ID card. He was glad Wilkins didn't give his name; if Valpariso filed a complaint, he probably wouldn't be able to name the rookie, which was all for the best. New cops took it hard when citizens filed complaints against them. "We're investigating the attack on Ben McGann, and I take it you're Rico Valpariso?"

"Get your hands off my bed." Wilkins let the mattress drop and Valpariso marched over and straightened the quilt. "I come in here and find cops touching my things, my personal property. Isn't there a law against this sort of abuse? I think so. Do you have a warrant?"

Cody straightened to his full height, turned on the old cop persona. "No warrant, though we're in a gray area here, Mr. Valpariso. Technically you're a guest of the college, and they allowed us to search the rooms of people who knew Ben McGann." Not completely true, but Cody had to run with it. "If it makes you feel any better, we're going through the rooms of all the Lakers players."

"I don't care if you're patting down the dean of students. Stay out of my shit."

"Good enough." Cody nodded toward the door, hoping that Valpariso wouldn't notice his bloody towel in the plastic bag swinging from Wilkins's arm. "Let's go, Officer." And he turned and stepped into the hall.

Wilkins had taken a single step when Valpariso pointed to

the bag. "What's that?" He glanced back toward the hamper. "Is that my towel?"

When Wilkins's jaw dropped, Cody stepped in. "It's a bloody towel. We're taking it to the lab to determine if any of that blood belongs to Ben McGann."

"It doesn't," Rico said sharply. "It's my blood."

Pausing, Cody looked from the bag to Rico. "That's a lot of blood. What happened? And don't tell me you cut yourself shaving."

"Maybe I did cut myself shaving," Rico hissed.

Wiseass. Cody frowned. "Okay. You want to come in and give us a sample of your blood? That way you can prove that is was just a simple cut."

Valpariso folded his arms, his dark eyes squinting. "You must think I'm crazy."

It was the last image Cody had of him before the door slammed.

Chapter 42

Kate McGann
Good Samaritan Hospital

The scurry of footsteps was the only thing that pulled her from the choppy bay of sleep. Footsteps might bring doctors with news of Ben . . . but usually they were just staff, people in scrubs or lab coats, aids in pink jackets pushing carts, men in neckties.

And when the footsteps produced nothing of value she stopped opening her eyes for them and let them wash past her. Her mind created new scenarios for the sounds around her: The retracting elevator doors were a revolving stage, a rumbling cart, a rusty bicycle creaking in the rain.

When the footsteps grew closer and whispered to a stop, she forced herself to look up. It was that detective, what was his name? Gorgeous man, tall and statuesque. Wise eyes, bad shirt. Oh, God, did she say that?

She took a deep breath, forcing herself awake. "Detective . . . I'm sorry."

"No, I'm sorry. I thought I'd check back with you, but when I saw that you were out I considered letting you sleep."

"It's a strange sleep . . . more like passing out." She shifted in the vinyl chair, stretched.

"I don't suppose there's any news from the OR yet," he said.

"Not yet, and it's been a lot longer than they said it would be."

"They lie." He sat down beside her, facing the hallway as she was. "They do that all the time."

Twisting in the chair, Kate wondered why hospitals felt so unhealthy. She pulled her legs up under her and hugged herself. The air seemed stale; the lighting had a sickly green tint. Her face felt oily, her mouth dry, and she tasted that slightly antiseptic tinge at the back of her throat. She didn't belong here. Ben certainly didn't belong here.

"Please," she told the detective. "Distract me. Tell me about your job."

"Not much to tell. Crimes are committed. The cases bounce upstairs to the desk of a detective and we try to find the perp." As he spoke he stretched out his legs, long legs.

"Am I picking up a trace of an accent?" she asked.

He nodded. "Brooklyn."

"I used to teach in New York City. The students kept me on my toes there. Such a vast cultural mix, it truly was a 'beautiful mosaic.'" She turned toward him. The way the overhead lights hit his hair, it seemed to be glowing. A halo of sorts. "Were you ever a cop there?"

"I was. Twenty years."

Twenty years with the NYPD: That could go into the positive category. At least he would know something about conducting an investigation. "Tell me about the investigation. Do you have any leads?" she asked.

"You don't want to hear about that. Not now, when you've got your son to worry about. There'll be time to go over it later."

"Please, Detective, indulge me." She pointed to the magazine rack against the wall. "I've read every article in three months of *Parenting Now!* I just about memorized their one copy of *Better Homes and Gardens* and I even perused *Car and Driver,* though I don't have a clue what they're talking about half the time. I need a distraction, something with relevance."

He looked nervously at the elevator. "What do you want to know?"

"I want to know who did this to him."

"I thought you were going to ask questions I can answer."

She paused. "Okay. Do you know how he was injured? I mean, what might have been used as a weapon?"

"It sounds like our theory about the baseball bat is holding true. The forensic techs found a bloody bat, no detectable fingerprints. We're thinking it belongs to Ben. Some of his teammates told us that Ben kept bats in his room. Brought them back to the dorm every night?"

"That was Ben. He took care of his equipment, maybe because it was hard to come by. The cost of wooden bats and batting gloves adds up, and he's had things stolen from the locker room before. That hurt." She thought of Ben's most recent treasure, a Rawlings bat at the top of his Christmas list two years ago. He loved that bat. Ben would be devastated if someone stole it. "You said a bat was vouchered . . . were there other bats there? I mean, I'm wondering if the rest of his collection was stolen. He had a laptop too, and a DVD player."

Detective Cody paged back through his notes. "Looks like three bats were vouchered, collected for evidence. The forensic team also took his laptop and cell phone. A DVD player is still in his room."

She sighed. "That sounds right. I'm just thinking about Ben's favorite. A Rawlings Blue Thunder. Ridiculously expensive, but we got it for him as a gift, and it seemed to be worth every penny. It's sort of his lucky bat."

"I'll check the inventory, make sure it's there."

She nodded. It seemed important to protect Ben's possessions right now, even if he wouldn't be healthy enough to use them for a while. For the first time she wondered at the long-term prognosis. If Ben survived, if he regained consciousness, what could she hope for? Normal? Would he be playing ball again this time next summer, this entire nightmare just a cautionary episode in her son's life?

"And what about the player I mentioned . . . the one who used to play first base?"

"His name is Enrico Valpariso."

"Have you questioned him?"

"Briefly."

He was hiding something. The one-word answer, the way he glanced toward the reception desk. "What? Did you find something?"

"Valpariso approached Ben at the party. One of the players, Zach Steiner, says he witnessed the exchange. Valpariso seemed sober but menacing. No fists were thrown, but Rico made some threats."

Kate's heart beat faster with each word. "It's him . . . he must be the one who attacked Ben. Are you going to arrest him?"

"Right now we're still investigating." He closed his notebook, now bulky with the folded papers shoved inside, and got to his feet.

Kate wanted to pounce on him and shout that he had to do something about this Rico kid, but she realized that he had stood up because someone was coming down the hall, the footsteps finally attached to someone with information.

Moving against stiffness in her hips, Kate rose to her feet as Dr. Zanth guided a short, bald man toward her. He wore green scrubs and his glistening scalp made Kate think how handy it would be to be a bald neurosurgeon, that you wouldn't be bringing all the microscopic bacteria that clings to hair into the operating room.

"Kate." Teddy Zanth seemed ghostly, her eyes small in the hollows of her face. "This is Dr. Carl Pruett. He's the neurosurgeon who operated on Ben."

Kate's heart was still racing, the noise of her pulse thrashing in her ears as she shook the neurosurgeon's hand.

"Ben's procedure went as well as could be expected," Dr. Pruett said. "I don't know if Dr. Zanth told you, but we have a state-of-the art neurosurgery suite. We have an MR scanner right in the operating room that allows us to get high-definition pictures of the brain during the actual surgery."

Kate read caution in his dark brown eyes. "And you drilled holes in his skull to relieve the pressure from swelling?"

"Actually, we were planning to drill burr holes, but the swelling was more extensive than the original scan indicated. We removed a portion of his skull, called a bone flap. Right now the bone flap is stored in his abdomen, which is the best way I know to keep it healthy. Eventually, when the brain swelling recedes, we'll replace the bone flap in his head. The original bone is far better protection than a metal plate."

He made it sound so simple, like a short vacation for the brain, then—good as new.

"Dr. Pruett?" Detective Cody stepped in, introduced himself. "Could you describe Ben's injury?"

"Right frontal lobe. Contusions consistent with blunt trauma. There may be some damage to the right optic nerve." Dr. Pruett turned to Kate. "It's too soon to address the optic nerve issues. Right now he's fighting to survive."

"But . . . what does that mean?" He was moving too swiftly for Kate. "Will he be able to see?"

Dr. Pruett shifted his weight, obviously weary. "He might have diminished vision in his right eye. We thought the eye socket was broken, but X-rays say no."

A broken eye socket . . . damage to the optic nerve . . . it is getting worse by the second. Kate sucked her cheeks in, trying to stop tears from forming "Where is he now?" she asked. "Can I see him?"

"He's in recovery," Dr. Zanth said, "but he'll be moved to the ICU soon, and you can see him there."

"He's sedated, and we'll keep him that way for the next twenty-four hours." Dr. Pruett's eyes were focused over Kate's head, as if he were reciting something by rote. "We want to give him a chance to heal."

Kate nodded. "And then? Then he'll wake up?"

"I expect that he'll regain consciousness," Dr. Pruett said. "If and when he does, he'll be moved to a neuro ICU. Right now we're looking for him to stay here for a month or so; then we'll reassess."

If and when . . . Did that mean he wasn't sure? Kate rubbed her temples. "I have to make sure I'm hearing you correctly. Ben is going to be okay, right?"

"I've seen head trauma patients make great strides in recovery. The brain can have a great deal of plasticity. Sometimes cells surrounding the damaged area undergo changes in their function and shape so that they take on the role of the damaged cells." He shrugged. "There are a lot of possibilities for your son's prognosis. Right now it's too soon to tell."

"Oh." Kate felt stupid. Was she asking the wrong questions or processing the answers improperly? "I don't understand what you're saying, Dr. Pruett. Is he going to be okay?"

"From the way the surgery went, I'd say he has a good chance of regaining consciousness. And that is thanks to Dr. Zanth here, who recognized the signs of intracranial bleeding and got him up to the OR stat. The surgery bought Ben some time; it may have saved his life. But we won't know about things like cognitive damage until later."

Cognitive damage.

Blindness.

Kate shook her head. She refused to accept that these were real possibilities for her son. "Is there a chance he'll recover? That he'll be normal again?"

Dr. Pruett sucked air in between his teeth. "I understand your anxiety, Mrs. McGann, but we just have to wait and see. The first six weeks is usually the time a patient makes his fastest recovery. If he wakes, he'll be tired, and his memory will not be at its best. The second six weeks of post-op is usually a time of improved stamina. After that, there's a three-month period of readjustment, sometimes longer, depending on the patient. This is all assuming Ben regains consciousness."

Twelve weeks plus three months . . . Kate quickly added in her head. Six months. Six months without baseball? It would kill Ben.

That was, if he came out of the coma.

Somehow, she'd expected a more definitive answer, a reassuring "Everything will be fine."

Pruett leaned forward to pat her on the shoulder. "We can talk more later. I'm going to check on Ben in post-op. Dr. Zanth can bring you up to see him when he reaches the ICU."

Kate glared at him, unsettled by the demeaning pat on the shoulder, but he didn't seem to notice as he walked away. She turned to Dr. Zanth, suddenly recalling her story.

The girl who had come back from the dead.

"What are the chances?" Kate spoke through her tears. "I need to know. What are the chances that he'll recover?" Kate extended an arm toward the disappearing Dr. Pruett. "Because I can't live with what he's telling me. I can't wait and see when my son's life hangs in the balance."

"I understand." Dr. Zanth's hands came together as if in prayer and she bowed slightly, touching her fingertips to her forehead.

Kate drew in a breath as Teddy Zanth lowered her hands and set her burning amber eyes on Kate. "I am not a neurosurgeon, and I don't know statistics. I do know that most recovery occurs within the first six months after the injury, and children tend to improve more quickly, so Ben has youth on his side. But recovery is possible. If I were you, that would be my focus: to make Ben a whole person again. Most likely your son will be a changed person, perhaps not as outgoing, perhaps not a ballplayer. But he will be your son; his essence will remain."

The words were a salve, not a cure, but an analgesic to take the edge off the pain.

Hope for the best, Kate told herself as she dug her fingernails into the palms of her hands. *Hope for the best, even when it defies science.*

Chapter 43

Teddy Zanth
Good Samaritan Hospital

If Dr. Cooper Smeltzer went door to door selling magazines or soliciting donations for wildlife preservation, Teddy was convinced that most people would have refused to open their doors and hear him out. If the name didn't put you off, there were the thick, black-framed glasses that magnified his eyes. His white jacket was always crinkled as if he'd slept in it, which he probably had. If he didn't miss a spot shaving he cut himself, leaving a series of garnet scabs at his jawline. And his physique—not terribly obese, but the freshman ten were now the residency twenty, hanging over his belt.

Lucky for Coop Smeltzer he was not selling magazines but instead was working as a new resident in the trauma department at Good Sam, as people here called it. The guy was a train wreck. Teddy had tried to avoid him in orientation, when he tried to recruit her for a pro baseball pool he was putting together. "Five bucks a week, random pick. You in?" Not even speaking the language, she had said no thanks and rued the day when they would be working the same shift. Like it or not, Teddy realized she would be seeing a lot of Coop over the next few years.

"Dr. Zanth, it says here that you're off." He stood at the Plexiglas board showing ER intake, no doubt sniffing around for interesting procedures he might be assigned on his shift. "And yet, somehow, you're still here. If I were off, I would not be here talking to a schlub like me. I would be far, far away. Or at least down the block at Martini's Bar."

"I have to do charts," she said. A lame excuse, but she no longer had the energy to get creative. The room seemed to tilt a little and she pressed her palms into the counter to steady herself. She would not let herself get sick in another trauma center, but the sour taste in her dry mouth was alarming. She pressed a hand to her forehead. No fever.

"Ho, there, whoa, there! Your name is on this board. A head trauma." He looked down at her, his blue eyes wide, flickering pools behind his glasses. "Is this true?"

She nodded, wondering when she last ate. Yesterday, right? She had breakfast before she came on shift, didn't she?

"So you caught a real case." Coop wasn't giving up. "How's he doing?"

"He's in recovery. An emergency craniotomy." The end of his playing season, but maybe he would survive. "But there was something else. . . ." She closed her eyes, trying to remember. A bowl of peppermints gleamed on the counter, and she quickly unwrapped one and popped it in.

"Zanth?" Coop's concerned voice was right beside her, and she realized her eyes were closed as she swayed over the counter.

"I need to make a follow-up call. A little girl . . . their daughter died last night."

"Zanth, you're talking crazy. It's not on the board and you're passing out. Come on now. To the lounge."

Strong arms pulled her upright and as she focused she was walking alongside Coop, one side supported by his warm body. Funny, she thought, but he didn't smell the way she had expected. There was no body odor, but a soft, sweet scent. Baby powder? No . . . fabric softener.

Laurel jumped into her thoughts. Laurel toddling through flowers. Laurel smelling of baby powder. Projections, not memories. She didn't know the first thing about the little girl, except that she was dead.

"Okay, now sit right down here. When was the last time you had something to eat?"

Teddy focused on Coop, or at least on the icy glare of his black glasses as she fell back onto the couch of the doctors' lounge. "I don't know." She felt the mint, stuck to the soft flesh on one side of her mouth. "Yesterday."

"Typical doctor. No clue that all the info in your nutrition class applies to you. No, you're superhuman. Nothing will stop you." As he spoke he reached into his locker, fished in a cooler, popped something into the microwave. He shook a pink bottle from the cooler, popped it open, poured some into a cup from the water cooler. "Drink this."

She spit the mint into a tissue and took a sip. It tasted of peach and tangerine, cool and soothing to the pucker in her mouth. She drank it all, easing back onto the vinyl sofa. "Thanks. You bring your own cooler to work?"

"Hell, yeah. I got sick of having my dinner scarfed down by refrigerator raiders."

The microwave beeped, and he popped the door open. "Now eat this—all of it. I don't like wasting food." He handed her a small brown patty on a paper plate.

The fork shook in her hand as she separated a piece and got it to her mouth. Savory and smooth, it seemed to warm her from the inside out. "It's delicious."

"Not really, but you're so hungry for nutrients you can't tell the difference."

She sighed as she chewed. "What is it?"

"Veggie burger. Mostly mushrooms, soy, and brown rice."

She took another bite. "I love it."

"It's manna from heaven when you're suffering malnutrition. Which you are, Dr. Zanth. You need to maintain an appropriate balance between personal health and work ethic."

"You sound like my grandmother."

"She must be a smart woman." He refilled her cup, poured himself some, and then sat down and toasted her. "To balance, baby."

"Okay, now you just sound like a weird granola resident." Her head was clearing, the room set and still now, and as her blood sugar level began to stabilize her focus returned, along with a haunting image of a toddler with tousled blond curls and blue lips. "I have to make a call."

"What? Are you talking gibberish again?"

"No. I'm okay now. Thanks." To demonstrate her competence she sat up straight and winged the paper plate like a Frisbee toward the trash can. It hit the side and fell to the floor, and she slid down on the couch with a groan.

Cooper laughed. "Okay, whatever. Why didn't you eat last night? I know it can get crazy, but you can sneak a granola bar while you're looking at X-rays or doing charts."

"I wasn't hungry, and then we got slammed in the early hours of the morning. And that was after I'd lost my first patient here. Well, officially it was Dr. Chong's patient, but she bestowed the honor of notification on me, and it was tragic. A little girl who died in the family swimming pool. She was eighteen months old, probably not even talking yet."

He let his head roll back on his shoulders. "Brutal. I haven't lost a patient yet. Well, not here. And never anything that sad."

She turned toward him, waiting to see the intelligence in his eyes. "That's the thing, Coop. The tragedy of it." He sat up straight, met her gaze with a curious look. "You go through the paces to treat a child who's already dead, all the while hoping for a miracle. And then, when it's over, to have to tell her mother and father, to see them so broken and know that you are more a part of the damage than the repair." Although Teddy had arranged for grief counseling for Tori and Stu Weissbaum, they did not seem keen on participating. She brought her hands up over her head. "I got clobbered last night. Hit hard by two kids, one who died and another who may be on his way out. Med school doesn't prepare you for it, and really, that's not why I wanted to be a doctor. I want to cure people, save them from death. I never expected to be the person standing by helplessly when they die."

He didn't answer, though she could tell he got it. There was an intrinsic flash of connection, the sense of a question asked and answered in the same instant.

And then he glanced at the big dial on his wrist. "Sorry to rush the existential, but I'm due for rounds."

"Thank you. Really." She arose with sure footing and a clear head. "You saved me from eating the floor wax."

"In this place? That wouldn't taste so good." He stowed his cooler back into his locker. "If you get on my shift next week, I'll bring an extra veggie patty. Or a whole grain pizza. Do you know if that stove works?" he asked, nodding at an old stove and rangetop beside the sink.

She shook her head. "No, but it's worth a try for pizza."

"And if the rangetop is good, there's always the incredible edible egg. I make a mean frittata." He turned the dial and blue flames burst forth in one of the burners. "Perfect. Get on my shift, Zanth, and you'll be eating in style."

"I'll see what I can do about that." She took the last sip of nectar, swallowed. "Do you ever wonder why you went to med school?" she asked.

Cooper snorted. "Every day. And just when I think I've answered that question the parameters shift and I find myself rethinking it all over again."

"Okay. I'm relieved to know I'm not the only one who lives in a perennial state of self-examination." She tossed the paper cup into the trash and headed out to grab her paperwork and check in with Tori Weissbaum.

Chapter 44

Kate
Good Samaritan Hospital

Not even ten a.m. and Kate was ready for bed.

Too bad there was no place to sleep. Wincing at the green fluorescent glow of the restroom, she took off her hooded sweatshirt, stowed it on a narrow shelf under the mirror, and passed her hand under the faucet to get the water flowing. Nothing. That always happened to her in public restrooms; as if she were invisible or lacking in enough atomic mass for the sensor to pick up.

Annoyed, she waved both hands, switched to the next sink, and finally got the water going. It felt good to suds her hands and forearms, bracing to rinse, as the hot water didn't seem to work. She leaned forward and splashed water on her face, feeling a small part of her come alive again. Pressing her face into paper towels, she sighed. So many things to wade through, it was overwhelming.

She needed coffee. She needed to book a hotel room. There had to be some way she could research traumatic brain injury. She dreaded the phone call to Eli, and she knew it was time to reach out to her sister Erin, who would do whatever Kate asked.

But first, there was Ben.

Watching the reflection of the strange woman with lifeless hair and puffy pink face, she tossed the paper towels, wrapped her hoodie around her waist, and headed out to the next challenge.

As visitors were not really allowed in the intensive care unit, there was no reception desk, only a nurses' station with a computer and some files. Dr. Zanth had explained when she'd dropped Kate off here, "It's not really the environment for visiting, but immediate family is allowed. When you're ready, just press that button on the wall and someone will come out and help you."

The man who peered through the windows reminded her of Mahatma Gandhi—short and bald, with the golden-taupe skin of an Indo-Asian. The doors slid open, and he stepped out. She assumed he was a doctor in his navy scrubs. "Can I help you?"

"Yes, Doctor, my son is in the ICU—Ben McGann? I'm here to see him."

His brows lifted. "I'm not a doctor, but I can help you. My name is Sonny—you probably won't remember that—and I'm a nurse. Please, would you sign in?" He motioned her over to the nurses' station and slid a clipboard across the counter.

Kate scribbled her signature. When she looked up his eyes were scanning the plastic chairs by the window, where a middle-aged couple sat, the woman doubled over to hide her face, the man talking quietly.

"Okay, Kate McGann. Are you here alone?"

She bit her lower lip, thinking of how Eli had fled. "Yes."

"That's fine. I can take you to see your son, but first you need to brace yourself for this. Ben is sedated, yes, but we don't know how much of your reaction his subconscious might detect."

"Does he look that bad?"

He tucked the clipboard under the counter. "He doesn't look good. I don't know how Ben used to look, but they shaved his head for the surgery. There's a lot of swelling and many tubes running in and out of his body. Just be prepared."

She took a deep breath, preparing herself for the worst. "Okay. Thanks for the warning."

"It's part of my standard spiel; more than one visitor has passed out in the ICU. It's a problem."

Bracing herself, Kate used the community hand sanitizer, then followed the man into the ward, an extended room of beds surrounded by tubing and poles containing bags of fluid and monitors. She tried not to look at the lumps in the beds, but instead focused on putting one foot in front of the other on the tile floor as the man led her to Ben.

"Here we are."

At first she felt nothing for the figure in the bed, his misshapen skull shaved down to a dark bristle, his swollen, half-purple face. Thin wires snaked under the sheets and tubes ran into his throat and chest, like tethers to keep the heavy body from sinking into the bed.

"Right now we have to be careful to avoid infection or pneumonia."

"Ben?" She moved closer to the bed, pressed into the silver bars that kept him from falling. Instinctively she reached to touch his head but knew she couldn't stroke the thick, dark hair that used to shine there; she didn't dare touch his brow or press the back of her hand to the unbandaged side of his face.

It frightened her that she would not have recognized him. She would not have been able to identify him as her son. But somewhere within this battered shell were the remnants of her boy, the hints of the man he was becoming. Somewhere . . .

"Oh, Ben." She let her hand fall to his arm. His skin was cool, distant and peaceful, she hoped. She rubbed her fingers over the dark fur of his forearm and sent him the message to heal. "It's Mom, honey." She bit back the desire to cry, sucking on her upper lip. She hadn't been allowed to call him honey since he started junior high. "I'm right here. You just rest now. Just rest."

The monitors above his bed were digital line graphs and readouts that showed his blood pressure, heart rate, pulse rate, and breathing, though, from the mechanical rise and fall of his chest, it was clear that a machine was pushing air into his lungs. She had no idea if the numbers were good or cause for alarm, but it reassured her to watch the moving lines of the monitors instead of looking at her son's ravaged head and face. When an alarm went off at a bedside behind her and three nurses responded, it seemed to confirm that things were under control. The monitors knew when to worry. The monitors were keeping things under control, watching over Ben. Small comfort, but relief nonetheless.

She had no idea how long she stayed there, watching, waiting, reassuring him with the touch of her fingertips. Ben probably could not hear her, but she believed that it mattered. He had to know someone was here for him; his spirit could sense it.

"Kate McGann." The Gandhi nurse stood at the foot of Ben's bed. "Can I get you a chair?"

"No, that's okay." Her fingers trailed Ben's forearm, the lean muscle and solid bone. "I'm going to go for a while."

"Good idea," the nurse said. "Get some food and rest. Your son will be here when you return. His doctor has prescribed a strong sedative for the rest of the day."

She squeezed Ben's arm. "Take care, honey. I'll be back soon."

As she followed the nurse to the exit the other patients didn't seem quite as horrifying. They were just people hooked up to machinery, patients struggling to survive, each with his or her own story.

"If you're back on my shift, my name is Sonny," the nurse said. "I'm here till midnight tonight. I'll see you later, Kate McGann."

Kate nodded. "Sonny." This time she would remember his name.

On the elevator ride down she turned on her cell phone and saw two missed calls from her sister. She was dialing Erin before she stepped out into the courtyard and took a seat on a cement bench in the sunlight.

They spoke in the shorthand of sisters, the language of twin beds, hand-me-down clothes, and shared dreams.

"Ohmigod, I got your text. Is he okay?"

"He's in the ICU. They say the surgery went well but it's sort of touch and go. Can you come?"

"I'm packing as we speak. In fact, I'm packed. Where am I going?"

"Good Samaritan Hospital in Syracuse."

"Syracuse. Shit. Do you think there's a direct flight from Baltimore? Oh, whatever. I'll figure it out and get my ass there ASAP."

"And bring your laptop. I need to do some TBI research." Kate had thought she would use Ben's, but then Detective Cody had told her that the police had taken it to look for evidence.

"Laptop . . . okay."

"I knew I could count on you."

"Be there in a heartbeat. I'll call from the road."

Kate ended the call and pressed her cell phone to her chest. She had to call Eli, but she wasn't ready; she didn't possess the energy to juggle his angst and her own fear. Instead, she crossed the courtyard to a red vendor's wagon that promised coffee and churros that smelled of sugar and crisped fat.

Ben loved churros. Although she wasn't really hungry, she would eat one in his honor.

Chapter 45

Emma Lenson
Good Samaritan Hospital

"**Y**ou must have it wrong." Emma stepped closer to the counter where the mousey-looking woman sat at a computer clicking away with her mouse. "He definitely wants to see me. I'm his girlfriend."

Marnie turned back to Emma and held her hand out in frustration, but Emma ignored her. Leave it to Marnie to screw things up. The girl didn't have an assertive bone in her body.

"I'm sorry, but it's hospital policy." Mousey pinched the tiny bauble dangling from her necklace. "Family only."

Emma nudged in beside Marnie and placed her hands flat on the counter, her "Pretty in Pink" nail polish gleaming in the fluorescent overhead lights. "But we're like family, and we came here just to see him." She pointed to the big double doors with square windows in the top half. "Is he in there, or not?"

The nurse stopped clicking on her computer and cocked her head at Emma. Her pursed lips and stern eyes were so obvious; she wasn't even trying to hide her annoyance.

Well, if Emma had her mousey brown hair and beady eyes, she supposed she'd be annoyed, too.

"What was the patient's name again?" the woman asked. She reached for the charm on her necklace and ran it back and forth on the chain, like a two-year-old revving toy cars on a track.

Emma folded her arms, satisfied to be making progress. "McGann. Benjamin McGann."

Nurse Mousey typed on the keyboard.

"And I'm Emma Lenson. Of the Lenson family. I'm sure you've heard of Lenson Crystal."

The woman didn't even look up at Emma, just kept her BB eyes on the computer screen. What was wrong with her? Did she drink out of jelly jars?

"Okay, we do have a patient named Benjamin McGann, but he's just out of surgery. There are no visitors allowed in the ICU." Mousey squeezed the charm again and started running it back and forth, back and forth, until Emma wished the woman would pull too hard and break the necklace. "Sorry."

The way she cut Emma off, zipping her little charm . . . Emma sucked in a breath, fanning the fury. "I don't think so. I don't think you're sorry at all."

"Emma . . ." Marnie cut in. "Come on."

But Emma wasn't going to be pacified. "I want to see my boyfriend. He needs me."

"Hospital policy," Nurse Mousey said without looking up.

"Well, at least can you tell me how he's doing? What happened in his surgery? Is he going to be okay?"

"I can't give that information out, young lady. A patient is legally entitled to privacy of records." And then Nurse Mousey had the gall to wheel her chair around to the desk behind her and face away from the counter, her back to Emma and Marnie.

"The drama queen thing isn't going to fly," Marnie said, gesturing her away from the counter. "We need to go to plan B."

"I don't know what you're talking about. I have to see Ben. I am freaking out here, and that one just spouts off hospital policy."

"That one is enjoying your freak-out." Marnie flipped open her cell phone and pressed out a number. "Let's find Dylan and see what he can find out. He's pretty tight with Ben's parents, right?"

"Excuse me, miss?" Nurse Mousey called from behind her counter. "There's no cell phone use in the hospital." She pointed to a sign.

Marnie glanced from the sign to Emma, then back at the nurse. "What are you going to do, arrest me?"

Mousey gaped at them, her beady eyes glistening with hatred in her piggy face.

That made Emma feel better. And as they headed down to meet Dylan in the courtyard, Emma realized that, despite what Marnie had said, she wasn't really freaking out. Her heart wasn't pounding at all, she could breathe just fine, and she hadn't even taken the two Valiums tucked in her purse.

What did that mean? She was doing an amazing job coping with all this. That was real progress. She couldn't wait to tell her therapist. Lucy would be so proud of her.

The elevator was huge, but smelly, and when it stopped on the third floor and a dried twig of a woman was wheeled in on a gurney, Emma realized that it was oversized so that sick and dead people could ride through the hospital. She held her purse close so that it didn't touch the wall and took shallow breaths, hoping not to take in any of the dead people's bacteria. This was a terrible place.

When the elevator doors opened at the lobby level, Emma bolted out and had to stop short to keep from falling on a fat man waiting there in a wheelchair. She turned to Marnie, her eyes wide. "Get me out of here!"

Thank God Dylan had told Marnie to meet him in the outdoor courtyard, away from the smells and germs. As the door opened, Emma sucked in a healthy breath of fresh air, glad to see the pansies and petunias growing around a bubbling fountain. "What a relief," she told Marnie. "Did you see all those sick people in there? Disgusting."

"Dylan said he'd be waiting by the fountain," Marnie said.

They started to circle it, but there was no sign of him. Off to the side was a vendor's cart shaped like a cute little red caboose, and people sitting at a handful of tables and chairs.

One woman sipping coffee looked familiar. "See that woman

with the hoodie around her waist? Who is that?" It was an older woman with short, dark hair. "Oh, wait, that's Ben's mother." Emma waved vigorously, hurrying over to the vendor's cart. "Mrs. McGann!"

Ben's mother turned her worried eyes toward Emma. Wow, she did not look good. She reminded Emma of that ragged stuffed penguin her dog Bitsy dragged around, but she would be happy to see Emma.

I can take over the bedside vigil, Emma thought, picturing herself sitting by Ben's bed, holding his hand as the sun went down, sort of like a sweetheart caring for a soldier in a Civil War movie.

"Mrs. McGann, I am so glad you're here," Emma said. "I came to see Ben, but the nurses won't even tell me how he's doing. I need you to tell them that I'm okay. I have to see him!"

Chapter 46

Dylan Kroger
Good Samaritan Hospital

When Dylan saw the girls talking with Ben's mom, it threw him for a second. Mrs. McGann was *his* family, *his* second mother; what were Marnie and Emma doing with her? Then it sank in. Emma had met Ben's mom, maybe once or twice in Boston. Still, it bothered him, the way Emma acted so bouncy and bright, as if she were hosting another party.

"Dylan, look who we ran into!" Emma reached for the strap of a little top that dangled over her shoulder. She yanked it up, but a second later it fell again. "And guess what? Mrs. McGann says that we can see Ben. Isn't that nice of her? She says she can get us in."

"Mrs. McGann is always nice," he said, turning to Ben's mother, who seemed small and shrinking by the moment, her petite hand clutching a paper coffee cup.

He hated seeing Mrs. McGann this way.

All pink around the eyes, her hair flat and lifeless.

"Mommyson . . ." They hugged, and he could feel her trembling in his arms. That scared him, because she had always been just a mother in his mind—source of compassion and discipline and reason. She was the mom who used to make them turn off video games and go to bed at one in the morning, the mom who had dispensed Motrin when one of them woke up with a fever or leg cramp in the middle of the night, the mom who had made them both sign contracts promising that they would not drink and drive, that if they ever got high or intoxicated they would call her for a ride home. She was Ben's mom, and Dylan never thought he'd feel her quivering like a kitten in the snow.

"I was trying to reach you the entire time we were driving here last night. I was so worried, thought maybe you were with him. That you got hurt, too."

"I'm fine. Sorry. I freaked out when I saw Ben in the ambulance. I just freaked. By the time I pulled it together, I had to go to practice. I'm sorry. How's he doing?"

She hesitated. "Not so good."

Dylan sucked in a breath. "Everything's going to be okay. Ben is one of the strongest guys I know. He won't let a knock on the head get him down."

"It's more serious than that, Dyl." Her bloodshot eyes filled with tears, making Dylan want to squirm. He turned to Marnie. "Would you guys mind getting me a Gatorade?" He nodded toward the vendor's cart, the hidden message being: Get Emma away.

"Sure." Marnie touched the strap of her small leather bag. He loved the way she wore it over one shoulder, the slim strap cutting a diagonal across her compact body. "Come on, Emma."

Dylan turned back to Mrs. M. "What did the doctors say?"

"He's suffered a traumatic brain injury. They . . . they had to remove a piece of his skull."

"Why would they do that?"

"To give the brain room to swell. They can replace the skull later. That's not the big problem. But there's a question of brain damage. It's possible." Kate McGann pinched her lips together, as if trying to suck back more tears. "I'm so worried about him, Dylan. I don't know what I'll do if . . ."

"Hey, don't go there." He dropped her hand and patted her back. This was awkward, treating Ben's mom like a little kid who dropped her ice cream cone. When was she going to pull herself together and be a mom again? "Hey . . ." He shook her shoulder affectionately and smiled. "It's gonna be okay, Mommyson."

"God, I hope so." She sniffed, then let out a breath. "I can't believe this is happening."

"What can I do to help?" He looked at the nearby benches. "Where's Mr. McGann?"

"He went home. You know he can't deal with things like this."

An image of Ben's dad came to mind: Eli McGann leaning over the light table in his studio, strong, quiet, reclusive. When Dylan was a kid, he had fixed on that image, imagined that Eli McGann was the perfect father. That was assuming Ben's dad was so quiet because he was at peace with himself, unlike Dylan's dad, who fell apart when Mom died. At least, that was the way Ginger told the story.

Dylan was just a baby when it happened, so he didn't remember his mom at all. His childhood memories of family swirled around his tired, chain-smoking grandmother and his father, who came by now and then to rail against the "idiot doctors" and "a bloodsucking medical monopoly." But his life had been saved by sleepovers at the McGanns'. He'd loved the way Mrs. McGann had taken over, moving Dylan into their house, giving him the bunk bed over Ben's. He stayed there for weeks, and even after his dad insisted he return home Dylan spent most weekends with the McGanns. He was her second son, that's what she called him, and he loved Ben's mom as if she were his own mother. He had to help her.

"Do you need anything?" he asked. "Need me to drive you around?"

She shook her head. "Thanks, sweetie, but you've got your own commitment with the team. I will need to get around. I suppose I can use Ben's car." She frowned, as if the possibility disturbed her. "But yes, I'll need a car."

From the pocket of his plaid shorts he extracted his keys and split the ring to remove the Ford key. "I think Ben's car is parked in the West End lot. That's near the dorm. The Ford might be a little messy, but it always starts up, and the AC works."

She stared at the key in her palm. "I don't think he'll be driving for a long time, Dyl."

He swallowed over the knot swelling in his throat. Things didn't sound so good. "So you take good care of his car."

Nodding, she slid the key into the pocket of her khaki jeans. "I've been talking with the police. Detective Cody. Did you meet him?"

"Not yet, but I need to talk with him. I'm scared."

"About what happened to Ben?"

He crossed his arms over his chest, not sure how to break this to Ben's mom. "I don't want to worry you more, Mommyson, but these guys, this team, they're relentless. When we talked about it last time you were here, I figured they were just blowhards, but it's worse than that. They targeted Ben . . . and look what they did to him. I'm definitely watching my back."

"Oh, Dylan, you've got to be careful." She grabbed his wrist, held tight. "Call Detective Cody right now. He'll come over and talk with you. You need to go on record with what you know."

"I will. The detective is coming to our practice this afternoon. I'll fill him in."

"Promise me." Her brown eyes pinned him. "Please, don't let these guys intimidate you into knuckling under."

"I would never do that. Not with the way they messed up Ben."

"Who, Dylan? Who did this to Ben?"

"I can't be sure, but this guy on the team, a senior, he's never gotten over the fact that Ben took his spot on first base. Enrico Valpariso is his name."

"And he would brutalize Ben over that? Over who plays first base?" Kate asked.

Dylan shrugged. "That's what I'm thinking. The senior guys, this is their last chance at summer ball, one of their last chances to really shine for the MLB scouts. And with Ben out for a few games, Valpariso gets first base back."

Ben's mom shook her head. "Ben is out for more than a few games. Dr. Pruett says he'll be in a neuro ICU for at least a month, and that's just the beginning. Six weeks rehab after that."

"Really?" Dylan refused to believe his best friend could be out of baseball that long. "Is it really that bad? I can't imagine Ben being out of the game for the rest of the summer."

Kate frowned. "It's that bad." She glanced over at the girls, then gestured toward the hospital door. "Let's go up to the ICU. Ben would want to know you're here for him, and I don't want to leave him for too long. Come up and you'll understand. Our Ben is fighting for his life."

Chapter 47

Eli McGann
Woodstock

The air vibrated with music as Eli paced through the house of glass. Boz Scaggs was singing "Lowdown," and Eli sang along, enraged that Bosley did not receive the accolades he deserved. One of the great works of its time, the *Silk Degrees* album reached number two on the charts, and what happened? Where was Boz Scaggs now?

Probably teaching band in some suburban high school. That sounded familiar.

The song ended and he changed the record, queuing up the Beach Boys' *Pet Sounds,* a masterpiece. Over the years he had played "Caroline, No," so many times that Kate accused him of wearing out the record. As he smoothed a soft cloth over the grooves of *Silk Degrees,* the song "Wouldn't It Be Nice" brought him back to his childhood in Oklahoma, dreaming of escape from a family of rage and a town of football. Memories of summer nights on the football field, running through drills, sweating and falling and getting kicked when he was down. "Nothing like football to fuel a young man's dreams," his father used to say. And Eli would run "Wouldn't It Be Nice" in his head, and plot his escape to a place where a boy could be a man without strapping on ten pounds of gear and banging into other boys like bumper cars.

Next he played Steely Dan's "Bad Sneakers" as he circled

back to the kitchen and examined the bottle of whiskey he'd removed from the cabinet, though had not cracked open. He held the bottle up to the sunlight and examined the hue—a ginger brown? Amber? Cinnamon? He wanted to have a drink, but worried that once he started he would not stop—his usual pattern.

And wasn't it bad enough that he was here, bouncing around the house like a flea, instead of back in Syracuse with his wife and son? Or at the very least on an overcast Saturday, he should be in his studio, cutting or soldering for firing a piece. When he first got home he had pulled in beside the studio and tried to get to work. He had fanned out some old cartoons, some of his most popular pieces built around clear colored jewels and stunning rondels. Tamara would love to have a piece like that for the gallery—simple and salable. But after driving more than six hours, after the sickening abyss of standing by as his son went free-falling through surgery, he didn't have the energy to start a piece.

He had come up to the house with the plan to take a nap. He put on a record to silence the noise in his mind, and now, many songs later, he was pacing the house, revisiting his earlier stained-glass pieces he'd done when they lived in Manhattan. They had held up: a cluster of grapes, a willow tree. His mandala beckoned—a far more complicated design of triangles and circles within a circle that utilized glass he had etched and stained himself. The mandala was a one-of-a-kind piece, a wondrous extension of the better part of himself, his essence. Every glimpse brought new licks of color, fantastic streaks of light given form by geometric shapes. Sheer brilliance.

Standing in its glow, he worried that he no longer possessed the fire to create a mandala.

His art had become work.

The song ended and he released the bottle to put on a Todd Rundgren song, not one of his earlier rocking jingles but the torch anthem "A Dream Goes On Forever." The crisp, lyrical piano could bring a man to his knees. Rundgren was another barely discovered genius, a studio wizard when he produced other musicians' albums. Todd *was* God; unfortunately too few people were believers.

The phone was ringing, which he realized only because he could see his illuminated cell, Kate's name on the screen. He sucked air in through his teeth and answered. "Yes, Kate."

"Ben is in intensive care," she said, launching right in. "The neurosurgeon, Dr. Pruett, said the surgery went well."

"Have you seen him?"

"He looks . . . you wouldn't recognize him, but they say that's normal. There's so much swelling, and all the tubes and wires . . ." Her voice broke, and Eli felt a stab of pain.

"Did he talk to you?"

"He's unconscious. He'll be sedated for the next day, and then they're not really sure when he'll regain consciousness."

"So it's a waiting game now." He pivoted and returned to the nook where the mandala hung, the wood floor sticky under his bare feet. If there was nothing to be done for Ben, he was glad he'd come back home. "You're going to hang out there until he wakes up?"

"No, I'm not just hanging out," Kate snapped. "I'm supporting him, trying to surround him with love and the strength to heal, even if it's on a subconscious level. Eli, they're talking about possible damage to his right eye, and . . . maybe damage to his brain."

"Oh, God." The words squeezed from his gut as he pivoted away from the mandala and stumbled back against a rectangular window. He felt the leading of the panel scrape between his shoulder blades. His weight slammed into the glass piece, pulling one of its anchors from the wall. A hook popped, a cord scraped, and then came the thud of lead onto the floor, the tinkle of breaking glass.

The piece he'd always called "Blood Rose" slammed down beside his bare feet, a smattering of glass tumbled around him like rose petals at a wedding.

And through the slam and clatter, Kate's criticisms strode on, a mad horse galloping through a forest. "I don't know how you can step away at a time like this. He's our son, Eli. He was our baby once, so tiny in my arms. Remember when we did everything for him? Feeding and diapers, twenty-four-seven? Well, he might need us to do everything for him now, too. That might be the case. I pray to God that it won't, but . . ." Her voice caught in a sob.

He slid down, sinking to the floor until he sat in the puddle of glass shards. He was useless. She wanted help, but he had nothing to give. "I can't do this, Kate. I can't do what you expect . . ." His teeth dug into his knuckles.

"You're not doing anything, Eli. I'm doing it all, but that's okay. I'll be a mother, father, and chief bottle-washer for Ben, if that's what it takes to get him through this. I'm going to stay here for as long as he needs me."

Eli wanted to respond, but he could not find the words.

Yes, he was a bad man, a failure as a husband and father. But what Kate did not understand was, though you failed, it did not mean you didn't care.

Chapter 48

Kate
Syracuse

Maybe it was a mistake.

She had let Dylan and Emma visit because she thought it would be good for Ben, that he would feel their presence and know that he was surrounded by people who loved him. However, she had not anticipated the toll that it would take on the nineteen-year-old visitors.

Emma did not last long. Although she had bobbed into the ward with a carefree flip of her blond hair, Emma's demeanor went flat when she stopped at Ben's bedside. "Are you sure that's him?" she had whispered. When Kate nodded, she said, "Hi, Ben. Hello in there. It's Emma. Okay, then. Get better soon, okay?" And she'd pivoted on her lovely heels and run out, shoes clacking on tiles.

Kate watched her leave. "Emma's worried about you, Ben, but Dylan's still here."

More stoic, Dylan had remained beside Ben's bed, shoulders hunched and head bent as if in prayer.

"He probably can't hear you, but you can talk to him if you like." Kate stepped closer to touch Ben's arm, which seemed warmer than before. She sandwiched his hand between hers and rubbed gently. "We know you're tired, Ben. It's okay to sleep. Now's the time to rest."

Hearing Dylan sniff, she turned and found his face dripping with tears. It was all too much.

She touched Dylan's shoulder. "You can go. You have a game today, right?"

Wiping his nose with his wrist, he nodded.

"Okay. I'll talk to you soon, Dyl. And you are going to speak with Detective Cody, right?"

"Right." His voice was hoarse. He touched the bed rail tentatively, as if he were going to say something to Ben. But instead he just sniffed again and headed out.

"People are worried about you, son," Kate said. "We're counting on you to pull out of this."

After a foggy, uncertain interval, Sonny joined Kate at the bedside. "You need to get some rest, Kate McGann. You'll be useless to this boy if you fall apart."

"I know. I just hate to leave him."

"Go, sleep now, while there's no chance of him waking up. Give me your cell and I promise I'll post it at the nurses' station. We'll call if anything changes."

Kate drew in a tired breath. "I'll go."

"Do you have a place to crash? I can look for an empty room."

"I'm going to get a hotel room." She thought of the motel she'd stayed in a few weeks ago. "But I don't think I can check in until four."

"Are you kidding me? I'm sure they can give you a room now. It's not like we got the Sundance Festival going on here."

Kate gave Sonny her cell phone number and extracted a promise that Ben was in good hands. Downstairs at the main lobby a receptionist helped her get a cab, which she directed to Hawthorne Hall, Ben's dormitory. The logical reason was that she planned to take his car from the parking lot, but she figured she should tell the police first. The emotional motivation was that she wanted to get a look at Ben's room in the dorm so that she could picture how the attack had played out.

As she paid the driver she got a glimpse of herself in the rearview mirror—shiny forehead, limp hair, puffy eyes. An unattractive stranger. She needed sleep and a shower.

The lobby desk, which had been manned by a college stu-

dent the last time Kate visited, was now staffed by a student
and an armed security guard. She identified herself to the student and officer at the desk. "Are the police still upstairs? I
wanted to pick up some of my son's things, and I'd like to
speak with Detective Cody."

"Ma'am, we're not supposed to let any visitors in after this
morning's incident," the officer said. "But let me call upstairs
and see what the detectives say."

While he made the call, the female student offered Kate a
seat and some water. "Mrs. McGann, we're all devastated
about what happened to Ben. I'm going into my senior year
and I've never heard of anything like that happening at Cross
College."

Kate nodded. "I hope it's an isolated incident," she said,
and her thoughts trailed off to what Dylan had said about
guys on the team targeting Ben. She had to talk to Detective
Cody.

"Mrs. McGann?" The officer was back. "Detective Cody
said that Chelsea here can escort you upstairs."

Chelsea had a key for the building's elevator, which took
them up to the fourth floor. The doors rolled open to reveal
Detective Cody, nodding as if Kate were an old friend.

"You haven't crashed yet?" he asked. There was a hint of a
smile on his face, and leaning against the dorm wall in his
sneakers and jeans, he seemed younger than his silver hair
would indicate.

"Back at you." She stepped off the elevator, thanking
Chelsea. "I came to pick up Ben's car. Thought I'd give you a
chance to have a look at it first if you think it might provide
some clues."

He rubbed the stubble on his chin. "Not a bad idea. I'll take
a look. Let me just tell the other guys that I'm heading out for
a bit." He walked down the hall, then turned back. "Do you
need a key?"

She started walking behind him. "Ben's friend Dylan gave
me his copy, but before we go . . . I want to see his room."

"That wouldn't be a good idea." His face puckered, as if he

were sucking a lemon. "You don't want to go there, Kate. It's still not cleaned up, and it's an active crime scene."

"This is something I need to do." Glancing away from him, she kept moving down the hall, fairly sure that Ben's room was somewhere in that direction.

"Kate, don't. It'll be too upsetting."

"I'm maxed out on upsetting today. The numbness has set in." She reached the end of the hall, a vacant corner of three shut doors, and turned left toward the male voices. The floor was eerily empty, but then it was the team floor and she knew the players had very full days of drills, batting practice, weight and agility training.

"Kate, stop. Really, I have to insist." Cody walked alongside her.

"Are you going to forbid me to see my son's room?"

"Yeah, if that will stop you."

"It won't."

"There's still some blood."

"Detective, I just saw my son in the hospital and he is so battered he's unrecognizable." Her voice was calm and distant, as if it weren't attached to her. "I can deal with some blood."

The room straight ahead had an open door, but she knew it wasn't Ben's. She passed right by it and saw the next doorway, blocked by a black uniformed cop and a man in a cornflower polo shirt with a gold badge hanging from a lanyard around his neck. Without a word Kate pushed between them and dared to look inside.

Except for the blood on the mattress, the room held no hint of violence. There were no scattered articles of clothing, no bloody bats. Nothing seemed damaged, though there were splashes of black or white powder on the walls and furniture. She squinted. "It looks like someone dumped flour and ashes."

"That's from us." Cody's voice came from behind her. "Forensics dusted for prints. So you've seen it. Are you done yet?"

She ignored him, trying to visualize how it happened in a

logical way. "So all that blood in the middle of the mattress . . . that would be from Ben's head."

"Right." Cody stood beside her; she could feel the electricity of his presence though he wasn't touching her. So he was annoyed about sharing his crime scene; at least there were no patronizing smacks on the shoulder, thank God. "Gibbs, the kid who found him, said that Ben seemed to have fallen back on the mattress, his feet on the floor over the foot of the bed."

"So the attacker would have only had to take a few steps into the room. He could have grabbed one of the bats from that dresser on the right. That's where Ben kept his bats," Kate said, thinking aloud.

"Right. That's consistent with the statements we've gotten."

"He grabbed a bat, turned to Ben, and swung." Kate covered her mouth with one hand. "Of course, I get it. The attacker is a baseball player, someone who knows how to handle a bat."

"Why do you say that?"

"It just seems to make sense; I can picture it. Anyone else . . . me, or the average geek, we're not comfortable with a bat in our hands. I could barely connect with the ball during parents' games in Little League. I wouldn't feel comfortable defending myself with a baseball bat."

"Good point. Do you want to go get that car?"

She stared at the mattress. "Why is there more blood on the near side of the mattress?"

"That would have been Ben's right side, consistent with his wounds on the right side of his head." He drew in a breath, hesitated.

"And . . . what?" she said. "What are you not telling me?"

"We were just talking about that. Most of the population is right-handed, and a right-handed batter swings this way." He took a step back and demonstrated. "So if the righty is facing Ben, he's going to swing like this and strike the left side. But Ben's injuries are on the right."

"So the attacker is left-handed?" she asked.

"It seems that way. Of course, the attacker could swing from his weaker side, but in the heat of the moment, that wouldn't make much sense, would it?"

"A left-handed ballplayer." She closed her eyes, blocking out Ben's empty room. "Okay, then. Have you checked the team roster for left-handed players?"

Cody scratched the stubble on his chin as he gave her a bug-eyed look. "Jesus, Kate, you're worse than my sergeant. You don't just take an isolated clue and run with it. We have some other evidence here that we're following up on; we're building a case. The left-handed thing, the notion that the perp is a ballplayer, that's just speculation right now."

"You're just annoyed because I barged in on your crime scene." She turned from the doorway, noticed the two cops hanging back, watching. She turned her back to them to stare down Cody. "Why is it so wrong for me to get a mental picture of what happened to my son?"

"Sorry, but we don't bring moms in for consultation on crime scenes."

She folded her arms across her chest. "Well, you should."

"Are you ready to go?" he asked.

Somehow leaving seemed to be conceding the point, but she needed to move on, find the hotel, recharge. "Whenever you're ready."

Cody turned to the other cops. "I'm going with her to check over the victim's car. Back in five."

"Do you want us to find Valpariso?" asked the uniformed cop. "Bring him in for questioning?"

Kate froze as the name hit her. "Wait." Her hands flew up. "That's the guy who threatened Ben. Dylan says he was targeting Ben because they had a rivalry for first base. Are you arresting him?"

"Thanks, Wilkins, but not now." Detective Cody glared at Kate. "Again, we're building a case, Kate. We don't jump on any one piece of evidence and make assumptions. If you don't mind, I have a few other places I have to get to before I can call it a day. Come on." He led the way toward the stairs, his long legs swallowing up the floor tiles rapidly.

"Wait." Kate hurried to keep up with him. "If you suspect Valpariso on your own, there's probably more than one piece of evidence here, right? What did you find?"

He descended the stairs without looking back. "Nothing conclusive yet."

"Would you stop being a sourpuss and tell me?"

"Sourpuss? Wow. I haven't heard that word since I was crawling on all fours."

"You're not that much younger than I am, and don't change the subject. What did you learn about Rico Valpariso?"

"If I tell you, will you stop playing Nancy Drew?" He bounded down the second flight of stairs.

"You are a sourpuss. You don't like me stepping in your territory, even though my son is at the center of this case."

"It's because your son is at the center of this case," he said, looking up at her from the landing. "Do you think cops work on investigations involving their own families? The stuff you see on television isn't real. Not to mention the fact that you aren't on the force, and you don't have a PI license."

"Stop making excuses and tell me about Valpariso."

"We found a bloodstained towel in his room, okay? It's being tested in the crime lab to see if any of the blood belongs to Ben."

"Oh, my God. You have to arrest him."

He threw his hands up. "You were going to butt out of this case!"

"I never said that. And Dylan said Valpariso had threatened Ben. Something happened between the two of them at that party last night. Did you talk to anyone who saw it?"

"We got it covered." They had reached the lobby level, and Cody flipped sunglasses over his dark eyes. He stopped at the turnstiles and asked Chelsea to sign Mrs. McGann out of the building, and Kate got directions to the West End lot.

The sun was stifling hot, waves of heat shimmering over the black asphalt. Fortunately, Ben's mandarin-red Ford Focus stood out in the sea of cars. The backseat was littered with take-out menus from Chinese restaurants; the floor held a variety of water and Gatorade bottles, most of them empty. Cody went through the glove compartment, console, and trunk, but didn't find anything suspicious.

A fine pattern of sweat gleamed on his upper lip as he shut the trunk. "You're good to go." He patted the rear end, beside the tail spoiler.

Really, the car was way too flashy for Kate's taste, but right now it was necessary transportation. She climbed into the baking car, pulled the driver's seat up, turned on the max AC, and rolled down the window.

"Get some sleep," Cody said, leaning down to the window.

"Get Valpariso," Kate answered flatly. She didn't know the kid and she was suffering from exhaustion, but this one thing she knew with conviction: He had to be stopped.

Cody sighed, wiping his brow with the back of one hand. "I'll try," he said. "But my job is to enforce the law, not make new ones up."

Chapter 49

Emma
Dining Room, The Regan Hotel

"**I** want to go home." Under the tablecloth Emma dug her fingernails into her palms and smashed her knuckles against each other. She knew her mascara was running but she couldn't stop crying, and one tear splashed on the menu that sat open in front of her. As if she could eat, the waiter had mentioned the specials, Maryland crabcakes and shrimp Caesar salad. After what she'd seen today, she doubted she would have much appetite for weeks. "I can't stay here."

"That's probably a good thing." Dylan closed his menu. "After what happened to Ben I don't know if you're safe here. I'm not sure anyone is. I say you two pack up and head back to Boston after lunch."

"I can't eat," Emma muttered. "I can't . . ."

The waiter came back and Dylan and Marnie ordered stuff while Emma held her water glass in two hands and tried to stop crying.

She had started the day with enthusiasm and strength. She had geared herself up to be Ben's rock, help him get through this difficult time. She had fantasized about climbing into the hospital bed with him and turning toward that crooked smile, those steely gray eyes.

But everything changed when she walked into that hospital room and saw what they had done to him. Barely human now, distorted and freakish. She didn't recognize him at all.

There was no chance of finding Ben in that swollen mass on the hospital bed, that perfect body tagged with tubes and electrodes topped by a hideously swollen head. There was no hope.

Her Ben was gone. Her summer was ruined.

There would be no stolen weekends at Martha's Vineyard. Their week together in Paris after summer ball ended? It would never happen.

"I feel pretty safe here," Marnie said. "It beats dealing with the weirdos I meet on mass transit when I get up at the crack of dawn to open Beantown Grind. I want to stay till tomorrow."

"Marnie, use your head." Dylan tore a roll in half. "What if the guy who attacked Ben goes after someone else?"

"You guys, stop fighting!" Emma protested. "I'm sick about Ben. I didn't recognize his face, and his head . . . his head was so huge. They took out part of his skull." She sucked in a breath, then sobbed.

"They'll replace his skull after the swelling goes down," Marnie said. "Actually, that's pretty cool, the way they tuck it into the abdominal cavity for safekeeping. The nurse was telling me they used to stick it in a refrigeration unit, but sometimes it was lost that way."

"That is so disgusting." Emma gulped some water down, tried to steady her breath. But these sobs weren't the desperate gasps of a panic attack. No, this wasn't her system shutting down over fear; this was emotion, pure and painful. "And you didn't see him, Marnie. If you saw him, you would know. Nothing about this is cool."

"I didn't mean it that way. I know it won't be easy for Ben after he wakes up. People with traumatic brain injury need therapy, and that can be really intense, for years. Even then, most people are altered. I'm not cracking jokes about it, Emma. I'm just saying, it's a good thing they've got ways to treat TBI." The waiter brought her salad, and she stabbed a few romaine leaves. "And I don't want to bail today. I want to stay, maybe see Ben tomorrow."

"Bad idea," Dylan said. "Marnie, think about it, you—"

"I *have* thought about it," Marnie snapped at him.

"Stop! Just stop it." Emma felt a cold tremble shudder through her body. She had just lost her boyfriend, and these two were going to snipe at each other?

"You guys keep bitching at each other and it's not helping me at all. Every time I close my eyes I see him, that bloated face and his head all shaved. I can't stand it. It's gruesome." She tore the linen napkin from her lap and tossed it onto the table. "I'm not going back to that hospital, and I'm not staying here. Keep the room if you want, Marnie. It's paid for till Tuesday. But I am out of here."

Emma shot up from the table and turned, knocking her chair over as she stepped away. Her second step was blocked by a tall man with silver hair. His sneakers and wrinkly shirt seemed sort of shabby for the dining room of the Regan Hotel, but she didn't have the energy to complain. She just wanted to go home.

"Excuse me," he said. "Emma Lenson?"

She paused. "How did you know my name?"

In one quick flick of a hand, he opened a small black leather case to reveal a shiny gold detective badge. "Greg Cody. I'm with the Syracuse Police Department. Would you mind answering a few questions?"

One minute. Just one minute sooner and she would have gotten away before all this cracked open. She bit her lower lip, pressed her eyes closed, and burst into tears.

Chapter 50

Dylan
The Regan Hotel

"I wish Marnie would go back with you," Dylan said as he helped the bellman hoist two heavy Louis Vuitton bags into the back of Emma's Mercedes.

The bellman got a folded bill from Emma; Dylan got more of her whining. "I don't know what I'm going to do without him."

"Don't talk that way. Ben's going to make it through this. You'll see. By the end of the summer we'll be back in Boston, all four of us, hanging out just like last year. That was great, right?"

Emma shrugged, her lips squeezed into a fat pout as she fished in her purse for keys. The purse that matched her luggage, Dylan noticed for the first time. He was glad Marnie had a looser sense of style. Marnie was smarter, more on the ball than Emma.

Marnie . . . in the midst of all the stuff with Ben getting hurt, he'd almost forgotten about catching Marnie kissing Ben. Last night he'd been pissed. So pissed he had considered telling Emma what he'd seen, knowing that she'd throw a major tantrum.

Now he felt pinched by guilt that he even considered ratting on his best friend and his girlfriend. One kiss. Maybe it was just an innocent hug. In retrospect it seemed small and trivial, not even worth mentioning to Marnie.

"Before I go." Emma stood beside the driver's side of the Mercedes, her nose red and moist like a dog's. It was a first, seeing Emma disheveled like this. "I just have to tell you something because I feel so bad about it. I feel like I'm partly responsible for what happened to Ben." She pressed a fist to her mouth. "I feel so bad!"

"Emma, I don't think you went after him with a baseball bat," Dylan said. "Don't blame yourself. Did those detectives twist your words around and make you feel like it was your fault?"

She shook her head. "I was afraid to tell them, but I gave Ben some drugs. I had the bartender make that drink he likes—grapefruit and cranberry juice together, always so healthy—and I crushed up three Valiums and slipped them in."

Dylan blinked in surprise. "Where'd you get the drugs?"

"From my shrink. It was just Valium, but I gave him a triple dose because, you know, he's bigger than me."

"So . . . okay. He didn't know he took the drugs."

"I know, I know, it was a stupid thing to do, but he was so keyed up. I couldn't get him to relax and come dance with me, and that was the whole point of the party. I mean, I drove all the way here for him, but he didn't get that. That was so Ben! Baseball on the brain. I thought the pills would make him kick back a little and have some fun, but it didn't work out that way. Instead, he just took his bats and slipped away while I was dancing. One of the guys, I think it was Kenta, said Ben was just too tired to party on."

"So that's why the doctors say they found drugs in his system."

Emma nodded. "I'm afraid it made him too drowsy to fight back when the guy came in and . . . and it's my fault he's in the hospital now." Her voice was raspy, her chin wobbling as she broke down again.

Dylan hugged her, let her cry against his chest as he thought about Ben . . . poor guy. Did the person who'd attacked him know about the drugs? Ben couldn't fight back because he was smacked on drugs.

Emma trembled against him. "I don't know how I'm going to get through this," she said.

"You'll be okay," he told her. It was a struggle to stay positive with Emma freaking out, but he held strong. "We're all going to be fine; you'll see. Marnie and I are going to get closer than ever because of this, and you and Ben will be back on track before you know it."

She pushed away from him, her eyes glistening with tears as she shook her head.

"It'll be just like before. I promise."

Without a word Emma slid into the driver's seat. A moment later the Mercedes peeled out of the hotel driveway with a squeal of wheels, merged into traffic, and sped down the street.

Chapter 51

Greg Cody
Syracuse

Coach Otis Ramsey stopped tossing the ball long enough to shake hands with Greg Cody. "Did you have trouble finding us?"

"It took me awhile. You're a good hike from the sports complex parking lot."

"Yeah, the baseball clubhouse was built long before that high-tech stuff. It's a stodgy old facility, not the Yankees' clubhouse, but it's got history. Lot's of blood, sweat, and sunflower seeds. I thought you wanted to talk to the players?"

"I'll catch them later. Better to start with you." Realizing that his presence in the team locker rooms would create a stir, Greg Cody arranged to meet Coach Otis Ramsey inside while the players were out on the field for practice. He figured he could get a better read on Ramsey minus the pressure of players, some of whom had probably figured out they were on Cody's informal list of suspects.

"Have a seat," Ramsey said, indicating the two steel chairs padded with vinyl. Ramsey sat behind an old metal desk that probably weighed a ton. "My kingdom for the summer."

"And after that? Are you returning to your job at the community college? Sociology, right?" Cody sat down and the vinyl of the chair made a farting noise as trapped air was pushed out. Charming.

Fortunately, Ramsey seemed too engrossed in repeatedly tossing a ball in the air to notice. "I am looking to make a change in the fall, as I have not been invited back to teach sociology this year. Some deep budget cuts going on there."

"Ouch." Cody stretched his long legs out, stacked his sneakers.

"Tell me about it. My wife is going back to her teaching job. I'm trying to view this as an opportunity to grow. A career shift. I've always preferred coaching to teaching. Been talking to some people about coaching one of the minor-league teams in New York state. Utica, Geneva, Binghampton . . ."

"Moving can be hard on the wife and kids."

"My kids are young; they'll adapt. And I'm ready for it, been working toward it." He dropped the ball into his lap and pointed both hands toward the door like a flight attendant. "This team, this year's Lakers, they were hand chosen to gain the attention of scouts, as well as to kick some ass on the field. These Lakers are supposed to be my ticket out of here. Now a day ago I would have said they are my ticket out, but then Ben McGann got hurt." Otis swirled a Sprite can, took a sip, shook it some more.

Cody was getting distracted by the man's constant movements, like following a kid with ADHD. He flipped through the roster the coach had given him, the batting order, the season stats to date. "But you've pulled together a stellar team here. Some of these guys got nice draft picks. Valpariso, Suzuki . . . Turtle is a solid catcher and you've got strong batting in the outfield." Cody had concocted this assessment with Fitz's help, as Fitz knew a hell of a lot more about baseball and the Lakers. "You've got depth. They're a kick-ass team, even without McGann."

"Ah, but Ben McGann was my centerpiece, the Lakers' keystone—that one piece that you tug out and the rest of the wall comes tumbling down? That's McGann. I honestly don't know how we're going to do tonight with Rico Valpariso back on first base for the first time in weeks. I'm bringing Webber in to play third, which means I have to put Harold or Kroger in the outfield, which I am not happy about. You know I lost two players today; Isaiah Gibbs quit the team."

"I talked with Gibbs in the dorm. He's still in shock."

"I tried to talk him out of quitting, but he already bought his ticket home, and it is *just* summer ball. He's still got a scholarship in North Carolina to go back to. Still, we'll miss him. Good, reliable performer. I'm running out of reliable."

"You couldn't cancel tonight's game?"

Ramsey shrugged. "What good would that do? The other team is already here from Ithaca. We played them last night, beat them, too. I didn't want to mess with the schedule."

Enough with the small talk, Cody figured. He had a case to work. "Coach, I'm sure you've heard the rumors and speculation that McGann was attacked by someone on the team."

Ramsey leaned back in his chair and tossed the ball high. "I've heard it all."

"What's your take on that?"

"It's possible. There isn't a lot of cohesion on a summer ball team, when your players come from all over to play ball. Most of these guys just met each other two weeks ago."

"Do you have a sense of who might have hated Ben McGann so much he'd take a bat to his head?"

The coach shook his head emphatically. "No patience for the personal stuff. I expect my team to be a machine out there. Baseball comes first."

"Still, you must have some sense of their personalities at this point. Allies. Guys that hang together at batting practice."

Ramsey groaned. "You put it that way, I suppose I know something. Half of these players were with me last summer. Turtle, Kenta Suzuki, Dozo. Valpariso was my first baseman, and Will Sager was here for part of the season. Kenta keeps to himself. Turtle is a leader of sorts, but something's little off about that guy. He doesn't keep a friend for long. That group got on okay."

"And then this year you brought in McGann."

"Right. Kroger came with him, sort of to keep the friends together and we wanted McGann that badly."

"Even though you had a solid first baseman?"

"Solid, but not exceptional. And McGann is a lefty." Ramsey sat up straight behind the desk. "Do you understand the advantages of a left-handed first baseman?"

"Don't know that I do."

"It's all about speed. Say you got a play where the first baseman has to field a ball, then wing it over to another base. A right-hander will have to catch the ball, turn his body toward the target, and make the throw. But not a lefty." He stood up to demonstrate. "A lefty like McGann catches the ball, then shoots it over to second or third in a millisecond. It's a thing of beauty. A guy like McGann also has the advantage when you want to pick base runners off first. Catch and tag in one motion. Saves a few seconds, and it gets the out."

"So why doesn't Valpariso decide to own third base? If he's right-handed, he'll have the same advantage there, right?"

Coach Ramsey wagged a finger at him. "You're catching on, and you're correct. As for Valpariso, I don't know his agenda. I'm here to make choices for the team. I'm trying to garner attention for our ball club, raising the bar for all of our players. McGann was the only topnotch player I could woo here. Would I have preferred to bring in a great second or third baseman? Sure. But it boiled down to McGann or no one. Maybe my move backfired, but it was an attempt to push our guys to the next level."

"Ultimately, Valpariso got stuck playing third."

"Which is not a bad position." Ramsey rolled the ball atop his desk, frowning. "And was he happy about that? No. Of course not."

"Was he unhappy enough to take a bat to a teammate's head?"

"I'm not a profiler; just a coach."

"True." Cody sketched a rough baseball diamond in his notebook and filled in the positions with Enrico Valpariso on first. "So I take it you're putting Valpariso back on first. Who will play third base tonight?"

"We're bringing Will Sager in from center field."

"And who takes center?"

"Right now, Dylan Kroger. We've lost Gibbs and so we're down to Kroger and Harold in the outfield."

"You are short."

"At least I've got pitching depth." He swirled the Sprite can again, then pointed it to Cody. "Something I forgot to mention earlier. We had a little incident here Thursday night, a practical joke that went south when the custodian discovered it Friday morning. Someone buttered the stairs outside our locker room."

"Really?" Cody stopped sketching.

"Not sure what they used, but it left the tiles slippery enough to send Seth sliding. He ended up with some bruises, but it could have been worse, and it could have been one of my players. They all have access to the locker room, day and night. Their key cards get them in."

"I don't know if it's related, but I'll see what I can find out. Any other pranks that you remember?"

"Nah. It's been like any other season until this week."

"Thanks for your time." Cody stood up and shook Ramsey's hand. "There are a few players I've yet to interview. Mind if I snag them as they come in?"

"Be my guest. They should be done with fielding practice soon."

While Ramsey made a call, Cody moved through the locker room. The smells of sweaty clothes and floor wax brought him back to high school, the last time he'd had to change clothes in a place like this. Above each locker was a player's name written on masking tape. The locker doors were made of mesh, so you could see through them from most angles, and the disheveled balls of clothes and dirty equipment added to the messy feel of the room.

He strolled down the row against the wall, looking for the name he'd heard over and over again.

Valpariso.

They'd found the bloody towel in Valpariso's room. The girlfriend he'd interviewed was concerned about the threat Valpariso made at the party last night. The best friend had told Fitz that Valpariso had been a problem long before last night. Kate McGann had been all hot to arrest him, and the coach recognized the problem when he brought in another first baseman to take Valpariso's spot.

At the moment, everything was pointing to Valpariso.

He found Valpariso's locker, third from the end of the row. Through the metal grate he could see two game jerseys on hangers. There was the usual jumble of water bottles, socks, and balled-up T-shirts at the bottom, along with a pair of sneakers which Cody assumed Valpariso would wear after practice.

Yes, he needed to have a more in-depth discussion with Valpariso.

Cody slid his sunglasses on and stepped outside. The field was a good quarter of a mile away, up a hill and along a path. By the time Cody got there he was sweating, from the heat, he told himself. Definitely the heat, not the fact that he hadn't been in a locker room in years.

Most of the team was still in fielding position, with Coach Ash pitching to alternating batters. Right now Kroger was up at the plate. Cody's gaze shot over to first base, where Valpariso stood beside the bag, digging his feet into the gravel.

There was the pitch. Kroger hit a pop fly just over second base. Dozo took two steps back from the bag, backed up more, but missed it. Quickly he scrambled for the ball and whipped it to first.

Valpariso caught it, dust curling from his glove as the ball hit just a second before Kroger reached the bag.

"Out at first," Coach Ash called. "And you have to make those catches, Dozo."

Lips puckered in satisfaction, Valpariso tossed the ball back to the coach.

But Cody did not follow the ball. His eyes were on Valpariso, who now pumped his bare right hand into his well-worn glove.

Right-handed.

Which meant Valpariso probably wasn't the one who hit Ben McGann with a bat. A right-handed batter would inflict wounds to the left side of the face.

Damn.

Chapter 52

Rico Valpariso
Syracuse

He owned this spot.

Positioned beside the bag, Rico worked his feet into the ginger-red gravel and socked his right hand into the pocket of his glove. First base fit him. Standing here, the pitcher and the rest of the infield on his right, he felt like part of a well-oiled machine, ready to swing into place when the ball or the runner came this way.

First base was his zone; he owned it. Five feet in any direction and he would snag the ball, whether he had to stretch, jump, or field it on a hop. This was his territory to defend against runners. Their journey ended here.

He anchored himself into position as Coach Ash wound up, snapped the pitch. The batter, Webber, grounded to Short. Kenta shot the ball over, right into Rico's sweet spot. The ball reached first base before Webber was halfway there, but Webber jogged through.

"Don't beat me up now," Webber said as he passed by. "I got no desires for first base."

Rico's head snapped to the left. "Shut the fuck up, Webber."

"At least here I got a helmet on." Kevin Webber's face split in a wide grin, a spiteful smile.

Rico hated Webber. He hated all of them, whiny babies who couldn't stop talking about McGann, big-mouth gossips who sucked their teeth and glowered at him, blamed him. Suspicion was a poison, and they had drunk the Kool-Aid. All of them, joking like he was going to raise a bat to them any minute and start hacking away.

They were trying to ruin this for him, but he would not let them. He was back at first base, back where he rightfully belonged, and these clowns could not deface the purity of that perfection.

While Coach Ash took Harold aside for some instruction, Rico went over to Turtle at second base. "Why is everyone blaming me?" he said. "Why do they think I took McGann out?"

"You hated McGann." Turtle hitched his hat back, staring at Rico like he was crazy. "You threatened him last night, and a lot of people heard it."

"*You* were rolling with him on the floor." Rico felt the heat of anger rising under his skin. "Nobody's looking at you."

Turtle shrugged. "That was different. Anyway, we resolved it."

"This is fucking crazy," Rico growled. He stepped to the side of second base and waved at the outfielders. "Hey! Everyone!" He turned to point to Kenta and Sager in the infield and Dozo, who had his mask off to chug a Gatorade at home plate. "Listen to me, and listen well, because I'm not repeating this. I didn't touch McGann. It wasn't me!"

Dozo nodded and continued drinking, but the other guys just stared at him. Fuck, they wanted to skewer him.

"I didn't do it, okay?" Rico pointed to his head. "Think about it. What player would cripple his own teammate? They say it was some homeless guy, a crazy who made his way into the dorm. Didn't you hear about that?"

People looked down in the dirt, punched their gloves. No one stepped up to support him.

"That's enough, Valpariso," Coach Ash said as he jogged back to the mound. "Let's get our heads into baseball, gentlemen."

Still seething, Rico trotted back to first base. As he got in position something moved behind the plate—a man behind the backstop. Rico squinted, groaning when he saw that it was that detective again. Great. The detective was here to shake them all down. Maybe he'd steal the locker room towels while he was at it. All thanks to McGann.

The Lakers got messed up bad by McGann. Worse than anyone realized. From the day he set foot on this campus, trying to suck everyone in with the nice-guy act, all smiles, and white-boy pep, McGann screwed them over. He wanted to be the star, and he didn't care who he stepped on to get attention. McGann was El Diablo, the devil that made his mother squeeze her eyes shut and cross herself against his evil.

Rico reset his cleats in the dirt as Austin Harold came up to bat. What a joke. Even though a coach was pitching fatties, Harold would probably strike out.

To occupy his mind while Harold choked at the plate, Rico counted the hours till his next cold beer. Nearly two o'clock now, he would have to play it straight until the game at seven, and then two hours. By nine he could have a cold beer in hand if he got one from Dozo or Harold. They both kept some beers in their dorm refrigerators, though Rico didn't have the money for a fridge. If those possibilities came up dry, he'd have to walk to a bodega off campus and score a six.

Because of McGann, he didn't want to chance sneaking off to Aunt Riya's place in town. Although he went there under the pretense of getting a well-cooked meal from Aunt Riya, the free tap beer from the bar was what kept him there most of the night. He had told his aunt he'd be there tonight, but now he didn't want to chance breaking rules and curfew with all these cops swarming on campus.

Another thing McGann had screwed up. Even from the hospital, the guy was still messing up the team, pitting guys against each other because everyone wanted to know who took down McGann. *And too many people have their eyes on me.*

As Harold swung and missed, Rico reached for the gold medal around his neck, Señora de la Alta Gracia. Our Lady of the Highest Grace was the reason he'd come this far. "It is because of La Alta Gracia that you received the scholarship, Enrico," his mother said time and again. "You will be the first in our family to graduate from college. Don't mess it up."

Rico pressed the gold plate between his thumb and fore-finger and sent up a prayer. *Please don't let them find out about me. Don't let them know what I've done.*

Chapter 53

Dylan
Syracuse

Dylan removed three jerseys on hangers, squinted at the labels and hung them back up for like, the eighth time. All the time spent sorting out his locker was just a pretense. He was waiting for the locker room to clear so he could talk to the cop. He wanted to do the right thing for Ben. But it was hard to take the first step.

The tall detective with the silver hair—that wasn't the one Dylan had talked to when the two cops had descended on them during lunch at the Regan Hotel. Dylan had talked to a Detective Fitzgerald, a shorter guy who seemed to care; sort of like a father.

Dylan had liked Fitzgerald. Just his luck the other guy was here in the locker room pulling people aside for statements. The cop vibe on this guy sent Dylan back to his locker, made him wonder if giving up Emma was the right thing to do. He wanted to clear Ben's reputation regarding the drugs, but if he had to tell that guy, he wasn't so sure it was worth sticking his neck out.

Dylan turned back to his locker, weighing his options. With people hurrying off to get batting practice in before dinner, the locker room was emptying out. Only the pitchers, Gilmer and Pettit, were left, comparing injury stories.

Closing his locker, Dylan felt that shot of adrenaline. Time to go for it.

He stepped up to the doorway of the coach's office and the two men turned toward him. "Detective? About the drugs found in Ben's system. I know who gave them to him."

Detective Cody's eyes went wide, but Ramsey crossed his arms.

"Good Lord, Kroger. Please tell me you're not involved. I can't afford to lose another player this week."

"I'm clean, Coach. And I'm not fixing to get anyone in trouble. I came forward because I want to clear my best friend's name and reputation. Ben would never take anything. Not steroids, not speed, and he didn't smoke weed. Ben was straight as an arrow."

"That's a very nice speech," Cody said, "but it still doesn't tell me how he had those sedatives in his system."

"His girlfriend slipped some crushed Valium tablets in his drink. He didn't know about it. She was trying to get him to slow down a little. To relax and join the party."

Cody clicked his pen. "So we have a poisoning and an assault." He leaned his head to the side and stared at Dylan, intimidating.

Dylan wished the other detective was here; Detective Fitz wouldn't put him in the hot seat like this. "Emma didn't mean to hurt him."

"Where did she get the drugs?"

Dylan glanced over his shoulder. No one was listening; the pitchers were engaged in conversation across the room.

"Kroger," the coach prodded, crossing to close the door, blocking out the scattered locker room conversations. "Answer the detective's question."

"I don't know." A small lie. Dylan knew they were from her personal stash. Emma was always talking about needing a Valium. The smallest ripple freaked her out. But he'd heard the rumors about Turtle, and he figured it was time for some payback. "Emma said the drugs came from Turtle. I'm not sure if she bought them or he gave them to her, but he was the source."

"Turtle?" Coach Ramsey yanked his baseball cap off and raked a hand back over his head. "Shee-it."

"Does he deal?" Cody asked.

Dylan shrugged. "That I wouldn't know about. I've tried to stay away from Turtle and Rico Valpariso . . ." His voice trailed off as he caught himself. Turmoil glowered, a hot ball of confusion and blame in his chest as he recalled the way they'd set him up. Christ, they'd had Dylan race across campus to roust Ben. They'd played him for a fool, tried to make him a part of hurting his best friend.

Ben had told him to shut up about it; that no good would come of ratting out the two guys.

But Ben was hurt. Attacked. It was time to talk.

"The hallway outside the locker room that was greased down?" Dylan nodded toward the door. "That was Valpariso's way of setting Ben up. Turturro was in on it, too, and they used me as a messenger." He folded his arms across his chest, wishing he could clam up tight, but knowing that he had to let the story spill out, how the guys came into the weight room, egged him on with the story, sent him running all the way back to Hawthorne Hall to wake Ben up.

Detective Cody remained silent, nonjudgmental as he wrote in his notebook. Behind him, Ramsey jiggled a pencil between two fingers and shook his head. Regretful? Disappointed?

Dylan couldn't tell, but he hoped the coach wouldn't end up pissed at him.

"Oh, God," Ramsey said. "I wish this season was over."

The detective turned to Ramsey. "Did you have any trouble with these two guys last year? Valpariso and Turturro?"

"None at all."

"Well. It looks like you've got some trouble now."

The coach let out a scorching breath. "Are you going to arrest them?"

"Not yet." Detective Cody closed his notebook and glanced over at Dylan. "So, Dylan. You're wise to keep your distance from these guys."

Dylan sank back into the chair, nodded.

"Let me ask you, Detective. You don't think they took out McGann, do you?"

"It's hard to say." Detective Cody scratched the silvery hair behind his ear. "Until we sort everything out, I'd remain cautious. Keep avoiding them, Kroger."

With a nod, Dylan glanced over at the window into the locker room, which had cleared out since their conversation began. Nearly empty, except for Rico Valpariso, his dead-eyed stare piercing Dylan, an arrow laced with malice.

"Shee-it." Noticing Rico at the window, the coach jumped up and eased the venetian blinds down, but not before Dylan caught the hatred there.

The threat.

The promise of violence.

Chapter 54

Kate
Good Samaritan Hospital

Sunday morning was like any other in the hospital routine. Amazing how all the details of an environment came rushing back at you: soft swish of Crocs on tile floor, antiseptic smells, beeping monitors. A new day, a new nurse, but when you stepped up to the bed the same panic rose.

With a deep breath to dispel her fear Kate leaned down to touch his arm—still thick with muscle and heavy bone. Such a strong boy, her son. She thought of all those hours in the high school weight room, following the weight training program prescribed by the coach. Maybe he'd be lifting again, soon. Maybe the doctors were wrong.

"Good morning, Ben. It's a sunny Sunday." She rubbed his furred forearm, hoping for some reaction.

There was none.

She told herself not to be disappointed, but in the back of her mind she had written a scenario of rapid healing that would defy science. Although she told Erin about the extent of Ben's injuries last night after her sister had arrived in Syracuse, she had hoped to enter Ben's room at the hospital this morning to find his swelling down, his face back to normal. She had this wild idea that he would power through the sedatives and awaken just to give them the message that he was fine.

That wasn't happening.

Stupid me, she chastised herself. She knew about hope, fear, anger, and denial. On an existential level she understood what people in crisis went through. She'd just never lived it before.

"Aunt Erin is here," she told him. "Right now she's back at the hotel, but she'll be here later. She needs to catch up on her sleep. Do you know it takes more than six hours to drive from Baltimore to Syracuse?"

She rubbed his arm, which was warmer than her cold hand. "Are you warm enough? Do you need another blanket?" She glanced up at the curtain that had been drawn between Ben and the next patient, whom two nurses had been working on when she arrived. The patient was an older man, unconscious, and they were turning him in the bed. "They keep it pretty cool in here, especially when you're not moving around."

The breathing apparatus made a whooshing sound as it pumped oxygen into Ben's lungs, and the other monitors showed jagged lines for pulse and blood pressure. Kate watched the electronic peaks and valleys, thinking that this was Ben's only expression right now. His steady heartbeat.

"How's it going?" The curtain billowed and the nurse who had greeted her today approached. The big-boned blonde named Diana hung a bag of clear fluid on the pole at the far side of Ben's bed. "This is just saline, but right now he's on a morphine drip. Dr. Pruett wants us to start switching him over to something milder, tramadol, later today."

Kate nodded. "Did you notice any change during the night?"

"No. Notes from the last shift said he had a quiet night."

"I was hoping he'd regain consciousness."

"Oh, no. That wouldn't be good." Diana looked up from the IV tubing. "He needs rest, and if he were awake right now he'd probably have a hard time managing pain. Let the morphine do its job, and give him a little time, Mom. In fact, I was going to bring a chair in for you, but really, I don't want to encourage too much stimulation for him right now. So, while you're welcome to visit, I'd recommend keeping it to short periods." She nodded toward the double doors. "And there's always the visitors' lounge outside. If you feel compelled to be nearby, you can spend as much time as you want out there."

Kate squeezed Ben's arm. Although she had errands to run, she worried about being too far away. She was Ben's advocate here; he couldn't speak for himself. "I'll wait outside until my sister gets here," she told the nurse. "But if anything changes, you'll come and get one of us?"

"Absolutely."

When Kate went back to the waiting room, Erin stood talking to a nurse outside the double doors. Her chin-length, straight hair was now highlighted so much that she was no longer a brunette, but a blonde with honeyed bronze streaks. Kate had noticed it immediately last night, but there'd been no time to comment on it with the other matters weighing in for discussion. Now she couldn't resist. "Hey, blondie," she said, moving to the counter beside Erin. "Have you revamped the face of health care yet?"

"Do you know this woman?" asked Isabelle, a petite nurse with fat red lips and black hair pulled back in a twist. "She's not here ten minutes and already she's making phone calls about getting better furniture for the visitors' lounge."

"I see you've met my sister," Kate said. "Causing trouble already?"

"I'm trying my best, but so far I haven't been able to get through to the mayor's office for the city of Syracuse." She glanced at the wall clock over the desk. "Might have something to do with the fact that it's a Sunday morning. I'll try him later." She hung up and smiled at Kate—the professional, I-can-do-it smile. "Can I heckle the boy now?"

"No heckling today. They want him to stay unconscious and unaware of pain."

"That's what Isabelle said. Sounds like we won't be playing Scrabble today."

It was just like Erin to remember that Scrabble was one of Ben's favorite games. "Apparently not while he's on morphine," Kate said. "Do you want me to go in with you?"

"I'll be okay. You go, take care of your errands." She lowered her voice, nudging Kate. "Buy some clean underwear, will ya?"

Chapter 55

Marnie
Syracuse

S he refused to meet him in Hawthorne Hall. Not that the sight of blood freaked her out or anything like that, but she had her reasons. She didn't want to encourage Dylan's fantasy that he actually had a chance of getting her in bed, and it seemed disrespectful to Ben to be meeting right next door to his room. But she didn't use those excuses. "They beefed up security in the dorms, right?" she had said. "We don't even know if they'll let me in."

Instead they met in the Franklin Library in the shadow of a statue of Benjamin Franklin. From a distance old Mr. Franklin seemed to have a bowling ball at his feet; up close she realized it was a turkey. Weird. She wiped the sweat from her upper lip and welcomed the cloud of cool air from the library door.

The guard at the desk told her she could enter if she signed in and showed him a valid ID. She showed him her Massachusetts driver's license and filled out a line in the log book, signed in at nine-twenty, and wondered how long this would take. She wanted to get this over with; she wanted to be straight with Dylan. Right now, guilt was eating away at her because her feelings didn't match her actions, and she hated being a fraud. Guilt painted everything a mucky brown. It made her grouchy, made her bite her nails.

"Hey, Marnie." He was waiting by the magazine carousels at the front of the library, just as he'd said. The baseball shirt he wore emphasized his flat chest and spare shoulders. Dylan was one of those naturally skinny guys who had to work at bulking up. Some of his damp curls fell into his pale blue eyes this morning. He seemed young and fresh.

He made Marnie feel so old.

"I found a spot upstairs where we can talk." He motioned her toward the end of the great room. "The elevator is this way."

She looked around. "Can't we talk here?"

He pressed the up button. "It's more private up on the fourth floor. Besides, my stuff is spread out."

Private . . . that was the last thing she wanted with Dylan. Besides, the library was so empty you could probably hear the dust mites working if you listened hard.

Inside the elevator, he slipped an arm around her waist and pulled her against him. "We never get to be alone like this."

And that's for a reason, Marnie thought as she put a hand up to his chest. Didn't he realize that all of their "dates" had been foursomes with Ben and Emma? That the few times they had been alone had happened because Dylan had insisted on seeing her home or had waited for her outside one of her classes at BC? "Dylan, not now," she said, relieved to hear the hum of the opening elevator doors.

Stepping out of the elevator, she thought it might be a good idea to use conversation to keep some distance between them. "So I've got to head back to Boston tomorrow and get back to work," she said. "With Emma gone, I wasn't sure how I could get back. Didn't think about that when I told Emma I was staying. My bad. I thought I'd have to take a bus, but I found a flight for a hundred and ten dollars. Not as expensive as I'd thought it would be, but my mother is mad, since I had to put it on her credit card. I'm going to pay her back, of course, but she still thinks it's a waste of money."

"What time is your flight tomorrow?" he asked as he pointed to a wall lined with doors.

"Leaves at seven-thirty p.m."

"So you can come to the game. We play early on Monday."

She shook her head. "I stayed on for Ben. He really needs us now."

"I know, but that doesn't mean you have to miss my games." He opened a door marked OCCUPIED and there was a tiny study room, a cell, but for the single window that looked out over the campus. His backpack, a paper take-out cup, and a bottle of Gatorade sat on the single desk that filled the space.

"Kind of nice, right?" he said as he closed them in.

The click of the door latch was a sickening sound. Marnie felt trapped in a prison of her own making. "Yeah. I guess this would be a great place for someone to study."

Dylan touched her shoulder as he shifted over to the desk. "I brought you some coffee." He picked up the cup, frowned. "It's sort of cold now. Sorry." He pushed the items to the side and perched on the desktop.

"That's okay." Her stomach couldn't take the acid right now, but she recognized the thoughtfulness that went into his actions. Dylan was a sweet guy, who really liked her. There'd never been a question about Dylan; the problem was that Marnie didn't feel that way toward him. The problem lay in her own lack of thunder and lightning.

She went to sit down opposite him in the chair, but he reached down and grabbed her hands. "Don't sit there. Come here."

And in a heartbeat she was in his arms, clamped in by his legs. She could feel him hard against her stomach as he burrowed his face to her neck. "Dylan, no. I'm sorry, but I can't. I can't do this."

"It's okay, Marnie," he whispered, his breath hot in her ear. His hands smoothed down her back to cup her butt, sending a shiver of revulsion through her. "I won't make you do anything you don't want to do. I've always respected that, right? Just relax, okay?"

"I can't." She twisted out of his arms, pushing back from his shoulders. "I can't be your girlfriend, okay? I just can't. I'm sorry, Dylan, but I don't feel that way about you."

"What?" His voice was small, childlike.

"I can't be your girlfriend. We—" She waved a hand between the two of them. "We're not a couple. It's just not working."

"Don't say that." He reached for her shoulders, his face awash with an earnestness that clutched at her heart. "We can make it work."

"No, Dylan. I'm sorry, really sorry, but we can't because it's not working for me. You're a really nice guy, a sweet person, and I'm sure lots of girls out there would flip if you even looked at them. But it's not working between us."

"You're breaking up with me? Just like that? I mean, don't I get a second chance?"

"There is no second chance." At Dylan's startled reaction, the shine of tears in his eyes, Marnie's right hand was at her mouth, her teeth closing on the fingernail of her pinky. Desperate times called for desperate measures. "There's no second chance because you didn't do anything wrong in the first place. I'm the fuckup, Dylan. It's me, not you. I wish I felt differently, and believe me I've tried to find . . . something between us. Some chemistry. Something. I keep trying, but . . ." She shrugged. "I'm sorry."

He covered his mouth with one hand, thoughtful. "Is this because I'm a scholarship student?"

"Dylan! That's not like me. Besides, I'm a scholarship student, too. Why would I break up over that?"

"Some girls want guys with more. Guys with successful parents, fathers who are doctors. Guys with money in the family."

She shook her head slowly. "God, have you seen the way I dress? I don't aspire to be some doctor's wife."

"That's a relief," he said, his tone easing. "Because I'm not going to be a doctor."

Her heart sank. "Dylan, no. I'm sorry."

"Come on. Why do you have to decide everything today? Don't ruin my summer, Marnie."

It struck her that Ben's summer was pretty much ruined; but

Dylan seemed to have forgotten about his best friend. "I don't mean to hurt you," she said. "Especially knowing how upset you must feel about what's happened to Ben."

"Well, yeah." He closed his eyes, lowering his head as if in prayer. "Ben is another issue. But . . . don't distract me, Marnie. Can't you see I'm trying everything to hold on to you?"

Her mouth felt pasty, her lips dry and sore, and when she brought her fingers to her mouth she recalled how Ben had kissed these same lips. She was such a fraud.

"Can we just let things ride? Give it some time," he pleaded.

"No. No, Dyl. I'm really sorry." Her legs wobbled beneath her as she evaded his reach, maneuvered around the chair, and fled from the airless cell. She could feel people watching as she raced past the elevator and bounded down the stairs. Let them stare. One more minute in that cell and she was going to explode.

Please, God, let him get the message. Help him accept the way things have to be.

She sent the impromptu prayer past the statue of Ben Franklin and his turkey, over the crown of foliage, and up to the blue sky. But as she walked briskly across the campus Marnie recalled Dylan's eyes, that pinched look of pain, abandon, and determination.

Dylan wasn't giving up anytime soon.

Chapter 56

Greg Cody
Syracuse

As Greg Cody moved to a shaded picnic table in the park overlooking Cayuga Lake, he wondered why he always pulled the weekend duty when the weather was so nice. Out on the lake a team of divers searched for the body of a boater who had fallen in while trying to drop anchor early this morning. The dispatcher had received the call of alarm just after three a.m. Patrol cops had responded immediately, putting search boats out, though the divers couldn't go in until after sunrise since this part of the lake was known for its dense aquatic plant life, likely to snag even an experienced diver.

As far as Cody could tell from the statements of the witnesses—three women and two men, all in their thirties, all who seemed sick about the missing man, Buford Monroe, "Buddy" as they called him—there'd been no foul play involved in the incident. Just a lot of beer and not enough life vests.

Whatever happened to boating safety?

"But Buddy could swim," the girlfriend had said. "He didn't need a life vest."

Apparently he did, Cody thought as he gazed out at the three boats, looking for some signal that they'd found the body in the thick underwater weeds. Still nothing.

He'd have to wait it out until they came up with Buddy. Might as well make good use of the time.

He leafed through his notebook, looking for loose ends to

follow on the McGann case. No use following up on the evidence from the crime scene, as the county lab was all but closed on Sunday.

There was a bit of a delay getting the records of who had passed into the dorm through the turnstiles, as the college's tech services department was also closed over the weekend. He did hear from the head of security that the guards had monitored videotape from the emergency exits of the building, and no one had passed in or out of them from noon Friday to noon Saturday, except for Fitz and the resident assistant checking them out.

He flipped to Dylan Kroger's statement from yesterday, that McGann's girlfriend secretly gave him drugs she'd gotten from Turtle, Joseph Turturro.

That Turtle was a pain in the ass. Flip and obnoxious when Cody interviewed him. A real snapping Turtle. He said he had put his own lock on his dormitory door because he had a bad experience with someone rifling through his stuff last year. When Cody mentioned that his was the only room that hadn't been searched, Turtle had countered that he wasn't going to let the cops in without a warrant. "I don't roll over like these Barbie dolls."

Yeah, a royal pain in the ass.

And then there was the girlfriend Emma, the dame who slipped McGann a Mickey, something right out of a Nick and Nora movie. Cody had worked cases that led to a female perp; he'd arrested women for assault and manslaughter. Really, Emma Lenson didn't strike him as the type. The girl was too soft around the edges to whack her boyfriend with a stick. Stereotype, yeah, but she might break a nail swinging the bat. Still, no reason not to follow up.

He flipped back through his notebook to the cell phone number Lenson had given him, gave her a call.

"Hello?" Her little voice was about as enticing as a lizard; he realized she couldn't tell who was calling from the caller ID.

"Good morning, Emma. This is Detective Greg Cody from

the Syracuse Police Department. How are you doing this morning?"

"Oh. Um . . . I'm okay. I thought I'd never make it home yesterday. I was so scared. After what happened to Ben, I didn't feel safe there."

"I can imagine. Emma, I'm following up on the conversation we had yesterday . . . a few things I forgot to ask you. Not sure if you heard, but the hospital detected some drugs in Ben's system."

"Oh. Yes, I did hear something like that. A rumor."

"It's surprising, because everyone we talked to said Ben didn't do drugs. His mother says he didn't even like taking over-the-counter meds for a headache. So it's really got me scratching my head here, trying to figure out what prompted Ben to go so far off track."

"Ben was completely straight. He was always careful about things like that," she said.

"Any idea what happened the night of the party?" he prodded.

Silence for a beat.

"Okay, I'll tell you. I was the one who gave him the drugs—three Valium tablets. I put them in his drink; he didn't know. He would never have taken them, but he was tense and not having fun at my party. I wanted him to relax a little. But I swear, I didn't mean to hurt him in any way. I didn't think anyone would ever find out. I mean, who goes to sleep and wakes up all swollen and unconscious in the hospital?"

The paradox of "waking up unconscious" was not lost on him, but he let it go since Emma was on a roll. "Where'd you get the drugs, Emma?"

"From my pharmacy. I've got a prescription for Valium."

"I don't have to tell you that his reflexes were probably compromised by these drugs."

"I only gave him a few. He should have been able to fight back and defend himself."

Maybe his attacker expected more of a fight, Cody thought.

Or . . . maybe Ben's attacker knew his reflexes would be diminished. Could he have underestimated Emma? Misjudged her?

"Let me ask you, Emma, have you ever played softball?"

"What? What kind of question is that?"

"Do you work out?" Cody asked.

"Are you kidding me? I work out with one of the best personal trainers in Boston. People would kill to have a session with Andre, and I get to work with him twice a week. I never miss it."

Cody's lips curled; he couldn't resist. "So . . . you're strong enough to swing a bat."

"What? I can't believe—" Emma's voice was muffled.

Suddenly an older woman's voice came on the line. "That's enough, Detective. Any further discussions with Emma will have to take place with her attorney present."

The line clicked off, and Cody dropped his phone away from his ear and let out a full belly laugh, so rollicking that the volunteers waiting in the ambulance looked over from behind the windshield. He was still laughing when his cell phone buzzed, the sergeant on the boat letting him know they'd found a body.

"I'll call the family, see if someone can meet us at the ME's office," Cody said. The coroner's report would wrap up Buddy's case.

Sending him back to figure out who had attacked Ben McGann.

Chapter 57

Kate
Syracuse

Heeding her sister's advice, Kate had driven to a nearby Target and purchased underwear and some simple clothes—cotton shirts and capri pants—to last a few days. She'd put together toiletries and grabbed some Coffee-mate. After Target she located a bookstore, where she found *Head Cases* by Michael Paul Mason and *In an Instant* by Bob and Lee Woodruff, only two of the five books she'd placed on her wish list after researching traumatic brain injury on Erin's laptop. It was a start.

Zipping along in Ben's lipstick-red Ford, she made it back to the hospital in minutes, even though she had not been summoned back by the phone call of her latest fantasies.

Your son is awake. He's awake and he'll be fine.

The more Kate had read from medical Web sites, the more she realized how fantastic that scenario truly was. Yes, people awakened from surgeries and comas every day. But when patients with traumatic brain injuries returned to consciousness they were significantly different, changed people, and she worried at what or who Ben might become.

When her cell phone jangled as she pulled into the hospital parking lot, she breathed in hope for the impossible call but steeled herself when Detective Cody was on the other end.

She really wasn't in the mood to talk to him. After talking with Erin last night she felt like it was better to get beyond thinking about the actual attack. "Do you have good news for me, Detective?"

"Only if you like Italian food. There's a restaurant two blocks from Good Samaritan, Mario's. I was hoping to meet you there this evening. I'd buy you dinner if you answer some questions for me."

"I'm sorry, but I'm not in the mood for going out to dinner. Besides, I need to stay near Ben."

"You'll be a couple blocks away, and you'll need to eat sometime."

"I'm eating just fine. My sister arrived last night, and she's forcing me to take care of myself."

"So she can stay with Ben while we talk."

She turned off the engine, the air suddenly stifling in the car. "I'd rather not."

"And I'd rather not conduct an investigation in the intensive care unit. Medical personnel get hinky about that sort of thing, and I prefer to give the patients their rest. I'll meet you at the hospital and we can walk to Mario's."

"Fine." She shouldered open the door. "If you think it's safe to be out in this neighborhood at night."

"Very funny. I'll be there around seven."

Chapter 58

Marnie
Syracuse

Marnie tipped back in the vinyl chair so that sunlight from the windows behind her fell on the open pages of *To Kill a Mockingbird,* the part where Atticus pushes back his glasses and lifts the gun to kill the rabid dog. This was her third time reading the book, but somehow it brought her comfort, being in Scout's shoes, knowing that Atticus would do the right thing.

It felt right to be here with Ben, even if he was in a room through those double doors, and that was a security hard to come by since Marnie had arrived in Syracuse. Other times her energy went to tolerating Emma, avoiding Dylan, or finding something to do in the ghastly spacious hotel suite Emma had rented for them.

This morning when Marnie had returned to the hotel, she didn't know what to do with herself. Usually Marnie's life did not contain free time; by daybreak she was at Beantown Grind. When school was in session she went straight to the BC campus from the coffee shop. Now that summer was here, most days she grabbed a quick lunch at the Grind and headed over to Storemart to work the photo processing counter or shelve inventory or—the most mind-numbing of all—scan items at the register. Moments not spent at work or school involved long train or bus rides. Home was just a place to recharge with a quick shower, a pot of mac and cheese, a dive into bed.

Rushed was normal. This elastic span of time stretching across the day—sluggish, syrupy time enough for thoughts to sag and loll—that was bizarre and strange.

This morning she had changed into shorts and a black T for a solid hour on the treadmill. That put a hurting on her feet, which she eased by doing laps in the hotel pool. Slogging through the water, she beat herself up for mishandling things with Dylan. Granted, she didn't initiate anything, but she also did not nix it, and her lack of action lulled him into believing she was his girlfriend.

Big mistake.

She chastised herself for five laps, then let it go. It was over; she had said her piece, and now was time to take action of a different sort. Time to reach out to Ben.

So here she was spending a quiet afternoon at the hospital, which didn't seem to be such a bad place as long as you weren't a patient. She had met Ben's aunt, a compact blonde who was an atomic cloud of energy compared to Ben's mother, Kate, who struck her as a cautious, careful planner. Marnie pictured them as the yin and yang sisters, dark and light, intellectual and impetuous.

Her legs began to cramp, so she shifted in the chair, sliding her feet into the flip-flops on the floor. She turned to the last page of the chapter when she noticed someone coming down the hall. Ben's mother. Today she was dressed up a little more in a loose raspberry shirt with a braided fabric panel for a collar. Something about the collar and the lack of that worn sweatshirt made her look younger today.

Their eyes met, Kate's swimming with disorientation for a minute.

"Oh, Marnie. Hi. I wasn't expecting to see you. I guess I thought you would have headed home."

"Emma left yesterday." Marnie rose, reached into the backpack for Emma's letter. She handed Kate the hotel envelope, bulging with Ben's high school ring and a mundane breakup note from Emma. "She asked me to give you this."

Kate shook the fat envelope. "What's this?"

"Ben's ring is inside, along with a note from Emma."

Kate frowned. "She's ending the relationship?"

"In a pedantic way, yeah. I only read it because she asked for help. She didn't know how to spell 'endeavors.'"

"Why doesn't that surprise me. I have to admit I'm relieved. I never connected with Emma. She was . . . I don't know . . . difficult to engage."

"Same."

Kate seemed distracted, and Marnie wasn't sure if she was lost in thought or subtly checking out her outfit, a black T-shirt smock over a white T and black bike shorts. Marnie was accustomed to the odd stares slanted her way on trains or streets in Boston. She knew her sense of fashion was offbeat, but with a pert nose and heart-shaped face like hers, you had to work to avoid cute.

"So . . ." Kate ventured back. "Did you see Ben?"

"Your sister didn't think it was a good idea, not without your permission. Which I get. She never met me before, and she didn't want to call you and freak you out. So I've been hanging here, which is cool."

"Would you like to see him?"

"I guess." Marnie fought the craving to nibble on her pinky finger and instead twisted the skirt of her black shirt around one finger. "I just want you to know, I was friends with Ben for a long time before Dylan and I started going out. Ben and I started hanging out to study during fall semester, and when it came time to register for the spring we made sure we got a class together. Nothing against Dylan, but Ben is my friend. He's one of the few people at BC that I trust."

Kate nodded. "Thank you. I have a feeling Ben is going to need a good friend in the months to come."

Marnie thought of Dylan. No doubt he would be sticking by Ben. It was going to be awkward and twisted, but she would stand her ground with Dylan, and she would be around for Ben. Right now this was the only place that felt right.

"Let's go see if this is a good time to drop in on Ben." Kate led the way to the nurses' station, where a big-boned, officious nurse said it would be okay, but not to try and wake him right now.

On the way in, Marnie held her two hands knotted together so she wouldn't bite her nails. After seeing the way Dylan and Emma had reacted yesterday, she felt the press of fear. She didn't want to fall apart.

Ben's Aunt Erin was at the foot of the bed with the sheets thrown off Ben's feet. Her fingers squeezed their way up Ben's ankles and calves, as if she were kneading two loaves of bread. "I'm massaging his legs," she said in a hushed voice. "They said it might be good for his circulation."

Seeing Erin work like a sorceress, Marnie snorted. Too funny.

It broke the tension for the moment when she looked up at Ben's face. White gauze circled his head, mummylike, and an eye patch covered his right eye. The bit of face that was exposed was grossly swollen, purple and puffy. It was bad; difficult to see Ben beneath all the swelling and bruising.

Marnie slid her fingers under his hand, squeezed. "Hey, Jock. Catching up on your beauty rest?"

Of course he didn't answer, but that was okay.

Marnie jiggled her fingers under his hand, amazed that she was able to touch him at all. "Get your rest. You're going to need it," she said. "Come September, we've got Economics."

Chapter 59

Kate
Syracuse

Although Kate had been dreading her appointment, a wind of change breezed into the hospital with Detective Cody. His dog-eared notebook and sneakers felt comfortable and familiar, and his presence somehow reminded her that someone else was looking out for Ben, at least in a punitive way.

Greg Cody introduced himself to Erin and spoke with Marnie, whom he'd met the day before. It surprised Kate that Marnie wanted to stay through the evening, but she planned to scout some food in the hospital cafeteria and bring dinner up to the waiting room for Erin.

On the way to Mario's, Kate updated Cody on Ben's status—mostly the sedation that would last until tomorrow. She was still talking when they arrived at a small storefront with a red awning. Inside, the narrow restaurant was dimly lit, the small space punctuated by conversation from more than half the tables adorned with the traditional candles, red carnations, and red and white checkered tablecloth. Although an air conditioner chugged under one window there was no masking the scent of garlic and warm bread. "Welcome, welcome," said a waiter passing by with three steaming entrées on his arm. "Have a seat wherever you like."

Kate declined wine, but Cody ordered half a carafe of red, as well as an antipasto.

"Wine on duty?" Kate asked.

"With the meal, and actually, today is my day off. It's just that I got stuck with the call-out duty, and I got another early call this morning. So tonight, technically, is off the record."

The smell of garlic awakened Kate's appetite as she ordered manicotti, and settled back in her chair. "So how are you holding up, Mom?" Cody asked.

"I'm better with some sleep. It's good to have Erin here. I've been researching Ben's surgery and brain trauma online, trying to get well versed in the field. It's a lot to bear on your shoulders, being responsible for someone else's life. I've never been a health advocate before."

The carafe of wine arrived, and Kate broke down and accepted a glass.

"And what about your husband. Eli, right? Doesn't he want a say in this?"

She swirled the claret liquid and took a sip. "Apparently not. He had to get back to Woodstock ASAP."

"Doesn't your husband's employer give time for family emergencies?"

"His teaching job is very generous that way. Right now he's working on some projects, a self-inflicted deadline, I think. He's a stained-glass artist. But the real issue is that he's a homebody. Slightly agoraphobic."

"Isn't that like being sort of pregnant?"

"Something like that. Eli gets anxious if he's forced to venture too far from home, school, or his studio." She let her gaze slide to Cody's left hand holding his notebook. No ring. "Have you ever been married?"

He placed his wineglass on the table. "How do you know I'm not married now?"

"No ring. And you're having dinner with a victim's mother on a Sunday night. Off duty. Not the act of a married man."

He snorted. "I guess not. My ex-wife and daughter live in New York City, Queens."

"Do you miss it? Being married, I mean."

"I miss my daughter, and I miss New York. I thought I would miss my ex, but once I put some distance between us, far enough to drown out the incessant whine of criticism, I realized I was okay on my own."

Kate picked at the glossy crust of a piece of sourdough bread, admiring Cody for making a move that big. If she'd had proper nerve and sense, she would have put Eli many miles behind her in the past year. The food arrived, and she held her words until the waiter departed. "My husband and I are working on a separation," she spoke into the warm steam from the manicotti dish. "Does that sound cliché?"

"Only if it's followed by a swell of music." He shook some cheese onto his clams in white sauce. "Actually it sounds civilized, to work on it. Most people just argue until one person leaves."

"It's not as civilized as it sounds. We've been together more than twenty years, good times and bad. The past few years things have disintegrated. This summer I realized I'm suffocating, choking."

"So you left?"

"I'm working up to that."

"So you stayed."

"I did. I stayed married but basically alone. That was when I realized the undercurrent, the hidden hook that was keeping me there."

"Ben?"

She shook her head. "Our house."

"You stayed in a suffocating marriage for a house." His bottom lip jutted out as he whistled. "Must be some mansion."

"It's a two bedroom shoebox, but a marvel in its way. It's built into a hillside, and most of the exterior walls are made of glass." Their very own house of glass. "When we first moved in I was worried about people looking in on us at night. As if any human being would end up within a mile of our desolate place."

"So you hung blinds?"

"We loved the light. We'd been in a New York loft before that, a dark apartment that faced an alleyway. To make the most of the light, Eli started creating custom stained-glass pieces. Over the years, he filled every window with art. The house is a masterpiece now, a jeweled box." Sparkling, dazzling, swimming with colors and iridescent light, the glass house had become more than a home; for Kate it had become the embodiment of their marriage.

Was that why she was having trouble letting go of the place? It did seem mercenary to want to hold on to the house, but she couldn't put her finger on the reason why it mattered so much to her.

Kate swirled the wine in her glass. "I must be punch-drunk with exhaustion, telling you this stuff."

"Nah." He put his fork down, surprisingly comfortable with the conversation. Kate figured that he'd probably heard it all, especially as a cop in New York City.

"I didn't even tell my sister until she arrived last night. It's the kind of thing that's hard to bring up in a phone conversation. *Oh, by the way, my marriage is over.* How do you segue to that?"

"Well, there's always the opening line. You start with: *I'm afraid I have some bad news.*"

"There's that." She swallowed a bite of food, considering. "Or maybe I should have said: *After years of torture, I've got some good news.*"

He laughed at that.

"That was easy. I should have said it years ago." She put her fork across her plate and pressed the napkin to her mouth. "Thanks for the distraction, Detective. So . . . on to the unpleasant business. Are you close to arresting someone?"

He rubbed his jaw, leaning back in the chair. "Still looking at two Lakers players, Turturro, the catcher, and Valpariso."

Kate folded her arms, trying to temper her annoyance. Cody should have locked this guy up already. "Valpariso is the one you want. He threatened Ben, he had a bloody towel in his room . . . what more do you want?"

"For one, I'd like to know where he got a pair of surgical gloves. And if he bothered to toss the gloves and a shirt into a washing machine, why didn't he throw in the towel, too? Pardon the pun."

"Wait, this is something new to me. What did you find?" She listened carefully as he described finding a pair of surgical gloves and a size large Lakers practice shirt in the third floor washer. "And you say Valpariso lives on the third floor?"

"Yeah, but you can't count that. There's no laundry room on four, so those guys have to use the one downstairs."

"Cody . . . Greg. Please. Everything points to Valpariso, and he's got the motive. He wanted first base."

"But Valpariso is right-handed, and Ben's wounds indicate that the attacker was left-handed."

"That is so frustrating." Kate finished her wine. "So what left-handed suspects are you looking at?"

"There's the catcher, Turturro. According to Kroger, Turtle and Valpariso had banded together against Ben."

Kate bit her lower lip. "Ben mentioned some trouble when I visited recently."

"Apparently, the catcher and the former first baseman staged a trick to get Ben out of the lineup. That misfired and injured a janitor instead, but Kroger is still upset about it."

She wished Dylan would talk to her about it. "So you're going with Turturro? I take it he's left-handed."

Cody nodded. "A lefty, and he's a big, strong guy. He's evaded a room search since he's got his own lock on the door. Something suspicious about that. Plus he has a record. Was brought in as a minor for drug and alcohol possession in some small Pennsylvania town. He may have provided Emma Lenson with the drugs that doctors found in Ben's system."

Kate put a hand to her chest. "Emma gave my son drugs?" She lowered her voice. "Were they doing drugs together?"

"The girlfriend copped to sneaking drugs into Ben's beverage."

"Actually, she's not his girlfriend anymore. She had Marnie drop off a note. A 'Dear John' letter."

"Typical. Now when I talked to Emma Lenson, she said she got the Valium from her stash. But Dylan Kroger, who tipped us off in the first place, claimed that Lenson bought the drugs from Turtle."

"Do you think Emma and Turtle plotted together against Ben?"

"My take on Emma Lenson? She's not a likely coconspirator. The girl can't see past her next manicure appointment."

"That's a bit of a stereotype, Detective," Kate said sternly. "Though in Emma's case, you may be right. And what was Turtle's issue with Ben?"

"Well, most recently they argued over the Blue Thunder, the bat you mentioned? Apparently Ben said the other guys could use it, then reneged on his promise."

"That stupid bat." Kate's fingers dug into the checkered tablecloth. "Where is it now? Do you have it with the evidence?"

"It wasn't one of the bats our forensic investigators found in his room. Any idea where it might be?"

She shook her head. "If Ben was attacked over a goddamned wooden baseball bat, so help me, I'll . . ." She bit back the ending, not wanting to go on record as vowing to tear a young man's limbs from his body. The logic was wrong, violence breeding violence—and yet she was beginning to understand the biblical law of retribution: An eye for an eye, a tooth for a tooth . . .

"Easy, Kate. You don't want to go there."

"Normally I subscribe to nonviolence. I'm a peace-loving person. Mahatma Gandhi said: 'An eye for an eye, and soon the whole world is blind.' Or something like that. And the man had a point. But as a mother, I'm determined to punish Ben's attacker. I want to see him suffer."

"So let him suffer through the criminal justice system. Trust me, Kate, I didn't start doing investigations yesterday. I'm on this."

She hoped he was, because she would never be able to sleep at night if the beast capable of such violence was free to walk the streets. "Don't let this happen again," she told Cody. "I'm counting on you."

Chapter 60

Greg Cody
Syracuse

Goin' fishing.

Cody didn't much like being in limbo on a case, but when you had to wait for things like lab results, better to go fishing than to sit at your desk and string paper clips together.

Which brought him to the Lakers' final game in their series against Ithaca, a day game so that the boys from the visiting team could catch their bus home. A one-thirty game on a humid, eighty-degree Monday. Cody was in for some sunburn and heartburn if he ate another one of those dogs with the works. Now that was good old-fashioned, smelly, sweaty base-ball. He liked the game, but in some ways it was a relief that he didn't arrive until the sixth inning; too hot in this stark mid-day heat. The bleachers were hot to the touch and he had to buy a Lakers hat from the concession stand just to keep the sun out of his eyes. The stands were quiet, nearly empty, though that was no surprise. Who could attend a ball game on a Monday at lunchtime?

Cody noted the way the coach had switched his players around to cover the hole left by McGann. Valpariso to first, Will Sager to third, Dylan Kroger to right field. Today south-paw Tobey Santiago was pitching. Nothing revolutionary.

Ithaca had runners on first and third, with a hefty batter at the plate. Cody sized him up as a potential home run hitter. Santiago threw a ball. On the pitch the batter smacked the ball, sending it sailing out to right field, where Dylan Kroger ran backward, stopped, ran back again. He seemed to lose the ball in the sun as he squinted below his outstretched mitt. Suddenly, he dove to the right, narrowly making the catch.

"Nice one." Cody clapped.

Kroger scrambled to his feet and shot the ball in, but after tagging up, one runner scored and the other was safe at second. Still, considering the sun and heat, not a bad play. Kroger may have saved his position off the bench.

"Looks like we're getting our money's worth," Cody told the Lakers fan sitting off to his left, an African-American man wearing the team cap and dark glasses.

"Looks like," the man agreed.

Santiago struck out the final batter and the Lakers jogged into their dugout. As the teams switched, Cody unfolded the seven-page printout from his bulging notebook—the list of times that residents and visitors checked into the Hawthorne dormitory in the twenty-four hours surrounding the attack. The list had been e-mailed to him early this morning by Devin Mains, the campus director of security, and the roster of names was extensive. Campus security required students in the dorm to scan in with their ID cards; any other students or visitors were required to sign in and leave their ID down at the desk. Not a bad system, as long as you could trust your residents, which was one of those sticky wickets of campus security. You had to allow students access, but what if one of those students was a security risk?

Cody had spent the morning checking out the nine nonresidents visiting the dorm that night. All the visitors had campus ID, so the rumor of an anonymous psycho stalking students— as had been circulating on campus—could be dispelled.

Four of the visitors were students meeting for a Bible study in the second floor lounge. Cody interviewed two Bible study kids at a deli on campus, and they seemed legit. "We were really scared when we heard about the attack," the girl, Charlotte, had said. "We're grateful he didn't come after us." That

group had signed out by ten-forty p.m., hours before the attack.

Two guys had signed in to play a computer game called
"Gothic Warcraft." "We were running a quest, and though
you meet online we always feel our pack has more power
when we're in the same room," said Brandon, the student
Cody had hooked up with in the dean's office. He was on campus to conduct summer tours for the month of July, and he
told Cody that a few kids on his tour had asked about the attack. "This is really more excitement than we've had here
since I was a freshman and the cafeteria food service went on
strike," Brandon said. This kind of excitement Cody didn't
need.

The remaining three visitors were young women signed into
three different players' rooms around the time the party would
have been winding down, and none of them signed out until
after four a.m., long after the attack. Intrigued, Cody checked
on the dorm policy, which specified that a resident could have
an overnight visitor as long as the visitor did not stay more
than one consecutive night. So overnight honeys were okay
with campus security; what about Coach Ramsey?

In any case, the young men with female visitors were Will
Sager, Trevor Dozneski, and Kenta Suzuki. In some ways the
girls could be alibis. He would have to locate and interview the
three women.

Although he had a few more calls to make, Cody considered
the guests to be clear. That left the residents of Hawthorne
Hall, and here Cody had a long list of names compiled from
each time a resident swiped into the building.

As Cody saw it, the only downside was that he couldn't tell
when residents left the building, as they weren't required to go
through turnstiles on their way out. That meant the DA
wouldn't be able to place any one person in the building at any
given time, though they could show proof that a person en-
tered.

As Turtle walked over to the batter's box Cody started

checking off names on the list that he recognized as players. He wanted to see who came back to the dorm after the party. Or who didn't even attend the party. He hadn't thought of the possibility of someone being pissed because he felt excluded by Emma Lenson.

Turtle had one of those interesting batting styles: butt out, bat sticking high up as if he meant to poke a cloud. Today the stance didn't work for him, as he quickly struck out. Turtle kicked at the dirt, muttering something about "useless" as he returned to the dugout.

Cody went back to the dorm list as the game moved quickly: three up, three out. Sometime during the next inning his cell phone rang, and Samira Goldwyn told him she had some results from the tests they'd run. Cody fished out a pen to take notes.

"The objects found in the washing machine, let's see . . . there was a pair of surgical gloves, a gray T-shirt with the Lakers baseball emblem on the front. Apparently those objects were run through a wash cycle, though it doesn't appear that detergent was used. We found dilute traces of blood on the items—Ben McGann's blood."

"So our guy is smart enough to know he had to get rid of the bloody evidence," he said.

"Can you identify who the shirt belonged to?" Samira asked.

"That shirt belongs to every player on the Lakers team. It's a practice shirt. One of the guys told me each player is issued three at the beginning of the season, and a large could belong to just about anyone."

"You'll have to keep digging, then."

"How about the towel? A small white towel found in Valpariso's room?"

"Yes, I have it. We know that it's the blood of one person, a male, and it didn't come from Ben McGann."

So Valpariso might have been telling the truth about the nosebleed. But Cody had looked into the causes of nosebleeds, and while some were random, others were caused by high blood pressure. Which could be brought on by stress or anxiety.

Cody's gaze moved over the field until he found Rico on deck, digging into the gravel within the lime-lined circle. Rico cocked the bat over his right shoulder and swung right-handed, the way Cody would swing if he got a crack at a pitch. The right-handed thing bugged Cody. Otherwise, he liked Valpariso as a suspect. The kid had motive, he'd made some threats, he even seemed to scare some of the other guys on the team. And maybe his bloody nose had been brought on by stress in the aftermath of the attack.

Ithaca's floundering pitcher had already walked a batter. The coach called him off the field and brought out a fresh player, a southpaw. The theory being that right-handers like Valpariso found it more difficult to hit a ball pitched by a left-handed pitcher. After a few warm-up pitches, Valpariso headed over to the batter's box . . . but he didn't stop.

He moved to the box on the catcher's right, dug his cleats in, and swung the bat over his left shoulder. He was going to bat left-handed.

Whoa.

A switch-hitter.

Cody squinted into the sun; he had to see if Valpariso was any good left-handed.

The first strike sailed past him.

The second ball seemed low, but it veered up at the last minute and Valpariso swung. With a crisp crack, he made contact, sending the ball to left field. It shot behind the fielder, hit the grass, and bounced over the short wall.

A home run.

Victorious, Rico pumped his fists in the air as he ran the bases.

A left-handed swing was no problem for Rico Valpariso. No problem at all.

Cody flipped open his cell phone and placed the call to his sergeant. It was time to make a move.

Chapter 61

Joe "Turtle" Turturro
The Locker Room

Turtle did not like cops under the best of circumstances. So it was no surprise that he had developed a particular loathing for Detective Cody, who had sat his fat ass in the bleachers to comb over the players for most of the game. The old intimidation behind sunglasses technique. Like that was going to work.

And then sticking around after the game ended, saying "good game" and shit, as if he were part of the coaching staff. It pissed Turtle off, but he had held back as he stroked the thin lines of his beard, all the time thinking about his stash.

Was it safe?

Had the cops somehow found it?

Was Cody here for him? Maybe someone had tipped the cops off. Not that too many people here knew, but all it took was one talker, one person who opened his or her mouth to the wrong person, and—blam!—your personal shit was out there, posted on some blog or being discussed over burgers in the dining hall.

Turtle took a swig of water, poured the rest over his head, and ducked into the shadowed coolness of the locker room. All around him guys were slapping five and talking about Kroger's home run, a run batted with Ben McGann's Blue Thunder. The little shit Kroger said McGandolf had said that

Kroger could use it. Yeah, sure. Turtle itched to mess Kroger up, put him in the hospital with his friend. The two could share a room.

But Turtle let the details of the game fall away as he approached his locker studiously, checking for signs of intrusion. Through the grated door he could see his royal blue bat bag propped toward the right, and down low, so low Turtle had to squat to see it; a small square of transparent tape was still affixed to both the door and the frame. So no one had been rooting through his stuff. Wow. That was cool.

Maybe he was being paranoid. The last time he'd tussled with the cops was more than five years ago when he'd been sitting in the front of a van outside a school dance waiting for his friend Ace to light up a pipe. Turtle had gotten into the vehicle for conversation, not dope, but the cops didn't buy his story.

"I'd love to lock you up and throw away the key," the cop had told Turtle that night, speaking with the passion of a TV evangelist. "Believe me, son, if you were eighteen, you'd be going off to the state pen with your buddy there."

But while Ace went to jail, Turtle went home that night. The cops didn't even make his mother leave her shift at the hospital, since they didn't have any charges that would stick. Yeah, it was no wonder Turtle hated cops. All the time he'd been growing up, they'd never been around when the apartment got broken into or Ma's Honda got stolen from right in front of their window. Cops were one of those nasty things that were necessary to keep the global ecosystem in balance, like cockroaches and snakes. Unpleasant, sometimes downright creepy, but you could survive them.

Normally he left his stuff in his room, but after he got word that detectives had been trying to get in he thought it was safer to transfer it to his bat bag, to that inside pocket that most players used for batting gloves and wallets. He figured it'd be safer there. You couldn't be too safe with detectives like Cody wandering around.

Turtle sat on the bench facing his locker and began to unbutton his jersey. *One button and Cody won't make any trouble. Two buttons and he's not on to me. Three and the old gus of a cop will be gone when I turn around.*

He finished unbuttoning the entire shirt, then turned around.

Damn. Detective Cody was still here, talking to Coach Ramsey. The detective was a minor annoyance, unlike the sight that emerged from the shadows of the locker room entrance. Cops . . . two in uniform, a guy and a woman, and they had some lemon-sour pusses on.

He rubbed the back of his neck, suddenly sweating. What did they need more cops here for?

Shards of memory stabbed at him. Pouring the oil on the steps. Getting Kroger all charged up. Turtle and Rico had doubled over in laughter when they saw Kroger running up the path, crossing the campus, and they had thought it would be just as funny to see McGann fall on his ass. When that didn't happen, it was a challenge to up the ante.

Then the girl stepped into the picture . . . McGann's rich girlfriend, acting like she was coming on to him when she really just wanted to score. That blond twinkie. He'd shut her down fast and wheeled on Dozo, who swore he hadn't said a word to her.

And McGann . . . Turtle had him in his sights since the day he arrived in Syracuse, leaping and rolling and stretching to field the ball. Fucking McGandolf. Turtle wasn't jealous, not really, but he didn't like to be outshined by a punk sophomore, and all that sour piss poured out the other night at the party, right in front of everyone.

For all the world to see.

Pretty stupid.

But motive wasn't enough to indict a dude, right?

The glimmer of gold on the female cop's uniform caught his eye as she stepped forward. Oh shit.

He'd hustled and busted his butt to get here . . . and for what? To get arrested? A pulse thrummed in his ears as his mind panned rows of bars, the jail cells of prison films filled with grisly, muscled men who sharpened pens into daggers and jumped you when you were trying to shower. He was strong, but no match for a gang.

He braced himself as the two cops approached . . .

And walked right past him, the guy's sleeve brushing his. They paused behind Detective Cody, who pulled a pair of handcuffs from the back pocket of his worn jeans.

"Enrico Valpariso?"

His back to the men, Rico pulled on a clean tank top before turning to the three cops.

Cody held up the cuffs, as if Rico had misplaced them somewhere and he needed to claim them. "You're under arrest."

"You kidding me?" Disbelief glimmered in Rico's eyes.

Turtle felt his jaw go slack as he watched it all unfold. They handcuffed Valpariso's hands behind his back and escorted him out the door. Just like on television. Shit.

Chapter 62

Kate
Good Samaritan Hospital

As Kate waited at Ben's bedside, time seemed liquid, like a puddle on the floor that spread when you tried to mop it up. Days seemed to stretch on forever and yet sunset came too early because it led to the inevitable hopelessness of night. With Ben unconscious, time was a paradox, slippery and illogical.

She envied Marnie her concentration. The girl sat on a chair with her legs tucked under her, seemingly engrossed in her book. Kate had been unable to escape the here and now since she'd received that call early Saturday morning. How many days ago? She closed her eyes, counting silently. Saturday, Sunday, Monday . . . two and a half days and Ben was still unconscious. In that time the only thing Kate had been able to focus on was her research—books and articles—a quest that had proved less than encouraging.

Many articles about traumatic brain injury described personality changes in the patients who survived. Most patients suffered agitation and restlessness, anxiety and depression. Families observed dramatic changes in social behavior, inappropriate behavior. Patients who suffered injury to the right frontal lobe often talked obsessively or perseverated, clinging to a single thought. And a recent study claimed that patients with injury to the right frontal lobe—Ben's injury—had trouble comprehending the punch line of jokes and showed a preference for slapstick humor. If that wasn't a wry twist; perhaps all those Three Stooges DVDs he and Dylan had loved in junior high would come in handy.

She had read highly literate accounts written by TBI survivors, stories of loss, pain, and long rehabilitations. Although she had tried to remain objective, she found herself picking and choosing, hoping for the best aspects from the success stories, praying that Ben would be spared the tragic circumstances of the worst cases.

If there was a lighter side, it was that Ben had not suffered damage to the brain stem, which usually resulted in two horrific states. In "locked-in syndrome," the patient is alert and cognitively healthy but locked in a paralyzed body with communication reduced to a basic response like eye blinks. Other patients with brain stem injury ended up in a persistent vegetative state, in which a patient's body manages to breathe and sleep but they are deemed unconscious of their surroundings. Brain dead.

Kate shuddered. Fortunately, Ben's prognosis was more hopeful. Hopeful, but still something of a mystery.

She peered into the shopping bag of magazines Erin had bought, grabbed *The New Yorker,* and paced to the foot of the bed. Maybe the cartoons would distract her. It tore at her heart to look at her son, the purple side of his face visible beneath the eye patch and bandages, the tubes attached to his mouth and arm, plastic appendages that gave a body the clinical look of a laboratory experiment. It hurt to see Ben this way, but whenever she looked away she felt sure she would miss something important—a sign or signal indicating that he needed something or that he was rising from the deep pool of unconsciousness.

Now she let her gaze move down the bed, past the flat broad chest and long legs outlined by a sheet, to where his feet nearly hung over the bed. Her tall son, the perfect physique for a first baseman. Everyone had told her that, from the high school coach to the formal pro ballplayer who ran a clinic in Woodstock. Ben had been born to play baseball.

Medical staff came and went quickly from the ICU, and Kate didn't look twice at the man and woman in scrubs headed her way until the woman called her name.

"Kate, how's he doing?" Dr. Teddy Zanth seemed petite and delicate beside the bear of a man who towered over her. He needed a shave and his eyes seemed watery behind his thick glasses, which he pushed up on his nose as he eyed Kate.

"This is Dr. Cooper Smeltzer," Teddy introduced.

"Are you a neurologist?" Kate asked.

"Just a resident. I work in trauma with Teddy." He glanced up at the monitor while Teddy leaned close to Ben's head. "His vitals look good," Dr. Smeltzer said. "Any sign of consciousness yet?"

"Nothing that I've noticed," Kate said. "They removed the tube last night and he's breathing on his own now."

With light fingers Teddy pried Ben's good eye open and shined a small light over the shiny surface. "Pupils are constricting," she said.

"That's good, right?" Kate needed a glimmer of hope.

"It's a good sign." Dr. Smeltzer turned to Kate. "And how are you holding up, Mom?"

"I'm . . . here. I wish we knew more."

He nodded, but unlike most of the other staff members who seemed to be afraid of Kate's questions he didn't look away. His dark eyes were heavy with intelligence and something else. Compassion, Kate thought. "We don't have all the answers when it comes to head injuries. Many aspects of the brain are still a mystery to doctors and scientists. Which is good and bad. There isn't a lot we can do for your son right now, but the brain has great potential in ultimately healing itself. The great plasticity."

Marnie had slid out of the chair and now stood beside Kate. "I wish you guys could be Ben's main doctors."

Dr. Teddy smiled. "We're training in trauma. The quick fix. Keep the patient alive. It's not often that we have the opportunity to follow through." She turned to Kate. "And this isn't a professional visit. I really just wanted to see how Ben was doing."

Kate was thanking Dr. Teddy when a nurse from the unit interrupted. "Kate, there's a phone call for you at the desk. A police detective?" Kate excused herself and took the call at the nurses' station.

"This is Kate."

"Greg Cody. I want you to know we've made an arrest."

Kate sank with relief at the news. They found him. The person who did this to her son would be punished. Leaning into the desk, she allowed herself a breath of calm. "Was I right? Was it Valpariso?"

"Rico Valpariso. He's a switch-hitter. When I saw him batting left-handed this afternoon, that sealed it for me. Sergeant Lopez agreed."

"Thank God. Oh, thank God."

"I just wanted you to know."

"And why did he do it? Just to get Ben off first base?"

"We may never know," Cody said. "The criminal justice system doesn't require reasons why; just the truth of the crime. Hold on." She heard voices in the background. "Okay, listen, Kate, I gotta go. Just thought you would want to know."

"Thank you. It's good to know he'll be off the streets." Kate had to bite back the notion that she wanted to see this young man punished. In all her years of teaching, she had argued against punishment, attesting to rehabilitation and behavior intervention instead. Now that her son was the victim, her desire for justice had sharpened. "Will you keep me posted?"

"Absolutely. And you'll keep me updated on Ben's condition?"

"I'll let you know when there's a change." She ended the call as Erin arrived, bagged sandwiches from Subway dangling from her hands.

"Five dollar foot longs, baby," Erin said. "Sorry I'm late. I got turned around and ended up on an expressway headed toward Rome. I thought you had to cross the Atlantic to get to Italy."

"You never were a driver, sweetie." Kate took two of the bags. "Ben's emergency room doctor is inside. Did you meet Teddy Zanth?"

"Nope." Erin looked around. "Are they going to freak if we bring food inside? The delicious smells might wake the dead."

"We'll take turns eating in the lobby." Kate snatched a bag of chips from her sister. "Just keep your mitts out of the bags till you're out of the ward."

"You're chipper."

"That was Greg Cody on the phone. They arrested the guy who attacked Ben."

"Really? And I thought you were just happy to hear from him."

"Maybe I am." In the hours of waiting Kate had told her sister how she and Eli had grown irrevocably apart. They'd also had a chance to discuss every aspect of what had happened to Ben, along with the attractive detective working on his case. "But mostly I'm relieved."

"I get it," Erin said, linking her arm through Kate's. "It's progress. Moving ahead."

Kate nodded toward the ICU. "Let's go tell Ben."

At Ben's bedside Kate introduced her sister to the two doctors, and Dr. Smeltzer—Cooper, he wanted to be called—announced that the sandwiches were making him hungry.

"We should put Subway in our repertoire," he told Teddy. "Semi-healthy."

Teddy nodded, mentioning that they were on their way to grab a bite, with her shift about to begin and Cooper's ending. Kate was recommending Mario's, the Italian place she'd gone to with Greg Cody, when one of the nurses, Sonny, joined them.

"Kate McGann, are you causing me trouble here in my ICU?" he asked with a deadpan expression.

"We're just talking," Kate answered. "Trying to give Ben some entertainment."

"At that you're succeeding," Sonny said, squinting from one face to another. "But I'm afraid it's getting a little loud here. Not that I don't love a good party, but we're only supposed to let one visitor at a time into the ICU. We're not set up to entertain."

"We're on our way out," Teddy said, motioning Cooper toward the door.

"And I have to head out to the airport soon." Marnie checked her watch. "I'd like to stay until the last minute. Do you mind if I eat the sandwich at the airport?" she asked Erin.

"No problem," Erin said. As she went on to tell the others how she had gotten lost on the way back from Subway, Kate turned to her son.

Something seemed different.

It wasn't just that the tubing had been removed from his mouth, making him look more human than alien. Some of the hue had returned to his skin, a more peachy tone on the good side of his face, and as she studied him she could have sworn his head moved. She stepped up to the bed. "Ben? Honey, can you hear me? It's Mom."

Silence whipped through the group and sent Erin and Marnie and Nurse Sonny and the two doctors rushing to surround the bed.

Suddenly it was all about Ben, who was indeed stirring, arms flailing. His left eyelid fluttered and finally fought its way open, just a slit, but open.

Kate leaned over him, moving into his line of vision. "Ben." Her voice was firm but encouraging. "Wake up, Son."

"I'd like to, Mom." His voice was dry, gravelly, his lips chapped. "But my throat is like a cement mixer. My eyes are glued shut."

"Well, yeah." Marnie pushed forward and squeezed the fingertips of his left hand. "That happens when you sleep for three days."

"Marnie . . ." he growled, that half-crooked smile recognizable amid the swelling on his face. "What are you here for? Busting my chops. Don't you have to go steam a latte or something?" He closed his eye, winced, then looked up again. "Somebody get me some water." And then he smiled.

That jagged smile was Kate's undoing.

It was Ben; her son was back. Certainly not 100 percent the person he'd been three days ago. There would be rehabilitation ahead, maybe years of mentally and physically taxing work for him, but the glimmer of energy, the essence of Ben, was there. Finally, after hours and days of uncertainty, her son was still there. She felt her eyes fill with tears.

Ben was awake, cracking jokes and asking the nurse for water. Kate clutched her chest, sure that she was witnessing nothing short of a miracle.

Yes, truly a miracle.

PART V

Chapter 63

Ben McGann
Good Samaritan Hospital

*S*ixth game of the World Series, and Fenway is roaring for the Sox, who are in the lead. On the field, the team is pumped. Revved and ready to win.

Ben faces the batter, thinking that this guy won't get much heat off their pitcher. He's right.

Mookie hits a short line drive toward first base.

Easy out.

Or it should be, but as Ben strides over to field the ball something is wrong with his legs. They feel wooden and stiff, and his entire body is slow, as if caught in a viscous solution, trying to move while encased in thick silt.

What the hell . . .

The movement kills him, but he gets there, gets to the ball in time. He leans down, mitt wide open . . .

And the ball eludes him, rolling right between his legs.

"Ahhh!" Ben thrashes, trying to spin around and snag the ball fast, trying to hustle. But he's stuck, cemented in place.

And the disappointment of the crowd and team pours down on him, batters him, causing a gnawing pain in his head. A god-awful pain . . . He can't take it anymore.

He gropes at the field under him, but there are no blades of grass. No turf. Just the crisp fabric of bed sheets . . .

Stray sounds pulled him from sleep, but the journey was tough. So hard to rise up to the surface under the weight of disapproval, both from the grumbling crowd and from his own conscience.

How could you miss that? Why didn't you get there?

When he finally was able to lift his head the hollow sound of footsteps on the tile floor told him he wasn't on the field but in the dorm, but some of the details were wrong, like in a dream where floors tilt and roadbeds drop off unexpectedly.

There was a curtain on hooks drawn beside his bed, a curtain with vertical stripes that brought to mind a circus tent. A television on the wall cast surreal light in the dark room, and the smell was more antiseptic than the usual dorm odors of old mattresses, ramen noodles, and solidified floor wax.

What the hell . . . ? Was it all a dream? He sat up with a stab of urgency. No clock in this dorm, but from the heaviness of sleep in his body he sensed it was late. He'd overslept and Coach was going to be pissed. No wonder he was having a nightmare; his body must have known he was oversleeping.

As he sat up a heavy pain dragged him down. Like someone was trying to claw his brain out from within. In slow motion he tossed back the sheets and slid out of the bed, but as he pulled away something tugged on his arm. He looked down to find a white surgical tape holding a needle in his arm.

What the . . . it looked like he'd been shooting up.

As he started to work the tape loose he noticed a note on the high table beside the bed. His name was written in cursive across the top in bold marker, his mother's handwriting, which he recognized from years of finding his name decoratively scribed over his brown lunch bags. Still, though he could read the words, they didn't completely make sense to him. Some of the lines wavered and went off on their own tangent, like ribbons flapping in the wind.

> *Ben,*
> *Please do not get out of bed.*
> *Do not remove the IV in your arm.*
> *You are in the hospital, recovering from a head*

injury. Coach knows, and you can go back to sleep.
If you need help, ring for the nurse.
See you in the morning. . . .
Love,
Mom

The letter is familiar, though its meaning is something of a mystery. Instructions . . . they seem important, but what do they mean? His fingers released the edges of the tape. "So this needle is supposed to be here. It's supposed to be here. Mom says it is, but it doesn't feel right."

Something wasn't right.

He took a deep breath, went to rub his eye, his fingers stumbling over thick padding taped there. He pressed on the bandage and sucked in a moan at the pain, ghastly tenderness that emanated from his head and threaded down his jaw.

"Shit. What happened to me?" He looked at the note again. "A head injury? She says head injury. What happened? I don't remember that. I just know Ithaca is in town, and they've got that left-handed pitcher that nobody can hit. An accident. Why can't I remember?"

It hurt like hell, but he didn't want to be here.

"Can't stay here. Got to get some air. Nothing that exercise won't cure, right? Once I get to practice, I'll feel better." He swung his legs down the side of the bed and fingered the printed cotton robe. A grandma robe with snaps. "What . . . Are you kidding me? Is this some kind of joke. Dylan . . ." He shot a look at the other bed, partially blocked by a curtain. "Dylan, is that you? You pranking me?"

He moved to slide out of the bed but the needle in his arm tugged him back again. "Pain in the ass . . . how do I get this thing out? Can't you see I've got a ball game to play?"

On the ball field he would forget about the pain. Making the out at first—three up, three down. Spanking the ball over the fence . . . that would make the pain go away.

He had to get to the game. With renewed resolve he picked at the tape on his arm.

"Ben?" A middle-aged woman with a pixie cut paused in the door. "I see you're up, but don't tell me you're trying to take the IV out. You are! Not again. No, no. Back to bed." She rushed over, shooing his hand away from the needle.

Who was this chick? "I have a game tonight," he said. "I need to get to practice or the coach is going to bench me. Just help me get this thing out and I'll be out of your hair."

"I don't want you out of my hair, Ben McGann. You just had brain surgery, for God's sakes."

"What are you talking about?"

"That get your attention? I said brain surgery, as in, you'd better get your derriere back into bed and stay there or I'm going to have to use the restraints, which nobody likes. Back in bed, Ben."

"Who are you?"

"I'm Jodi, a nurse here." She smiled, hands on her hips. "You still don't remember me? We go through this every night. I'm beginning to think you don't like us here at Good Sam."

"I don't dislike you. I don't even know you," he said.

"Yeah, well, you've seen me every night around this time for the past three days. Did you see the note from your mom?"

"What note?"

She held out the note from his mother.

"Oh. I saw the note. Yeah. I saw it, but it didn't make sense. How did I get here?"

Jodi motioned him to move back in place on the bed. "You got hurt, sweetpea."

"In a car?"

"You got hit in the head with a baseball bat. Do you remember?"

He let his thoughts drift back to the game that day, the party afterward at Emma's hotel. What happened next? When he tried to think back, his memory rammed into a barrier, solid as a brick wall. "I don't remember."

"That's normal, given your condition. You just rest now, and leave that IV alone, you hear me? I'll be right out in the hall if you need anything."

"Thank you." He decided to go along with Jodi the nurse's instructions, though it didn't feel right. Nothing felt right; everything was spinning out of orbit at the wrong speed, compounding the pain in his head and the shredded anxiety in his gut.

He gripped the sides of the mattress, trying to recall a few threads of the event that was unraveling his life. "Something happened. Something happened." Talking helped, even if no one was listening. "Hit in the head? How did I get hit? Must be the reason my head hurts. Must be. Did it happen during a game? Why can't I remember? Show me the replay. Why can't I remember?"

Chapter 64

Kate McGann
Good Samaritan Hospital

At times he seemed normal.

Gathered around his bed, the visiting players listened intently as Ben recalled a fantastic triple play they'd made earlier in the season. Ben rattled off the details, calling the play as if he were a radio sportscaster, gesturing with both hands. The table with his dinner had been slid out of reach, as Ben now had a tendency to knock into things on his right—the spatial issue. But the visiting players wouldn't have noticed that. Kenta Suzuki, Chad Gilmer, and Zach Steiner nodded and grinned, awed by his retention of information. They even joked about Ben's bandaged eye—a pirate, they called him—and they threatened to bring in Ben's batting helmet to replace the dorky yellow one. They didn't seem to mind Ben's excessive talking, brought on by his brain injury.

It made him sound a bit manic at times, but Kate dismissed it as a minor consequence, one that would fade over time with rehab. These past few days, Kate had come to appreciate so many things that she'd once taken for granted. She loved the sound of Ben's voice, his tone a mixture of enthusiasm and confidence. Instead of worrying about the excessive talking she thanked God that his ability to talk had been spared, as right now it served as Ben's only source of relief and expression. And his crooked smile could bring tears of joy to her eyes.

But that joy was tempered with concern and a hidden measure of devastation for the permanent losses. After almost two weeks in the neuro ICU, Ben had been moved here, to the surgical ward. At that time, Ben's neurologist had sat Kate down in a conference room to lay out the facts of his injury.

The real prognosis.

Although Dr. James Paulo, the personable neurologist who reminded Kate of Captain Kangaroo, approached everything with a calm manner, the news could not be detoxified by his warm smile.

"First, let's talk about his vision." Dr. Paulo sighed and looked down at the file that lay open on the table. "We were hopeful about the recovery in his right eye, but it doesn't seem to be improving. There may be damage to the optic nerve. If that's the case, and we'll have an ophthalmologist check him, he may be blind in his right eye."

"Oh." Kate nodded, swallowing over the thickness in her throat. She pressed her fingernails into the table, needing something to hold on to, a baseline. "But he would still be able to see, with one eye, right?"

"Right . . ." Dr. Paulo nodded. "But there's a major adjustment that goes along with that. Often depth perception is affected, which is one of the reasons you see Ben stumbling into things, knocking them over. Driving may be an issue, as well as sports."

"He won't be able to play ball . . . baseball." Kate saw where this was going. How could a first baseman react in a split second with limited vision? How would Ben see a ball coming toward him, from any position on the field, if his peripheral vision was damaged? "Oh." Why hadn't she seen this coming, and why did it matter so much? He was alive, his personality intact . . .

So much of his persona revolved around the game; she couldn't imagine what his life would be like without it.

Kate felt herself sag in the chair, hope draining, but she had to hear the rest. "What else?" she asked Dr. Paulo.

He turned the page in Ben's file, but Kate knew he wasn't reading. He knew the case; he was just gauging her state of mind. "That's some pretty heavy news for starters. As for the brain trauma, I can still only tell you patterns we've seen in these cases. Ben sustained damage to the right frontal lobe. This is the same injury many people sustain when their head hits the windshield in a car crash. The frontal lobes play a major role in executive functions. We're talking about organizational skills. Adapting and multitasking. The ability to initiate and complete tasks. Ben will need weeks, probably months of physical therapy. He might need to relearn how to dress and feed himself, take care of basic functions."

"But Ben is a very independent guy. He's always been that way. I know he needs help now, but—"

"Let's try not to compare Ben to the way he used to be. Our most realistic goal is not to return to former function, but to help Ben utilize the function and abilities he can access right now. Sometimes a frontal lobe injury takes away a person's inhibitions, bringing on inappropriate behaviors, but that doesn't seem to be the case with Ben."

Thank God, Kate thought.

"In fact, from what you've said, his personality seems to still be intact, and that's fortunate. Patients with frontal lobe injuries often have a flat affect, expressionless and unemotional. But we've seen Ben passionately plot to escape. We've even seen him laugh and cry. For someone in his state, that's fantastic."

Kate nodded, thinking that it didn't feel fantastic.

Dr. Paolo talked about the possibility of depression, as well as nightmares and flashbacks of the incident. Seizures were a possibility, and Ben would stay on the anticonvulsion medication for at least a year. After the flap of his skull was replaced and he recovered, he would have to move to a rehab center, where he would relearn basic daily tasks: how to clean and dress himself, how to shop for groceries, prepare a simple meal.

At the end of her meeting with Dr. Paolo, Kate was angry, convinced that he was a terrible doctor, cold and ruthless. Erin sympathized and restrained herself from pointing out the obvious truth: Dr. Paulo had given Kate information she did not want to hear.

The difficult truth.

Since then, each day, Kate steeled herself, ready to defy reality and find signs of improvement. Ben's memory was sharp, up until the time of the attack. Since he'd awakened he'd been slow to process and learn new facts such as nurses' names, where he was, or what had happened. Nearly every time he woke up he was riddled with anxiety, sure that he was going to be late for a game or a practice. A few times he'd removed the IV line and made it out to the hall—a concern, since the unprotected side of his brain was quite vulnerable without a helmet. When Kate was there she could usually calm him, but he often awoke with the same questions: "Where am I? What happened? Where's Dylan? Where's Marnie? Why does my head hurt?" Oddly, Emma was not on his mind, and so far he hadn't thought to ask what day it was. It was as if he'd awakened to the same day over and over again. One perpetual day.

Sometimes restless energy tore at him, and the staff was happy to walk him down the hall as long as he wore the yellow helmet he'd been given to protect his head. With his strength and stature, Ben required a guardian on each side, and Kate had learned firsthand the difficulty of trying to support him when he broke into a spontaneous skipping motion or slumped down from exhaustion.

He wasn't able to stay awake for more than an hour at a time, and when he was awake he tired easily. Restlessness, agitation, memory loss, and excessive talking—these seemed to be Ben's deficits at the moment, though they were all normal at this stage in his recovery. Dr. Paulo had said that Ben might overcome these problems with the help of physical therapy, and Kate held on to that hope.

On the other side of Ben's bed, Kate and Erin sat quietly, letting the boys' conversation wash over them. Kate doodled on the note advising Ben to stay in bed. The nurses thought it was overwhelming Ben with too much information, and they'd advised her to cut it down so that Ben got the main point before he ripped his IV line out.

When Ben first regained consciousness Kate had been worried that Valpariso would show up at the hospital and try to hurt Ben again. Word was probably getting out that Ben was remembering bits and pieces of that night, and she suspected Valpariso was getting nervous. She had notified the hospital staff of the security risk, and they'd been happy to take her list of approved guests.

Someone paused in the doorway, catching Kate's attention. Detective Cody.

She could feel heat flare in her cheeks at the sight of Greg Cody across the crowded room. Granted, she was happy to see him, but nothing like wearing your feelings at the age of fifty. How embarrassing.

Erin leaned so close her breath grazed Kate as she lowered her voice. "Are you blushing?"

"Stop." Kate beckoned him inside. "Good afternoon, Detective. Come join us."

The players tightened up a bit, but their conversation kept going.

"I thought there were no more than two visitors per room," Cody said.

Kate winced. "We're bending the rules, just a scooch." She stood up and bit her lower lip, feeling awkward and hating herself for it. She wasn't a fourteen-year-old crushing on a boy. "You want to interview Ben?" Of course he did. Ben's memory of the attack had been blank the first day when Cody spoke to him, but details seemed to be falling into place.

"I can wait, give them time to hang out. Should we step outside?" the detective suggested.

Erin's eyebrows wiggled suggestively as Kate passed.

"I'll deal with you later," Kate told her sister. She smoothed her blouse over her dress shorts and faced Greg Cody. "So how's the case against Valpariso going?"

"It's going. His parents posted bail, and he's been ordered

off the Cross College Campus, and he returned home to the Bronx. His attorney is claiming an alibi. I'm checking on it."

"What?" Kate didn't want snags. "What kind of alibi? Where does he say he was?"

Cody's hands went up. "Easy, Mom. I'll let you know when I have the details."

"Well, thank God Ben is starting to remember some of the details of the attack. Maybe his testimony can help you nail Valpariso."

"If Valpariso is guilty," Greg said. "One very important detail. We don't want to 'nail' the wrong guy."

"Talk to Ben. It's surprising what details are coming back to him."

Cody nodded and followed her back into the room, where the guys were bumping fists with Ben.

"Feel better, man," Zach Steiner said.

Kenta clapped him on his good shoulder. "We miss you out there."

"Yeah, this is killing me," Ben said as the guys headed out. "Smack one out of the park for me, will ya?" He shifted in bed, wincing with pain. "Mom, I swear, if I wasn't so tired, I'd break out of here."

"You've tried." She looked over his lunch tray. "You didn't finish your salad."

"Like there's nutrition in iceberg lettuce."

Kate shrugged. He was right. Sometimes he made perfect sense. "Do you remember Detective Cody? He talked with us earlier this week."

Ben scratched the stubble on his chin as he checked out Cody. "Umm . . . I don't remember."

"Greg Cody." He extended a hand to Ben. "You were kind of groggy the last time we talked."

"Detective Cody is trying to figure out who attacked you." Kate leaned close to her son to make eye contact. Ben had trouble recalling the attack unless he was cued properly. "Remember that night? You were in the dorm, in your room."

"Oh, that. That night . . . parts of it are hard to remember.

But sometimes certain moments are so clear I can feel the warm blood on my cheek. I was in my room in the dorm; that's right. I can see his silhouette against the light from the hallway."

"His silhouette?" Cody's pen was poised over his notebook. "You saw the guy who attacked you?"

"Not his face. I didn't see his face. I only saw that there was some guy standing in my doorway, in a T-shirt and boxers, I think. It was dark in my room. I was lying down, not in bed, but stretched out on it. I don't know why. I wasn't drinking at the party, but I didn't feel well. Yeah, that was it. I didn't feel well to begin with, sort of sick and dizzy on my way into the dorm. I sat down on the bed and sort of passed out."

"And then . . . ?"

"He called my name. I do remember that. He called me Ben. I knew him. I mean, I wasn't really scared because he was someone I knew, but I don't remember his face." Ben's head lolled against the pillow; he seemed exhausted again. "That's the last thing I remember . . . him calling my name."

"If we ran some names by you, do you think you might remember?" Kate asked.

Cody was shaking his head. "Not a good idea. You're leading the witness, Kate."

Ben's eyes opened a sliver, and Kate realized he was getting tired. "I wish I could remember." He knocked his fists together.

"Would you recognize the sound of his voice if you heard it?" Kate asked. When Ben shrugged, she turned to Greg. "Maybe we could arrange something . . . a way for Ben to identify the attacker. We could have the team drop by. Or make a tape with each player saying hello to Ben."

Cody winced, sounding as if he were sucking soup between his teeth. "The DA would kick my ass. A voice match is a little more difficult than a lineup. It's been done, but not often, and in this case Ben isn't even sure he could identify the assailant's voice."

Ben let out a heavy sigh, and Kate realized he was snoring—

fast asleep. He'd been awake for more than an hour, which was exhausting for him.

"Let him sleep," Cody said. "If we're going to convict Valpariso, we can do it based on the evidence we've already collected."

"What about his alibi?"

"I'll keep you posted." Cody tipped his chin toward Ben. "All things considered, he's looking much better. What are the doctors saying?"

"It's still too early for an accurate prognosis. Ben is exhibiting some behaviors of traumatic brain injury such as excessive talking, anxiety, sometimes agitation. Right now they're still watching for infection, pneumonia . . . it's one day at a time. Down the road, he'll need to be transferred to a neurologic rehabilitation facility. Dr. Zanth says there's an excellent center right here in Syracuse, and I made a few calls. Ben's on the waiting list. Recovery—whatever that means for Ben—is going to take some time."

He nodded. "But he's got you on his side."

"And most of the Syracuse Lakers," she said, leaning over her son to brush some hair from his eyes.

"Most, but not all." Cody sighed. "And I'd love to find the one bad apple."

Chapter 65

Marnie Epstein
Storemart, Boston

"What a loser." Marnie grabbed a shopping basket and dropped in the dozen or so boxes of condoms that some moron had moved to the candy aisle. Really, people didn't have enough constructive things to do with their day; they had time to go through her store and rearrange the merchandise for shits and giggles. Well, she got the same hourly wages whether she was restocking items moved by pranksters or just swiping at the register, so it was no big deal. In fact, she'd actually been getting into work the past day or so, liking the distraction it provided from the weirdo who was hounding her.

She cleaned up a spill in the housewares aisle and unloaded two boxes of school supplies in the front display. She was just breaking down the boxes when George called her from the main register. "You got a call on line three. Says it's an emergency."

Thinking that it could only be Ben, Marnie hurried over and picked up the phone. "This is Marnie."

In the disturbing silence she sensed that someone was on the other line. "I'm watching you. I see you," hissed a slow, deliberate voice. Male or female? She couldn't tell, though she'd guess male. It sounded like it was altered in some way. "I see you . . ."

Oh, God . . . not here at work.

"Oh, yeah?" She squeezed the receiver as she turned to look behind her. "Then what am I doing?"

"I know what you did," rasped the voice.

Scanning the aisles, she walked across the front of the store. This was all just a bluff; it had to be. She swallowed back fear, reassuring herself that she didn't see any creepy people in the store. Although two people, a woman in the cosmetics aisle and a man looking at greeting cards, had cell phones pressed to their ears.

"So since I have you on the line," she said, working hard to keep her voice steady, "why don't you tell me exactly what I did that's pissing you off? Because I've examined my conscience, really racked my memory, and I'm not coming up with anything that bad. Bottom line, I have a really boring life. I didn't rob a bank. Didn't steal a yacht or kidnap a millionaire's baby. So maybe you have the wrong person."

The answer was a click disconnecting the call.

She sucked in her cheeks and hung up the phone.

"Everything okay, Marnie?" George asked from behind the register. A retired city clerk, George was the unofficial caretaker at Storemart.

"Fine." For a moment, she considered telling him what was going on. It would be a huge relief to have one other person know about the threats, and George had expressed more interest than anyone else so far.

"Just saying," George went on. "I don't mind if you get a call now and again, but just warning you, Mr. Merritt doesn't like it."

Of course, he was worried about their manager finding out. "It won't happen again," Marnie said as she grabbed the two empty boxes and lugged them back to the stockroom, eager to get out of sight of the mystery caller.

In the back room she took her time breaking down boxes, thinking. The threats had begun the night she returned to Boston. When she turned on her cell phone coming off the plane, there were two text messages from a restricted number, Boston, MA:

"I know what you did."
"You'll pay in blood."

At first she wondered if it was a joke, or messages sent to the wrong number. Possible. But early the next morning, while she was alone in Beantown Grind setting up for the day, the shop phone had rung and that dry, wispy voice sank its fangs into her.

"I know what you did.
"You will suffer for what you did."

That first time he called she didn't respond; she simply paused at the coffee bar and chewed down a fingernail until it bled. Who was mad at her for something? Who knew her well enough to know she would be the one to answer the phone at Beantown Grind before the coffee shop opened?

Those questions had throbbed in her mind these past few days until tonight's call at Storemart added a new dimension of fear.

He knew her schedule, and that scared her more than his fake-oh wispy voice.

When Marnie honestly examined her conscience, only one sin gave her a pang of regret. An image of her dad came to mind, dark hair falling over his forehead. She could see him as he'd looked on their last outing in his blue cashmere sweater, his skates making him tall as he circled the rink. They'd had to cut the session short because he had to take Little Petunia to some party. Little Petunia wasn't his daughter's name, but that was what Jade called the kid and it had stuck in Marnie's mind.

Leo Epstein had been furious with her that afternoon; she had seen the sharp fury in his eyes, the muscle flickering in his jaw. But that was years ago . . . she'd been in seventh grade. Why would a man hold a grudge all these years? Besides, what

Jewish accountant in his fifties threatened his teenaged daughter?

As she was chucking the boxes in the Dumpster outside, her cell phone buzzed in her smock pocket. "Oh, God." How creepy that it rang when she was out here alone.

Although she expected to see "restricted, Boston, MA" again, she saw that it was Dylan. With a relieved breath she called in to George that she was taking her break and sank into some lawn furniture in the stockroom. "Dylan, hello."

"Hey. Do you miss me?"

How to answer that? "It's only been a few days."

"It seems like forever. I'm calling to give you another chance."

"That's really sweet, but . . . you know. How's Ben doing?"

"Ben isn't why I called." He seemed wounded by her question.

"But he's your best friend. Come on, Dylan. Give me the update so I don't have to bug his mother."

"You were there when he woke up, right? What else is there?"

"Is he beginning to remember what happened to him?"

"He remembers the attacker called his name. A lot of good that does."

"How's he doing otherwise?"

"I don't know, Marnie. I've got games and practices going on, not a lot of time to babysit Ben." His voice was tight, his annoyance obvious.

"Yeah, we're all busy." Marnie trod cautiously. "Just so you know, I'm planning a trip back to Syracuse, just as soon as I can schedule a few days off."

"You want to watch me play? I can get you tickets."

"I want to visit Ben. Come on, Dylan. He's my friend and he was in a coma for three days."

"And suddenly you're Florence Nightingale?"

"See? I'm trying to keep things friendly and you're already mad at me."

"You'd fly all the way here to visit a guy stuck in the hospital?"

"Well, duh. When Ben got hurt I realized how fragile our lives can be. You gotta live for today, enjoy the moment."

"Sounds like you've been reading Hallmark cards."

"Dylan, what do I have to do to stay friends with you?"

"You don't have to do anything because I love you, Marnie. I'll always love you."

So much denial! She stuck her pinky between her lips and ground the stubby nail down; she hated it when he didn't listen but bulldozed right over her.

"I can't wait to see you again," he said. "Hey, did you know that I've been playing third base? Do you want me to get you some tickets for the game?"

She stood up and kicked at a cardboard box. "I have to go. I'm at work and I have to get back. I'll talk to you later," she said, hanging up abruptly.

Much later. Like . . . never.

Chapter 66

Kate McGann
Woodstock

As Kate soared down the New York Thruway, her hands gripped the steering wheel with a sense of control she hadn't experienced in years. Yes, she was headed back home to Woodstock, but only for a brief stop to pick up her clothes and toiletries for a long-term stay in Syracuse. As Erin would have to get back to her life in the next day or two, and Eli was attending a craft show in New York City, Kate saw this as a good time to grab her belongings and put the McGann family's glass house behind her.

"It's all good," Kate said aloud as she turned off on the exit toward Woodstock. Although she was heading home, it was a move forward, a step toward departing her old, staid life.

When she'd stopped for gas she'd had a text message from Marnie, asking if Kate would be willing to sublet half of her hotel room when Marnie visited this weekend. Kate had texted back that Erin was leaving and Marnie would be welcome to stay as her guest. In fact, Kate was relieved to have the company, and since Marnie lacked the pretension and façade of Emma, Kate suspected she'd be easy to room with.

Kate turned onto the meandering gravel drive to the house, slowing as she passed Eli's studio. Once upon a time she had sensed magic in that stoic building; she'd been sure that something her husband produced would be discovered and placed in the foyer of the United Nations building or the Capitol Rotunda. Had she been a naïve romantic, or did Eli actually possess a limitless, vaulting talent?

As the car climbed the hill and the house came into view, she sensed the difference. The stained-glass jewel box she had once cherished now seemed gaudy, like a schoolgirl's cell phone covered with stick-on gems. Kate kept her gaze on the house as she stepped out of the car and slammed the door. "It looks like a kaleidoscope barfed," she said aloud, smiling.

The house no longer held her in its throes. She was released from its power.

Inside, she sensed the wicked *her* in the flowers on the table, the graceful drape of a throw over the sofa, the way the magazines were stacked and fanned, as if the place were a dentist's office. She told herself that none of these things should bother her. Intellectually, she should be glad that Eli had found someone to take care of him. But it hurt. Within a week, another woman had moved into her spot—into her bed, as evidenced by the long red hairs on her pillow. Eli had stolen her home away while their son lay unconscious in a hospital bed. Although Kate was glad to be moving on, she couldn't deny the tug of exasperation she felt at her husband's lack of sensitivity. Clueless.

Three LP jackets were stacked beside the turntable—three of Eli's favorites. She slid the records from their sleeves, took them to the kitchen counter, and pursed her lips. Yes, she had to do it.

She reached into the cabinet under the sink for an abrasive sponge and gave the Eagles a brisk rub. Todd Rundgren received a good scrubbing, as did Boz Scaggs. That was mean and immature. Totally rotten. But it felt good.

She began loading up two large suitcases and a duffel bag, packing not only clothes, toiletries, and jewelry but also favorite sheets and blankets, her pillow (minus the pillowcase), a few choice novels, and towels. Was this all there was to her? How could it be that a few worn items made up the life of Kate McGann? Was this all she had accomplished in fifty years?

As she cleared off her dresser her hand closed over a photograph of the three of them taken at a gallery party in SoHo when Ben was still an infant. Funny, but Ben had that crooked grin even back then. She swiped the dust off to study Eli, looking cool and sexy in shades and a leather jacket. Something sank deep inside her. God, how she'd loved him back then.

Holding the photo close, Kate dared to face her own image: apricot lipstick, one cocked eyebrow, and round brown eyes, two deep pools of mystery.

She knew the secret behind those eyes. For years she couldn't look at herself, sure that the guilt in her eyes was so obvious, like an announcement blaring over a loudspeaker: "Kate lied! She's a Liar with a capital L! Tricked Eli to get the baby she wanted because she was so desperate to be pregnant."

For twenty years it had been her secret, her source of guilt. But now, looking at the photograph, she didn't see guilt in her eyes at all. A sob escaped her throat as she recognized happiness.

The woman in the photo was happy.

It wasn't a bad life, living with a creative man who loved her, raising a son in this progressive, often charming community.

And now . . . that life dangled from a precipitous cliff. Or maybe it had gone over the edge. Wasn't she here searching through the wreckage?

Kate tucked the photo of that happy family into her suitcase, sure that Eli wouldn't miss it and unwilling to let it fall into the hands of a stranger like Tamara. She zipped up the luggage, pulled the bags to the door, and hobbled down the steps with one suitcase in hand.

The sky had changed, royal blue giving way to a field of pewter pounded by blue-black thunderheads to the east. She wanted to get back on the interstate before the sky opened up. But wait . . . she didn't need to keep Ben's car. She pulled her Volvo out of the garage, grateful for its low, steady purr.

As she switched the vehicles, she noticed how damp the hill was. The grass slicked down to mud in some spots, and many of the flowers she'd planted this summer had lost their blossoms, their leaves grayish green from water rot. She sighed. More erosion on their hill.

Symbolic of their lives together.

Grunting, Kate hoisted the first suitcase into the trunk of her car. The second one was lighter, easier to wedge in the tight space. As she placed the duffel bag on the backseat, she felt lighter inside, empowered by the realization that these items did not represent the sum total of her life; they simply contained a few props to make each day easier.

With a freedom she hadn't felt since she'd snuck into a cinema to see the R-rated *Butch Cassidy and the Sundance Kid* when she was thirteen, she climbed into the Volvo and rolled down the hill. She pictured herself as a river, one of the small rivers that sluiced down this hill, making its own path when nothing worthwhile had been carved out for it.

Yes, she would find her own path.

Chapter 67

Greg Cody
Syracuse

The fluorescent sign of the Shooting Star Saloon glowed in the gray of dusk. Just down the hill from the campus, the bar was the black eye on an otherwise quaint block of storefronts housing a florist, a Realtor, and a bagel shop. Cody pegged it as a typical neighborhood watering hole for old drunks, derelicts, and deviants that had nowhere else to go.

"Should have been called the Dying Star," Cody muttered to himself as he stepped away from the glaring din of the jukebox by the door, his sneakers sliding with the help of sawdust on the checkered tile floor.

Cody took in the patrons, a typical group: two men at one end of the bar listening to a third. A group of younger guys in basketball shorts and tank tops sat around a table laden with pints of beer. In the corner booth, an old man stared into his beer.

Cody sat on a stool away from the others and reached into his jeans pocket.

The bartender was a petite, round woman with painted-on eyebrows and gray crescents under her eyes that made her look old, in her forties at least. "What can I get you?" she asked.

"Just looking for some answers right now." He showed her his shield and ID card. "Greg Cody, Syracuse Police."

Her eyes flared. "You're here about Rico."

"Do you know Mr. Valpariso?"

She nodded, and he noticed crow's-feet at the corners of her eyes. "He's my nephew." Looking down at the counter, she grabbed a rag and began wiping the old, pitted wood. "I already talked to the lawyers, Detective. I don't want no trouble in here. I run an honest business here. Plenty of work and not much pay, but we do our best."

"And your name is . . . ?"

She lifted her chin, facing him. "Damita Arechia. My husband and I own this place."

"I'm not looking to cause you any trouble, Mrs. Arechia. I just need you to tell me the truth about your nephew. Are you sure you saw Rico in here in the early morning hours of July tenth?"

Her eyes were locked on him, calculating. "Saturday, yes. He was in here just before midnight Friday. Came behind the bar and started helping out. Since Rico got here in June we let him tend bar for us a couple of times. The kid needs some spending money, and he's twenty-one. It's all legal."

"Was he tending bar for you Friday night?"

"Nah. He just showed up and set to work. Or so I thought. Come one or two in the morning, I find him lining up shots on the side bar, for customers I think. But was I right? No, I was wrong. He picked them up and drank them, every last one of them. Three or four." She shook her head. "For such a smart, talented boy, he can be very stupid."

Greg flipped open his notebook on the bar and wrote: "Drank shots @ 1-2 a.m." Would that allow Valpariso enough time to haul his ass up the hill and whale on McGann with a baseball bat? Seemed that way.

He glanced up to see Damita Arechia watching him, arms folded. "What you writing there?"

"Just my notes. Chicken scratch." He needed to engage her. "Could I have a glass of seltzer, please?" While the woman filled the glass he tried to keep her talking. "So Rico came in Friday and ended up doing some shots. Did he leave after he got drunk?"

She snorted as she slid the glass of seltzer in front of him. "Maybe I shouldn't say this about my own nephew, but Rico doesn't know when to stop. He likes to get his load on."

"You've seen him get drunk before?"

"Plenty of times. Drinking up my profits. I tell him he got a problem, but he don't want to hear it. He is all head up his ass about being famous. A big shot baseball player, too important for anybody to bother him about what he is drinking. Dominicans think everything centers around baseball. I don't know what my sister taught him, but that boy was not raised right."

He sipped the seltzer, cold and bubbly. "He's got a drinking problem."

"That and no respect for his elders. If it is not about baseball, that boy is lazy. He's got the *mañana* attitude."

"*Mañana*, as in tomorrow?"

She nodded. "As in, if he can put it off till tomorrow, he will."

He nodded. "Lots of people suffer from that. From what I hear, your nephew is an awesome ballplayer."

She tossed the rag onto the counter. "Lot of good that will do him after he falls into the bottle."

It seemed ironic, a bar owner complaining about the effects of alcohol. "So that night, July tenth. A week ago. Did Enrico head out of here after he did the shots?"

"I wish. He hung around, trying to weasel some more booze from behind the bar. I wasn't putting up with that. I sent him to the back room to sleep it off." She nodded to a door behind the bar. "In the office back there. That's where he spent the night."

"Maybe he went out the back door," he suggested.

She smiled. "Mister, there's no door or window. He was back there, sleeping on the cot until five, six in the morning. This I know because I worked closing that night. After last call, a few customers hung on till morning and I was here waiting on them forever. I offered to make him some breakfast, but he had to get back right away. Something about the rules and the coach."

"Yeah, the players are supposed to sleep in the dorm."

"Ridiculous rules for grown men."

And it doesn't keep them from getting wasted, Cody thought. He scribbled the time line Damita had detailed in his notebook. "One thing I don't get; why didn't Rico mention this when I first interviewed him about the attack?"

"Because he broke the rules. It's all about baseball for him. He's afraid that if the coach finds these things out, he'll get kicked off the team for breaking curfew and drinking. Now, instead, he is in trouble from here to Sunday. Nothing but trouble because of his lying and drinking."

Pretty much, yeah, Cody thought as he placed a few dollars on the bar and thanked Mrs. Arechia. "One more thing," he said. "Did anyone else see Rico here in the early hours of Saturday morning?"

"Sure." She pointed to two of the patrons sitting at the bar and mentioned her daughter Alicia, Rico's cousin, who had arrived in the morning to clean up as Rico was leaving. "She works in the bakery next door. They're closing soon, but you might be able to catch her."

A short conversation with the men at the bar convinced Cody that Rico had indeed spent most of that night here.

As Cody finished his seltzer he thought about the records from the turnstile at Hawthorne Hall and tried to piece together Rico Valpariso's path that night. First to the party at the Regan Hotel. Then back to the dorm. Then here to Aunt Damita's saloon. Then back into the dorm right around six a.m. It jived with the dormitory records. That put Valpariso back in the dorm after the attack, with just enough time for a harried shave, during which he cut himself, before hustling off to breakfast or practice or whatever mandatory activity the coaching staff insisted upon. Cody agreed with Damita Arechia that the team rules were a bit juvenile, though it was also clear that some of these boys needed babysitting during their stint here in Syracuse.

Next he stopped by the bakery next door and resisted the urge to stock up on pastries while Alicia confirmed her cousin was sacked out in the back room of the bar last Saturday morning. "He was there, giving my mother grief. She wanted to make breakfast for him and he thanks her by walking out the door. Do you know what? I'm glad he's gone. No one should treat my mother that way."

Alicia Arechia sealed the deal. On the way back to the precinct he called ahead to Sergeant Lopez to let her know how things were developing. "We need to drop the charges against Enrico Valpariso," he said. "His alibi looks good."

"How good?"

"Airtight."

She sighed. "Don't you know better than to call me with bad news?"

"It's good news for Valpariso."

"Any more bad news?" she asked.

"The Dow is down twenty points."

"Wiseass. I'll call the DA."

Chapter 68

Rico Valpariso
Bronx, New York

It wasn't so bad being kicked out of Syracuse.

It got him here to the Yankees game, right? He tossed back beer and shuffled his sneakers on the peanut-shell-strewn cement and tried to imagine himself at the plate, just like Posada, waiting on a three and two pitch. Monster pressure, man, but he could do it.

The pitch drew a swing, that popping sound as the ball struck wood, and Posada was stepping slowly toward first, watching as the ball sank into the bleachers. Home run, baby!

"Yes! Oh, yeah!" His shout blended into the chorus of approval as everyone celebrated the go-ahead run. It choked Rico up to watch Posada run the bases. He pressed his lips together and tried to ignore the tears that filled his eyes at the glory of baseball and the death of a dream.

His dream.

Grinding to a halt because of fucking McGann. An arrest, and now he'd have to go back to Syracuse for a trial, maybe miss school. Even without a conviction, Baruch might not let him play. His scholarship was a big question mark, and his lawyer said there was nothing he could do about it. "They can pull a scholarship if you make the school look bad," Paul Jimenez had said, his doleful brown eyes making him look like a sad old dog.

If he got convicted, he'd be looking at time in the big house, a jail sentence, and of course the MLB draft pick would be null and void.

Either way, Rico was going to lose his lifeblood, his backbone, his soul.

They were going to strip him of baseball.

He let the tears roll down his cheeks, drop onto his lap and into his open cup of beer. He'd really fucked up.

As the roar died down and another player came up to bat, Rico felt the buzz of his cell phone in his pocket. He put the beer down by his feet and fished it out. Just his bad luck, it was his lawyer.

"Paul. *Como Estás?*"

"Good news, my brother. I just got a call from the DA's office in Syracuse. They're dropping the charges."

"What?" Rico plugged his other ear, tuning out the action on the field, the stadium noise, the sensory overload. "What are you saying?"

"You're a free man. Your alibi checked out. The assault charges are dismissed."

"Yes!" Rico closed his eyes, crossed himself. "Oh, *Dios!* Thank you, God. Thank you!"

Two men sitting in front of him turned; both shot him a skeptical look. "Chrissakes, it was only a single," said the grizzled one.

"I don't know what you want to do," Paul was saying. "I can get them to give us an apology in writing, but I'm not sure the Lakers will reinstate you."

"Forget it," Rico said, snapping his fingers as the path became clear. "No way am I going back to Syracuse. I don't need the Lakers anymore."

And he wasn't taking his chances on another year with Baruch baseball.

Down on the field someone clobbered the ball and it bounced like a pinball, ricocheting off second base, the shortstop's shoulder, then down to the grass. The crowd went wild as the batter—Rico didn't even know who was up anymore— raced to first base and made a single out of a shitty grounder.

That was what baseball was all about, man. Turning it all around when you look like you're going down.

"Rico?" Paul's voice squirted from the phone. "You still there?"

"I'm here. I'm really here. I'm watching the Yankees game."

"What do you want me to do?"

"Get the letter of apology. I'm good with that," Rico said. "You gonna send me a bill?"

"Your parents paid me a retainer."

Rico thought of the sour homecoming he'd had just a few days ago, his father's stony puss, his mother crying into a hanky as if he'd died or something. They would come around quickly. They would be dancing and laughing when he announced his decision, the news that every Dominican father wants to hear about his son. All this time he had been holding on by his fingernails at Baruch, determined to be the first person in his family to earn a college degree, and for what? So that he could put on a suit and ride an elevator to some desk job five days a week?

That grind was over.

The time to start his life was now. Now, before it got derailed again.

"Have you ever been to Pittsburgh?" he asked the attorney.

"What? No, I haven't."

"I hear it's a baseball town. They love their Pirates," Rico said. One day it would be his town. People would know his face; kids would know his name. "I've been drafted by the Pirates, and I'm going to sign. I'm going to be a pro baseball player, on the same team that the legendary Latino Roberto Clemente played on."

"Really?" The lawyer sounded skeptical.

"Yeah, well, I gotta start in the minors. Everybody's got to start somewhere."

"Good luck, Rico. I'll look for you on TV."

"I'll be there, man. I'll be there."

Chapter 69

Kate
Good Samaritan Hospital

After a day of driving, Kate slipped into Ben's hospital room and found both Ben and Erin asleep in the shifting illumination from the television screen. Ben's face was a mask of tranquility and Erin was curled up in a chair, snuggled in a hospital blanket.

Relieved to be back, Kate let out a sigh and lifted her face to the TV screen, where Hugh Laurie was ranting on about possible diagnoses in a rerun episode of *House*.

"Dr. House," Kate said, "where are you when we need you?"

"Really," Erin said without stirring. "But I have to say, Ben's doctors are much kinder and gentler." She opened her eyes. "How was your trip?"

Kate sank into the chair beside her sister. "It was good, actually. Sort of a purging. I thought I'd have so much to pack, but everything I really needed fit into three suitcases."

"I guess you and Eli won't be fighting about the Mikasa? No bickering over the Lenson Crystal?"

Kate smiled. "I thought I'd want some of his stained-glass pieces, but when I took a look at them this time, I saw how intrinsically they represent him. They belong to him, no question about it. So the glass house is over for me, and I don't think I'll be returning to Woodstock."

"And your job?"

"I guess I'll have to give notice at work." She had thought about that during today's car ride. In a few weeks the teachers would be back to school, attending in-service training and preparing their classrooms for the new year, but she would not be among them. Perhaps the hardest part of all of this would be saying good-bye to her colleagues at school, giving up the connection she always forged with her students during a school year. During the past few years teaching had allowed her to lose herself and shift focus away from her disintegrating life with Eli. "I'll miss the kids, but Ben is going to need an advocate here when he's going through rehab. *If* he gets in the program. Dr. Zanth thinks he's a good candidate, but to think it would be so competitive to get help. I had no idea that there's a shortage of treatment facilities for patients with TBI."

"That is a surprise." Erin peeled off the blanket, leaned down and mussed her hair, then flopped back up. "I need to get back to the hotel. I know it's not even nine, but I have to pack and get over to the airport hotel. My flight's at six."

"Six a.m.? I thought it was in the evening. Oh, Erin, I didn't know you had to go this soon." Kate fished the car keys out of her purse and handed them to Erin. "Take my car. Just leave the keys in the hotel. If you want to take my car to the airport hotel, just—"

"Calm down, sistah. I'm not late yet." Erin jiggled the keys. "The Volvo? You traded cars back in Woodstock."

"Yup. The lipstick-red Ford with the spoiler is taking a break."

"God bless it." Her fingers closed around the keyring. "I wish I could stay and talk longer. He hasn't been asleep that long. And when he woke up after dinner, he wasn't in a rush to get out of here. He actually seemed to remember why he was here. That's progress, right?"

"God, I hope so."

"Anyway, maybe his night terrors will fade, too. The restraints are on now, just in case." Erin held her arms open for a hug. "Sorry to rush off, but if I don't get back I'm afraid the mayor will crash and burn."

"No doubt."

"We've got a big event at the aquarium this weekend, and an international lacrosse tournament at Johns Hopkins."

Kate was reminded of her sister's very full life in Baltimore, a schedule jam-packed with meetings and luncheons, ball games and parties, sailing regattas and festivals at the Inner Harbor. That Erin could tear herself away for a week was nothing short of a miracle. "How do you keep these things straight in your head?"

"I don't. They're in my BlackBerry."

"I don't know what I would have done without you." Kate embraced her sister, letting her chin linger a moment on the bony knob of Erin's shoulder. "Geez, Erin, you dropped everything and came up here and kept a vigil for Ben and patched my life together."

Erin sighed. "You did the patching, Kate."

When they separated they both turned to him. His body lay still but for the rise and fall of his breath. The swelling around his face had reduced, but the bruising had turned sickly shades of purple, green, and brown. The beard that was growing in had earned him the nickname "Abe Lincoln" among the nurses.

Kate bit her lower lip at the vulnerable expression of his lips, the ghostly hollow beneath his good eye. When he was awake he talked excessively, but he seemed to find peace in sleep.

"Take care of our boy." Erin touched Kate's shoulder and they leaned into each other for a long hug. "I'm going to miss you guys."

Kate nodded. "I don't know what I would have done without you."

"You're so strong. You're my hero."

"Hardly!" Kate swallowed hard, trying not to get emotional. After all Erin had done, she didn't want her leaving on a sad note.

Erin squeezed her arm. "You call me if you think of anything I can do, okay?"

"Always."

And then, she was gone, her footsteps fading down the hall.

Alone with her son for the first time that day, Kate went over to his bedside to check the monitors and the restraints that were now necessary. From her limited knowledge everything seemed fine. The drive had zapped her energy, but she wanted to be here for Ben's inevitable night terror. The nurses had reported that he'd been waking up every night, usually more than once, and it was getting more and more difficult to calm him.

Kate grabbed the blanket Erin had abandoned and snuggled into the chair, pulling her legs up to her chest.

Night terrors . . .

When Sonny, the nurse, first mentioned that Ben was having episodes, the image of her son, wild-eyed and manic, had blossomed in Kate's memory. Ben was about to start fifth grade when the night terrors began.

The first time, Kate had been straightening up the house—tossing cleats into the mudroom, newspapers into the recycling bin—when Ben emerged from his bedroom.

"It's after midnight, sweetie. Is Dylan asleep?" It was a sleepover night, typical of their summers.

Ben didn't answer, but kneeled down beside her and tilted his head over the magazine rack. His eyes were impossibly wide and blue, like one of those waif paintings. "You're working much too hard."

She laughed, partly because it seemed like such a grown-up thing to say, and partly because Eli liked to tease that she didn't work during the summers. As if chasing two fourth-grade boys with their science experiments, affinity for fireworks, and calendar full of baseball games and practices weren't enough.

Ben had fooled her that first time, when he'd reached out to pat her head, such a parental gesture. But as soon as she told him he had to go to bed, his demeanor changed. Tears pooled in his wide eyes, eyes that held a frantic plea.

"I want to go, but I'm just so afraid. So afraid I'll have an outburst, that I won't be able to control myself." A shudder rippled through his body and he began to sob.

Kate folded him into her arms, but there was no soothing him. Through his tears he told her he needed a bath, and she guided him to the tub and got the water running. She watched as he climbed into the tub and hunched near the faucet, soothed by the water falling through his fingers. After a few minutes he said he felt better and returned to bed without incident.

The following night, about an hour after Ben went to bed, he sought her out, his eyes wild as he babbled about not being able "to find the right one." This time he paced, his voice so loud it drew Dylan from his bed. Again, he wanted a bath, which soothed him. And so began the regular pattern of Ben waking up each night, ranting and sobbing, as if possessed by a soul-sucking demon. Frightened and wary, Kate didn't understand what was happening, though she could understand how episodes like these could inspire movies like *The Exorcist* or *The Chosen*.

In all her years of teacher's training Kate had not heard of night terrors, but Ben's pediatrician had some experience with the phenomenon. "It's something he'll outgrow, probably by the time he turns twelve," the doctor had explained. "Your job is to keep him safe while he's acting out. Contrary to popular myth, it's fine to wake someone up while they're sleepwalking, so feel free to get Ben awake so he can return to bed and a sound sleep."

When Kate did further research, she found a dearth of information on the subject. The few accounts she came across reiterated the one-page handout the doctor gave her, which she found to be true. Despite the nightly frequency of Ben's night terrors, they subsided completely by his twelfth birthday.

And that was the end of it . . . until this brain injury.

"Do you think it's a reoccurrence of the night terrors he used to have as a kid?" she had asked Drs. Pruett and Paulo, who both shrugged off the question as irrelevant. "Hard to say." This nonanswer was typical of the communication Kate had experienced with most of the doctors—excluding Dr. Teddy Zanth, who remained in close touch regarding Ben's care. The other doctors were aloof and hard to pin down during their daily rounds in the company of a dozen doctors or more. Kate was learning that the doctors were more like distant gods, issuing edicts from afar, bristling when their decisions were questioned.

If the hospital was a war zone, the doctors were generals who passed orders down to the front line soldiers, the nurses, who stayed in the battlefield to make sure orders were carried out. The nurses—Sonny, Diana, Isabelle, Jodi, and Oliver—were open to discussion on any topic involving Ben. Oliver and Diana agreed that Ben might be prone to the reoccurring night terrors because of his childhood experiences with them. It had been Jodi's idea for Kate to leave Ben a note that explained what had happened to Ben, and for a while that seemed to calm him when he woke up in the middle of the night. Sonny had shared anecdotal stories about brain injury cases he had worked on, a vast range of injuries, disabilities, and recoveries. Every day Kate learned something new from the nurses, the true caregivers.

Kate didn't know what time she dozed off, but suddenly Ben's voice was pulling her from a deep sleep.

"Somebody help me. Get me out of here. I'm going to be late and I am so fucked."

She checked the clock: almost ten. "Ben, it's okay." In an instant she was beside his bed, her hands cupping his shoulders. "You're not missing anything. You are right where you're supposed to be, in a hospital, recovering from an injury."

"But Coach Ramsey said no excuses. *No excuses.* And I screw everything up by sleeping in. Help me get out of here."

Desperation glinted in his eyes, and she longed to sweep through the webs of damage caused by his injury and connect with him, really connect. "Ben, you need to stay in bed, okay?

You need rest so that you can get back to the game. Do you understand? Rest."

"Don't you understand, Mom? I've been resting! I've been in this bed so long my ass is getting sore."

Kate bit back a smile. This sounded more like her son. Maybe this wasn't a night terror.

"Sounds like someone is getting a better grip on reality," Jodi said, joining them. "You know, we have noticed some pressure wounds developing. We try to shift you around, but you flop right back on your ass."

Ben flailed, tugging against the restraints. "If you let me go to practice, it'll solve that."

"Can't let you do that, A-Rod, but we might be able to increase your physical therapy, get you walking around more. Long as you wear your helmet. We need to get you fitted for one."

"I got a batting helmet that fits better than that one," Ben said. "How about it?"

"I like the way you're thinking, sweetpea, but you need a special helmet to protect the vulnerable area in your skull. We can't do anything right this minute, but I'll make sure Dr. Pruett knows you're feeling energetic."

Ben braced his arms and nodded down at the restraints. "How about these? Can you cut me loose?"

Jodi put her hands on her hips. "Well, I s'pose I can do that as long as you promise me you won't bust out of this joint."

"I won't. I promise."

"That means you stay in bed, Ben," the nurse warned.

"Really," Kate added. "You could get seriously hurt if you start walking on your own."

"Christ, Mom, whose side are you on?"

"I'm here for you, Ben," Kate said, rubbing his upper arm. "We're all here for you."

Chapter 70

Marnie
Boston

Overworked and overtired, Marnie pulled herself out of the seat and braced herself on the pole as the well-lit Brookline Station rolled into sight beyond the train's windows.

Her shoes seemed barbed with needles and hot coals. Ignoring the pain, she hopped off the train and crossed the platform. These shoes didn't have enough arch support for twelve hours on your feet, the abuse she had just subjected herself to. She wasn't supposed to work a full shift at Storemart, but George had asked her to stay to cover for a sick employee, and she figured it was worth it to get some time off at the end of the week. It seemed like a good idea, but ouch.

Inside the pocket of her shorts her cell phone hummed, signaling that she had a text message. Great. Another nasty message would be just the thing to cap off a rotten night.

Although it was dark, the air was still soupy humid, and the occasional breeze only scattered dust and hot, smelly air. Marnie pushed herself toward the apartment, wishing she could be anywhere but here. Not that Brookline wasn't a great place to live. Lots of scientists, musicians, and basketball players made their homes here. But in the last few days she'd been feeling Boston closing in around her. The heat, the grime, the threats. Even the crazy guy who lived in the alley behind Beantown Grind had spit at her yesterday when she tried to get past him.

She'd been thinking that it was all a sign from the furies or something; a message telling her to get out of town, now.

At the corner she stayed out of the crosswalk while a shiny white pickup truck made the turn, the rear of the truck fishtailing with a squeal of brakes. Asshole.

As she plodded down the street toward home, she felt a stab of guilt.

These things wouldn't be happening if you hadn't done the wrong thing, all those years ago. Right, Marnie. Blame yourself for the humidity.

Her logical mind knew that there was no connection, but she still felt the brand of guilt, a scar you couldn't keep your fingertips from tracing.

The last time she had seen her father, she had argued vehemently with her mother. Marnie didn't want to go. Brittany Nelson had invited her to come along on a family shopping trip, and Mrs. Nelson was the nicest mom at school, with a seemingly endless supply of hot cocoa, grilled cheese sandwiches, and grape soda. Mrs. Nelson didn't work, so she appeared outside the school in her minivan on rainy days to drive the children home. When the Nelson kids went shopping, they got to stop for lunch at the food court. The Nelsons had a beach house in Cape Cod and an enormous tree filling their vestibule at Christmas time.

At last, the invitation had come for Marnie to do something with Brittany, and she was sure that after this one foray the Nelsons would fold her into their perfect family so that she could pretend to have a brother and sister and a mom who cared.

But it was not to be.

"You've got plans with your father," Jade Epstein had said. "Tell Brittany you'll hang out another time."

Marnie was crushed. It had taken months to hook Brittany. But no amount of arguing could make her mother change her mind. That day when Marnie's father arrived with "Little Petunia," Marnie noticed things. She saw the disgusting red blood vessels in his eyes. The bristly skin on his neck reminded her of a turkey wattle. And then, when he told her they could only skate for half a session because his daughter—his other daughter—had a party to attend, Marnie felt a stab of injustice.

It wasn't fair. At this very moment she could be shopping with the Nelsons, and no one cared. But drop everything when Petunia got an invite to a pathetic kiddy party. It wasn't fair, and she was done with the fake-oh father thing.

That afternoon when she returned home, she had stood beside the television, arms folded across her chest, until her mother noticed her glum expression.

"What's the problem, Marnie?" Jade Epstein did not like to be interrupted when watching the soap operas she'd missed all week.

"It's him. My father. I never want to see him again."

"Well, he's got a right to see you, as long as the court sees fit."

"I'm not going next time. I hate him," Marnie said, knowing her words would have no effect. She couldn't stand being powerless over her own life. There was only one way to stop him . . . an ugly, deceitful path . . . and she took it. "You don't see the way he looks at me, Mom. He's . . . disgusting."

Jade's gaze snapped up. "Did he touch you?"

"I . . . I don't want to talk about it! I'm not going near him again!" With that, she had stomped into her bedroom and slammed the door behind her.

Through the thin wall of the apartment, she heard the progression of calls. First to her father's cell, then to Leo Epstein's new wife, whom Jade rarely dealt with. "You tell Leo that this is the end. If he wants to stay out of court, hell, if he wants to stay out of jail, he had better stay away from Marnie. I don't care what the custody agreement says! And if you care one whit about your Little Petunia, you'd better haul his ass into therapy!"

That afternoon, because of a small, twisted lie, it was all over. She was free to accept any invitation she wanted, though

Brittany Nelson did not ask her over again. And she was done with the tired stranger who smelled like peppermint.

She didn't miss her father, and that did not bother her. No, the tight kernel of guilt she harbored was over that lie, a wicked implication that had charged him with heinous things. That was definitely a sin.

She turned the last corner and fixed her gaze on their apartment house two and a half blocks ahead. So close, but still many painful footsteps away. She paused by a small tree and thought about shedding her shoes. They were killing her, but the street was so disgusting. She just had to get home.

The traffic was light, and she cut across instead of walking up to the light three blocks ahead. She was on the double yellow line when two headlights came zigzagging toward her. A wild driver, wheels squealing.

Adrenaline shot through her veins as the lights closed in on her. Gasping in a huge breath, she sprang ahead and lunged across to the other side. Her feet pounded painfully on the sidewalk, where she ducked behind a small tree and dared a look at the vehicle. It was a white pickup, soaring past her on the wrong side of the road. The windows were tinted, too dark to see inside in that brief moment when it was close enough for a look.

"Oh, my God." Marnie pressed a hand to her chest.

A couple who were down the block hurried toward her, the mountainous woman struggling to keep up.

The man stopped a few feet from her. "You okay?"

Marnie nodded, unconsciously sliding off her backpack to reach for her keys.

"That was so scary! I thought he was going to hit you." The woman's thick jowls were beet red. She adjusted her cotton shirt over her belly. "Where are the police when you need them?"

"They should be patrolling here," the man said. "Didn't you read that in the paper? They've had trouble with drive-bys lately. Teens, they think, but still."

As they talked Marnie found her keys and gripped them so

that one key protruded between each knuckle. It wasn't much in the way of defense, but it might buy her a minute or two if someone got close.

"That was a close call," the man said. "Stupid kids."

She swallowed, her mouth suddenly dry. She wanted to tell the young couple that the man in the truck was not a kid pulling a prank; he was out to get her. She'd been getting threats. She was a target.

"I think I might know who it is," Marnie said.

The woman's eyes widened. "You want us to call the police for you?"

"No, no, I have a cell phone," Marnie said as the three of them stared down the street where the truck had disappeared.

"He's long gone," the man said.

He was right; she was safe now. "I'm going home." Marnie thanked them and started walking again, wishing she had worn better shoes so that she could run the rest of the way. There was no slowing her breath or calming her jittery nerves, but soon she would be able to soak her feet and stretch out in bed, plugged into her iPod.

Behind her an engine roared, causing goose bumps to form on her upper arms despite the hot night. It was nothing; probably a car that needed a muffler.

Like a growling monster, the loud car approached from behind, unnerving her as it seemed to linger behind her. Gulping air, she stepped up her pace.

Don't turn around. Don't turn around. She was almost home, and to acknowledge him would be to encourage him.

"Hey!" a low, gravelly voice called out.

He's talking to me, Marnie thought. A car passed on the other side, but no one else on the street seemed to notice her now.

"You want a ride?" he asked.

Worried that he might try to grab her, Marnie caught a glimpse of the vehicle in her peripheral vision. A white pickup, a few feet away, but edging alongside her.

Oh, God.

"Come on," he said, his voice sounding friendly. "I'll give you a ride."

Ignoring him, she moved toward the apartment door. Long strides, rapid pace.

"I'll ride you all night!" he growled. "Freak!"

Swallowing air, Marnie steeled her muscles to run for the door. Her panicked mind processed the sound of the truck door opening and slamming. He was coming after her! Her fingers tightened around her keys.

Crossing the path to the building, she made it to the lobby door and spun around, wielding her sharp-edged fist in the air.

A laugh rang out from the shiny white steel and tinted glass. She was trying to memorize the vehicle when the blast made her jump. Her heart raced, but she realized it was just the engine of the truck. Motor gunning, wheels squealing. It raced off down the road, the taillights glowing as it turned the corner by the old church and disappeared.

Marnie keyed her way into the vestibule, sank down onto the floor, and burst into tears.

Chapter 71

Kate
Syracuse

"Did you see how quickly he went back to sleep?" Nurse Jodi seemed pleased as she made notes on a laptop—Ben's electronic chart. Watching Jodi's reflection in the glass, the way her dark fingers danced over the keyboard, Kate was increasingly in awe of her range of skills. All the nurses here had been great—positive without mincing the facts.

"I hope that's going to be the new trend." Kate stood in the hall of the neuro ICU, where she could watch Ben from the glass window without disturbing him. The metal frame of the interior window felt cool against her cheek as she leaned against it, not sure where to go from here.

"Sugar, if you think it's a positive, who's gonna prove you wrong? You've got some good times ahead with your son, some bad times, too. When it's good, you got to celebrate. Whoop it up. You're going to need those good news moments to get you by."

Kate forced a smile. "Consider this my happy dance. It's hard to muster enthusiasm right now." Like a sopping wet sponge, her brain could not soak up another ounce, good or bad.

"Did I hear something about good news?" Just the sound of his voice offered her a sense of relief, a window opening down the hall.

"You again? Get out of town!" Jodi pushed at Greg Cody's upper arm. "I heard you already solved this case, Detective Cody, but you're still coming around?"

For me, Kate thought hopefully. *He's here to see me.*

"A good detective always comes up with more questions, Jodi."

"Is that so?" She closed her laptop, turned to Kate. "I'm going to put those restraints back on, just in case, but I don't expect he'll wake up again till morning."

Kate pushed away from the window. "Thanks, Jodi. I'll see you tomorrow." She turned to face Greg Cody, immediately noticing the pinched look around his eyes, the tension in his face. "Something's wrong. What happened?"

"Talk about cut to the chase. I'm fine, how are you?"

"Tired. Hungry. Exhausted, really. I drove to Woodstock and back today, wanted to pick up my things before Erin left. She's on her way now." Kate felt a sting of loneliness as they started walking down the hall, but she didn't want to suck Greg Cody's soul just because her sister was leaving town. "Can you give me a ride back to the hotel?" She hoped that sounded casual enough.

"I'll do better than that. We can stop at this bistro along the way and grab a bite to eat."

He had taken the bait. "As long as you tell me why you look so awful."

"Flattering, too." He pressed the elevator button. "I'm afraid my bad news is contagious." He turned to face her, his eyes dark, rueful. "It's Valpariso. The DA dropped the charges against him when I learned that his alibi holds up. He was down the hill, off campus, at the time of the attack. A few people saw him, and the scanner in the dormitory turnstiles backs up his story."

"Damn it! I wanted him to fry."

"Kate? I think you want to catch the guy who did this to your son."

A hot breath hissed through her teeth. "Yes, of course.

Nothing personal against Rico Valpariso. I was just so sure he was guilty and now if it's not him . . . It's a huge disappointment knowing the investigation isn't over yet."

"There's that. And because of our mistake, Valpariso got kicked off the Lakers and sent home to New York City. I feel bad about that, though the kid was sinking himself, drinking and breaking curfew. The team administration wasn't on to him yet, but it was only a matter of time."

"So . . . now Gibbs and Valpariso are gone. Two down. It reminds me of that Agatha Christie mystery, *Ten Little Indians*."

He winced. "Not really."

The elevator doors opened and they maneuvered around a gurney and a handful of hospital staff.

She spoke quietly, not wanting to attract attention in the elevator. "So the next question is, if not Valpariso, then who?"

Cody nodded, his silver hair glinting in the fluorescent light. "We're casting a wider net now. I discovered an interesting detail about the girlfriend today."

"Emma? Currently the ex-girlfriend."

"Did you know she was left-handed?"

"Really? I didn't know that, but do you think she's even strong enough?"

"Strong enough to swing a bat. If she took him by surprise attack in the dark. . . . it's possible. She was the one who slipped him the drugs."

Kate nodded, although she found it hard to believe Emma would have the fortitude to carry out such an attack. The patient on the gurney, a young twentysomething woman wearing a turban, stared at Cody and Kate sharply, as if they themselves were suspects. Kate waited until the woman was wheeled off on the next floor to ask about Turtle.

"Yes, Joe Turturro is still a suspect. There's been a delay getting into his room. With the personal lock on the door, my boss wanted a warrant, and we stopped pursuing that when we had Valpariso." Cody shrugged. "We're back on it. Should have a warrant to get into his room in the dorm tomorrow. But

Turtle, he's a left-hander, not a switch-hitter. Doesn't really match up with the angles of the blows."

"Not the perfect suspect," Kate said. Though she didn't know who qualified for "perfect" at this point.

They didn't talk on the way to the parking lot, where Cody stopped at a late-model Jeep. The canvas top was down, the roll bars exposed like a skeleton.

She climbed into the passenger seat, which, she noted, was absent of the paper cups, newspapers, and take-out containers you'd expect in a single man's car. "A convertible. Is this your midlife crisis?"

"Yeah, and a rather poor one at that." As he backed out he slung his arm onto the top of her seat, making her feel for a moment like part of a couple again. She settled into the stiff seat, wondering how it would feel to be loved by Greg Cody . . . thoroughly, voraciously ravaged.

"You okay?" he asked as he turned out of the hospital parking lot.

"Fine." She immediately turned to the right, grateful for the air blowing over her heated face. *Don't go there,* she told herself. *Don't torture yourself with romantic crap just because your husband has been withholding since the fall of the Berlin Wall.*

The Elephant Bistro was exactly what Kate needed. Greg ordered a few light dishes for them to share: a wedge salad, crab spring rolls, crusty warm bread, and two bowls of squash soup.

"This place is an amazing find," Kate said. "Do you come here often?"

"Is that a pickup line?" He seemed to be working hard to keep from grinning. "Seems to me you're moving toward the singles scene, right? Didn't you go back to Woodstock today to clear your stuff out of the house?"

"I did."

"How did that go over with your husband?"

"My guess is he's relieved to have me out of his hair without a fight. I'm always the person who wants to define things. I'm the one who needs parameters and closure." She broke off another crust of bread. "So he's probably thinking he got off without the endless series of soul-searching conversations I require before making a huge decision. So yes, 'relieved' is a good description. I'll take the initiative to get the divorce, and Eli can just keep on keeping on. And, from the evidence left in my former home, I can see that he's already moved on."

He nodded. "Does that bother you?"

"A little. Mostly because he was obviously involved with her months ago, and I just turned the other cheek rather than point it out and argue about it. I suppose I wanted the marriage to be over back then; I just didn't know how to make that happen."

"It's always hard to end a relationship, especially a long one." He stared off at another table, perhaps another lifetime. "Things get even more complicated when there's a child involved."

"I think it was Ben who kept us together. Now, it's as if what happened to Ben has given me permission to separate from Eli. Ben needs me now. It's a pure, genuine need, and any fake attachment I had to Eli pales in comparison." She squeezed the white center of bread into a dough ball. "I know I'm doing the right thing being here, but my overloaded conscience won't allow me to sleep."

"Worried about Ben?"

"I know he's in good hands. It's . . . everything else."

"Tell me. What thorny items weave their way between you and a night of sound sleep?"

It was a crazy question—way too personal—but the words left Kate's lips before they could be filtered. "My marriage . . . my failed marriage. I'm almost fifty years old and I don't know how to tell my mother I'm getting a divorce."

"If she's got a good, strong heart, pick up the phone. Otherwise, maybe she doesn't need to know. Full disclosure isn't always required with an elderly parent."

Kate nodded. "Then there's the selfish me. Fifty years old and I'll be in the singles scene again. That is just not going to work for me. I've seen the commercials for date dot-com. There is no way I could sell myself in a sixty-second video that people can tune into on YouTube."

He tore into a crust of bread. "No, I don't think the singles scene is for you, Kate."

"Maybe you know someone. A nice cop you can fix me up with?"

"Cops aren't nice. They're worse at marriage than celebrities and politicians. Real swordsmen."

"Nice medieval terminology." Kate caught herself smiling. "Was the end of your marriage difficult?"

"Aren't they all? I'll never understand those people who divorce and stay friends. How does that work? Once someone's been under my skin, a part of me, I can't say I'll ever be comfortable dealing with her across a table, but that's just me. Set in my ways, I guess. Not very good at redefining myself or my relationships."

"You sound fairly articulate about relationships."

"Yeah, my therapist did a good job. Had to leave her behind in New York. My ex-wife got to keep our daughter and the therapist. Come to think of it, she got to keep New York City. How'd I screw that up?"

"Do you miss New York?"

"Every day, but I needed to move on. Coming here was good for me. It was the first time I had to stand on my own and put a life together, get an apartment, start from scratch. I really miss my daughter. Not that we were that close when I left, but we've developed a thing, and now I kick myself for moving so far from the city."

"Do you think you'll stay here?" she asked.

"Stay, as in forever? I'm not that committed. For now Syracuse is great. You've seen the great hospital system firsthand. There are jazz festivals and a symphony if you like that sort of thing. Lots of comedy clubs. A couple of restaurants like this. I know my neighbors. I have friends to hang with from work. It's all good. But before I start sounding like the Chamber of

Commerce, tell me what happened with Eli today. Was he nasty? Helpful? A pain in the ass?"

"He wasn't there. One of the reasons I chose today was because Eli had to be in New York for a craft fair."

"Really? Does it bother you that he can zip down to New York but when it comes to seeing his injured son in Syracuse he can't seem to make the trip?"

"That didn't even occur to me at this point." She pressed a hand to her temple. "Honestly, I've given up on Eli's parenting skills. Fortunately, Ben doesn't seem to miss him. He's been asking about Dylan and Marnie all week, but hasn't mentioned Eli."

He stacked their empty soup bowls. "I haven't had an update for a few days. How is Ben progressing?"

"His head is healing, and so far no sign of pneumonia and infection." Emotion flooded Kate, pooling as tears in her eyes. "I'm sorry." She swiped at the tears, surprised by the sudden onslaught.

"Don't clam up because of me."

"It just hit me that I really don't know how Ben is doing, beyond my own instincts. The doctors are distant and the nurses remain positive. We're still in 'wait and see' mode, and I'm sick of it. I want some answers. I want to know that he's going to recover. I want someone to reassure me that his injury won't keep him from living a fulfilled life, and . . ." She bit her lower lip to keep from crying.

"And no one will say the word, because no one knows what the future holds for Ben."

She nodded. "I don't mean to complain. I'm grateful that he's alive. But it's hard to look ahead, make plans. I'm not even sure what to hope for anymore."

He rubbed the stubble on his beard. "Seems to me you should shoot for the stars. No one can fault you for wanting the best for your kid."

"You would think that, but sometimes I talk about Ben's recovery and the doctors look at me like I'm in denial. It makes me wonder what information they're holding back." What did they know that they weren't saying? Kate's hours of research in the hospital library would never make up for all the things she didn't know about brain injury. So she stayed on guard, vigilant, to make sure the decisions made were in Ben's best interest. "It took me years to learn how to be the mother of an athlete; now, I'm suddenly the mother of a critically ill patient, and I'm afraid I'm not very good at it. Overnight I'm supposed to be an expert in TBI. Arguing, questioning . . . it's all beyond my comfort level."

"Ben is lucky to have you as his advocate. Makes up for that half-baked husband of yours."

"Don't get me started on Eli. I'm trying to stay positive, wish him the best."

"Give him the rope so he can hang himself."

She smacked his shoulder with the back of her hand. "You have a dark sense of humor." She drew in a deep breath, soothed by food and conversation. "I feel better. It's amazing what a good meal and a little black humor can do." She put her credit card in the leather folder and handed it to the waiter. "My treat tonight. You saved me from dining on Cracker Jacks from the hotel snack machine."

"Been there, done that," he said casually.

Being with Greg Cody required so little effort; one conversation flowed into another with ease and alacrity. She dreaded spending the night alone, and as the server ran her credit card a plan of sorts took shape in her mind. Some people would condemn her for it. After all she was the mother of an injured child, not even divorced yet. But really, did anyone else need to know her personal business? Pushing fifty, she was old enough to make choices and live with the consequences. It had been awhile and she was out of practice, but what the hell. Just like riding a bicycle, right?

She wiggled her toes in her sandals, traced her water glass stem on the table, and resolved to make Greg Cody her first. The seduction of Detective Cody would be the opening act in the new life of Kate McGann.

Chapter 72

Greg Cody
Syracuse

He kept his eyes straight and tried to focus on driving, tried to pretend that he was listening to Kate's stories about her students and not suffering sensory overload from the smell of her shampoo or perfume, lilac and vanilla, mixing with the night air, the sight of her petite frame in the passenger seat of his Jeep, the electric sway of her elbow next to his as she made a point. The entire atmosphere of the vehicle was transformed, as if the molecules moved rapidly, bouncing against each other and exploding, or whatever molecules did when they were passionate and unstable. It was all Kate, changing the air that he breathed.

God, he wanted her. He'd always felt that physical tug with Kate, even before he had a sense of her spirit and personality. Now, as he had witnessed her courage and personal strength, his attraction had increased exponentially, despite the stigma of being thought of as a potential home wrecker (her home had already been wrecked) or unprofessional because he was sniffing around the mother of a crime victim. Yeah, he wanted her . . . but he had a better chance of getting struck by lightning on a clear summer night like this.

She was wrapping up a story when he pulled into the hotel drive, shifted the Jeep into park, and cut the engine. "Oh . . . we're here." She frowned at the building's double doors. "I'm not ready to go in there yet. Now that Erin has left . . ." Her voice trailed off, giving way to the group song of crickets.

Her dark hair caught moonlight, a pure sheen. She looked like a pixie, petite and glittery.

"Why are you staring at me?"

"I'm not . . . okay, I am. But is that not okay?"

"It's more than okay. I guess you've figured out that I like you, too."

He scratched his head. "Now, see? There you go and try to reduce it all into words, which makes it kind of awkward for me."

She laughed, a jingling, hearty laugh. "Right. And our language is lacking in this area. There's 'I like like you,' which is still used in grammar school, and the more recent 'you're hot,' which I've also overheard on the playground. Not much between there and 'I love you,' which is riddled with minefields."

"Exactly."

"How about . . . I'm strangely attracted to you?" She spoke with an Eastern European accent, swaying so close he could feel her breath on his cheek.

"No. That won't work at all." He lied; it was working, all right.

"No? Then why do I get the distinct impression that you want to kiss me . . . and you're thinking that it's not a good idea."

"Because it's true, on both counts." He shifted in the driver seat, trying to face her.

"And why is that a bad idea?"

"I'm thinking that once I get started, I might not know how to stop with you."

He cupped the back of her neck as he covered her mouth with his. The kiss was soft, tentative, until she slid back into his chest with a sigh. He cradled her there, savoring the feel of her, the smooth shift of skin and bone and muscle, so compact in his arms.

Kate McGann was in his arms, kissing him. He felt an unaccustomed giddiness, like one of the students she spoke of. This . . . this was a fantasy come to life. Not just some woman to hook up with and go through the motions. This was Kate.

"Mmm." She turned her face so that her lips ran along the line of his jaw, exploring the tender area in a way that drove him wild until she sighed and stopped. "Greg?"

"Yes?" His voice was a raw rumble.

"I'm getting stabbed by the gearshift. Can we go upstairs?"

He released her, then took in a good amount of air, oxygen for sanity. "What about your sister?"

Kate rubbed the side of her hip. "She's already at the airport hotel . . . early morning flight."

"Oh. In that case, maybe I should let you go. Get a good night's sleep."

"Are you kidding me? One of Syracuse's Finest is going to leave a job unfinished."

Another deep breath, though it didn't seem to clarify his logic. "You got a point. I can't let the brotherhood down." He turned the engine on. "Let's park the car."

Chapter 73

Kate
Syracuse

Falling against the rock-solid wall of his chest, Kate lost herself in the feel of his lips against her neck. Wondrous, warm sensation. It flared in her core and flamed through her belly, slowly melting a part of her that had gone stone cold.

All because of Greg Cody.

While his lips teased the sensitive tendons in her neck, his fingers moved under her cotton shirt, massaging her bare skin, pulling her body up to his so that she could feel him against her pelvis.

She moaned, stirred by the evidence that he wanted her, too. Thank God for that. And for his sense of humor. And for the wine she'd had with dinner, which helped dissolve her inhibitions.

His fingers dipped into her denim shorts, running along the waistband to the front snap. "Can we get rid of all this?" The slight touch of his hand made her gasp as he eased the zipper down.

"Am I scaring you?" he asked.

"I think I'm scaring myself."

He pushed her shorts down. She quickly stepped out of them, feeling a stir of awareness as he looked down at her. "This isn't something I do every day."

"I'll say. If you would have told me this morning that I'd end up with you, getting naked in a hotel room, I would have told you to go scratch." He slid a hand behind her back and easily lifted her into his arms. "And now, here we are."

"Here we are." She looked over at the bed, flush with excitement and wariness. "Please don't drop me."

"I wouldn't dare."

"And can we turn the lights down?"

"Eco-minded are we?" He grinned. "I think we can feel our way in the dark."

Chapter 74

Marnie
Beantown Grind, Boston

"Holy shit! You were accosted by the Brookline marauders." Chaz ducked under the counter and started taking chairs down from tables, preparing to open Beantown Grind. "Did you call the cops?"

"I didn't," Marnie admitted. "It was late, my mom was asleep, and, I don't know. By the time I got inside I felt kind of stupid. This morning when I told my mother, she thought I was exaggerating. Who are the marauders, anyway? A gang?"

"Nah, just the name some reporter coined for these guys who've been harassing people on the street late at night in Brookline. They run people off the roads, shout out derogatory things from the car, sometimes toss beer bottles out the window."

Marnie pulled plastic sheaths over her hands, opened a giant box Chaz had brought, and started loading pastries into the case. There were two boxes today, extra for the Saturday crowd, who had time to linger over an almond croissant or muffin. "How do you know about these guys?"

"Don't you read the paper?"

"Like I have time for that? When I'm not here I'm working at Storemart."

"Sorry, Cinderella. I'm just saying, last night fits in with the marauders. You said a white truck? I think that's one of the vehicles mentioned in the article. Here . . ." He switched on the coffee house's computer. "We'll check it out online soon as we set up. That other stuff—the text messages and threatening phone calls—that sounds like something different. You got any friends who are into pranks?"

"Not really." Aside from a few clownish boys from high school, Marnie didn't know anyone who liked pranking people, and even those guys had grown out of it. "The text messages, they're just not funny. No laugh potential in '*I know what you did,*' and '*You'll pay in blood.*' "

Chaz tucked the last chair under a table, considering. "Yeah, you're right. That would be an amateur prank." He flipped on the neon OPEN sign and ducked under the counter. "So . . . who do you think is playing with you? Sending the threats?"

Marnie closed the pastry box and sighed. "I don't want to think about it."

"Mmm. If you've got a gut feeling, you're probably on to something." He opened the register drawer and dropped the cash box in. "So they keep saying, 'I know what you did. . . .' Is that what's getting to you? You're remembering some huge mistake. You wronged someone and you feel bad about it. Is that it?"

"I hate you."

"Bull's-eye."

"So what did you do?"

"It was years ago." She shook her head, grateful to hide behind her dark bangs as she measured beans to start a pot of coffee brewing. "Ancient history. I was just a kid."

"It must be really bad if you remember it from that long ago."

She thought about the incident that ended her father's visits, the small lie that had the potential to blossom into a poisonous situation. "Child abuse" . . . "incest" . . . toxic phrases. If the slightest inference of impropriety had gotten around, it would have threatened Leo Epstein's marriage, his life in the community, maybe even his job.

"It was pretty bad." She met Chaz's eyes. "I hurt my father."

"Really? I didn't think you had a father."

"I haven't seen him since the whole thing went sour." *From my lie.* "He probably hates me."

"Enough to threaten you, after all these years?"

"Maybe." Marnie felt the desire to bite her nails, but she stopped her hands midway and got busy restocking the sweeteners. "You know that expression 'blood is thicker than water.' "

"I've heard it. Never gotten it."

"I think it means that, when it's your family, the bond is strong."

Chaz handed her the carton of Equal packets. "Get real. If you haven't seen the guy for years, the bond isn't that strong."

"Still . . . if I had to choose my greatest sin of all time, that would be the one." She dumped sugar packets into the bin. "I wish I could locate him, just to find out if he's behind this."

Chaz snorted. "That's easy. You can find anyone on the Internet."

Although their conversation dried up as customers trickled into the shop, Chaz's words stayed with Marnie. Was it possible that she could meet with her father, apologize, and end this insanity?

During a lull she went to the shop computer, Googled her father, and came up with five Leo Epsteins. She narrowed it down to an address in Malden, a suburb north of Boston. Could it be that easy?

She checked the subway map on the bulletin board. The Orange Line would take her to Malden. It was crazy, thinking that the address was correct and that she'd find her father at home on a random Saturday afternoon. Still, she had to give it a shot. She needed some peace, and if facing her past was the only way to get it, well then, Leo Epstein was going to get a surprise visit.

Chapter 75

Joe "Turtle" Turturro
Moyers Corners, New York

Time to cut his losses.

Pedal to the metal, Turtle flew down the highway at a smooth sixty miles per hour, not so much for the thrill of it as for speed. He needed to take care of business fast—quick and clean—before the cops got on his case, figured him out, and threw his ass in jail. Up ahead a light turned yellow, making him squeeze the brakes. What the . . . He didn't have time for a red light.

Damn McGann. Turtle wasn't one to blame all his own petty shit on someone else, but really, if the excellent first baseman hadn't come along, they'd have a better than average team at this point. Valpariso would be playing first; a very tidy job he'd do. Gibbs would be swallowing flies in center field and belting them out of the park. And Turtle himself would be cracking the bat on a few now and again. It would have been good, solid, summer ball. But no, McGann had to come along and throw things all out of whack. And now they were down two players—three if you counted fucking McGandolf—and everybody eyeballing each other like they knew who did it when nobody knew shit. And when you had to rely on beef jerkies like the guy with two first names, as well as McGann's useless sidekick Dylan Kroger, it was no wonder they were on a losing streak.

The team was shot to hell, and Turtle's own livelihood was

being threatened. Not that he'd made a fortune dealing, but his bit of side action had bought him this awesome Mustang. Used, but it was wheels. Now his next insurance payment was in jeopardy because of the mess with McGann, but that couldn't be helped. Not with Detective Cody breathing down his neck. The stuff he'd heard this morning about the police trying to get into his dorm room had made his head spin. He'd told the coach he wasn't feeling well, threw all the shit he could find into the trunk of the 'stang, and headed toward Moyers Corners.

Right at the gas station, left at the DQ. Two more lefts landed him on Scott's street, a quiet cul-de-sac where you'd never suspect a small fortune in prescription drugs was changing hands.

He made a one-handed turn into the driveway and scrambled to get the stuff out of the back. "Scotty!" he yelled, scurrying down the driveway to the basement door. His cousin Scotty lived in the downstairs apartment of a split level. Aunt Peggy lived upstairs, but she never bothered Scotty as long as he didn't make too much noise after midnight. "Scottee, my man! Open up!" Scotty had to be home. Scotty was always at home when he wasn't at dialysis, and today was not a day for liquid ice. He banged on the crappy screen door, making it rattle in its frame.

The steel door opened and Scotty stood there in orange boxers. "What the hell?"

"Scotty, I'm so glad to see you. I gotta hand this stuff back to you for now, my brother. I need a break from business for a while. Just a short while, till things cool down."

Scotty grabbed a clear Ziploc bag of pills from Turtle, eyeballed them, then tossed them onto the kitchen table. "Fine. Just pay me for what you sold and I'll find someone else who wants to get rich."

"Now just wait. Don't get me wrong. I want to make the money. I'm going to move the stuff. Just not right now."

"What, you want a vacation?"

"The cops are on my case."

"The cops! The police are on you and you led them right here to me?" Scotty smacked the top of Turtle's head as he scuttled over to the window.

"Hey!" Turtle protested. "They're not that close."

"How would you know? You sure no one followed you?"

"Yeah, I'm sure." Turtle rubbed his head. Fucking Scotty.

When Scott folded back the curtains sunlight illuminated swirling motes of dust and a network of stains on the kitchen Formica. How did Scotty live in this dump? Turtle had tried to help him clean up a few times, but Scotty seemed to like living in a cave.

"I can't believe you could be so stupid. What are you, brain dead? The Vicodin burn a hole in your brain?"

"You know I never use the stuff." Turtle had tried some Percocet once and the couch he flaked out on was spinning and flipping through the air for hours. It was not a fun ride. "I got health issues."

"Yeah? And I got kidney disease. That's how we got the drugs in the first place." He poked at a bag of shiny caplets on the table. "All the stories I had to tell to get this stuff. Sitting around in waiting rooms, sucking up to windbag doctors. 'Just get the stuff and we'll make a shitload of money.' That's what you said, Turtle. So where's the money, man? Where's the green?"

"We've seen some of it, right?" Turtle hated the way Scotty turned the tables on him. He'd done that since they were little kids, making things look like they were Turtle's fault. "Didn't you get that new flat-screen digital TV?"

"Yeah, but the digital doesn't work right. Got to change the whole service with the cable company."

"So change it!"

"Ma thinks it's too expensive."

"I don't have time for this." Sometimes, talking with Scotty, he felt like he was trapped in that old TV show *The Beverly Hillbillies*. Turtle stood up, cleared the old take-out containers and french fry wrappers from the counter, and stuffed them into the trash. "Look, I gotta get back. There's a game to-night."

Scotty took a can of Coke from the fridge, snapped it open. "There's always a game."

"Because I play baseball, moron."

"Don't patronize me. I'm your bread and butter."

"Yeah. And that's all going to work out, down the road. Just . . . just hold on to this stuff, okay?" He turned toward the door, grimaced at the grime on the frame. Went for the Windex. "And don't let your mother see it. She'll freak."

"She never comes down here."

Turtle scrubbed the smudges off, knowing it was true. Aunt Peggy probably suspected that one look at Scotty's place would send her running for Lysol and roach motels. "Hold on to the stuff till things blow over, and we'll get back on track, okay? I promise you. Big payday ahead. Big money. All right?" Turtle dropped the dirty paper towels in the trash, rinsed his hands, then gave his cousin a thumbs-up. "We're good, right?"

Scotty considered. "Long as you run and get me some McDonald's before you go."

Chapter 76

Marnie
Malden, Massachusetts

With dove-gray siding and black shutters, Leo Epstein's house was not the grandest or friendliest house on Boylston Street. Mildew dripped from the shutters, and the gutters were so backed up that small saplings had taken root in the dam of debris near the garage roof. Still, Marnie could imagine her mother stewing with jealousy that her ex lived in a house in the suburbs while she remained in a tiny apartment.

Marnie slowed in front of the house, not quite sure what to do. She had planned to sit in a nearby café or park, try to catch her father coming or going, but there were no businesses within three blocks, and she could hardly park herself here on the sidewalk without causing a stir.

She would have to ring the doorbell.

Steeling herself, she climbed the front porch, wood stairs creaking under her clogs. There was a flash at the window as someone pulled the lace curtains aside, then silence. Marnie rang the bell again, heard muffled voices. *Come on,* she thought as the sun burned through the dark batik print of her smock.

Marnie was looking over her shoulder at the grander house across the street when she heard the door budge. The wooden door had been pulled open and a young girl in that odd age approaching adulthood peered out. She had their father's eyes, brown and doleful, and a slash of a mouth that gave her a permanent pout. A Red Sox T-shirt was stretched wide over her mushy middle.

Little Petunia. Marnie struggled to remember her real name.

"What?" the girl barked through the storm door.

"Hey. Is your father home?" Marnie wiped her sweaty palms on her denim shorts. "I'm looking for Leo Epstein."

The girl glared at her, then closed the wooden door.

Nice. Dad should have taught his daughter some communications skills. Like, maybe using a few words?

The door opened a second time and Marnie was face-to-face with a stretched-out, tired version of her father. His dark hair was silvered white now and receding far from his forehead. Rocking back on her clogs, she realized she was the same height or taller than he was.

He fixed her with a glare as he pushed the storm door a crack. "Marnie." It was a statement, rife with disappointment and disdain. "Please, go away."

"We need to talk."

He let his chin drop, and she wasn't sure if he was checking his watch or just meditating on the horrible thing she had done to him. "That's not a good idea. Haven't you caused enough trouble already?"

"Please . . . just for a few minutes." She shrugged, trying to keep it casual. "What else are you going to do on a Saturday afternoon?"

"We're going to Fenway," he said, his voice full of scorn. "And I'm not going to be late for the game."

"Please, just ten minutes? Dad, come on. No one else can help me sort this out. I need to talk with you."

"Fine. Ten minutes." He pulled on a Red Sox hat and stepped out, letting the storm door fall behind him. "But we're sitting out here, for all the world and my nosey neighbor Mrs. Altoona to see. I'm not going to take the chance of you screwing me over with another lie, Marnie."

"I understand." She turned away from him, lowered herself down to the top step. "The thing is . . ." What could she say?

Someone's been threatening me, and I'm sure it's you? If that didn't send him fleeing into the house, nothing would. And face-to-face, in the light of a summer day, one thing was very clear. Leo Epstein was not harboring a bitter resentment for what Marnie had done to him. Instead, he seemed well settled into another life, one that didn't allow him the time or energy to include her.

"What, Marnie?" He spoke from behind her. "What drove you to make an appearance after all this time? Curiosity? Repressed father issues? Or did you just want to threaten my marriage and my family again?"

She turned to face him. "Maybe I came to say that I'm sorry."

"Seven years too late," he hissed.

"Yeah. I guess I needed some time to grow up."

"Marnie." He let out a gust of breath, sat beside her on the stairs. "I guess you're entitled to that. You were just a kid when Jade and I split up. I guess it was hard."

She shrugged. "That's ancient history."

"How's your mother?"

"She's . . . fine. Still making bad marriage choices. You were her best husband."

"That isn't really saying much."

Marnie hitched her thumb toward the house. "Does your daughter know about me?"

"Sonia? She knows you exist. Believe it or not, she remembers you from when she was little. She used to admire you, I think. Like an older sister."

"That is hard to believe."

"She was a little disappointed when you couldn't join us for outings anymore, but she was too young to get the full explanation."

They sat side by side for a few more minutes, talked about the possibility of doing something together in the future, maybe a Sox game, but Marnie knew it was just idle conversation. They were strangers, and though she was relieved to know her father was a kind, decent person, she saw no purpose in trying to build a relationship from scratch.

When she stood up and dusted off her hands, there was a feeling of finality and closure between them. "I'm going to go. You guys need to get on a train if you're going to make the first pitch." Jealousy tweaked at her, and for a second she wished she were going to the Sox game.

"Thanks for coming by." Leo Epstein patted her squarely on the back, the safe, paternal touch of a trusted doctor.

Petunia appeared in the door, her eyes scouring Marnie. "Daddy, are you ready?"

"Just let me grab my wallet." He headed inside. "See ya."

"See ya." Marnie wiped sweat from her brow and replaced her sunglasses as she moved away from the house. Any kid that age who called her father "Daddy" needed serious socialization.

As she reached the sidewalk she extracted her cell phone from her pocket. One text message:

"You will pay for what you did!"

Wow, an exclamation point. Now he was getting pissy.

She looked back at the house. The message came in while she was with her father, though she didn't need that evidence to know he wouldn't hurt her.

So now the question was, who was threatening her?

Pausing at the intersection, she looked twice before crossing. After last night, Boston wasn't proving to be the safest place for her these days. Time to get out of town, chill awhile. She needed to get online and book that flight to Syracuse.

Chapter 77

Greg Cody
Syracuse

Although Saturday was supposed to be Cody's day off, he didn't mind coming in to work the McGann case. His night had been consumed by Kate McGann, and by day he knew he'd have a hard time shaking off thoughts of her. The smell of her skin, the curve of her body against his, the thrill of her touch . . . memories of last night sat on his shoulders like a magical cloak that baffled him even as he struggled not to let it slip away. All things considered, he wanted to do right by Kate McGann, and if that meant working a Saturday, so be it.

Something had been dogging him, something he didn't want to verbalize to Kate before he had any solid information. Something didn't line up with Dylan Kroger, the left-handed pitcher turned third baseman who was Ben McGann's friend for years. A best friend who'd only made it to the hospital once since the attack. Some guy. Cody knew the coaches kept the players busy, but Kroger would have been allowed a few visits to his teammate.

He spent the morning trying to get a bead on Dylan Kroger. There was no listing for the grandmother, Ginger Mayers, though his database showed a Woodstock address for her, a post office box and rural route number. He called the Woodstock Police Department and talked to an officer from the local force. Sergeant Ed Gunther didn't know Ginger Mayers, but he did recognize the names of the two local baseball players who'd won scholarships to Boston College.

"We're looking into Dylan Kroger's possible connection to an assault," Cody explained. "I'm not finding any criminal records. I'd love to know if you've got anything. Also, if you could save me some legwork and a trip down there. The grandmother, Ginger Mayers, has no phone. I'd like a sense of where and how this kid lives at home."

"I can get an officer out to talk with Mrs. Mayers," Sergeant Gunther said. "But I can't promise it'll happen right away. This is our busy period—tourist season. Our local population doubles during the summer months."

"I'd appreciate it," Cody said, making an entry in his notebook.

He leafed through the open file on Dylan Kroger, one of the two dozen or so team profiles he'd gotten from the baseball league director here in Syracuse. Kroger was an excellent student, a three point nine. Premed, and getting some hands-on experience working in a laboratory near the campus. His boss had written him a glowing recommendation. His coaches called him dependable, determined, and bighearted. Reading between the lines on that, Kroger was not an inspired player, but overall his profile was pretty damned good.

Premed. And what was his buddy McGann's major? He flipped over to Ben's file. History.

He pulled all the left-handers' profiles and was mulling them over when Fitz appeared waving a document, his jaw slack with a dopey grin. "You ready for a peek inside the turtle's shell?"

It was a warrant to search Turtle Turturro's room.

"Perfect," Cody said, shoving his notebook into his back pocket. They headed over to Hawthorne Hall and hooked up with a resident assistant, to make sure everything would be respectful and by the book. Cody had promised the school he would enter with a minimum of damage, which proved difficult considering the lock Turtle had installed on his own.

"Hmm. I'd bring in a locksmith, but he won't be able to do much for a dead bolt," Cody told Fitz as they tried the master key the dorm had provided. "Short of turning this door into firewood, I say we try the window."

With a warrant in his pocket and his favorite resident assistant in tow, Cody rounded the corner of the dorm building and checked the blueprint in his hand.

As usual, RA Ronnie Leonard was unruffled as he pointed to a set of windows in the dead center of the building. "If he's in one-seventeen, it'll be that one there, with the shades pulled down." Ronnie dug his hands into the pockets of his baggy jeans. With his washed-out jeans, T-shirt, shell necklace, and a braid down his back, Ronnie actually reminded Cody of the hippie dude who had watched him and his brother when they were kids, some forty years ago.

"X marks the spot." Cody folded the blueprints as Fitz opened up a six-foot ladder they'd borrowed from campus maintenance. "Let's see what our security buff is hiding."

As Cody scaled the ladder, he could see that the window was open a crack. "Looking good. It's open, but there's a screen. Maybe I can pop it off."

"Probably not." Ronnie shielded his eyes against the sun. "The screens are bolted on."

From up close, Cody could see the student was right. "We'll have to cut it. Shouldn't cost too much to fix the screen." With a box cutter from his pocket he sliced into the mesh, cutting a flap. In a matter of seconds he eased the window open, handed Fitz two spider plants blocking the sill, and climbed in.

"Neat as a pin." Somehow, he'd expected much worse from Turtle, the big bruiser. The bed was made. Toiletry items lined the desktop. Baseball gear was squared away in the open cubby that served as a closet.

"Jesus H Christ, I'm getting too old for this," Fitz said as he squeezed in through the window.

Behind him, Ronnie appeared on the ladder and peered through the torn opening. "I'll just watch from here," he said stoically.

"Not a lot to see," Greg said. "Mr. Turturro is a tidy house-keeper."

Fitz and Cody pulled on rubber gloves and divvied up the room.

"The guy's a Felix Unger," Fitz said, dipping into the top drawer of Turtle's dresser. "Even his underwear is folded."

"What's a Felix Unger?" Ronnie asked.

"A New Yorker with OCD. You should Google it." Cody checked the slender desk drawer, then rolled out the deep side drawer. "Wow." He lifted a box out of the drawer and opened the lid. Dozens of syringes twinkled in their individual plastic wrappers.

"Holy shit." Fitz's jaw dropped open. "You hit the mother-lode."

"Syringes?" Ronnie asked, leaning in through the window for a better look.

"That's right, a whole box of them." Cody checked the side of the carton. "The box contained a hundred syringes, half-inch needles."

"He must be a junky," Fitz said. "Or else he's dealing. How do you play competitive ball nearly every day of the week and shoot up opiates? I'll bet he's a dealer."

"Maybe." Cody reached into the drawer and removed a box of latex gloves.

"Just like the ones we found in the washing machine, right?" Fitz held up his right hand for a high five. "Looks like we found our man."

Cody bumped fists with him, but he was shaking his head. "I don't know, Fitz. Something isn't right here." The box that remained in the drawer was smaller. Cody picked it up and read the label aloud. "Quick Check Strips."

"What?" Fitz dropped the syringes back into the box and squinted at Cody. "He's taking pregnancy tests?"

"No, no. Now I get it." Cody leaned down to open the small fridge stowed under the desk. There it was, just as he expected. "Insulin." He held a vial of clear liquid up for Fitz to see. "He's diabetic. The Quick Check Strips are to test for glucose levels. You check the blood sugar to see how much insulin you need to inject."

"Really." Fitz crossed his arms, shoulders sagging. "So he's a diabetic. I gotta admit, I thought we were on to something." He swung around to face the window. "Did you know about this, Ronnie?"

"No, I did not. And something like that is supposed to be reported to the resident hall staff. It's hard for us to help when people keep us in the dark."

"I wonder if Coach Ramsey knows." Cody closed the fridge. "Maybe Turtle was hiding his condition. Didn't want people to feel sorry for him."

"Or discriminate against him," Ronnie added.

Cody nodded. "It's possible."

A series of clicks and pops at the door caused Cody and Fitz to turn quickly. Cody removed his shield from his pocket and faced the door, which quickly opened to reveal the triple-XL frame of Turtle.

"What the fuck?" Turtle's face puckered in a scowl. "What are you doing in my private room?"

"We have a warrant." Cody pulled it from his back pocket, extending the paperwork.

"Fuck! You guys scared the crap out of me."

"It's all legal, with a warrant," Fitz said. "And we wouldn't have had to get one if you didn't add your own lock to the door."

"You're not supposed to do that, man," Ronnie advised from the window. "If we need to get in here and help you, you're screwing yourself."

"What, I can't have a little privacy?" Turtle raked his fingers through his hair, pacing in front of the desk to inspect the damage.

"Yeah, but you can't put locks on your door, man," Ronnie said. "How are we supposed to get in if you need help?"

"Just . . . just get out of my window, okay?"

Ronnie ducked away. A moment later he reappeared with

one of Turtle's spider plants, which he replaced on the windowsill.

Cody turned to Turtle. "Why didn't you report your diabetes to the residential staff?" he asked. "Does the coach know?"

"Ramsey? No. I don't go advertising. It's my private business. And it's diabetes, not leprosy. You make it sound like I'm going to spread some toxic disease."

"That wasn't our intention," Cody said. He could see where Turtle was going with this. "We didn't single you out, Joseph. It was a matter of investigating every player's room, and you shut us out."

For what reason? Cody smelled something foul here. Turtle had been too secretive to just be hiding that he was diabetic. The guy had some racket going; exactly what, they might never know.

"Yeah, I'm not big on having cops put their paws all over my stuff." Turtle's brows arched as he pulled the box of syringes away from the cops. "You done here?"

Although something was hinky about Joe Turturro, Cody sensed that it didn't have much to do with the attack on Ben McGann. Certainly there was no evidence in this room that pointed to Turtle.

"We're done," Cody said, extending his hand. "You take care of yourself, okay?"

Turtle rolled his eyes, but he shook on it. "Yeah, whatever."

Chapter 78

Kate
Syracuse

"On a personal level, this is the best Sunday morning I've had in years." Kate adjusted the sheets over her bare breasts and accepted a mug of coffee from Greg, who stood before her, a wall of dark boxers, muscular legs, and beautiful bare chest.

"On a personal level . . ." He lifted a corner of the sheet and sneaked a look before sliding in beside her. "I have to remind you, the morning isn't over yet."

Sipping the coffee, she sighed and closed her eyes as his hand slid over her bare thigh. It was a reminder of the wild, skin-on-skin romp they'd just completed, as well as the intimacy of sharing a bed with Greg, welcoming him through that vulnerable window of sleep alongside her. She felt close to him, her muscles and nerves still singing with pleasure. Greg Cody was an addictive drug, a haven of escape, a kind person, and it was scary how comfortable she felt here in his "bachelor pad."

"I have to admit, I feel a little guilty," she said. "It seems wrong to feel so good while my son is in bad shape."

He nodded. "I get it. Our kids are our kids, a part of us we'll always worry about." He withdrew his hand from under the sheets and picked up his coffee from the nightstand. "But you can't be with him twenty-four-seven. He's in good hands. And sex is a great de-stressor."

Kate cupped the mug. "I miss him. That may sound selfish, but I miss having my son healthy. I want to see him laugh and stay awake for an entire day. I want him to have the chance to return to school and play baseball. I want to see him hit a home run and explode off the bag when he's running the bases." A month ago, all those things were a given; today, they would have to be hard won over time.

"Are those things possible with Ben's prognosis?" he asked.

"The doctors are hopeful but cautious. And some of it depends on the extent of damage to his eye. You need vision in both eyes to play baseball. Peripheral vision is key. He's getting a thorough eye exam today."

"It's progress. Gotta walk before you run."

Kate knew he was right, though she was always the one trying to pick up the pace. "Did I tell you Marnie is coming today? She's going to stay with me in my hotel room."

"She's a good friend," he said, "making the trip back just to see him."

"She is. Emma completely dried up, though that's probably a good thing. Ben doesn't seem to miss her, though he's always asking about Dylan, who disappeared." Her voice trailed off as she thought of the boy she'd nearly raised, her second son. "I can't believe he hasn't come around since Ben regained consciousness. They've always been best friends. Like brothers."

"Some guys get freaked out by hospitals."

"But not Dylan. He's premed. He's wanted to be a doctor since he was a little kid with a toy medical kit." Something had to be keeping Dylan from coming to see them. "I need to talk to that kid. Give him a little kick in the fanny."

"Now you sound like a mom." He touched Kate's shoulder, and she had to bite back a huge smile at the thrill of being touched. "Just don't do it in front of the rest of the team. Guys hate that stuff."

"I'll be a model of diplomacy." She covered his hand with hers and squeezed. "Can we talk about the case?"

"D'oh!" He winced. "And I thought you were here because you liked me."

"I do. But you offer gratification on so many levels." She put down her mug and propped herself up on her right elbow, facing him. "What was it you found in Turturro's dorm room that made you discount him as a suspect? He's a strong guy. A left-hander. And he was at odds with Ben."

"Though they made up after their fight, a scene witnessed by many. I think they were actually hugging at the end. And there's the matter of the articles we found in the washer with traces of Ben's blood. The shirt, which we speculate the attacker was wearing? It's a large, and Turtle is a big guy. Most of the T-shirts in his room are triple-XL. He's just not fitting the profile. Certainly wouldn't fit the shirt."

"That's disappointing." She stared down at the bed. "It takes us back to the question: Who did this to my son?"

"I still think it's someone on the team. I still think it's a left-hander, though we're down to a handful of lefties who haven't been ruled out. One of them is your second son Dylan."

"And . . . I'm supposed to take that seriously?"

"Just saying. He's left-handed. He had access and opportunity."

"But motive?"

"You tell me."

Kate didn't want to think about it. It seemed like a waste of time to pursue something that wouldn't pan out. Also, she felt a niggling instinct to protect Dylan, who hadn't had the easiest upbringing. "Putting aside my resistance to the notion of Dylan as a cold-blooded monster?" She shrugged. "What do you want to know?"

"Just the basic profile. Parents weren't around?"

"I never met his parents. Dylan was only a few weeks old when his mother died, and since then he's always lived with his grandmother, Ginger. When Ben met Dylan—that was in Pre-K, sandbox days—Dylan's father was supposedly trying for custody, but I suppose it didn't work out. Eventually the dad moved to California and got married, had two more kids, I heard."

"And has the father been paying child support? Helping for college?"

"I doubt it. Dylan's always scrambling for money. He was the kid who always needed a ride, didn't have a car. He wore Ben's hand-me-down jeans and cleats. He's at Boston College because they helped him patch together some academic awards with a baseball scholarship."

"Hmm. You know, very often in violent crime, it's someone the victim knows well." Cody stretched over to the nightstand and exchanged his coffee mug for his notepad.

"Oh, please, Detective." She pushed herself up, tugging the sheet along as she settled against the headboard. "You bring that thing into bed with you?"

The look in his eyes was languid as melted chocolate as he grinned. "Only when there's something worth noting." He clicked the pen. "But don't distract me. What's the grand-mother's name?"

"Ginger. Ginger Mayers."

"Are you friends with her?"

"Friendly. Acquaintances through Dylan, really. Ginger is sort of a loner, sometimes a little paranoid, but for a woman alone raising her grandson, I think she's held it together. She waits tables at a place in Woodstock. Has three dogs that she adores but generally she likes to be left alone. A few years back, the county went through and paved some of the back roads around Woodstock, and she had a fit. She kept calling the new curb 'the curb to nowhere,' and she was sure rats were going to invade her property from the new rain gutters. Over the years I've tried to engage Ginger, and while she let Dylan have a lot of freedom to be with Ben, she's always kept me at a distance."

He was jotting things down.

"What are you writing?"

"Don't get all defensive. Just indulge me while I check out Dylan Kroger."

Kate folded her arms across her chest. "Fine, but you're barking up the wrong tree."

"I'm used to that. I just keep barking."

"Meanwhile, the guy who attacked Ben is out there. Free to go after someone else."

"Kate . . . it's my job to find this guy. Along with the perps from about ten other crimes."

"Just saying."

He leaned closer and pressed his lips to her cheek. "Let me do my job." His hands moved over her tummy and around her waist, leaving breathtaking pleasure in their wake. He pulled her hips toward him, and they both shifted so that their bodies lined up, skin on skin. He nibbled the sensitive flesh of her neck, then lifted his head so that his sky-blue eyes shone over her. "Just let me do what I do best."

In his arms, making full-frontal contact, she had no choice but to trust him. "Okay," she whispered as his hands swept down her thighs, stoking the fires that had lain dormant for so many years. She closed her eyes, giving in, seeing herself as she stepped through a window to his world. "Okay."

Chapter 79

Eli McGann
Good Samaritan Hospital

Nothing Kate said had prepared Eli for his first sight of Ben that Sunday morning.

The strong body of a handsome athlete had suddenly morphed into a delicate creature defined by pasty white skin and bloated extremities. A body in decline, a life in ruins. His own son was Jekyll and Hyde, both incarnations at one time. The right side of his face held the deformity of a hideous monster, swelling accented by tracks of staples, eye covered with a white patch. A beastly pirate. The left side of Ben's face was cloaked in peace and godly beauty, maintaining a slight hint of his former self.

Leaning against a patch of bare wall, Eli niggled at a swollen cut on his thumb as he watched the rise and fall of his son's chest. A man's chest, so hard to believe Ben could have grown into such a big guy from the freckled pipsqueak who used to be afraid to get out of bed in the middle of the night. Yes, Ben was a man now, at least physically.

Psychologically? No one could quite say. He had thought Kate was being overly dramatic, but now, seeing Ben, he understood.

His son's life was over. All the things that had mattered to Ben had exploded with one crack of the bat.

He turned away from the tragic sight, from the possibility and promise that had been snuffed out by the very instrument

Ben adored. A baseball bat. Eli never had much tolerance for the useless game, and now this.

Thank you, Kate. She'd been the one to marvel at how well Ben threw a ball when he was a baby. She noted his wide-eyed fascination with sphere-shaped objects and his attempt to pronounce the word "ball." She brought home the first Wiffle balls and plastic bat. She stood on the side of the hill, showing Ben how to turn his body into a batting stance, reminding him to keep his eye on the ball. Goddamned Kate. She set him up for this, thrust him into the testosterone-laden world of competitive sports.

During the past week Kate had been good about keeping him updated on Ben's condition, but that news always came with a price. The wrath of Kate: a formidable battleship that brought Eli an onslaught of guilt and self-loathing.

"When are you coming to see him?" she kept asking. "Is any of this connecting?"

And he came back with logical, pragmatic answers. Summers were the busy season for his stained-glass art, and his free time dissipated once school started. Teachers had to report to school the second week of August, and she didn't want him to lose that job, right? If Kate wasn't going back to school, someone needed to hold on to a job that provided medical benefits, right?

Sound, practical answers. Shoveling against the tide.

And now, he'd driven two hundred miles to watch his son sleep. A complete waste of time and source of endless pain. Ben wouldn't even know he'd been here.

A man in navy scrubs came into the room. Stocky, with a wide physique, he wore his dark hair long, with a beard that reminded Eli of Wolfman Jack. "Hey, how's it going? Are you related to young Ben, here?"

"I'm his father. Eli."

Wolfman nodded as he snapped on a glove. "I've met Kate. Has Ben been awake for you?" He flipped the bottom of the sheet up and began to massage Ben's legs.

"Not yet."

"Ben? You have an important visitor here." When Ben didn't respond, Wolfman rubbed his knuckles down the center of Ben's chest. "Wake up, young man."

There was a heavy moan and Ben's eyelids lifted, just for a moment. "Dad . . ." He slid away again.

"Wake up, Ben," Wolfman coached him. "Your lunch will be here soon. How's that for motivation?"

"My head. Someone take the ax out of my head. It hurts!"

Eli shrank back, panicked at the ferocity of his son's pain.

Working the muscles of Ben's calves, Wolfman stared up at the monitors at Ben's bedside. "We're trying to wean him off pain meds, but it's not easy finding the right balance. We want him alert, his pain tolerable." He pressed a button on the touchpad.

"Can you give him something to help him feel better?" Eli asked.

"I just did."

Ben stirred, arms tugging against restraints. "Take these off?"

Eli shifted from one foot to another. "Do you have to tie him down?"

"Did you know your son tries to get to the ballpark just about every time we wake him?" Wolfman asked.

Kate had mentioned that, but it had slipped his mind. "Still . . . to tie him down?"

"Mr. McGann, your son is missing a piece of his skull. If he were to fall and injure that part of his head, the injury could kill him."

Ben writhed against the cuffs, and Eli noticed that his hands were swollen, his fingers fat. "Let me go."

"I can take them off for now." Wolfman got right up in Ben's grill. "You stay in bed, or we'll have to strap you in again. Deal?"

"Yeah, sure." Ben's head lolled against the white pillow, his single eye glossy. "Dad?"

Eli stepped into his line of vision. "Hey. How's it going?"

"Just an explosion in my head."

Eli gestured toward the nurse. "He says it should feel better soon. I'm glad to see you awake."

"Yeah, but I'm missing a game, right?" Ben rubbed his wrists, flexed his shoulders. "I know I'm missing something, but everyone keeps telling me that's okay."

"It's fine, Ben. You just rest up. Get better."

"I'd be fine if my head didn't hurt so much." Ben reached up with one clamped finger and gingerly touched the eye patch. "I'm so messed up, but you've been great, Dad. Like a rock. I don't know what I'd do without you."

Ben had to be hallucinating. Eli sucked in a breath, hesitating. What could he say? *Sorry, I couldn't be here. Mrs. Rosenberg—you remember her? Cadaverous woman with a lazy eye and a penchant for American Gothic architecture? She ordered a rose window that I can charge her a fortune for. And I'm up against a deadline for a competition in Cologne, Germany. Can't miss the deadline . . .*

As if entering a contest could compare to the pain Ben was struggling through right now. All the things of import in Eli's daily life now sounded crass and fickle.

Ben rubbed the back of one hand against his jaw, which glistened with oils from a moisturizer. "You're the best father in the world," he said groggily.

Someone must be shaving him, Eli thought, and his eyes went to the other tubes, to the bag of urine hanging on to the side of the bed. *Oh, dear God. My son has been reduced to that. A body in a bed. Like an infant to be fed and nursed, bathed, and wiped.*

How could Ben endure it? Minimal function. Trapped in a damaged shell.

"My memory sucks." The words floated on a weary breath as Ben melted back into the sheets. "Have you been here the whole time? Ever since the accident?"

Eli could not drop the weight of the truth on his shattered son. Instead, he swallowed back the truth, feeling small as he answered, "Yes. Yes, I've been here."

"I knew it." Ben let out a sigh, a shadow of a smile crossing his face. "I knew you'd come through when I needed you."

Eli felt his soul shrivel to a small, dry kernel. He nodded at his son, gripped the shiny bed rail, and imagined himself miles away from here, a patron in van Gogh's "Café Terrace at Night," just another dark figure safe within the framework of pavement and streetlamps under the stars. He was the old man in Hemingway's "A Clean, Well-Lighted Place," a man who suffered but was reassured that everyone suffered.

He was safe within the framework of his own composition.

Chapter 80

Marnie
Syracuse Hancock Airport

Late Sunday morning, when Marnie's plane touched down with a dull skid, she breathed a sigh of relief to be in Syracuse. It would be good to visit with Ben, who sounded like he was getting a little bit better every day. Plus it was a great time to get away from the menace at home, the unnerving threats that cloaked all her actions in Boston. God, it was good to feel free again.

She took her backpack from the overhead bin, turned on her cell phone, and eased into the aisle. On the jetway she heard the signal that she had some text messages. The first was the usual threat . . . "You will pay for what you did."

"Not here, not now," she said blithely and went to the next message.

"You can't get away. I will follow you anywhere."

She gasped, stabbed by a pang of wariness. Did he know? Did he know that she had left Boston for Syracuse? Her spirits sank as she slipped the phone in the deep pocket of her peasant skirt and plodded into the terminal. Buzzkill.

As she passed out of the security zone she hitched up her backpack and headed toward the shuttle services. She was circling a slow-moving family clustered together when she heard her name.

Snapping out of her haze, she scanned the carpeted landscape and noticed Dylan waving, looking bird thin in his Laker cap and a baggy T-shirt. "How's it going?"

"Dylan . . . hi." She slowed her pace, not wanting to stop for too long. "Some coincidence, huh? What are you doing here? Flying home for a break?"

"Silly. I came to pick you up."

"What?" Marnie stopped in her tracks, reflexively grabbing the straps of her backpack. "Say again?"

"I came to meet your flight. No one should fly in without someone to meet them." He reached for her backpack. "Here, let me take this for you."

"I'm fine."

"No, really. That's why I came."

Reluctantly, she slid the backpack from her shoulders.

"Anything else? Do we need to stop at baggage claim?"

"Nope. We can head out." Her hand snaked up to her mouth, and Marnie couldn't resist nibbling on the pinky nail she'd been growing. "This is kind of weird, Dylan. How did you know I'd be here?"

"You told me."

"I did?"

He nodded. "When we talked on the phone."

"Oh, yeah." Marnie remembered talking to him from the storage room at Storemart. "But I didn't even have my flight booked then. How did you—"

"I talked to your mom. Jade was happy to hear from me. She was grateful to know someone would be meeting you at the airport."

"And why didn't she mention it to me? Just wondering."

"I asked her not to. I wanted to surprise you."

Marnie didn't like surprises. Just proved how little Dylan knew about her. "Okay. I'm surprised."

"And a little bit confrontational," he teased.

"Look, I came to see Ben, okay? I'm not your girlfriend any-more, so back up and give me some space."

A woman rolling her luggage turned and shot Marnie a curious look. Nothing like airing out your differences in the middle of an airport.

"That's harsh." Dylan looked down at the floor. "I thought we were going to be friends."

Marnie gritted her teeth, trying to reel in her frustration. "I'm just a little on edge. I've been getting these messages and . . ." She noticed the woman with the rolling luggage; she was really eyeballing her now. "We'll talk about it later. Which way to your car?"

Dylan bit his lower lip. "I don't have a car here. We're taking a cab."

"Okay. So let's find the taxis." She found an arrow pointing toward ground transportation and marched off in that direction, annoyed that Dylan had bothered to come. What kind of person took a cab to meet someone at an airport? Why didn't he just back off?

There wasn't much of a line, and soon they were in the cab, arguing about whether to go to Dylan's dorm or Good Samaritan Hospital.

"You don't need to go straight to the hospital," Dylan argued. "Let's hang out for a while. I'll get you a ticket for tonight's game."

"Dylan, you need to back off. I'm not here for your games," Marnie said, trying to keep the annoyance from seeping into her voice. "Please, take us to Good Samaritan Hospital," she told the driver. "Do you know where it is?"

"Yes, ma'am."

She turned to the right and focused on the landscape . . . buildings and trees and cars. Nothing too exciting, but she pretended to be riveted. Something about Dylan coming to the airport, pressuring her to be his friend, irked her to the marrow.

"Wow. You really do hate me," he said.

"I don't." Big lie. "I just have things to do here, okay?"

"And you're stressed."

Although she didn't really want to talk about it, she gave

him some details. "I've been getting these text messages, a couple of phone calls. Threats. It's scary."

"What do they say?" When she told him, he winced. "I don't know. I can't be sure, but, the thing is, I have a feeling I know who's been sending you those threats."

"Really? Who?" Marnie leaned toward him, engaged.

"I can't tell you. If I told you what I know, believe me, things would be worse for you. All I can say is, I think it's the same guy who attacked Ben."

"Really." Marnie downplayed her panic, though her mouth went dry as she assessed him. He leaned back against the seat, trying to look casual despite the stains she noticed breaking out on the armpits of his shirt. "Are you serious?" He didn't flinch, didn't waver. He wasn't kidding. "Dylan, if you know who attacked Ben, why haven't you told the police?"

"It's not like I saw it. I just have this sense . . . and some details back up my feeling."

"Okay, then." She tried to ignore the swell of fear in her chest, the hammering beat of her heart. "And you think this person is threatening me, too." She'd been so sure the sicko lived in Boston. Why did she think that? Because the source of the number was Boston, Mass.? She shifted her knees toward Dylan, no longer so interested in facing out the window. "Why? Why me?"

"That I don't know. But I could talk to him . . . about you. I mean, I'll do it if you want me to. Or maybe you want me to back off. . . ."

Marnie stared at him, torn. Of course she wanted him to intercede, make the phone stalker stop. Yes, she needed help, but no, she didn't want it from Dylan. At this point maintaining contact with him was just going to lead him on.

But really, did she have any choice?

She gathered her skirt as the cab pulled in through the decorative main gate of Good Samaritan Hospital. The neuro ICU where Ben was recovering was probably half a mile across campus, but Marnie didn't care; she wanted out.

"Tell me what you want me to do," he said.

"I need you to help me. If this guy is the one who's been hassling me, maybe you can talk some sense into him."

"Maybe. I can give it a shot, for you."

Again with the moonface expression. As if he were only doing it out of some extraordinary love. What a load of crap.

She unzipped her backpack and fished out a twenty for the driver. Then she gathered the voluminous fabric of her skirt and scooted out of the taxi. Dylan followed with her backpack.

"Oh, God, I almost forgot that." She snatched it up, getting flustered with herself as the taxi drove off. She unzipped the top compartment of her pack for her cell phone, but it wasn't there. "Where is it?" She bit her lower lip. "Did I leave my cell in the cab?" A thrum of panic edged up her spine, gaining momentum as she realized she wouldn't be able to reach Kate McGann. There'd be no calls home, and good luck finding a pay phone. "Oh, God, I lost my phone."

"You keep saying that," he said, his fingers closing over a silver cell phone so shiny it had to be new.

She started checking other compartments of the backpack, burrowing a hand in to check around rolled-up T-shirts. "Call my cell, would you?"

He pressed a few numbers and Marnie's chime came alive.

"Oh, thank God." She felt the buzz low on her thigh, reached into the deep pocket of her skirt, and fished it out. Without looking she turned off the ringer and put it back. She was falling apart, so easily rattled.

And Dylan was still standing there, waiting for some kind of answer.

"Can't you go to this guy and tell him you'll kick his butt if he doesn't leave your ex-girlfriend alone?" she asked as she zipped up the many compartments on her backpack.

He frowned, his lips forming a ripple.

"Just do what you can." She hitched her pack onto her shoulder and turned toward the towering building. "You coming to see Ben?"

"Not right now. I need to get back . . . practice."

She shot him a look, unable to read the lie in his eyes. "Just thirty minutes ago you said you were free to spend the afternoon with me."

"Okay, you caught me." Dylan raked his curls off his forehead. "I don't want to see Ben. It's too . . . too painful."

"Oh, you big baby! You're supposed to be his friend."

"I am. It's just hard to see him that way."

"Fine, stay away. But just know that actions speak louder than words, and your actions are shrieking."

She turned away and strode off, glad to be done with him. As she reached the door she heard footsteps on the pavement, and suddenly Dylan was holding the door open for her.

"Okay, I'll do it. It's hard, but I don't want to let him down."

Forging ahead, she reminded herself that Dylan was an asshole when it came to relationships. Thank God she'd broken up with him. Thank God it was over.

Chapter 81

Teddy Zanth
Good Samaritan Hospital

"Hey, I brought you a gift." Teddy reached into the pocket of her scrubs and held up a blue, squishy ball. "Think fast." And she tossed it, not sure if Ben McGann would be able to respond.

But his left hand snapped it out of the air. "You brought me a ball!" His grin warmed her to the bottom of her toes. "I love you."

She rolled her eyes, staving off a yawn. "It's just a ball." Her shift had ended ten minutes ago, and though she had a pile of patient charts to update, she had decided to stop in and see Ben, the patient who, selfishly, she wanted to believe she had helped along the way.

"It's awesome." He cradled it in his palms, then tossed it back to Teddy.

"You can keep it," she said.

"Duh. Throw it back to me. We'll have a catch."

"As long as you go easy on me." She tossed it, and he caught the ball and gave it a squeeze.

"A stress ball?"

"It could be." She noticed his head moving with each throw; he was making adjustments, following the ball with one eye.

In a smooth, liquid motion he whipped his left arm back and sent the ball flying straight to her. "Hey!" Teddy reached up and missed; the ball deflected off her hand and bounced off the television mounted over her head.

They both laughed as Teddy scrambled to retrieve the ball. "Easy, there. I'm in big trouble if we knock out one of these high-tech monitors."

Ben caught the ball. "God, I need to get out of here and play some real ball."

Teddy wondered if that goal was realistic for Ben. She didn't know how his prognosis had changed since her last visit, but she remained positive. "That's what we like to see, a motivated patient."

He held the ball a moment as someone stopped in the doorway. "Dylan?" Ben turned his head, staring intently with one eye. "Is that you?"

Teddy shot a look at the door and did a double take. The curly-haired kid looked barely old enough to be a teenager, but there was something about him—his prana, his aura—something she found highly disturbing.

"This is Dylan . . . my best friend," Ben said in a voice strained by emotion.

"Hey, Dylan." Although she tried to appear friendly Teddy was cautious with the boy. She had heard of cases in which auras—or maybe ghosts—take over bodies that play host to them for centuries. Her grandmother told her of times when an unhealthy life force had sucked the health from another being. However, she had chalked those stories up to folklore. Cultural legends.

Not real-life scenarios. Not something she could see happen across the room.

Uneasy horror pushed her toward the wall, an observer of the visitor, who was followed by Marnie, a friend Teddy had met before. With her prana-vision oddly engaged today, Teddy noted that Marnie's aura was cheerful and solid, a warm orange blossoming into coral tinged with red, the colors of a magnificent summer sunset. Marnie threw off positive energy, but Dylan . . .

The curly-haired kid's bilious green and gray set her teeth

on edge, and the movement of his aura kept her on guard, watching as he leaned close to Ben and began to suck the vibrant blue glow from Ben's body.

"That's enough." Teddy stepped forward, not sure how she could explain herself but knowing she had to intervene. "Ben's had a lot of visitors today, and . . . and he has a test coming up soon."

"S'okay." Dylan stepped back, scraping off a dancing blue spark from Ben in the process. "I got a game."

"Man, I wish I could play." Ben sank back against the pillow, noticeably winded.

Teddy stepped between Ben and the thief. This had to end now. "Okay, then." She pretended to check his lines and monitor as Dylan said a quick good-bye and exited.

"Prana sucker," she muttered under her breath.

"What was that?" Ben's eye was closed, his arms crossed over his chest defensively.

"Nothing." She noted that his stats were back to normal.

"Is it okay if I stay?"

Teddy turned to see Marnie in the doorway, her aura plump and healthy in pink and crimson . . . the colors of love. "You're fine," Teddy said, anxiety draining away as Marnie picked up the ball and tossed it to Ben.

Chapter 82

Greg Cody
Syracuse Precinct

He spent the morning digging into the backgrounds of left-handers on the Lakers.

There was Tobey Santiago, the pitcher who had played both varsity baseball and soccer in high school before he'd focused on perfecting his sinker. As a kid he'd attended countless baseball camps and clinics. This was a nice Catholic boy from a fairly well-off family in a Pennsylvania suburb.

Fellow New Yorker Kevin Webber hailed from a family of baseball players. His uncle was still playing in the majors for a West Coast team, and his father had played minor-league ball until he blew out his shoulder.

Turtle Turturro had been featured in a few magazines as the rare left-handed catcher who might make it into the pros. Although Cody didn't think Turtle had attacked Ben McGann, he smelled illegal activity swirling around the big catcher. Making book? Dealing drugs? Whatever was going on, Turturro would have to wait until more pressing matters were handled.

And then there was Dylan Kroger. The mother was dead, the father into the wind. He wondered about Dylan's relationship with the grandmother. Whatever it was, the kid had managed to hold down a well-paying research job while he was going to school in Boston. He decided to give Sergeant Gunther from the Woodstock PD a call.

"You were on my list," Ed Gunther said. "I managed to pay a visit to Ginger Mayers. I don't think she was too happy to see us. She didn't like being disturbed."

"What did she have to say about her grandson?"

"Nothing good. The lady was pretty sour all around," Gunther reported. "But you need to take that with a grain of salt. Her house is a hovel. Newspapers stacked almost to the ceiling. Not a bare inch of floor. A handful of growling dogs, and you can imagine how the place smells."

"Yeah, been there, done that," Cody said, recalling the houses he'd tried to avoid entering in his years on patrol. The piles of junk, the scattered feces, random roaches and rats. "Yeah. So I can see why her grandson wasn't so high on coming home for the summer."

"Lucky for the grandson he didn't have to stay in that hellhole. He had his own space over the garage, and she let us have a look. Get this . . . the place was neat as a pin, except there's this little psycho corner. An altar there, strands of hair. Tickets from some events at Boston College. Photos of some girl, most of the shots look like they were downloaded from a cell phone."

Cody wondered who that might be. "Some movie star?"

"I don't think so. Just your average twentyish kid."

"What did the girl look like?"

"Dark hair, big smile, multiple piercings . . ."

"Really. Did you happen to take some photos?"

"Got some on a cell phone. You want them e-mailed over?"

"That would be great." As Cody gave Ed Gunther his e-mail information, he combed over Dylan Kroger's profile one last time. Was it really possible that this kid, Ben's best friend, would attack him in cold blood?

Considering that Kroger had nothing and McGann had it all . . .

And keeping in mind that most victims were attacked by someone they knew well . . .

Kroger was rising to the top of Cody's list.

Chapter 83

Eli
Good Samaritan Hospital

"It's so much worse than you let on." Eli tried to focus his gaze on a piece of bad art, an autumnal landscape dripping with dots of fluorescent color, sort of a sixties pseudo-impressionist piece. If he stared at the painting, perhaps Kate wouldn't hear the sliver of accusation in his voice. "I think he's hallucinating part of the time. You didn't mention that."

Kate held up a hand, her mouth open in feigned shock. "If that's your way of making this all my fault, you can eat your words and go right back home. I gave you the facts, Eli. I passed on everything I was able to learn through the doctors' conferences and leg massages and hysterical episodes and endless hours of waiting. If you want a second opinion, feel free to conference with the neurologists on your own."

He ran his hands over the short hair on the sides of his head and sighed. "I'm sorry. I just didn't expect . . . I didn't think a hit on the head could cause so much damage."

"There were probably three blows to the head," Kate said slowly, "and he was fortunate to be near a facility with a state-of-the-art neurological surgery suite." She squinted at him. "Do you hold the phone away from your ear when I call?"

"It's hard for me to process everything. You know me."

"All too well."

"I'm not good at conflict, Kate. I run from crisis. I know that about myself."

"That doesn't make it acceptable. When your son is trying to punch a nurse or ripping tubing and needles out because he thinks he's missing a game, when he's fighting off an infection, when he's clinging to life, it's not okay to run in the other direction because you're scared."

"What could I possibly contribute here?" He hated it when Kate put him on the defense. "My place is at home, working. I got two hefty commissions in the past week, and Tamara sold three of my pieces in the gallery. You're taking a sabbatical from school, right? Someone needs to earn a wage. Someone needs to keep a regular job, with insurance benefits, and it looks like that someone is me. In a matter of weeks I'll be back at Woodlands Academy."

"Wait. Suddenly you're all about being the breadwinner? Money and insurance? Don't abandon Ben just because you're finished with me."

He swirled the coffee cup, wishing he hadn't bothered to buy it at all. He wouldn't drink it, and now here was another waxed paper cup, another stirrer and plastic lid to go off to the landfill. "I'm sorry, Kate."

"I don't think so. If you were sorry, you would be here for him. If you were sorry, you wouldn't be hours away with her while your son is going through the nightmare of his life."

He turned his gaze back to the pop-art print, deciding it was less nauseating than discussing Tamara with Kate.

"Look, I know she's been sleeping in my bed already. But pushing us aside, Ben needs you, so stand up and be a father to him. Is she the reason you're staying behind?"

"It's . . . complicated." He rubbed his temples with the butt of his hands, wishing he could open his eyes and find himself vanished from this scene. "I was in pain. I needed a release that didn't involve alcohol."

"Damn it." Kate's fist pounded the table. "You're not answering my question. Why aren't you here for him?"

"I needed some consolation. . . ."

"You want consolation? I'll give you the ultimate consolation prize. Ben isn't even your biological son. Got that?"

Eli stared at her face, trying to read between the lines. "What?"

"Remember all those years of trying to get pregnant? More than three years . . . and all the while I was getting older and older, aging out of motherhood. You didn't want to go through in vitro—you wouldn't even go to get checked out. And I was so furious with you. The thing I wanted most in life, the miracle of life, was slipping through my fingers, and you didn't seem fazed at all."

"But then it happened. You were pregnant, and I got into it."

"I got pregnant because I purchased viable sperm. After years of trying, I went searching online. I found a reputable sperm bank in Spokane, Washington. It was expensive and I didn't want you to know, so I cashed in part of my 401K to pay for some samples." She looked down at the table. "I conceived on the first try."

"With who?"

"An anonymous donor. I only know part of his medical history. The thing is, you're off the hook if you want to be. You were there when he was little, and I'm grateful for that. If you need to back off now . . . it's going to disappoint Ben, but . . ." Her voice grew hoarse as her eyes grew glossy with tears. "Just go. He's got bigger disappointments than that to overcome. He'll deal with it."

A sperm bank . . . Eli wasn't as surprised by the facts of her story as he was by Kate's long-time deception.

So she had lied, too.

"You know, I always wondered about it when you got pregnant. I thought that maybe you slept with someone else, though it seemed so unlike you, and I didn't get any hints that you were having an affair."

"I wasn't. I just wanted a baby, Eli. I wanted your baby, but when that didn't happen, I did something about it. In the end, it's about creating a life together, isn't it?"

"I thought he was a miracle," he said, recalling the soft, warm aura that had surrounded Kate from the time she told him she was pregnant.

"What?" She squinted.

"When you got pregnant, I thought there was someone else because I knew the baby wasn't mine."

Disbelief shadowed her face. "How could you have known that?"

He sucked air through his teeth. It was a day for spilling secrets. "I had a vasectomy before I met you. I was shooting blanks for years."

Her arm flailed out and caught the side of his face before he could lean away. The hard, bracing slap stung his cheek.

He closed his eyes and pressed the back of one hand to his face. "Sometimes it feels good to be punished."

But Kate was not up for philosophizing. "All those months and years of trying . . . the bitter disappointment every time I got my period. You knew what I was going through, and you didn't say a word." She exploded from the chair, jolting the table. Coffee spilled from his untouched cup. It formed a small, muddy puddle, a reflection of their mutual perfidy.

When he looked up the fury was gone from her eyes, washed away by tears.

"How could you do that to me?" she asked.

"Because I loved you. Because I didn't want to lose you."

She shook her head. "And when I finally got pregnant . . . when Ben was born . . . you had to wonder. Where did you think he came from?"

Visions of the baby days arose in his mind. The baby baths and silky skin, Ben's baby scent, so distinct at the top of his head or nape of his neck. The flash of intelligence and wonder in his silver eyes . . .

"He had my eyes," Eli said. "I thought he was mine."

"How could you think that?" Kate shook her head. "What were you thinking?"

"I thought he was mine," he said, a hoarse quaver rippling his voice. Although it was not in his nature, he had made a leap of faith nineteen years ago and accepted something that defied explanation. "I thought he was a miracle."

Chapter 84

Marnie
Good Samaritan Hospital

"This is Marnie, Mom. My good friend Marnie."

"We met." Marnie stood up, shook out her peasant skirt. "How's it going?" Stupid question. From Kate's bloodshot eyes and cowed posture, she could see that things had taken a toll on Ben's mother. "Are you okay?"

"Fine. Just . . . I'm just a little rattled." She closed her eyes and took a deep breath. "Ben, you were scheduled for your eye exam twenty minutes ago. Didn't anyone come to get you?"

"Marnie came," Ben said, a hint of his crooked smile returning.

"Someone on staff was supposed to come with a wheelchair." Kate checked the clock on the wall, her mouth twisted in anxiety. "We don't want to miss that appointment. Let me go see what's going on." She turned to leave but paused in the doorway. "I almost forgot." She handed Marnie a small paper sleeve from the hotel. "Here's the key. Feel free to take over half of the room. Call my cell if you need anything."

Marnie thanked her, then turned back to Ben. "So what can I do for you? Need water? Something to read? Want me to sneak you a latte from the coffee shop?"

"Did you bring your textbook?" Ben asked. "We need to study for the psych exam."

It took Marnie a moment to process what he was saying. "Oh . . . no. I didn't bring it. We're not in psych till next semester, Jocko. It's still summer." She felt the buzz of her cell phone against her thigh, and fished it out. Another threat, same old, same old.

"What's up? Is something wrong?"

"I'm getting these messages." She waved her cell phone at him. "Text messages. Threats. I don't know who's sending them, and they're beginning to scare me."

"Let me see." He held the phone in front of his good eye. "You'll pay? Pay for what?"

At least he could still read. "I wish I knew. For a while I thought it was my father. I thought he was trying to get back at me for something rotten I did."

"Your father?"

"I know, I never talk about him." She told him how she had tracked Leo Epstein down outside his home and realized he was harmless. She told him how the creep had called her at work. "Pretty scary. I was so glad to get on that plane this morning. And then, listen to this, I'm in the airport and who do I see? Dylan. He came to meet me, and I didn't even tell him I was coming."

"But he should pick you up," he said. "He's your boyfriend."

Marnie's jaw dropped, and she had to reel herself in. Ben had missed a few chapters of her story. "Well, the thing is, Dylan and I broke up." Her right hand slid up to her face, her lips opening to her fingernails.

No.

She pulled her hand away. She didn't need to resort to nail-biting with Ben. He was her friend. He had always understood her take on things. Ben was on her side.

"So you and Dylan are over. He must be really upset about it."

"Yeah, I guess. He's kind of mad about it. Did he mention it to you?"

"Dylan . . ." He grimaced. "I don't know. My memory sucks now."

"But he's been here to see you, right?"

"Not for a while . . . I think. I don't think so. I don't re-member."

She retrieved the call log on her cell phone. "Why don't I just call him right now and you two can talk? That's what best friends do, right?" It was time to put Dylan on the spot. If he was a real friend, he would support Ben now, when he needed it. But as she scrolled back through missed calls, the only number that came up belonged to the Boston cell phone, the anonymous caller. "That's weird." She switched to her address book, but Ben was getting agitated.

"No, no, put the phone away. I don't want to talk on a phone. You're here, Marnie. I want to talk to you."

He reached out to her, and she stood, dropped the phone into her pocket, and watched as her hand folded into his. She choked up, relieved that he still valued her friendship, but also antsy about all the things that had not been said.

"You're still pretty strong." She gave a tug on her hand, sandwiched in his. "Don't worry. I'm not going anywhere."

"Good. I want you to stay. Can you visit me every day?"

"I wish. But your mom told me that you get lots of visitors. Your friends from the team, and your aunt just left, right?" Suddenly Marnie wondered if he knew Emma had dumped him. It wasn't the sort of news you would tell a very sick pa-tient, so Marnie wouldn't blame Kate for holding back. "Has Emma been here?"

"No. Emma was my girlfriend, but we broke up. I don't re-member it. Mom told me about it, and really, that's embar-rassing."

"Do you remember her?"

"I don't remember breaking up. I remember Emma, who definitely had her moments. Annoying and needy, but cute."

"That's Emma." Marnie let out the breath she'd been hold-ing. At least he wasn't mooning about Emma. But did he re-member what had happened between them the night he was attacked? She bit her bottom lip. Did he remember the kiss? And really, did it matter? That night seemed like eons ago and so much had changed.

Get real, focus on the here and now. What remained? Ben was going to be feeling his way back for a while, and she wanted to help. They had been friends first, right?

Ben pushed the sheet back, and Marnie's gaze slid to his lean legs, well muscled and furred with dark hair. She'd seen his legs before, plenty of times, as Ben favored shorts in warm weather, and they'd run into each other working out at BC. But this felt intimate.

The side rail of the bed was in his way. "Can you help me? I need to walk. It's good for me."

"Well, sure. But aren't you going for an eye exam?"

"I need to walk."

Ben pointed to his yellow helmet, which covered the sunken section of his skull completely. With the helmet on, there were traces of the old Ben, that crooked smile and angular jaw.

As Marnie was helping him strap the helmet on, one of the nurses came in to help. "You taking a walk again, Ben?" A gold tooth was evident as the woman gave him a broad smile. "I guess it's okay. Your exam was pushed back till five. But all's you do these days is walk. At the rate you're going, you'll be walking right out the door soon."

"That's what I'm going for, Nella. I'm going to run out of here and back onto the baseball field."

Positioned beside Ben, supporting him as he rose to his feet, Marnie wondered if Ben's dream was possible. Would he recover his agility and skill? Could he grow strong again, strong and quick enough to snap up balls and move with speed? She hoped so.

"Slow down, now," Nella said as Ben surged forward. "We got plenty of time here."

"I'm going, Nella. I'm ready to run."

"Child, you got to walk before you run," Nella said brightly. "Walk before you run, babe."

Chapter 85

Dylan Kroger
Franklin Library

The text message was short and to the point.

"Found the guy. He's willing to talk. Meet us outside library. Back door @ 4."

And she had agreed. Easy as that.

The hard part was setting everything up in time. Weeks ago he had found this storage room under the eaves on the fourth floor, a dusty room with a door marked EMPLOYEES ONLY, though he doubted that any employee had trod here for months.

He put down his gym bag and tried to see the room through Marnie's eyes. Musty and dark, its air vents blocked by boxes . . . she wouldn't like this. Once she stepped in, he would need to move fast.

The zipper of his bag purred under his fingertips. He pushed past his balled-up practice uniform and a towel and pulled out his shaving kit. The wrapping of the disposable syringes crinkled as he reached for the vial of morphine. The clear liquid glistened in the dim overhead light.

Liquid gold.

Not an easy task, pilfering this magic medicine from the Medford Lab. He'd had to switch miniscule vials of morphine with saline before they were injected in the lab rats. A quick switch, a sleight of hand, a little joke to distract his boss Leanne, who was so eminently distractible if you asked her a question about her three kids or the dog or the amazing discount she'd gotten on carpeting. Sometimes Dylan wondered how Dr. Leanne Robbins had completed her PhD with her penchant for filling every blank space with chatter.

Still, Dr. Robbins had been easy to work around, a real pushover. Once she gained confidence in Dylan, she gave him the key to the drug closet and let him sign out the morphine for the trials scheduled that day. Dylan always stole only the prescribed amount; he knew narcotic supplies were carefully monitored. Since the rats were injected with such low doses, it took awhile to stockpile a significant amount, but he was consistent, diligent.

A shiny orange in the gym bag caught his eye, and he tossed it in the air and caught it. He'd snagged it from the dining hall, wanting one last practice. Yeah, he'd injected a hundred mice, but people? Not one.

When students were trying to learn how to administer a shot, they practiced on oranges. He filled the needle with saline, tapped the air bubbles out of the barrel.

You used your wrist, as if you were throwing a dart. The deltoid muscle was a fine location. You had to insert the needle at a ninety-degree angle, aspirated to make sure you weren't in a blood vessel, then push the plunger.

He held the orange in his right hand and jabbed the hypodermic needle into it.

Bull's-eye.

Chapter 86

Marnie
Franklin Library

"What the hell?" There was no back door to the library. Her clogs shifted underfoot in the clumpy grass as Marnie descended the steep hill leading to a loading dock and a Dumpster. She clambered onto the shimmering black asphalt and stared up at the monster building. What was Dylan talking about?

She had expected to find a rear entrance, where Dylan and the asshole would be waiting for her, but this was all wrong.

As she turned away she heard a click. The brown door at the top of the ramp opened a sliver, and Dylan peeked out. "In here . . . he's in here." He waved her in.

"This guy is one weird dude," she muttered as she hustled up the ramp and into the cool of the library basement. "What was that about? There's no real back entrance," she complained.

Dylan shrugged, his pale blue eyes sad, earnest. "That was the way he wanted it. I'm just following along. It wasn't easy to get him here."

"I bet." She moved past Dylan to the main aisle, sauntering past rows of books. "Where is he?"

"On the fourth floor, by the carrels."

"And for that I had to come in the back door?"

"He's very particular."

"He's very whacked," Marnie said as she punched the up

arrow for the elevator, then wheeled on Dylan. "So is this the same guy who attacked Ben?"

"I think so. I'm pretty sure."

"And have you called the police yet?"

"I don't know for sure. Look, I'm just trying to help." He gestured to the elevator doors as they rolled open.

"Fine." They stepped in, and Marnie punched four. "But this better be good. I have to get back to the hospital. Ben is having an eye exam, which is a crucial factor in whether or not he might be able to play ball again. Did you know that? Did you know there may be damage to the optic nerve? No, because you haven't been to see him. Your best friend has been in the hospital for two weeks and you go there *once?* Once, Dylan?"

"Wow." He folded his arms, retracting. "I'm just trying to help, and I don't have a lot of time either. I have a game tonight. I'm on third base."

Whoopee, Marnie thought, but she clenched her mouth shut as the elevator doors rolled open to an empty floor. The stacks of the library stood tall and silent, a ghost town of shiny acetate covers and old embossed bindings.

Rubbing the goose bumps from her arms, she followed Dylan over to the carrels. This was weird. When Dylan had suggested the library, it had seemed like a good idea. They'd met here before; it was a public place. But today was Sunday, summer session, not a study day. And this floor was deserted.

Hugging herself, she took a calming breath as he led her through the stacks. "Dylan?" Her voice fell flat in the dead room. "You're going to stick around, right?"

"Of course." He stopped in front of a door and looked around nervously.

"What happened, did he leave?"

"No, it's fine." He put his hand on the knob of the door, and for the first time she read the sign. EMPLOYEES ONLY. "He's in here."

But the door says . . . oh, what the hell. Maybe he works here.

She stepped into the musty space, stepped past Dylan, and eyed the stacks of boxes and files. "Hello?" A driving pulse rose inside her, the steady bat-wing beat of fear and anticipation as she waited for an answer.

"Marnie . . ." Dylan fidgeted with something on a shelf beside her. When she shot him a glance, he jerked one hand behind his back, concealing something. A ring, maybe? Oh, please. "Don't get mad. I just wanted to explain some things."

"Are you kidding me?" She wheeled on him. "Oh, don't tell me you dragged me up here to try and kiss me or something. God, Dylan. Get over it, would you?"

"You don't understand. We have a destiny to fulfill, and I know if you search deep inside, you'll feel it, too." Sweat cast a sheen on his face, matting curls to his forehead. "Marnie, you and I, we've been chosen to—"

"Dylan, shut up. Are you crazy?"

"Don't say that. I'm just trying to get us back on track here. There's a tie between us that you can't ignore, a sacred—"

"What are you holding behind your back?" At his piqued response, fury solidified in her chest like a trembling fist. "Never mind. I am out of here." She pushed past him, ignoring him as he swung around to grab her. "Cut it out." She tried to shove him away as he squeezed her arm and pinched. "Ouch! Get off me or I'll have security in here so fast, you'll . . ." She stepped away from him and stumbled.

Something wasn't right.

The burn in her arm . . . she rubbed it vigorously even as her ears began to ring, a deafening roar, a puff of white noise that was closing in around her, lifting her, releasing her. She caught herself on the edge of a shelf and turned to look back at him.

That sad puppy look, slash of a mouth . . . and the plastic glint of a hypodermic needle in his left hand.

Oh, God . . . he'd injected her.

"What? What did you do to me?"

"You'll be okay, Marnie, I swear. I don't want to hurt you, but I have to help you find the way. I'm going to keep you safe until you learn to understand."

Her hands grew too weak to hold on, and she slid down, down along the shelf, grateful for the support of the old wood floor under her, the shelves behind her.

"Just relax, okay? I'll take good care of you."

As if his simpering voice was not repulsive enough, she could feel him touching her, his clammy fingers lifting her hair from her face and tucking it behind her ears. His fingertips closed over her earlobe, lightly pinching the studs and rings there as if counting them. Taking inventory.

He sat cross-legged, facing her, his bulbous eyes prying into her soul. "Don't you feel it, Marnie? It's like a steel rod that shoots through both our hearts. We belong together."

"You . . ." The word tore from her hoarse throat as reality began to sink in. He was the one who had been stalking her. Dylan had been calling her at work, texting her. Of course. He must have bought a second cell phone in Boston. He'd used it to unhinge her. He'd made her think she had to get away, and she'd fled right into his trap.

"Yes, it's been me all along," he said with a giddy grin. "I'm the one who loves you. The one who has always been there for you, even though you've been dense about understanding that. But you have to stop fighting it, Marnie. You can't tear apart an organism, and that's what we are, a whole being. Together, we are a thing of beauty."

He reached across and cupped her face, his hands repulsive on her skin. "Don't fight it, Marnie."

She tried to protest, but only a moan pealed from her throat.

"Don't fight it," he repeated. "Because when you deny it, you force me to do those cruel things. The text messages and threats."

The stalking. She glared at him, wishing she possessed the strength to lift her hand and smack that pitiful expression from his face.

"When you tried to shake me loose? That hurt. It derailed me for a long time. But I worked through it."

Marnie pressed her hands into the floor, trying to push herself up . . . up and out of here. She had to get away! Dylan was a psycho, a sick individual.

Scraping together resolve, she tried to lift herself up. She pressed her palms down and strained against the wood floor. But as she shifted her weight she no longer possessed the strength to support her own body. Like a sack of grain, she slid quietly to the ground.

"That's right, Marnie. That's it. Relax." His hand was a dull clamp on her head as the floor came up to meet her.

Prone, paralyzed, she tried to make sense of the inanimate world around her. Her mouth was slack, open to the floor, and her tongue felt heavy with drool.

A few feet away, under the shelf near her face, an orange sat on the wood floor, its textured surface gleaming in the shadowed light. An orange. A bitter taste stung the back of her throat, and she longed to wrap her fingers around the orange and launch it toward Dylan's head.

The toxic fear and fury and panic that had welled inside her suddenly began to drain from her body, ebbing away to a distant shore. In its place came a cool bottomless hole . . . a universe of darkness.

Chapter 87

Kate
Cross College Stadium

The smell of warm grass and popcorn brought Kate back to the years of summer ball as she made her way into the stadium in search of Dylan. The sound of practice bats cracking, the feel of fine gravel underfoot, the smells, the heat . . . it was all so blessedly familiar that tears welled in her eyes. She turned away from the field, facing the empty stands as she swiped at the tears. Thank God for sunglasses. Coach Ramsey had told her it was okay to talk with his player, just for a few minutes, and Kate didn't intend to spend a long time here. She wanted to meet with the eye doctor when he finished examining Ben. But when she'd heard that Dylan had stopped in to see Ben at the hospital, she thought it was time to reconnect with her second son.

She found Dylan off to the side, shagging balls. "Coach said I can borrow him for just a minute," she told the trainer as Dylan came bounding over.

"Mommyson Two!" He pushed his sunglasses onto his Lakers cap and grinned. So happy, so unaffected.

How did he escape unscathed? The thought disturbed her as he pulled her into a quick hug. The attack on Ben had torn through her life, sent waves rippling everywhere, to everyone he knew. Eli and her, Marnie and Emma, the guys on the team, the coaching staff and BC . . . Kate had even gotten calls from moms and friends of Ben's back in Woodstock. But here was Dylan, Ben's best friend, removed from the crisis.

"Did you come to watch me play?" he asked. "I'm on third now."

"I have to get back to the hospital. Ben has . . ." She stopped herself before saying that today they expected to learn whether or not Ben would regain vision in his right eye. Such an important day, a huge verdict, but somehow, in his state of mind, she didn't think Dylan would understand. "I haven't seen you for a while, though I heard you stopped in today."

"Yeah. I went up for a while with Marnie."

"I'm glad. Ben and I have missed you, Dylan."

He stared down at the dirt track. "Yeah. It's hard . . . I can't stand to see Ben that way. It feels like I lost a brother." His sorrow seemed sincere, but it bothered her that he'd switched it on, as if on cue.

"It is rough." Kate reached for his hand, surprised to find it cool and dry in this heat. "But Ben is still alive. He's making progress, and his chance for recovery looks good. Did you see him walking? He can walk and talk. The things he can do . . . I'm amazed every day."

He nodded. "That's great, Ma. It's not that I don't care. It's just hard to take, and I've made a commitment to this team." He gestured toward the players running through warm-up drills on the field. "They need me now."

Now that Ben has been knocked off the roster, Kate thought bitterly. Perhaps it wasn't fair to twist Dylan's good fortune that way, but she wasn't feeling especially judicious at the moment.

"Are you sure you can't stay?" he asked.

It was her turn to look away. "I really have to get back."

"Yeah, me too." He stepped back. "Tell Ben I'll stop by soon."

She didn't say a word but pursed her lips as he jogged over to where the players were warming up and took his place in line at the batting station, where one of the trainers was pitching. Her second son. Kate wanted to yank him back and dress him down for being so inconsiderate, so self-absorbed. Was this the rite of every teenaged boy, to separate himself from misfortune, keep it at a distance, deny it?

As Dylan picked up a bat and stepped up to the plate, Kate felt a stab of recognition. It couldn't be . . . But as she moved closer, fury sparked inside her. That was Ben's bat—his favorite Blue Thunder bat.

Kate marched up to the assistant coach and nodded toward Dylan. "What do you know about that bat?" she asked.

"It's sweet and it's hot; it's caused a lot of controversy on this team." He turned to face her. "Your son shared that bat with a few players, and they all came to love it. They'd fight over it, but then Ben told them they could use it as long as they shared. But after Ben got hurt, Kroger claimed ownership. Said Ben told him he could have it, and honestly, no one has the guts to dispute that claim."

"I don't believe it," Kate said under her breath. "My son would never give that bat away."

"And shame on his buddy for taking it." The coach shook his head. "Really. Shame on him."

From the stadium, Kate stopped in at the hotel, where she noticed that Marnie had dropped off a few things. A few gauzy overshirts hung in the closet and an empty backpack sat on the closet floor. It struck Kate that Marnie had finagled time off from her two jobs to make this trip, and she appreciated the sacrifice. Marnie was a real friend. She wished Dylan would pull his head out of the sand and take a lesson.

Back at the hospital, Kate met with the ophthalmologist, who did not have good news. She believed the damage to Ben's right eye had caused permanent vision loss.

"There must be something," Kate said. "I mean, they can transplant corneas, right?"

"A few years ago some researchers at Harvard were able to regenerate the optic nerves of laboratory rats," Dr. Quince explained. She struck Kate as a practical person in her J. Crew skirt and clogs with a strap on the back, and Kate sensed that she would like the woman more had she delivered better news. "But even in that study they were not able to restore the rats' vision. I'm afraid there's nothing we can do for Ben just yet, but in the future, I'm just as hopeful as you are."

So it was over; Ben's dream of playing major-league ball would never be fulfilled.

Kate set her gaze on a poster illustrating the parts of the eye and burst into tears.

Chapter 88

Marnie
Franklin Library

Her mouth was dry, cottony. She struggled to open her eyes and pull herself from the depths of sleep. *Wake up . . . get up!* shrieked a voice in her head. *Get up and get away from him . . . who?* She searched the endless stacks of memory as she sucked in a breath.

Get away from Dylan, she realized as her eyes opened and took in the boy sitting cross-legged in the dancing light of votive candles. The shifting orange light made him look young, like a kid, really. Curls fell against one cheek as he leaned into his hand, his eyes round as nickels.

That wounded, innocent look.

It was all a lie.

She forced herself to take another breath in the hopes of calming the flurry of panic rising in her chest. Oh, God. What did he want from her?

The floor felt hard and sandy under her palms as she tried to push up. . . . Nope. She didn't have the strength for that right now. She eased back against the hard wood and sneaked another look at him. No one would suspect the skinny kid with the tumbled curls of kidnapping. No one would think he was deranged enough to capture his ex-girlfriend, drug her, and sequester her in a musty attic.

Oh, God. She didn't want to think about the fact that no one knew she was here. No one could help her.

She had to do it herself . . . had to get out of here. From the way she was sprawled, she realized he hadn't tied her up. That was good. But if she made a break for the door right now, she wouldn't have the energy to fight him. She let her gaze sweep across, to the dark rectangle on the wall that seemed to be the door. It was probably just twelve feet away, though it might as well have been twelve miles.

He straightened. "You're awake. Good. I was beginning to wonder if I screwed up the dosage. I did the calculations and everything, but I had to guess your body weight, and it's a little different converting dosages for lab rats to humans."

She tried to speak. She wanted to ask him why? Why did he do it? Why did he inject her with that drug? But her tongue, so thick in her mouth, refused to move.

"Can you sit up?" he asked her.

She pushed against the floor, but only shifted on the wood.

"Okay, then. I'll come to you." His face came into full view as he slid down on his side, flattening his hands under one cheek. "That's better."

Inches from him, she wished for energy to slap that loving look right off his face.

"So." His once dreamy smile now seemed twisted. "I guess you're wondering why I brought you here. I'm not going to hurt you, Marnie. I know, the shot wasn't nice, but that's a necessary evil for now, while you're learning. I've got this whole plan for us. We're going to be together. We're destined to be together. I know, you probably don't feel that just yet. You wanted to break up with me. And I have to say, it really hurt when I saw you kissing him."

Kissing him? She squinted at Dylan.

"Yes, I saw you kiss Ben."

Oh, God . . . was that what this was about? He was jealous of Ben?

"I saw you kissing him, and that really threw me. I mean, my best friend and my girlfriend . . . you can imagine how I felt about that. Wow. Standing there on the hotel patio, I was devastated. At first I didn't think I could do anything about it, and then, there was this lightbulb moment, and I thought, yeah. I can fix this. I mean, was I supposed to sit back while Ben stole you out from under my nose? No way. I had to make a move."

He swiped some curls away from his face . . . that boyish face. "That's key, Marnie. When things go wrong, you can't sit back and moan about it. You've got to take action. Be the aggressor. And that's exactly what I did."

She watched, mesmerized, as he rolled onto his back, his voice soft, as if telling a bedtime story.

"It started out so easy. Ben's door was unlocked. No one locks their dorm room. And the weapon was right there in front of me, shiny and new. Those expensive bats that he always set up in his room like a friggin' shrine. That always pissed me off. Ben and his killer bats."

A chill shuddered down Marnie's spine. She should have known. . . .

He paused, his thin lips curving in a giddy smile. "Killer bats . . . get it? Anyway, I just figured I'd give him a whack, make him see stars, but I guess I don't know my own strength." He lifted his arms to the left and swung through the air. "Whoosh! I guess you could say I hit a home run. Yeah." His laugh was a loud, manic chuckle.

Fear clawed at her from the inside out. He had tried to kill Ben . . . and he was laughing about it.

"A home run! A few swings, that was all it took. The first crack of the bat . . . that bothered me a little. But then I really got into it, really put some muscle into it, because I knew he deserved it. Man, that felt good, seeing Ben get what was coming to him."

She couldn't believe he was boasting, bragging. A champion in his own delusions.

He wriggled closer to her, his face flushed with exasperation. "You see, that's the thing people don't know. Ben deserved it. For as long as I've known him, he's always bested me. He always got the very best bat, while I got his hand-off from the year before. I got the leftovers from his school lunches, and all his old clothes. No matter what, Ben got anything he wanted, and all his old crap got kicked over to me. Do you have any idea how that makes a person feel?" Suddenly he gripped her shoulders and shook her.

Marnie was trying to keep her teeth from rattling when he abruptly released her. Malice flared in his eyes; then he abruptly pushed her onto her back and sprang to his feet. Although the distance was some relief, his shifting manic moods terrified her.

What would he do next?

"After I clocked him, I realized people were going to ask questions. It wasn't just one of those wrestling matches guys have." He started pacing, his sneakers squeaking on the floor as he came within inches of Marnie's head. "There was so much blood . . . Jesus, what a mess. But I planned ahead. Used surgical gloves. Got those from the lab where I work, just like the sedative I gave you. It's good to plan ahead. Since I didn't leave any fingerprints, I left the bat for the police. Figured they'd have fun with that. But the blood . . . all over my shirt, and then it got on a towel in my room. I couldn't have bloody stuff in my room. I thought the community washer was brilliant. Pretty smart, right?"

Brilliantly insane.

Marnie tried to stay calm by letting her eyes follow the encased wiring on the concrete ceiling. If there was wiring in here, that meant someone must occasionally use this storage room, right? Maybe they would find her tonight . . . or in the morning.

"And do you see how everything worked out? Ben doesn't remember a thing, and I got you back." His shoes squeaked close to her head, and she felt pressure on her face . . . his hands.

"Marnie, look at me. It won't work if you don't look at me."

She stared at him, trying to express blistering revulsion through her eyes.

"The thing is, I've worked really hard to keep us together. I've been planning, building this relationship. You may not see it now, but if you try, really try, you'll see us, Marnie. Our love, our union, it's a sacred thing, something that can't be denied. You can try, but what happens when you fight me? Look at yourself. Just look."

She tried to tip her chin to observe her paralyzed body, but her head wasn't moving.

"Right . . . you can't look. Not until I give you your power back." His fingers smoothed back a strand of her hair, so gentle, so repulsive. "But you'll get used to it. You'll adapt. That's the beauty of the human race, you know? Didn't you pick that up in Sociology? Everyone's got two choices. Adapt or die. Adapt or die."

For the first time in her life, Marnie closed her eyes and wished for death.

Chapter 89

Kate
Ben's Hospital Room

*H*ospital rooms are not conducive to good health. As Kate struggled with the blinds on the window she noticed that the center pane was an old stained-glass panel, a white bird set against a cobalt-blue background.

A dove of peace. A knot of anger throbbed in her throat as she thought of her son, the peacemaker, leveled by violence. Someone out there was cruel to the marrow.

She wrangled the shade down and collapsed in the single comfortable chair, trying to sort through the events of the day in her mind. There were only three people she wanted to share her thoughts with: her sister Erin, Greg Cody, and Marnie Epstein. For the past two hours she had been on the phone with Erin. Greg was working on an investigation of a missing child. And Marnie . . . where was Marnie?

Before he fell asleep, Ben told her that Marnie had gone to meet Dylan at the library, and she would be right back. "That's what she said," he kept repeating. And Kate had sucked down a retort, not wanting to tell her son that the hospital staff last saw Marnie hours ago, around three. Marnie was not coming right back.

Kate had left voice and text messages on her cell, which seemed to be on. She had stopped back at the hotel, where Marnie's things had not been touched. She had left a message at the desk for Marnie to call her as soon as she got in. At first she'd been eager to get in touch just to share the news about Ben, but now Kate was beginning to worry about Marnie.

"I really should take up knitting," Kate said aloud to no one. Ben was just a few feet away, but he was sleeping soundly. With visits from Eli, Marnie, and Dylan, plus the eye exam, he had spent a good deal of time awake today. He was able to stay awake for longer periods now, but it still challenged his energy.

The phone on Ben's bedside table bleeped, and Kate picked it up with some relief. "That must be Marnie," she told her sleeping son as she picked up the phone.

"Do you have Prince Albert in a can?" asked a familiar male voice.

Not Marnie, but one of Kate's top three. "Prank calling, Detective?" Kate couldn't help but smile. "I think there's got to be some law about that."

"I'm feeling festive. We found our little girl."

"Oh. That's a relief. Did she wander off?"

"The mom picked her up from school on the dad's day. Or at least that's what he's saying. Anyway, it's the rare positive outcome. So what's your story?"

"I'd like to tell you over a glass of wine."

"That could be arranged."

"Just as soon as I find my roommate. She appears to be a missing person, too."

"Marnie? You sure she's not out in the waiting room?"

"I haven't seen her since this afternoon. The nurses saw her leave the hospital around three-thirty . . . and that's it. Ben is asleep now, but he keeps insisting that she's at the library. He says she left to meet Dylan at the library, and she said she'd be right back. That had to be this afternoon."

Kate buried her face in one hand, trying to de-stress. Hopefully, she was wrong about this, but her instincts usually were reliable. Something had happened to Marnie. She could feel it in the marrow of her bones.

"Maybe I'm overstepping my bounds," she said. "But I'm

worried about her. I just think she would let me know if she had a change of plans."

"Your instincts make sense," he said. "She went to meet Kroger? That I don't like. But let's not jump the gun. Maybe her cell's battery is out, or maybe she's back at the hotel."

"She checked into the hotel this afternoon, but hasn't been there since. I've got the front desk on the lookout. I know she's nineteen, and I'm not her mother or guardian, but I'm honestly worried. I just thought she'd give me a call or even text if she wasn't going to be here. Okay, I thought she would be splitting her time between the hospital and hotel. But no one I've talked to has seen her since this afternoon."

"We don't know about other friends she might have here?" he asked.

"I don't know. I don't even have her mother's number to call her home in Boston."

"Okay, sit tight. Let me do some checking and I'll get back to you."

As soon as Greg ended the call Kate dialed Dylan's cell phone and checked her watch. Almost ten o'clock. His game had probably ended awhile ago. No answer. She hung up and sank back into the chair. "Yes, I need to take up knitting."

Kate was leafing through yet another magazine when a cute, petite woman stepped into the room. Dressed in denim overalls with a turquoise tank underneath, Dr. Teddy looked more like a teen than a physician.

"I almost didn't recognize you," Kate said.

Teddy smiled, hooking her fingers over a thick strap of her overalls. "I'm off duty, but I couldn't leave the hospital without talking to you." She pulled the second chair closer to Kate and sat down. "Kate, I need to talk to you, unofficially. Off the record, I guess. What I have to say has nothing to do with medical science or my opinion as a doctor. Do you follow?"

"I get it. What's up?" She suspected that Teddy was going to make a pitch to enroll Ben in some sort of study.

"The boy who was here today . . . Dylan was his name. Is he friends with Ben?"

"Best friends," Kate said. "Or . . . at least, they were before the accident. They've been friends since grade school. Though I have to say, I'm disappointed in Dylan's lack of support since the attack."

Hunkered over in a thoughtful position, Teddy closed her eyes. "My mother's side of our family is from Bali, and my grandmother, she's a spiritual woman. A shaman, I guess you'd call her." She sighed, opened her eyes. "I don't know how to make a long story short except to say that she had always practiced an Eastern form of medicine, and growing up around her, I came to practice and understand it, too. So . . . cutting to the chase—I can see auras around people. As a kid I never thought much of it, though when I was bored in class I made it a game to explore the different colors and watch the flickering glows. Sort of like staring into a fire."

"You see auras," Kate said slowly, trying to follow this off-beat track. It didn't really bother her; as a teacher, Kate read attitudes, which, in her experience, could completely alter the features of a person.

"You probably think I'm crazy . . ." Teddy said.

"Not really. When you have friends who've been cured of chronic pain by acupuncture, you start to accept things you don't understand. Actually, I don't understand half the technology hooked up to my son right now, but I accept it."

"I want you to know that what I see of Ben's aura is healthy. Healthy and healing, rebuilding and transforming. That part is all good."

"But . . . ?"

"His friend Dylan has an aura that . . ." She stared up at the ceiling, at a loss for words. "It's positively wicked. Hungry. Greedy. I've only seen it once before in my life. A man in a grocery store, who I was sure was trying to attack my mother. In truth, he just stole her wallet. But Dylan's aura, it's greenish black, and menacing. Like a dense, sticky cloud of negative atoms pulling objects into its frenzied path. I could see Dylan's aura sucking away the edges of Ben's prana, like a parasite. As if he were trying to consume Ben's spirit."

Kate squinted at Teddy. "You could see this?"

"I know it's hard to believe, but . . ." Teddy shook her head. "It just is. And it unhinged me. I got between the two of them, chased Dylan out, told him he had to leave. But I couldn't get it out of my head. I still can't. I had to tell you, though it's not very orthodox. As I said, it's off the record. You can laugh it all off if you like."

Kate shook her head. "Can I ask you something? What color is my aura?"

"A rich, royal blue. Almost purple."

"That's reassuring." Kate thought of the way Dylan had acted that afternoon, so self-absorbed. Cheerful. So far removed from Ben. She let out her breath, surrendering. "I've been missing it all along. Since Ben was attacked, I just assumed that Dylan was on his side, that he'd show up here any day. I've been making excuses for him, but . . ."

"You said he was like a second son to you. Ben's best friend. Maybe he's just too close for you to see him objectively," Teddy suggested.

Too close . . . like family.

Greg Cody had been saying that all along. *The majority of assault victims are attacked by people they know well. Husband, wife, father, son, brother . . .*

He was right. "I've been in denial. I didn't want it to be Dylan, so I never considered him and . . ." She looked up at Ben, his face peaceful now, almost normal in size, the eye patch removed. "I think Ben saw it coming."

"I'm lost." Teddy touched her wrist. "What are you talking about?"

"I think Dylan came into Ben's room that night and hit him with his own bat. And Ben saw the warning signs. Just before they went off to college, Ben went into panic mode. He seemed annoyed that Dylan had chosen to go to BC. Dylan had asked Ben to put in a good word for him with the coach, and Ben was fed up with Dylan riding on his coattails." Ben had paced the living room that night, recalling Dylan's bad choices through their childhood. The time they climbed onto the overpass to swipe a banner and Dylan wanted to drop a brick on a passing vehicle. When a group of boys set pennies on the railroad tracks for the train to flatten, and Dylan brought a lead pipe in hopes of derailing the train. "And remember that rash of bomb threats at the high school?" Ben had asked. Kate had tried to deny that Dylan had committed a crime. She didn't want to believe it. Instead, she reassured Ben that he was just going through the typical freshman freak-out, and they drove into town to purchase some last minute supplies for his dorm room.

"Oh, Ben . . ." Kate chastised herself now, studying her son's face in the blue shadows of fluorescent light. "You knew things were getting strained between you and Dylan. I should have listened."

Kate bit her lips together as Ben stirred, maybe disturbed by the sound of his name. He turned away, then back to face them. "What?" he asked, his voice cracking.

"It's okay." Kate stood over him and began her soothing wake-up spiel. "You had an accident, and—"

"Yeah, yeah, I know."

"Oh." Kate blinked. That was progress.

His brows lifted as he surveyed the room. "Is Marnie back?"

"Not yet," Kate said as her pulse began to accelerate. "But that's a short-term memory. That's good, Ben." She reached for the phone beside Ben's bed. "I'm calling Detective Cody." She dialed Greg's cell from the business card he'd given her. "Are you sure she went to meet Dylan?" she asked sternly. "Do you remember that, Ben?"

"Yeah, yeah. She went to meet him . . . at the library."

That was hours ago, Kate thought as she listened to the purring phone. It was getting late; she would have to go search for Marnie if Greg hadn't come up with anything. She turned to Dr. Teddy. "Would you stay with Ben?" Suddenly the thought of Dylan on the loose unnerved her.

Teddy nodded solemnly. "I'll keep an eye on him."

"Detective Cody," he answered.

"It's Kate. I've been wrong all along. I think it was Dylan. Dylan did this to Ben, and it sounds like he's after Marnie now. We have to find him." She grabbed her purse. "I'll meet you outside his dorm."

"I'm already there. I just checked out his room, but Kroger's not here. And it's after curfew. Any idea what might lure him away from the righteous path?"

Kate pressed a hand to her temple. "Marnie."

Chapter 90

Greg Cody
Franklin Library

Kate's was the only car in the parking lot as Greg pulled into the library lot.

"I wish you hadn't come," he groaned, catching Lamont Bostwick's attention as he killed the engine and reached into the console for a flashlight. Cody didn't want Kate involved at this level of the investigation, securing data and combing an empty building for evidence.

"A friend of yours?" Lamont asked. He was a retired cop. A lieutenant on the campus security force, he probably enjoyed working in his more casual uniform—khaki shorts and a navy polo shirt with Cross College Security embroidered on the breast. Lamont had keys to the building and the means of removing a disk with programmed footage from that day's library cameras. Cody felt lucky that Bostwick was on duty tonight; he was in no mood to wait until Monday morning.

"Yeah, she's a good friend. Ben McGann's mother. She shouldn't be here." Cody flung open the door and climbed into the cool night.

Kate was out of her car now, presssing the keypad to lock it.

"I think you'd better wait in your car." Cody closed the distance between them quickly, feeling the reassuring weight of his five shot in its holster at his waist as he moved. "Really, Kate." He stepped close enough to feel the warmth coming off her body. Pointing the flashlight at her, he said, "You know I love you, but you can't be my partner in this investigation."

"Bullshit," she said, shocking him. "It's about more than Ben now. Marnie was in there with Dylan, and I'm not stopping until I find her."

"Kate . . ." He pointed to the dark glass-and-cement building. "Marnie's not in there. The building has been closed for hours. No one is in there. We're just going to retrieve some records. You can come along and review the recording at headquarters, if you want."

She snatched the flashlight and pushed past him, joining Lamont at the curb. "You have keys, I hope?"

"I do," he said, walking with her to the front door.

Mulling over fantasies of tying Kate to her steering wheel, Cody followed past the statue of a man and a turkey. Although he wasn't a stickler for procedure, he wasn't comfortable bringing a civilian along for the ride, especially one who not only distracted him but who also had a vested income in the outcome of his investigation. Sergeant Lopez was going to rip him a new one.

"Last chance, Kate," he said. She was holding the flashlight on the door while Lamont worked the lock. "I'll walk you to the door."

She folded her arms across her chest, staring down at the lock. "No, thanks, Detective."

Of course, she wasn't budging. She was Kate. "Just don't touch anything, okay?"

"Fine."

Lamont looked from Kate to Greg with amusement as he held the door open. "If you want to wait here in the lobby, I'll go disable the alarm and find the light panel."

Kate handed him the flashlight. "Sure."

As they waited in the red glow of the exit sign, Kate looked up at him. "Don't pull the big bad cop act, okay? Did you ever think I might be helpful? An extra pair of eyes."

"No doubt. But it's . . . complicated." He stopped short of

explaining that it was like bringing your mommy along on a job interview. That would not sit well with Kate.

The overhead lights flickered and held. A moment later Lamont returned and handed the flashlight back to Kate. "The alarm shows an amber light on the basement door," he said. "Must be a jammed door or something."

"We can check it out later," Cody said as they approached the security desk situated just beyond the main entrance. "I'd like to see the desk log first. Marnie doesn't have campus ID, so the guard must have had her sign in rather than scan through the turnstile. It will help us narrow down what times we want to cue the camera footage up to."

"Right. This girl's not a student, right? She would have had to leave her license with the guard here." Lamont reached behind the desk for the large, spiral-bound book and opened it. "You say sometime this afternoon?"

"Three to five." Cody sat in the guard's chair and perused the entries. Only eight visitors had signed in this afternoon. None of them was Marnie Epstein.

"She's not here." He pounded a fist on the desk. "She didn't make it in. She must have met him outside the building." He turned to Lamont. "You have outside cameras around the perimeter of the building?"

"Only one. It rotates from the front entrance to the statue of Ben Franklin, which our campus fraternities used to tag a few times each semester."

Greg sighed. "We'll need to look at those images, too. Damn. I was hoping the video from the library would help us."

"Maybe she did come in," Kate suggested. "What if the guard was busy and just waved her in?"

Cody hated to disappoint her. "Unlikely."

"But we have had some students piggyback their friends through the turnstiles." Lamont pointed toward the center of the building, the staff office. "We'll take a disk with the video from today, just in case. The system for the first two floors is down here. There's a unit that collects data from the top two floors on the fourth floor."

"Just show me the way," Cody said.

Lamont took them into the back of the library offices, to the computer that collected digital images from all the cameras on the first two floors. Cody watched as he typed in a few commands and a password to bring up a sharp black-and-white video of the front desk.

"That's what we're looking for," Cody said. Bostwick showed him how to enter the date and time of videos they needed, then burn it onto a disk. "I'll review this back at the precinct." Greg tucked the disk into a sleeve. "You want to hit the unit upstairs next, or check that basement door first?"

"Why don't you go upstairs and start downloading what we need. I'll check the basement and meet you up on four." Lamont explained how to access the upstairs unit, which was stored in a small attic room under the eaves.

Lamont took the stairs down to the basement, while Cody and Kate waited for the elevator, uncertainty straining the air between them. Cody was aware of Kate's every move. Kate stowing his flashlight in her purse. Kate staring at the elevator indicator overhead. Kate clearing her throat.

"Can I ask you something?" she said. "Where do you think Marnie is? What could have happened to her?"

"I don't have the answer. Ben gave us our only lead, and now . . ." He let his voice trail off as the door opened and they stepped inside. He didn't want to go over the statistics about finding a missing person within the first forty-eight hours. He wanted to believe that Marnie Epstein would turn up with some other friends, that they would find her back home in Boston, that she'd met a boy and headed out to a comedy club for a few laughs. *Anything.* Anything but seeing the image that perched at the edge of his consciousness—Marnie Epstein in a body bag.

He punched the button for four. "After this we may need to start from point A. Scour the campus, beat the bushes."

"I . . . I was afraid of that." Kate pressed a fist to her mouth.

He slid an arm around her and tipped his face down to her hair and breathed in the scent of Kate, vanilla and flowers, backbone and concern. This was insane. Once they were through here in the library, he would have to push her away and get moving.

Find Marnie Epstein.

Snag Dylan Kroger.

Chapter 91

Marnie
Franklin Library

Marnie felt the presence of people before she heard anything. The wood floor under her ear rumbled with the hum of machinery . . . the elevator. Was it morning already? It was impossible to weigh the passage of time in her groggy state, though she could make out the red glow of light through her closed eyes.

Cautiously, she forced her heavy lids open just a slit, not wanting to alert Dylan.

Still here. Just inches away, his angelic face filled her view. Somewhere amid his nattering tales of the mythology of love, he must have dozed off. No wonder. His dogma was maddeningly repetitious, like the extended-play version of an annoying song. All this crap about the two of them fulfilling their destiny together, finding the perfect love, a sacrament. At first Marnie was afraid that he planned a murder suicide, but as he rambled on she wasn't so sure. Or maybe he wasn't quite sure yet.

Through it all, he had held out the hope that she would suddenly click into place and join him in this sacrament. She'd played along a bit, but mostly pretended to be asleep to avoid his insipid logic and vacuous kisses.

Her wrists ached, and she realized they were bound together. A glance at the eaves told her it was still night, though a few of the votives still burned and there was a strip of light under the door. Someone was in the library. Hope sparked in her chest, a delicate flame.

Voices floated like a melody. There were no words or characters to attach, but people were there. Help.

Suddenly Dylan jerked and snapped awake. "What's that?" His eyes flared, suspicion sizzling. "Did you hear that?" He pushed up from the floor, worked his cell phone from his pocket. "It's the middle of the night. Who is that? They won't come in here, but what are they *doing* here?"

With one eye open, Marnie watched as he scurried to the door and listened. Suddenly he stiffened and shifted toward her. "Shit! We've got to hide you . . . get rid of this mess. Fucking people in the middle of the night." He punched a fist through the air, then wheeled and bent over her.

"You need an injection." Despite the cool night, beads of sweat were gathered on his forehead. "That'll keep you quiet." He yanked open a file cabinet and fiddled inside, his back to her. A moment later he leaned down and plunged in the needle, liquid ice.

She wanted to cry. He'd ruined her chance! Her one chance to call out, but now she'd slip away, fall under the ice to oblivion. Her dry throat swallowed over a lump as he scooted behind her and tucked his claws under her pits.

You vicious, stupid boy. You monster!

She remained limp as he lifted her under the arms and dragged her across the dusty wood, around behind a bank of tall metal file cabinets. Spongy insulation chafed against her bare skin as he shoved her in there, but she bit back the reaction.

"I'm doing this for your own good, okay?" Suddenly a dry, dense rag was stuffed in her mouth, exploding her cheeks. She moaned, objecting.

"So you are awake?" He moved away from her. "Sorry about that, but we all have to suffer a little for the ultimate goal. God, the candles. I'm gonna burn my fucking hands off," he muttered under his breath.

She wanted to object, to kick and scream and scratch like crazy. She wanted to punch him, but she was losing strength.

Just play dead. Pull inside. Withdraw, and he'll leave me alone.

Although she could not see him she could hear Dylan scurrying to clean up, cursing as he burned himself on a hot candleholder. She wondered who was in the closed library at night. Maybe some students had snuck in to fool around. Maybe it was a sorority or fraternity thing . . . though this was summer and campus life was sort of dead. The last of the candles went out, the room going dark.

"People hate the dark," Dylan muttered. "That'll scare them." The door opened to a shaft of light overhead, and closed to silence.

Dylan had stepped out; she could feel real peace hovering in the empty room now.

This was her chance. With all her might she pushed away from the flakes of insulation, muscles straining. She rose an inch, maybe two . . . then collapsed.

Too weak.

Out in the library the voices gained strength and delineation. Voices of a man and a woman.

Please, come closer, she begged. *Over this way . . .*

She listened intently, wishing that the drug wasn't already burning through her system, pulling her beneath the surface to dark oblivion.

She tried to make a small noise, but the plaintive bleat that emerged was meager and pathetic, barely a whisper.

Over here . . .

She tried to summon them even as the attic room was suddenly enfolded into a bubble and sealed into a snowglobe where she lay, exposed and alone, and fading to white under a dusting of wax snowflakes. Fading, slipping into white.

Chapter 92

Kate
Franklin Library

"When will you look at the video?" Kate asked as they threaded through the stacks, toward the fourth floor staff room Lamont had told them about. Cody had given up on finding anything in the video, but Kate was convinced that Marnie and Dylan had met here. Call it instinct, call it blind hope. From here she didn't know what order of things Cody had planned; she just knew she needed to be involved.

"When I get back to the precinct. I might reach out for a little help, someone to go through the video while I put out the missing persons report on Marnie."

"I'll help."

"Kate." He sucked in a breath, preparing the speech. "I really appreciate—"

"Don't say no. I'll just be reviewing video, not bagging evidence or taking out a sniper. Besides, it's Sunday. You've got a skeleton crew."

He rubbed his chin. "You're right."

"Just think about it. We'll talk about it when—"

The lights cut out, sinking them in darkness.

"Whoa."

Fear snapped in Kate's chest as she lost her bearings and bumped into Greg. "Sorry." She fumbled in her bag for his flashlight, but he stopped her.

"Hold on," he said quietly, sliding his arm around her waist to hold her in place.

What happened? Was someone there? Her pulse tapped urgently, and yet, over the roar in her ears, she could hear it.

Someone walking nearby.

She sensed the presence, the static.

"Do you feel that?"

"You, pinching my arm?"

Kate's shoulders tightened and she pulled back. "Someone else is here. Someone just walked by," she whispered.

Cody pivoted, announcing, "Syracuse Police. Identify yourself."

They waited; no answer.

"Do you smell that?" Greg spoke quietly, his lips near her ear. "Burning wax . . . candle wax."

Yes, she smelled it. That soapy odor that reminded her of a chapel. Her fingers snaked into her bag, closed around the flashlight. Her eyes were beginning to adjust, but the only light in the room came from splashes of moonlight near the windows, most of which were blocked by shelves of dense books.

"You're right." Cody's form moved beside her, black on gray. He felt around them and pulled her into an aisle between shelves. "Someone else is up here. He cut the lights."

She heard the whisper of fabric moving, saw Cody push aside his shirt, watched as he became a different person, a leonine hunter, arm extended, eyes sharp in the darkness.

His gun was out, ready to fire.

Oh, God.

She pressed her back against the bookcase. What should they do next? She had a million questions, but she didn't dare speak. Would Cody fire into the dark, not knowing who was there? She didn't think so. Should she shine her light, try to find out who was there? But then that would give up their location, and maybe the other guy had a gun.

Or maybe it was Lieutenant Bostwick. Right. The campus

security lieutenant was going to kill the lights and pull a prank. Not.

Cody's hand gently cupped her cheek, then pressed on the top of her head. "Get down," he breathed, and they both sank to the floor.

Kate found his face in the darkness, leaned close to his ear. "What do we do?" she whispered.

"Wait," he answered. "And be careful."

Taking a breath, she shifted from a squat to a kneeling position, resting back on the soles of her feet. She wanted to believe he was gone, but she sensed a presence in the darkness, a wild and poisonous thorn. Cody leaned out from behind the bookshelves and peered toward the right. She turned the opposite way, searching the monochromatic shadows for a hint of motion.

Quiet prevailed for a heartbeat, a moment, a minute, two.

Then she heard it, a high-pitched thread of sound, like the whimper of a trapped mouse. She leaned into Cody. "What is that?" she whispered.

Silence, then an eerie, muted wail.

"Someone in distress," he mouthed and pointed to the right. "From over there."

Marnie? Please let it be her.

She was listening intently, focusing on the sound when she felt him again. A cold presence slithering behind her, sending a tremor up her spine. Shivering, she angled her body so that she could see down the aisle behind them.

Fluid darkness, gray and moving. Looming closer.

Gasping, she wheeled and pointed the flashlight. The high-intensity light clicked on, the beam exploding a circle of stark white.

"Ah!" the man cried out, blinded by the light.

The man's face looked skeletal, all sharp planes, deep eye sockets, and shiny dark eyes. The face of panic. The face of Dylan Kroger.

"Dylan!" Kate blurted out, emboldened by outrage as she

rose, pinning him with the light. "What the hell do you think you're doing?"

His arm wheeled back, ready to strike, but something threw him off. "Kate?" Frozen in attack position, Dylan's left hand grasped something small and shiny.

A knife?

Details shrank against the swell of fury that brought Kate to her feet and propelled her toward him. "Stop! Just stop it, right now. . . ."

"Drop the syringe, Kroger," Cody said, as Kate felt herself swept back, away from Dylan. "Drop it and don't move."

Blinking against the light, Dylan let his hand unfurl and the hypodermic needle clattered to the floor.

Kate held the light on him, staring.

Were you going to stab me? Kate studied the boy she had once known so well, the child she had cared for and cajoled, her second son. The ground seemed to sway and rock beneath her as her mind raced over the terrain of Dylan's childhood. The bond between them . . . had that been a lie? A fabricated relationship? Or had something changed, Dylan's core morality disintegrating over time?

"Hey . . ." Shielding his eyes against the light, Dylan cocked his head. "Wow, Mommyson, am I glad you're here. There's some lunatic running around on campus. He tied me up, but I managed to get loose and . . . I'm just really glad you're here."

"Oh, really." Kate didn't believe him for a minute.

"I'm just relieved." Dylan patted his chest as if to still his racing heart. "That was scary."

"You're lying." Tears welled in Kate's eyes, blurring her vision.

Dylan cocked his head. "Don't say that, Mommyson."

"It's an act. I see that now." The edges of the light beam trembled as Kate was overcome with emotion. He was lying, and lying so gracefully. Dylan was an actor, a player who could recite lines rather convincingly. The boy she had nurtured had grown into a gutless, soulless man.

As Kate used the back of her hand to wipe away the tears, there was a blur of motion before her—falling books and footsteps—and suddenly Dylan was running, headed down the far aisle.

"Stay here," Cody barked from behind her. By the time she turned the flashlight his way, he was gone, too, his footsteps whispering away.

She pressed her face to one arm, composing herself with a quick breath. Then . . . the lights. She had to get them back on for Cody. Using the flashlight, she quickly navigated her way to the office at the center of each floor. The panel was off to the side, and she quickly threw each switch, reassured as lights began to flicker on, overhead fluorescents and green shaded reading lamps.

Outside the office there was no sign of Cody and Dylan beyond a few toppled stacks of books, but she felt a rising urgency to get to the source of the moaning. Retracing her steps, she found the shelves they'd hidden in when the lights went out, but the noise had stopped.

"Marnie?" she shouted. "Marnie, is that you? Where are you?"

Leaning against a wall of a bookcase, she closed her eyes and listened. Dylan must have fled to a lower floor, as it was quiet here.

Suddenly it occurred to her that the cry they had heard might not have been Marnie at all. "Hello?" she called. "Is anyone there?"

No answer. Damn.

She began searching, scouring the aisles, examining the walls for hatches to air vents or water supplies. Recalling a news story about a killer who had stuffed the body into a recessed ceiling, she looked up but found exposed beams and a fairly solid plasterboard ceiling. Still . . . there might be a crawl space. Her search led her to a closet filled with brooms, buckets, and cleaning supplies. Then she found the door marked EMPLOYEES ONLY.

The minute she pushed open the door she knew she was on

to something, as the room smelled strongly of wax and hemp—that old chapel smell—and even in the dim light she could see marks on the dusty floor, footsteps and trails where something heavy had been dragged.

She followed the widest swath to the back of the attic room, where it curved behind a bank of file cabinets and into the exposed wood beams of the roof, dusted white with blown insulation. A dead end.

Sagging in disappointment, she clicked her flashlight on for one last look at the lumpy insulation. In the stark white light, she noticed some of the texture was different . . . softer. A bedsheet. Her pulse skittered. Squinting, she took a step closer. Was that a bedsheet and . . . ?

Squeezing behind the cabinets, she saw that the white fabric blended perfectly with the insulation. Her heartbeat was thrumming in her ears as she leaned forward and reached down. The sheet pulled back to reveal dark hair and a pale face.

Marnie.

Oh, God!

The girl's skin was cool to the touch. Kate felt for a pulse on her neck . . . yes, yes! There it was, slow but steady. Without knowing why Marnie was unconscious, Kate didn't dare move her.

She called 911 and requested an ambulance at the Franklin Library. "It's a medical emergency, an unconscious young woman, nineteen. She's breathing but I don't know what happened. And her body is sort of wedged into a tight spot."

The dispatcher told Kate not to move her and asked her to stay on the line for further instruction.

"Marnie . . ." Phone pressed to her ear, Kate squeezed in under the eaves and pressed her hand against the girl's ivory cheek, which bulged unnaturally. Something was stuffed in her mouth. "Oh, Lord." Running a finger over Marnie's lower lip, she poked at a crusty cloth, pinched the edge of it, and tugged it out.

The action seemed to prod Marnie awake, and the girl sucked in a ragged breath.

"It's okay." Kate gently stroked her shoulder. "An ambulance is coming. You're safe now. Everything is going to be fine."

"He wouldn't . . . wouldn't let me go," Marnie sobbed. "I was . . . ssstupid."

"It's not your fault. Don't blame yourself. It's Dylan. He's . . ."

He's a sociopath. Dylan Kroger, my second son, is a conniving, vicious psycho.

"It's okay," Kate tried to reassure the girl, frightened by how close Dylan had come to altering yet another life. "You're safe now. Everything will be all right."

Chapter 93

Greg Cody
Franklin Library

"Y ou want to tell us what you did to her?" Cody stood over Dylan Kroger, who sat on the curb, wrists cuffed behind him, head sagging toward the ground. So far Kroger wasn't talking, but Greg Cody could be patient. He'd seen the spent syringes in the attic room and the needle marks on Marnie's arms. He knew there was bound to be some camera footage of Kroger doing the wrong thing. Kroger could stall, but Cody had waited out the worst of them.

Energized by the chase, the rush of adrenaline and endorphins, Cody observed every nuance of body language as he interviewed Kroger in the swirling wash of light from one of the patrol cars. Two patrol units and an ambulance had arrived at the scene within three minutes. It was good to know the guys had his back. "What did you give her, Dylan?"

"I'm telling you, I didn't do anything." Kroger's boyish face, his whole adolescent demeanor, could have won him an Oscar had he taken a different path in life. "I was just . . . just walking by the library when I heard something. She was crying, so I tried to help."

"Right. You were outside and you heard her moaning from inside the fourth floor storage room. And then you broke into the library to check it out instead of calling campus security."

Dylan didn't respond.

"Nice story, though impossible."

"I didn't do anything wrong," Dylan muttered without looking up.

Cody would have loved to smack the truth out of those boyish lips. "We know you broke the law. We just don't know how far in you are, yet. But we have you on camera. Now, I can take some time to piece everything together from the footage, but it would help the docs treat Marnie if we knew exactly what you gave her. We found the used syringes up there. We got you anyway, so you might as well tell us what you injected. It could save her life, Dylan. Tell us and I'll tell the judge that you helped us. Might make him or her feel a little more warm and fuzzy toward you."

"I didn't do anything."

"Look, I'm just giving you a chance to help her, and maybe help yourself. You say she's your girlfriend. You want to know if she's okay. I'm saying she has a better chance if you tell us what you injected. If she dies . . . I don't want to think about how that would look for you."

Dylan straightened, then hunched back down, muttering into his hand.

"What was that?" Cody asked.

"Generic morphine. I got it from the lab, but it won't hurt her."

Cody squinted down at him. The lab he worked in, back in Boston? That would point to premeditation. It was a good question, but Kroger was on a roll, and Cody was ready to listen.

"She'll sleep it off eventually. It's not gonna hurt her. I would never do that. I just gave it to her to keep her calm . . . just for a while. Until she could understand how things are supposed to be. How we're supposed to be together."

"Generic morphine. How many doses?"

"Three today, starting at four. The last injection was way early, but that's not my fault. I had to keep her quiet because I heard someone coming. I had to keep things under control." Kroger went on to describe exactly how many CCs he'd administered, how he'd learned how to give shots while working at Medford Laboratories. Cody scribbled the details in his notebook, and Officer Wilkins stood by, recording with a small digital camera. Normally Cody would wait to interrogate back at the precinct, but in this case the information regarding Marnie was vital.

"It was my job to inject the mice," Dylan said, almost proudly. "Some of the girls were squeamish about it, but not me. I'm premed. I can do it, no problem."

I don't think you'll be premed for too much longer, Cody thought as the double doors of the library opened wide and a stretcher pushed through.

Clutching her purse and the flashlight as if it were a scepter, Kate walked steadily behind them. Cody cut away from Kroger and intercepted them by the ambulance. He touched Kate's shoulder as he told the paramedic with a clipboard what he'd learned about the injections.

"I'm going to ride with her to the hospital." Kate's voice sounded flat as her gaze combed the parking lot, locking on Dylan sitting on the curb. She squeezed her eyes shut, took a breath. "Can I talk to him?"

Cody shrugged. "For a minute."

She shoved her bag and flashlight into Cody's arms and jogged over to the curb, reminding Cody of a teacher reeling in an errant student. "Dylan . . ." She paused before him, shoulders back, petite and dignified. "Look me in the eyes."

Slowly, his face lifted, the mask gone. The youthful, wide-eyed innocence had faded, giving way to sunken eyes and a grim slash of a mouth. "What?"

"I need to know why." Her voice was rough, barely controlled. "Tell me why."

He laughed. "Are you that stupid? Because I love her! She is everything to me. My world. We have something beautiful ahead of us . . . and it was all going so well until he butted in. Ben tried to take her away from me. Same old, same old."

"Ben didn't take from you, Dylan. He shared. He treated you like a brother. He—"

"Don't make him out to be some saint. Christ, how many years did I have to hear about how wonderful Ben was?"

"He loved you," Kate said quietly.

"He had everything. I had nothing. I just got his leftovers. That doesn't say love to me," Kroger snarled.

If the kid could spit venom at Kate, Cody was sure he'd be striking now.

Kate opened her mouth to answer, but then thought better of it. She bit her lower lip, then backed away in silence.

Cody helped her into the cab of the ambulance, handed her the purse. "Better buckle your seat belt," he said, tugging it down. "It's dangerous out there."

She nodded, squeezing his wrist as he reached across her lap.

He wanted to kiss her. He wanted to hold her in his arms and shield her, to tell her the worst was over and he would protect her. Of course, he couldn't do any of those things right now, and that would be a lie, the words of overblown male pride.

But he would hold her again, long into the night, for many, many nights.

As he watched the ambulance drive off, he recognized the precious value of a single person in his life, perhaps for the first time since his daughter had been born. The answer to so many questions. The light to his darkness.

Kate McGann.

Chapter 94

Marnie
Good Samaritan Hospital

Marnie was sitting on the edge of her hospital bed, trying not to look like a patient when Kate appeared in the doorway.

"Hey, you're up and moving around." Ben's mom looked fresh this morning . . . almost cheerful. "How are you feeling?"

"Better. I had a weird night, though. Kind of floating in and out of sleep, spinning. At one point I was sure the whole hospital bed was rotating. I'm wiped."

"Probably the drugs Dylan gave you," Kate said.

"Yeah. I guess it's proof that I would fail as an addict. I hate that feeling of being woozy, under water all the time."

Kate held up a white paper shopping bag. "I brought you some clothes from your backpack, assuming you wouldn't want to leave here in the things from yesterday."

"You got that right." Marnie slid down from the bed and padded over to Kate in the paper slippers the nurses had given her. "Thanks. I thought I was going to be strolling out of here in these old lady jams, and the nurses told me there are some reporters outside."

"There are, but you don't have to speak to them if you don't want to. Greg . . . Detective Cody will escort you out, if you like."

"I don't know. I don't mind talking to them, but I don't want to get too personal." Marnie thought back on what Dr.

Zanth had told her; when she was examined in the ER there had been no signs of sexual molestation or rape. Thank God. From what Marnie remembered, Dylan wasn't focused so much on being a pervert as he was on adoring her, like they were two players in some sacred ritual. "Do you think they'll ask me how I could have been so stupid to be Dylan's girlfriend and not know he was a psycho creep?"

"It's not your fault, Marnie. But there might be one or two reporters who'll try to make a love triangle out of it."

"I don't think I want to talk to any reporters until I've had some time to really sort things out."

"That sounds reasonable. I'll let Detective Cody know." As Kate handed her the clothes Marnie noticed that she even moved with more grace. Her eyes were clear, her hair shiny and curled neatly at her chin. "Marnie, I'm so sorry. You're not the only one who didn't see this coming—Dylan's breakdown. For many years he was like a son to me, but once the guys headed off to college, I lost track of him."

"It's not *your* fault. You didn't date him. I fell into a bad situation, and I just couldn't dig myself out." She thought about those rotten text messages, the threats. "You know, he said it had all started because he saw me kissing Ben at a party a few weeks ago. That set him off, but he must have been close to the edge."

Kate touched her shoulder. "Don't blame yourself. Dylan's jealousy of Ben has been escalating for years. It's not your fault Dylan targeted you as a point of competition. Besides, Dylan is responsible for Dylan's mental illness." She winced, shook her head. "That sounds ridiculous, but I need to blame someone for everything that's happened. I'm so angry with him right now. He's hurt Ben in ways that can never be repaired."

Marnie nodded. "Yeah, I get that." She thought of Ben that first time she'd noticed him, hanging at Beantown Grind. A fiercely cold day and he wore only that baseball jacket. "Do you think Ben will be able to go back to school? Back to BC?"

Kate's jaw clenched. "Honestly, I don't know."

"Wow." Marnie stashed the bag of clothes on the bed and

leaned back against the steel bedside. "I can't imagine how it would be without him." Her voice broke suddenly as tears flooded her eyes. Oh, God. She was crying in front of Ben's mom.

"It's hard, I know." Kate was suddenly beside her, rubbing Marnie's back between the shoulder blades. "The doctors keep telling me to stop trying to re-create Ben as he was. Instead, we've got to establish new goals, look for him to achieve the best success he can attain with his new abilities. Ben's attack has changed so many things, for all of us. I think he'll emerge with a new sense of values. It sounds corny, but I'm trying to value each moment, cherish each day. Trying to appreciate the new person Ben is becoming."

"I get it," Marnie said, swiping at her eyes. "I know that I've been changed by the bad things that have happened in my life. When you're going through it, you fight like crazy, but in the end, you turn around and realize you've learned from it. I've evolved." She looked up, drew in a deep breath. "The thing is, if it's okay, I'd like to stay friends with Ben. I think I can be good for him, and I know he's good for me. His honesty keeps me grounded." Recalling that nauseating sensation of her bed flying through the sky, Marnie knew she needed Ben in her life. "Ben is sort of like my anchor. He gets me, and I've always helped him figure things out. I think I can help him navigate this, too."

Kate nodded. "I'm sure you can."

Kate gave Marnie's shoulder a squeeze, and for a moment Marnie let herself suck in a little reassurance from Kate McGann, who seemed to have more nurturing to share in this moment than Marnie's mother had dispensed in her entire lifetime.

"Ben could use your help, your strong sense of direction," Kate said quietly. "With a good navigator, you can go anywhere you want."

Epilogue

June 2011
Kate McGann

Kate didn't want to admit that she was feeling an edge of anxiety over her son's departure. She bit back emotion and kept herself busy in the kitchen while Ben, Cody, and Eli carried duffel bags down the stairs and began to pack Eli's new car with Ben's gear for summer session at Boston College. Back to school and on to a new life, Kate thought, well aware that there was no returning to the lifestyle Ben once had on campus. Ben had not been back to Boston since he came here to play summer ball last year.

A single year . . .

The changes in Ben's life had been inevitable, but in some ways he had grown into a kinder, more considerate person. He laughed more. He wasn't so hard on himself or on the people around him. And he was able to take time for things that mattered. Last week while on his run he had come across an elderly man with a flat tire, and though Ben didn't know how to change the tire, he used his cell phone to call for help and stayed with the man until a tow truck arrived. The old Ben would have been too intent on his vigorous workout to slow down.

As Kate shoveled the last cookies into the container and sealed the lid, her throat constricted at the thought of goodbye. It was the end of an era, and it wasn't easy to let Ben go, despite the fact that his doctors and therapist were in agreement that it was time to give college a try once again. Although his intelligence had not been affected, Ben's skills and cognitive thinking were altered. Months of hard work in rehab had brought progress, and Ben was still working on some of the executive functions like step-by-step procedures and multitasking. The injury had also diminished Ben's inhibitions by a small measure, and Kate worried that, with his trusting nature, he would be taken advantage of. It made her apprehensive but then she figured that worrying was part of a mother's job.

"Kate?" Eli's voice called up the stairs.

"Coming." She grabbed the cookies from the counter of Greg's kitchen and hurried to the top of the stairs.

Eli met her on the top landing. "We're just about packed," he said. "Can you think of anything else he'll need?"

She shrugged. "There are stores in Boston, and Marnie will be there to help him settle in. She's whipping up a veggie lasagna and salad for your arrival."

"Rabbit food?" Eli cocked one eyebrow. "Can't wait."

Kate looked toward the door, then back to Eli. "Sit for a minute. We need to talk."

She sank down onto the landing, and he sat beside her, his bare arms dangling over his knees. The scar on his arm seemed like a part of him now, an angry three-inch gash that jutted down from his wrist. Funny, but the scar was hardly as noticeable as the other changes in Eli since the landslide—the catastrophic event that had sent mud, water, and rocks sluicing through their house of glass. The torrent of earth had cut through the center of the house, pushing Eli's BMW out through the garage wall. Fortunately Eli and Tamara had survived relatively unscathed. The destruction of the house had reminded Eli that his heart and soul—his creativity—was not of this earth. He had learned that he could live without the material creations that bound him to that house, and somehow that loss had freed him.

"Have you made a decision about rebuilding?" Kate asked. In the terms of the divorce, Eli had bought her out of the glass house on the hill months before it had been destroyed.

"Not yet. The geophysicists are still duking out whether it's safe to rebuild. Meanwhile, I've got a lawsuit going against the town and the county. They never should have approved the construction at the top of the hill without adequate trenches for drainage and runoff."

"I'm sure no one expected twenty inches of snowmelt, along with all that spring rain," she mused.

"The perfect storm, but still . . ." He scratched the back of his head. "I always knew there was a reason I was so resistant to change on that hilltop."

"Very resistant," she said.

"I'm on the plot, using my studio every day, but honestly, even if I rebuild, I'm not sure I'll feel comfortable living in the blueprint of that house again."

Kate nodded. Trauma had a way of carving out new dimensions in a personality, like a gemstone cut into a new shape.

Eli gestured toward the parking lot. "So what's this about? You worried about our boy heading off again?"

"Absolutely. But I know I have to get over that." With Dylan in jail for at least eight years, Kate was learning to let Ben live his life with a feeling of safety. Yes, he had learned to take precautions, to lock doors and stop initiating conversations with strangers.

Kate put the cookies on the step beside her and hugged her bare knees. "I wanted to talk to you about that conversation we had at the hospital . . . the ugly one."

Eli nodded. "Yes. That one sucked."

"When I told you that you weren't Ben's biological father? I'm sorry it came out that way. You were always a father to him. You *are* his father."

"Not always the best father . . ."

"But you were his father. You filled that role, Eli, and you two had such an amazing bond when he was a baby. Remember how you used to take him to the gallery with you?"

"Those were some sweet times. I suppose that in the back of my mind, I always suspected as much. No, wait. I didn't think you'd go so far out of your way to purchase sperm. I mean, that's way out your safety zone, Kate. But when you were pregnant, I guess I thought it was one of those flukes. Magical realism."

"An immaculate conception?"

"Hardly immaculate, but yes, some fantasy like that. When the truth was that we both lied to each other."

"We did." Kate squirmed, still uncomfortable with her own subterfuge. The action didn't bother her nearly as much as the lie. "I'm not proud of what I did, but I also don't regret having Ben. And I don't regret our relationship, either. We learned a lot from each other, Eli. We had some good times."

He leaned toward her, giving her a friendly bump. "We did. And I'd like to think I've contributed something to the person Ben has become. Is becoming."

"You have. Despite your reservations. You're his father, Eli, and I'm glad you're not giving up on him. He's come a long way, but recovery from a traumatic brain injury is a long process." She fixed her ex-husband with a hard stare. "He's going to need our support for a long time to come."

Eli frowned, the lines at the edges of his eyes deeper than she remembered. "I'll do my best. At least I know what he needs now. He does need us, Kate."

She nodded, swallowing back a twinge at their son's new vulnerabilities.

Downstairs Greg Cody stepped over the threshold, his silver hair glimmering in the summer sun. "You might want to get out there before Ben goes overboard with his masterpiece."

"What?" Kate rose to her feet, shooting a look at Eli, who just shook his head. Downstairs in a burst of yellow sunlight, Ben drew exclamation points in purple paint on the back window of Eli's new Subaru.

BOSTON OR BUST!! was scrawled across the wagon's rear window.

"Oh, no! Ben!" Kate's jaw dropped as she joined her son. "Your dad is going to kill you," she said under her breath.

"It's okay," Eli said from her elbow. "I told him he could decorate the windows."

"Gotta get psyched, Mom." Ben laughed and turned back to the window to paint a squiggly line under "Boston." "It's summer session and the campus is going to be dead. Give me a break."

"I'm trying," Kate said, trying to clear the hoarseness in her throat, "but honey, it's hard to say good-bye."

Ben turned to her, his eyes squinting as he tried to gauge her emotion. "Don't feel bad, Mom. You can visit me."

"You can count on that," she said quietly, then held up the bin of cookies. "For the road. Double chocolate chip."

"Mmm. Thanks." Ben opened his arms wide and she stepped up to him for a crushing hug. Sometimes it was refreshing to encounter unfiltered emotion, so pure.

"Hold on to those cookies, Ben." Eli opened the driver's side door. "I don't want them to disappear in the first ten miles."

"I'm on it, Dad," Ben said, cradling the container. "We'll crack them open at the first rest stop." He hugged Greg, then paused at the passenger door and flashed a wicked grin. "Hey, you know I could have driven myself. I still have one good eye, and that's all you need in New York state."

"You wouldn't take away your old man's rare chance for a road trip, would you?"

Ben grinned, that crooked smile that bolstered the mom in Kate's soul. "Nah. But you're going to let me drive, right?"

"Maybe later." Eli patted the rooftop. "The car's still in its break-in period."

Eli and his car obsession . . . some things never changed. Kate stepped back to the curb and folded her arms, as if to hold herself in place. She could imagine herself leaping forward and tearing after her son as he disappeared down the street . . . no, that wouldn't be good. Time to let go.

Suddenly Cody was beside her, one arm loosely slung over her shoulders.

Eli leaned across Ben's lap. "You sure this talking navigation screen works?" he asked.

"I use it all the time," Kate assured him.

"All the time, Dad. Don't worry, I know how to program it," Ben said. "And don't start asking me if we're there yet till we cross the state border. You're not the best traveler, Dad. You lack patience and focus."

"I'll do my best," Eli said.

It's a milestone, all right, Kate thought as she leaned into Greg. A day of change, with Ben off to college and Kate staying in Syracuse, living in the home she'd made with Detective Greg Cody. They had spent the past year wrapping their lives together, staking themselves on each other like one of her purple clematises climbing the garden fence in Cody's small yard. Kate had made friends through the hospital and rehab center here, but she and Cody had also talked about relocating. Recently Cody had applied for positions in Chicago, Phoenix, and Baltimore. She favored Baltimore, with her sister there, and Cody agreed it would be nice to have family nearby.

A year ago . . . who could have imagined it?

Ben waved as Eli started the engine.

"Drive safely," Kate called as the car pulled out and cruised down the road, taking her son on his way to a new life. God, it was hard to let go, but it was the right thing to do. The only thing she could do. "Stay safe."

Please turn the page
for a special conversation with
Rosalind Noonan.

What first sparked the idea for In a Heartbeat?

The plot idea came from a real event: A young man was attacked while sleeping in a frat house during summer ball season. He suffered serious injuries that ended his baseball career, but the attacker was never found. That aspect of the story intrigued me: an unsolved crime, a mystery, despite the fact that there were other people in the building at the time and the police found the weapon. Whenever I come across an unsolved crime in the news, I feel compelled to jump in. As Detective Greg Cody would say, I need to "play Nancy Drew."

But at the heart of this story is the issue of human aggression. What fans the fires of hostility to the point where an individual will behave violently and assault a person? As this was also a motif in my first novel, *One September Morning,* I am beginning to realize that it's a theme that intrigues me as a writer. The origins of aggression and the aftermath—the pain that ripples through a community when tragedy strikes—these are themes that resonate for me. Perhaps it's part of my own pursuit for peace that motivates me to write "cautionary tales" about violent behavior. So far, I haven't analyzed it too much; I just want to write the stories.

The hospital scenes have an authentic feel. How did you research them?

For me, research is a time-consuming labor of love that involves searches on Amazon, gathering bundles of books from my local library, and looking for any films that might be pertinent to my topic. Sometimes I'll come across a treasure trove of anecdotal information that helps me visualize something I know nothing about, like the atmosphere in an operating room or the relationship dynamic among players on a summer team.

In an attempt to get the medical facts about traumatic brain injury correct, I read several books written by doctors and experts in the field, some of which included specific cases. To depict Teddy, I tried to throw myself into the role of a resident in a hospital, realizing that the people making decisions in hospitals are not always 100 percent sure they're making the right call. Here's where the high school actor emerges in me. I can really get into the role playing in my imagination. The span of careers I've researched does make me laugh. For my last book, *One September Morning,* I was a soldier in Iraq, a clinical psychology student, and a newspaper reporter. For *In a Heartbeat* I became an ER resident, an elementary schoolteacher, a stained-glass artist, a detective for the Syracuse Police Department. If I can nail the details of a profession, it helps me flesh out characters I can believe in.

Of course, practical experience helps, and I am always incorporating experiences in my writing. Both my children needed MRIs while I was writing this book, so I learned a lot about that firsthand.

Multiple points of view have been an integral part of your first two novels. What is your goal in switching viewpoints?

When a story unravels through various points of view, there can be a certain full-bodied richness to it. As a reader I love stepping into someone else's shoes and learning about opinions and qualities different from that of my own. As a writer I've found that writing in multiple "voices" helps keep the narrative alive for me; it reminds me there are many facets to a story, and it helps me keep the plot from being "manipulated" by the protagonist, who sees the world through a very specific lens. It can be very satisfying to show the two sides of a character like Eli, a failure as a husband and father when you observe him from the outside, though when you share his thoughts you understand that he has hidden his emotional life in his art to escape his childhood and inept parenting. Ultimately, seeing the world through someone else's viewpoint builds empathy inside all of us, and I hope it leads to an understanding and celebration of the different qualities that make each person unique.

After *One September Morning* was published, readers responded well to the multiple viewpoints. Many readers wrote that they felt a strong connection to Abby, the protagonist. To my surprise, quite a few readers related to Madison, John's younger sister, who was the Stanton family rebel. I was glad to hear it, as Madison was a fireball to write. The minor characters of Marnie, Teddy, Rico, Detective Cody, and Turtle really came alive for me while writing *In a Heartbeat*. I'm hoping younger readers will connect with Marnie.

Many of the characters in this book feel like people I know. Do you base characters on your friends and family?

Although I might be inspired by someone I know, once a character steps into my story, he or she needs to be redefined and shaped to fit the plot. Although I might start out depicting the school librarian, or a nurse at the pediatrician's office, while I'm writing a character he or she must be molded to the story.

I must confess I relied heavily on my husband's experiences as a former New York City Detective when I was shaping Greg Cody's character. Like Cody, my husband relocated to another part of the country after he retired, and we have learned that, although you can take the boy out of the city, you cannot take the city cop out of the boy. People will interrupt a business meeting to point at him and bark, "East Coast!" or, "New York!" Now that the novelty has worn off, he's a little weary of being pigeon-holed and is surprised that it seems okay for people to discriminate against him because of where he was born and raised. It's doubtful someone would stop a meeting to point at a new business associate and shout, "Puerto Rico!" or, "Milwaukee!"

With a character like Cody, it's helpful for me to know how a former New York City cop might think and behave, but the similarities usually end there. As my story progresses, the character takes on a dimension of his own so that the final outcome—Greg Cody, in this case—has very little to do with the person who inspired the character.

You might say baseball is another character in this novel. Are you a fan of the sport?

Love it! It's America's sport, and nothing says summer like a player kicking up dust as he slides into home.

When I was growing up in Maryland you had to be an Orioles fan. I can still sing the Os' radio jingle from the sixties—don't ask! During the 1969 World Series someone had set a small black-and-white television set on the counter in our school's office, and I remember gathering there after the dismissal bell rang to watch, aghast, as our birds were losing. "You'd better say a prayer, Sister," one of the kids told our principal. We expected Sr. Mary Angela to laugh, but instead, she chased us out the door. There's still a soft spot in my heart for the Orioles, who gave us kids Brooks Robinson, Jim Palmer, Frank Robinson, and Boog Powell to cheer on.

Years later, I married a Yankee fan. When we were still dating my husband and I made it a personal quest to attend a ball game in each city we visited, and we found it was a great way to put a finger on the pulse of a community and check out the local team. We experienced ballparks in San Francisco, Los Angeles, Seattle, Chicago, San Diego, and Baltimore, and we were in the thick of a few games at the old Yankee Stadium in New York. Those are sweet memories.

Most recently we've been getting our baseball fix at the Mariners' Safeco Field in Seattle. Hats off to the architects and planners of that stadium. You feel like you're on the field with the players. There's a bubbling atmosphere on the mezzanine, where the food is varied and delicious and where you can watch the game while you wander. Since Baltimore is almost never there, it's easy for me to root for the Mariners.

And then there's minor-league ball, which can be that much sweeter because the guy on the field could be your next-door neighbor and admission to the stadium won't break your budget. Minor-league ball and summer-league games can be fun because the players have to really hustle if they want to get somewhere. That's the spirit I tried to capture with the Lakers in this book.

Do you ever get carried away by subplots or minor characters while writing a novel?

It happens all the time. In this novel, Dr. Teddy Zanth stole my heart away during the first draft of this manuscript, even after my esteemed editor had warned me to "focus on Kate." As a result, I wrote wonderful scenes that followed Teddy home to Chicago to explore the conflict amid her family steeped in the medical profession and her nurturing grandmother who never abandoned the quest for balance of elements prevalent in Balinese culture. I enjoyed flashing back to Teddy's earlier crises in med school, to match day, when she learned where she would be doing her residency. Since I missed seeing *ER* on television, I conjured up some exciting hospital drama to keep Teddy on her toes. Nice scenes, but they were not essential to the main plot, and when I turned in my first-draft manuscript, it toppled the scales at nearly seven hundred pages.

In an attempt to carve the book down to a manageable size, my editor suggested I cut those extraneous scenes, and as they sliced away with very few adjustments to the text around them, they seemed to shout out, "We're extraneous!"

And to his credit, my editor never once said, "I told you so."

Do you choose the photograph for the cover of your book? And who is the woman depicted on the cover of In a Heartbeat?

I have to laugh because the cover-art question always comes up when I'm visiting a book club, and readers are genuinely surprised that I do not design my own book covers.

Although I am invited to submit ideas for my covers, they are designed and created by the publishing team: designers who are looking for balanced, eye-catching compositions; editors with a sense of how to pique readers' interest; and booksellers who understand the market. The publishing team knows how to package books and I'm glad it's not the job of the author. Can you imagine if authors had to do covers? We'd all have to take courses in graphic design.

As to the woman depicted on the cover . . . it's Kate, of course. The photo was chosen for the intriguing expression on the model's face. At first I was a bit concerned that Kate does not sit near a lake or ocean in the course of this novel's action; however, my friend Shannon and I decided that it's a metaphorical ocean and she's contemplating a sea of change.

Do you ever visualize an actor or actress playing one of your characters when you're writing a character?

When I'm brainstorming a character, different aspects of his or her personality come to me at different times. Usually I'll get a chunk of their moral code or a glimpse of their face or a sense of the way they move. But as I was starting to write this book, Michael Cera came to mind when I visualized Dylan, and that made things click for me immediately. Cera played a stunningly convincing adolescent member of the *Arrested Development* dysfunctional family, and he also sparkled in *Juno* and *Superbad*. I still laugh when I think of that innocent, benevolent quality of Michael Cera's face. Perfect for Dylan. Visualizing the actor made Dylan's scenes easier for me as I kept imagining how he would play it—low-key and vulnerable, very likable.

I was about halfway through the first draft when I walked through the family room one night while my daughter was watching *Miss Congeniality* on television. We commented on how Sandra Bullock would make a great Kate. This was before her Oscar for best actress in *The Blind Side*. Since then, I pictured her when I imagined dialogue or worked through her emotional responses in the second part of the book. Would I like Sandra Bullock to play Kate? Call me crazy, but I can dream. Although most books do not have a film incarnation, I feel fortunate that my "inner filmmaker" helps inspire a visual dimension in my characters.

The demise of the "stained-glass jewel box" at the end of the story surprised me. How realistic is the possibility of a landslide?

It happens! In fact, last year I attended a reading group meeting held across the street from a house that had had its core blown out by a landslide. "Take a look at it," said Bonnie, the book club host. "It hit with such force, it tore into the back of the house, knocking the kitchen into the foundation, and pushed the car right out through the garage door." I confess it gave me the idea for the culmination of Eli's story.

Having grown up on the East Coast, I admit to being skeptical about such things in communities that are not right on the coastline. But the landslide in our town was caused by a number of factors that aligned for "the perfect storm" as Bonnie told me. The runoff trenches built into the hill to catch any falling debris were full of mud from a previous slide. A few feet of snow had fallen, making for lots of moisture and snowmelt. And rain had fallen every day for weeks, making the ground wet and muddy. The landslide hit late at night, blowing through the center of the house, sending a fat ribbon of mud down the center of the street. The angle of the street diverted the mudflow so that other homes were not hit. Fortunately, no one was killed, though the home was destroyed and a few people were injured.

What are you working on for your next novel?

I'm tweaking two plot ideas in development stage right now. One takes place in the world of cops in my beloved New York City; the other examines the pervasiveness of bullying in schools and society. Right now I am so jazzed by both story ideas, I'm not sure which one to pursue next; I may have to flip a coin with my editor.

IN A HEARTBEAT

Rosalind Noonan

ABOUT THIS GUIDE

The suggested questions are included to enhance
your group's reading of Rosalind Noonan's
In a Heartbeat.

DISCUSSION QUESTIONS

1. The call Kate McGann receives at the beginning of the book sets inevitable changes in motion. Have you ever received a life-changing phone call like Kate's? Or was there a defining moment in your life that set off major changes?

2. *In a Heartbeat* is written from multiple viewpoints. Did you find it jarring to transition from one character's point of view to another's, or did you enjoy jumping into a different person's thoughts?

3. Which character(s) did you most enjoy spending time with? Do you find that you prefer reading about people you relate to, or characters who expose you to a different culture or worldview?

4. Eli McGann escapes the real world through his art, as evidenced by this quote: "Music, paintings, a certain slant of light through colored glass—these were stored in his mind as sanctuaries, a place to go when life grew flat and sour." Did you find Eli self-indulgent, or do you think art is a healthy outlet for a man struggling with issues?

5. With much advancement in medicine, health advocacy has become more important than ever. Do you think Kate made the right choices as her son's advocate? If you were in her place, what might you have done differently?

6. Dr. Teddy Zanth's Balinese grandmother holds fast to the ancient way of accessing the "dis-ease" in a body. As Teddy muses, "Ether, air, water, fire, and earth . . . to Nyoman's way of thinking, those elements held the keys

to good health, to happiness, to life." Do you see a conflict between Nyoman's way of thinking and Teddy's Western practice of medicine?

7. Although Emma is quick to remove herself from her relationship with Ben, what do you think she learns from this experience?

8. Revenge is a recurring theme throughout *In a Heartbeat*. Explain how it applies to the players on the Lakers team. How does it affect Kate? Would you say revenge is Dylan's primary stimulus, or were his actions the result of complex motivations?

9. When Marnie searches her conscience for someone who might have a vendetta against her, she comes up with an incident from her childhood when she caused emotional harm to someone. Considering her age at the time, do you think her mother should have pursued it further? Do you think her father's response was appropriate?

10. While raising children, it often "takes a village" to sustain their physical and emotional health through adulthood. Compare the nurturing that Teddy received from her grandmother Nyoman to the care Dylan's grandmother Ginger Mayers provided.

11. Both Kate and Eli have been keeping secrets through the course of their relationship. If they were honest in the beginning of their relationship, do you think things would have turned out differently?

12. At the end of the book, when Kate and Eli talk about fathering Ben, there is a new dimension to their discussion. How has Eli's approach to parenting been changed by the events of the story?

13. How do Kate's feelings toward Eli evolve through the course of the novel?

14. If you were casting *In a Heartbeat* for a film, whom would you choose to play Kate and Cody? Marnie and Ben?

Acknowledgments

I am grateful to live in a community of creative friends who are willing to share their discoveries, pain, personal stories, and flashes of brilliance with me. Many thanks to Mike, Carly, Alex, Susan, Nancy, Wendy, Shannon, Keith, Elizabeth, Denise, Larry, Maureen, and Jack. To Mike Slavin, Vicky, Bill, and Cory, marrying into your families has raised our cultural IQ! And to my mom, the Mayor of Baltimore (just kidding, Ms. Rawlings-Blake!), thanks for keeping a spare room ready!

My editor, John Scognamiglio, has a great eye for story and a sharp red pencil for all those extraneous scenes. Thank you, John.

With love and admiration for the Harker family, who maintained a sense of humor and a positive track in the wake of crisis.